THE SPELL FOR UNRAVELING

THE *BURIED AND THE BOUND* TRILOGY

The Buried and the Bound

The Summer Queen

The Spell for Unraveling

THE SPELL FOR UNRAVELING

ROCHELLE HASSAN

ROARING BROOK PRESS
NEW YORK

Published by Roaring Brook Press
Roaring Brook Press is a division of Holtzbrinck Publishing Holdings Limited Partnership
120 Broadway, New York, NY 10271 • fiercereads.com

EU representative: Macmillan Publishers Ireland Ltd, 1st Floor, The Liffey Trust Centre, 117–126 Sheriff Street Upper, Dublin 1, D01 YC43

Library of Congress Cataloging-in-Publication Data is available.

First edition, 2026
Book design by Samira Iravani
Printed in the United States of America

ISBN 978-1-250-82227-7
10 9 8 7 6 5 4 3 2 1

For those of you who have followed Aziza, Leo, and Tristan from the beginning to the end.

CHAPTER 1

AZIZA

DION LEGRAND WAS ignoring her messages. She would have taken his silence for an answer, but when the wind sprites told her where he was, she had little choice but to go after him.

It was the day after her return from the Summer Court. There had been endless questions to answer last night, plus a trip to the hospital to treat her injured leg once the others had realized she was limping. The doctors had proclaimed her phenomenally lucky; after she'd been stabbed in the thigh with a glass shard from a broken wine bottle, messily bandaged the wound with the help of her friends and the first aid kit in her backpack, and then walked around on it for an entire night as they'd crossed state lines to get home, the damage could have been much worse.

She had collapsed into bed after dawn and woken again after noon. No one would reasonably expect to see her up and about for another few hours. So she took a train to the end of the line and continued into the woods on foot, her leg complaining the whole way. The old scars on her right hand ached, too; the pain radiated to her elbow. It didn't hurt all the time, but it acted up when she pushed her body too far.

A short hike southwest from Blackthorn took her through a part of the forest that looked as if it was in recovery from a terrible fire. It was cluttered with fallen trees, or those that had decayed standing up. No blade of grass or patch of moss was more than a few months old. One clearing was all verdant new growth aside from a great black mark in the center, like a puncture scar where a thumbtack had been plucked from the skin of the earth. This was the hag's graveyard, and it was where she found Dion.

His back was to her, his shirt soaked through with sweat and a shovel in his hands. Its blade was wedged into the scorch mark where the gateway tree had once stood. Salt water bubbled up out of the shallow hole he'd dug, steam rising off it.

"I hope you're not planning to go down there," Aziza said. "It's deeper than it looks."

"I can't find him," he said. "I tried digging—there are bones—but none of the clothing matched his. He must be down there."

"He could be," she conceded.

He exhaled hard, ducking his head as if to shield his eyes from a flash of sunlight. "Why are you here?"

Because it was a bad idea to dig up dead bodies, especially alone. She knew this from experience.

"Why didn't you tell Anne the truth?" she asked.

"What would that have accomplished? Emil was never spiteful. He wouldn't want me to be, either." He gave the shovel a yank to free its blade from the ground and came to the side of the clearing where she stood. "Forget it. I'm done here."

When Aziza had talked to Anne Sterling last night, she had confessed everything that had happened in Elphame. Then she'd backtracked to her encounter with the hag that terrorized Blackthorn last year. But she had omitted a crucial piece of context: her covenmate Tristan had been the hag's bondservant. He was no trueborn witch. His necromancy was a gift the hag had stolen from one of her victims—Emil Wulfsige, Dion's adoptive father. The last time they had spoken, Dion had been furious with Aziza for concealing the truth of Emil's fate from him.

He passed her now without waiting for her response—without even looking at her. The emotion he had displayed before had been put away and shelved cleanly out of sight, with the same efficiency he applied to everything from running a library to digging up unmarked graves.

He was icing her out. The least she could do was let him.

"There's one more place you could look," she said, and didn't know whether to feel relief or regret when he stopped walking.

A stone's throw away from what used to be the edge of the hag's territory, a break in the forest floor revealed an underground passage. Leo had fallen into it once and been caught in the hag's thrall, but there was no danger anymore, now that she was gone. They jumped down and ventured deeper, away from the weak sunlight pouring in from the woods.

"Emil *was* here," Dion said.

"How can you tell?"

She was starting to wonder whether she should have brought him here after all. If she'd thought about it for even a second longer, she would have waited for him to leave and then come back by herself to search.

"The same way you can sense Elphame's boundary or your grandfather's wards. Magic has a feeling. The more familiar you are with someone, the easier it is to pick up on the way *their* magic feels."

In his distraction, he'd forgotten to be curt. He had reverted to the patient, didactic tone of voice he had used when he was teaching her spells. The memory stung, so she brushed it aside.

The tunnel ended at a staircase made of packed earth. The opening at the top was a crevice barely wide enough for a person to squeeze through. And off to the side of the stairs, discarded in a shadowy corner, lay a body.

It was mostly a skeleton. It wore nondescript black trousers and a dusty jacket. Dion went so still she was certain he wasn't breathing.

"Let's go," she said quietly. "We'll get someone to help you move him."

His lips parted, but it was a moment before any words came.

"Emil left no instructions about what should be done with his remains. He never indicated a preference for burial or cremation," he said, as if in response to a question she'd asked. "His will said that I should do whatever would comfort me the most. It made me so . . . angry. The idea that anything other than finding him alive and well could bring me comfort."

"Dion," she said insistently.

"I don't see his grimoire, either," he muttered. He bent as if to look for it.

This was too much for her. She pushed in front of him. "Let me."

Her own parents had once risen from their graves to tell her how they'd died. At least this skeleton wouldn't talk. It wouldn't reach for her with grasping fingers. It was just a body; Emil wasn't here, and wouldn't be disturbed when she knelt beside his bones and checked inside the jacket, gingerly lifted each of the brittle arms in turn, felt in the shadows behind him.

"I can't find it," she said.

"He must have left it at home," Dion said distantly. "That's not like him."

She stood and brushed her hand off on her jeans. "We should go. Come on."

They went to Bishop Library, mainly because she didn't know where else to go. But she was stunned when he took his seat at the desk and turned on the computer as if he seriously intended to have an ordinary workday.

"You're still opening the library?" she asked.

"What else should I do?" he said. "I have to get things ready for my replacement."

"Replacement?" she said. Then it clicked. "You're leaving."

She had no reason to be surprised by this. Dion had gotten the answers he'd come here for, if not the ones he'd wanted.

"In a few days or so." Stiffly, he added, "Thank you for helping me find him."

How could she possibly respond to that?

"I tried the trap spell again," she said in a clumsy non sequitur. "It worked even better the second time. It's the only reason I survived last night. I owe you for that."

He scoffed. "You hedgewitches and your bargains. No, you don't owe me anything."

A debt was a kind of bond between two people—an assurance that, one way or another, they must meet again. By his reply, she understood that he wished to sever it. Honoring this implicit request, then, would be her only means of repaying him.

"I guess you're right," she said, and left.

THAT SHOULD HAVE been the last she ever saw of him.

A few days later, the three of them—her and Leo and Tristan—were letting themselves into the library after dark. The fire door opened with a clatter. The office, which contained the boarded-up entrance to an underground saltwater river, was locked. The lights were off in the reading room, the lancet windows afloat in the darkness, as if they hung suspended in midair. The beam of her flashlight slid over the labyrinth pattern on the tiled floor, its twists and turns disappearing at intervals under the bookcases. Meryl had been gone for about half a year, and no trace of her remained. But under the dusty vanilla scent of old books, she imagined she could still pick up a whiff of sea salt and tea tree oil.

Anne's instructions had been both specific and highly cryptic: *Come inside through the back. Go to the biography section. Have Leo look around.*

"Oh. I get it now," Leo said. He had taken the bandage off his amber eye. It was healed and didn't need to be covered, but he couldn't let it be seen in public. It would be impossible to explain to most people. The eye had been a gift from a grove of wood nymphs in Elphame. It granted him truesight, and now he could *see* magical energy. In things, in people. Apparently in places, too.

"What is it?" Aziza asked. Tristan was at her side, a hand on Lucky's flank, his fingers buried in its thick black fur. They hung back as Leo hesitated, blinking as if to bring his vision into focus. He touched the wall lightly with his fingertips, as if expecting it to ripple like water, its surface tension broken. When nothing happened, he flattened his palm against it.

"Follow me," he said.

He walked through the wall and vanished.

Her own surprise was overshadowed by the bond between her and Tristan snapping to attention. There was no circumstance where the sight of Leo disappearing before their eyes wouldn't disturb him, even when he had done it on purpose. Aziza touched the wall where Leo had; it was solid enough, but when she gave it a push, she sensed a kind of give—as if, the more certain she felt that there *wasn't* a wall there, the less like a wall it became. She stepped forward, Tristan right on her heels. When she should have smacked headfirst into solid stone, she instead had to squint against the sudden burst of light as she emerged into another room—a space that shouldn't have existed. Lucky's guttural, chainsaw growl sent a chill through her, but Tristan said, "*Hush*," and the hound subsided into a sort of sulky grumbling.

The library had transformed around them. The stone walls and rib vault ceiling still *looked* like they belonged to Bishop Library, but they were in a room she'd never seen before. There were no windows. The bookcases were pushed against the wall, and the open space in the middle was occupied by a long worktable identical to the ones in the reading room. An old chandelier hung over it, its teardrop prisms catching the light of actual candle flames. Across from them, a doorway opened onto an unlit passage.

Two people—and one pooka—were waiting for them.

The pooka sat in Anne Sterling's lap, wearing its preferred form—the form that had earned it its name, Fox. It was a young pooka, still learning many of its transformations, and had recently grown very attached to Coven Blackthorn. When it was older, it might wander away for good, but it was content to stay close for now.

Dion stood by the shadowed exit, leaning against the doorframe, as if he'd been on his way out. His cold gray eyes flashed up at her the moment she focused on him, as if he'd felt the brush of her attention. Her gaze skidded away at once, like a stone skipping across a smooth pane of water.

"Welcome," Anne said. Fox jumped off her lap and scampered up to Leo as she got to her feet. She was striking—almost a match for the Fair Folk in height, with dark brown skin and gray hair pulled tight into a sleek wrought iron twist.

"What is this place?" Aziza asked. Fox was settled happily in Leo's arms, making the oddly mechanical rumbling noise that was its version of a purr.

"This is the *other* Bishop Library," Anne said. "It's a collection of magical texts written and curated by witches, and others just like it exist all over the country. The largest ones tend to be found at universities. This is how we preserve and pass on our collective knowledge to the next generation."

Leo wandered over to one of the shelves as she spoke and ran a finger along the spines.

"I've seen this one before," he said, taking one of the tomes off the shelf and holding it up so that Aziza could see the title. It was called *Taming the Hounds of Hel: Portents of Death in the Medieval Period*. It had been among the books Meryl had pulled for her when she had been researching blækhounds. If she took the time to look around, how many other titles would she recognize? Her heart constricted. Meryl had been coming down here for years, picking out books on magic and setting them aside for Aziza. Working around the rules set for her by the captor who possessed her sealskin—which forced her to obey his every command—Meryl had still secretly found ways to teach her witchcraft.

"Are there grimoires here?" Tristan asked, his eyes sharpening with wary interest.

"No. You'll find spell books, but not grimoires," Anne said. "Spell books contain the words or instructions for casting spells—but, unlike grimoires, they have no magic stored inside them. They're only ink and paper. You won't find any grimoires in a public collection. They are generally passed down between family members, or from master to apprentice."

"Is that why Meryl was here?" Aziza asked. "To guard . . . all of this?"

"I doubt it. I truthfully don't know what she was here for," Anne said. "I'm looking for her, but our priority is to resolve the disaster in Elphame. That's why I brought you here. I can't afford to sideline anyone who can help. The three of you can be useful—with supervision. If you think you're up to the challenge."

As the most renowned hedgewitch on the East Coast, Anne was the one to whom all the others turned for advice when their own skills fell short, and who acted as the human realm's unofficial ambassador to the high court of Elphame. Earlier this week, she had swept into Blackthorn to interrogate Aziza about the events of the summer solstice—and to offer her an apprenticeship.

The disaster she was talking about was the failed coup at the Summer Court. In the aftermath, King Ilanthus and his son were dead; Princess Narra was on the run, along with her right-hand man, Viren; and the solstice ceremony that would have replenished the Summer Court's magic and affirmed its rule over Elphame for another seven-year cycle had been interrupted. Since then, a kind of wasting sickness had taken root in the fairies of the Summer Court, a corruption known as the jade rot.

"We're up for it," Leo said. For him, the fate of the Summer Court was personal.

"I'm glad to hear it," Anne said. "Because I'm afraid I am going to be asking a lot of you. Dion, why don't you start?"

"Of course," he murmured. "Follow me."

He took a stick of chalk from his pocket, and the matchbook he used to cast his spells, though Aziza had yet to see a demonstration of his witchcraft. It looked like that was about to change. He stepped into the semicircle of flickering light that spilled from the *other* Bishop Library into the dark passage beyond the open door. There, he paused as if to orient himself; then he turned down the corridor, disappearing from view, his footsteps echoing a long way.

CHAPTER 2
TRISTAN

He didn't have much to move. All of his belongings fit into a couple of boxes—mostly clothing, his old sketchbooks, and a few second-hand paperbacks he'd picked up from the one-dollar cart outside the craft store where he used to work. He had been unceremoniously fired upon his return from Elphame, because managers didn't tend to like it when their employees up and vanished for a week without a word of warning. He'd expected to spend the rest of the summer job hunting. But Anne had solved that problem for him last night.

Leo helped him haul the boxes up the stairs to the one-bedroom apartment above Bishop Library, where Meryl had lived for almost twenty years. Meryl must have had time to pack, since the cabinets and the closet were empty. Dion had never made use of the librarian's quarters, so it was visibly neglected, cobwebs in the corners, dust motes drifting through the murky light coming in through the little turret window. There was a bricked-up fireplace on one wall and a combination washer-dryer beside the kitchenette. In one of the drawers, Tristan found a pouch full of seashells, which he ran a finger over before carefully replacing.

"Bishop Library has been witch-owned for almost as long as it's existed," Anne had said. "The man currently responsible for its care is my colleague, Theodore Serapion. I've found no evidence that he has Meryl." This she had added for Aziza's benefit. "I walked in his dreams, and sent wind sprites to look around his residence and office. Theodore prefers to take a hands-off approach when it comes to the library's upkeep. I wouldn't be surprised if someone else sent Meryl to him, and it wouldn't have mattered who or what she was, as long as she kept the place in decent condition." Anne had paused, her eyes settling on Tristan. "I can send someone his way, too. He will take my recommendation."

"*Me?*" Tristan had said. He hadn't even finished high school.

"I hear you've lost your job," Anne had replied. "You'll be paid a fair salary. It's a full-time position."

Whatever protest he might have made about his lack of qualifications vanished from his mind.

"Full-time?" he had said hopefully. "With . . . health insurance?"

Needless to say, he was sold. Or maybe bought.

"Are you sure you want to move out?" Leo said now. It was not the first time he'd asked. Or even the second. He was still holding the last box, as if letting go would make it final. "You could've stayed at my place for as long as you wanted."

"I know," Tristan said. "But it was only supposed to be until I figured something else out. That was always the plan."

Tristan had moved into the guest room in Leo's house a few months ago. In that time, the friendship they'd had as kids had fallen naturally back into place, even though only one of them remembered it. When neither of them could sleep, they'd stay up together listening to music, sharing Leo's headphones with a blanket draped over both their shoulders, or watching awful three a.m. reality TV on mute so they wouldn't wake anyone. But it was easy to be in sync when they lived under the same roof and all either of them had to do was look for a light on under a bedroom door to know his company would be welcome. There were so many more chances to second-guess yourself when you had to go out of your way to pick up the phone.

But Leo had done it before, even if he didn't know it. He used to bike over to Tristan's house and text him from the street corner in the middle of the night. Or he'd wait up because Tristan had promised to come over, stealing downstairs to unlock the back door for him. It could be like that again. Just like before.

Tristan took the box from him and put it down on the table. Leo didn't step away to give him space, so when he straightened, they were very close. He had been an adorable kid, but now, almost eighteen, Leo was steal-your-breath handsome. He had grown into the strong, broad-shouldered frame it had always been apparent that he was going to have, even back when he was a gangly preteen with thick-rimmed glasses, scraped knees, and a wardrobe that consisted almost entirely of basketball shorts and baggy T-shirts, kicking around a soccer ball with an ever-present gaggle of friends. His asymmetrical gaze was mesmerizing—the otherworldly golden gleam of the amber eye with the thin vertical scar across it and the familiar warmth of his natural brown one. And it was fixed on Tristan.

"Just tell me you're not leaving because of . . . what happened the other night," Leo said, a flush creeping above the collar of his shirt.

Tristan widened his eyes in an expression of seraphic innocence. "Something happened? I don't know if I remember. Could you be more specific?"

"I mean it," Leo said, fighting a smile. "Because you know you can just tell me to fuck off, right? If we—moved too fast, or—"

"Anyone would think you threw me over your shoulder and carried me away by force. Feel free to do that next time, by the way," Tristan said. The color rose in Leo's neck. "But I'm pretty sure *I* was the instigator. Do *you* think it was too fast?"

"No," Leo said emphatically, almost before Tristan had finished speaking. He wasn't blushing anymore; he looked almost grave.

"If anything, it's harder to leave now," Tristan said, keeping his hands to himself with monumental effort. "But it's not like I need to be down the hall to sneak into your room."

It was a careful, exploratory flirtation. Maybe he'd get to act on it, or maybe they'd laugh it off and never speak of it again. He couldn't be sure yet. The other night had been a spur-of-the-moment decision. Leo thought he was in love with someone else—or maybe he *actually* was in love with someone else, since Tristan probably had more in common with a stranger on the street than he did the naïve sixteen-year-old he'd been when Leo's memories of their relationship had been wiped. It left Tristan in the mind-bending position of being jealous of his own younger self.

But that person wasn't here. *Tristan* was. And he was going to win Leo back.

Leo hesitated a moment before he relaxed with a laugh. "Never thought a boy would resort to necromancy just to see me. I'm flattered."

"You should be," Tristan said, turning back to the box Leo had abandoned and letting the moment pass. But what he thought was: *You have no idea what I'd resort to.*

RAIN SOUNDED DIFFERENT in Bishop Library. It echoed off its high stone ceilings, clinked against the leaded windows, and dripped off its spires and cornices. Once he'd finished cleaning to the ambient music of the downpour, he went downstairs to poke around in the circulation desk and figure out how one went about running a library. It was closed today; Tristan should have been the only person in the building. But he wasn't.

The intruder was an older man with slicked-back white hair and a tailored suit. He ran a finger along one of the bookshelves. With his long neck, sagging cheeks, and hooked nose, he resembled nothing so much as a judgmental condor.

"Dusty in here," he said, rubbing his thumb and index finger together, nostrils flaring with disapproval. His voice was smooth and refined, with a faint rasp, like a bowstring that needed tightening. "You'll take care of that shortly, I presume."

"You must be Theodore Serapion," Tristan said.

"Indeed. I thought it was high time I paid this place a visit." He smiled thinly. Something about him bothered Tristan, like a tag in the back of his shirt—he wanted to scratch at it.

As far as Tristan was aware, Serapion hadn't made an appearance at Bishop Library in several years. He never bothered to come by when Dion took over for Meryl—in fact, he didn't *know* Dion had taken over. Serapion had hired someone else to fill the post, and Dion had quietly paid that person off so that he could take their place and use Bishop Library as his base of operations while he investigated Emil's disappearance.

"Your predecessor left on short notice, which was . . . inconvenient. Fortunately, you came highly recommended by Anne Sterling." Serapion advanced slowly, hands clasped behind his back. "I had my misgivings. But when she told me I would have the opportunity to watch over a young, untrained summoner in need of a firm guiding hand, I considered it my duty to take you under my wing."

The itch at the back of his collar became so pronounced Tristan had to dig his nails into his palm. He understood what it was now—recognition. A kind of unwelcome kinship.

Serapion snapped his fingers. "That hound in your shadow. Bring it out. Let me take a look at it."

How could he tell the hound was there? Tristan hadn't meant for him to know.

With a nudge at his mental link to the hounds, he summoned Lucky—the first hound he'd truly tamed, and the first with which he'd formed something like a bond of loyalty. But even his most docile hound—if it could be called that—was a terror to behold. It swept out of the shadows in a rush of black fur, twisting around him until its full physical form had emerged. It was taller sitting down than Tristan was standing, its teeth bared in a sharklike grin.

Serapion's lip curled. "There is a reason blækhounds have fallen out of fashion among most practitioners of the infernal arts. They're unsophisticated. Too . . . bestial. My late friend Emil Wulfsige had a fondness for them. But he was an eccentric, and master enough to exert absolute control over his creations. I forbid you from making more."

"Is that in my employment contract?" Tristan asked.

Serapion's mouth stretched in that thin smile again. It was the movement of a predator that hunted by mimicry, and held no true feeling. "You don't have a contract. We are making a gentlemen's agreement, you and I. Now, how many of these do you have?" He gave a careless wave toward Lucky. He wore a number of rings on his hands, pearl bands stacked like rosary beads, clicking with the movement of his fingers.

"Three," Tristan lied.

Serapion raised his eyebrows.

"Three? At your age? Impressive," he said, though it didn't sound like a compliment. "Emil was twenty-five when he made his first hound."

Tristan didn't reply; he didn't dare.

"Show me the grimoire," Serapion commanded.

"Grimoire?"

"Anne already told me everything," Serapion said impatiently. "You come from a largely nonmagical line, and your parents forced you to suppress your gift. You happened upon a family grimoire in a deceased relative's belongings and began to teach yourself. Well? Let's see what we're working with."

This was the cover story the three of them had told Anne, to explain how a necromancer Tristan's age had gone undetected for so long. Of course, the grimoire didn't exist.

"No," he blurted. "It's private."

A vein jumped in Serapion's temple. "Excuse me?"

"It's a family grimoire, like you said," Tristan told him, doing his best impression of a sullen teenager, which, in fairness, he was. "No one touches it except family."

Serapion's eyes hardened. His rings clicked on his fingers, though his hands hadn't moved from his sides. They weren't pearl, Tristan realized, but bone. When Serapion took another step toward him, Tristan backed up reflexively.

"Think carefully," Serapion said, "before you say the word *no* to me again."

Tristan knew without a doubt that he was about to be fired from his second job in as many weeks. He'd have to pack his measly few boxes and turn back up on Leo's doorstep after all.

Then one of the drawers in the desk popped open.

It made no sound, or none that could be heard over the rain; it had only moved an inch, but it *had* moved, completely by itself. Serapion couldn't see it from where he was standing. But he saw where Tristan's gaze went. He strode to the desk, pulled the drawer open all the way, and reached inside. Tristan watched, bewildered, as he took out a book bound in black leather, which Tristan had never seen before in his life. The embossed lettering on the front cover was in a language Tristan couldn't read.

"You'll need to hide it better next time." Serapion smirked, no doubt taking Tristan's stunned silence for dismay. As he flipped through the grimoire, his long white fingers barely touching the pages, he *tsk*ed disapprovingly.

"Of course it had to be a *Book of Fenrisúlfr*. This is not a training grimoire, to be sure. But I suppose we all must make do with what we have." He snapped the book closed and shoved it into Tristan's chest. Tristan caught the grimoire before it could fall. It warmed in response to his touch, until it was so hot it felt like pressing his hand against sunbaked asphalt. "I intend to keep a closer eye on this place for the foreseeable future. We'll see each other soon."

He gave a shake of his fingers, as if flicking off a drop of water, and a cloak of shadow unspooled from the air in a velvety cascade. He flung it around himself and it fell to his feet, just short of brushing the ground. Then he had vanished through the shelves, in the direction of the other Bishop Library.

Tristan stood there holding the strange grimoire, mystified, until a new voice said: "He's gone."

It was Dion Legrand.

"How long were you . . ." The question died in his throat as he looked down again at the book in his hands. It clicked; Dion had planted it in the desk, and he'd somehow drawn Tristan's attention to it—and Theodore Serapion's—just in time to extract Tristan from what was about to be a very tight spot.

"I came here to speak with you, but then Professor Serapion showed up," Dion said. "I decided to stay out of the way until he left."

"With me?" Tristan said. He and Dion had never exchanged a word before this moment. Yesterday, with Anne and the others, had been the first time they'd been in the same room together, and Dion hadn't so much as looked at him. But he had seen Dion before through the hounds' eyes and heard Dion's voice in the messages he'd sent to Aziza through the wind sprites. He knew Dion uncomfortably well, actually, for someone who hadn't officially met him.

But Dion knew something about Tristan, too: that Tristan carried a dead man's magic within him, bound into his soul so thoroughly it was as if Tristan had been born with it. Or reborn.

Tristan had been anticipating a confrontation of some kind. Maybe Dion had kept his secret only because he planned to take the matter of retribution into his own hands. But Dion only sauntered over and held out his hand.

"Professor Serapion was right about one thing," he said. "That really isn't a starter grimoire."

"Uh—right, sorry," Tristan said, returning it to him. "Thank you for letting me . . . borrow it. I don't know what he would have done if he realized . . ."

Tristan trailed off, not wanting to finish that sentence.

"He would have killed you," Dion said. It was clear he wasn't exaggerating.

But it wasn't the first time an elder necromancer had hated Tristan on sight. Beor the Huntsman had nearly snapped his neck when they'd met. Compared to that, Serapion had been downright affectionate.

"You called him 'professor,'" Tristan said, desperate to change the subject. "Is he your teacher?"

"No. He teaches an osteology course at Yale," Dion said, pivoting and walking away, the grimoire tucked under his arm. "He finds it flattering when people who aren't his students use his title. Try that next time instead of picking a fight you won't win."

"Someone was picking a fight, but it wasn't me," Tristan objected. "Where are you—Didn't you say you wanted to talk to—"

"Are you coming or not?" Dion said.

He had gone down the hall to the office; when Tristan caught up, he was busy drawing a series of symbols on the closed door with a piece of chalk. Four sigils inside of a circle—at two, four, eight, and ten o'clock—and two outside, at three and nine. The chalk didn't show up very well on the paint, but it didn't seem to matter. His black hair fell into his eyes as he bent over his work. He wore a distinctive watch, old-fashioned, with an engraved case and a wide leather strap.

He was composing a spell. Tristan had watched him do something similar last night, but these markings were different from the ones he'd used then.

"Are you going to make this door take us somewhere other than the office?" Tristan asked, hazarding a guess based on what he'd learned of Dion's craft yesterday.

"Yes."

"Can you go anywhere? Is it like shadow travel?"

"No. It's a spell to take me home." He straightened, dusting the chalk off his hands and striking a match. "There are exactly two places in the world that I can get to this way."

He tossed the match at the door, and it burst into flames.

A wave of heat rolled down the hall, but the fire didn't spread beyond the limits of the doorframe, and it only lasted a few seconds, giving off neither smoke or ash. It ate away the paint and left behind gleaming golden-brown wood with a spiraling grain pattern and a shiny brass handle that turned with stately silence in Dion's hand. The new door glided open with a *shush* of air, like a sigh of relief.

Behind it, instead of the cramped little office, there was a well-appointed study lined with bookshelves. A bay window overlooked an expanse of picturesque countryside—downy meadows and tumbling knolls—instead of the grid of storefronts, schools, and row houses surrounding Bishop Library. The sky was gray all the way to the horizon, and thunder rumbled in the distance. Any other summer, the room would have been pleasantly sunlit.

Dion shut the door and went to the bookcase behind the desk. "You'll be able to shadow-travel here from now on, I presume."

"Yes," Tristan said uncertainly. "But why would I . . . ? This is . . ."

"My home, yes. Emil's, really. But he left it to me."

That name, *Emil*, fell like an anvil between them.

"And . . . why did you bring me here?" he asked.

"Because it's where Emil did most of his work."

Dion pulled on the edge of the bookcase, and the whole thing swung aside to reveal another door. He held up a tiny bronze key.

"It's warded," Dion said. "You won't be able to shadow-travel inside. That's why I'm giving you this key. I have a copy, but try not to lose it."

He unlocked the secret door and then passed the key to Tristan, who accepted it mostly because he couldn't think of anything else to do. A short spiral staircase led down into a room about twice the size of the study, full of even more books. They had cracked leather-bound spines and yellowed pages, and not one of them, going off the titles, was written in English. On a hook in the corner hung the cloth-of-silver cloak that had saved Leo during the Wild Hunt.

While Tristan hovered by the stairs, Dion made his way to the back. He slid the grimoire he'd shown Professor Serapion into an empty space on one of the shelves, wandered down the row, and selected a slim, dark green volume instead, which he brought back to Tristan.

"Start with this," he said. "They're basic spells for communing with spirits—nothing too dangerous."

Understanding dawned. It was a few moments before Tristan could do anything but gawk at him.

"These are his grimoires?" he finally managed. "You're *giving me* his grimoires?"

"I certainly won't be using them." When Tristan didn't move, Dion held the grimoire out impatiently. "Take it."

Warily, Tristan did. A jolt went through him. It felt—alive. Like it was only asleep, and would move in his hands if he held it long enough. Khaled had told him once that a necromancer's grimoires were made from animal remains. He flipped through the book—leather, parchment, and a dark red ink that he strongly suspected contained blood. Whatever had died to make this grimoire, its death was the offering for the spells written inside, and its spiritual energy—anima—was preserved within its pages.

"I can't read any of this," Tristan said.

"Necromantic spells can only be written in dead languages. Most of what's in that one is Latin," Dion said, with a flicker of amusement at Tristan's incredulous look. "It's common for master necromancers to study linguistics so that they can better compose their own spells. You'll have to translate them to figure out what they do." He tapped the cover of the grimoire in Tristan's hands. "Latin. Not too difficult. Then look for the ones in Old Norse. That was Emil's preferred spell language. Maybe you'll take to it, too."

"But you haven't told me why you're doing this," Tristan said, clutching the grimoire so tightly that the soft cover bowed under the pressure. "How can you—even stand to be in the same room as me?"

"I can't," Dion said.

He let it hang between them, not looking at Tristan. Tristan was silent, waiting as if for his sentencing.

"But I also can't let Emil's gift go to waste," Dion continued. "If he were here, he would have taken you on as apprentice in a heartbeat."

But Dion was wrong. If Emil were here, Tristan wouldn't be his apprentice, because he wouldn't be a witch at all. He probably would've frozen to death on the streets last winter.

"I won't waste it," Tristan said.

Dion inclined his head in a curt nod. "I should be going."

"You're leaving?"

"Yes. Stay as long as you like. I'm rarely in the house, and when I am, I won't be in here. You won't see me much, if at all." At the stairs, he stopped, hesitating. "One more thing. Emil had one particular grimoire that held his rarest spells. He usually had it on him, and when he didn't, he hid it so well that even I don't know where it is. It wasn't with his remains."

He said it so casually. *His remains.* Aziza had told him what she and Dion had found under the hag's graveyard the other day, but it was still a shock to hear Dion say it like that, without flinching.

"And you think it's hidden in here?" Tristan asked.

"I hope it is," Dion said. "If you find it, could you tell me? It's an Old Norse book of the infernal arts. I just don't want it to fall into the wrong hands."

"I'll tell you if it turns up," Tristan said. He would have probably agreed to anything Dion asked of him.

Dion thanked him politely and left him there alone.

Tristan spent hours going through the grimoires that day, using an online translator to puzzle out some of the titles. It was going to take him weeks to get a fraction of the way through all of this. But as he combed through the wealth of knowledge around him, his mind turning over the possibilities, he began not just to look . . . but to search. His fingers traced over covers bound in flexible cowhide and glossy snakeskin and something that felt like emery paper but which he suspected had come from a shark. A few locked in glass cases contained whole pieces of bone and muscle—this one was studded with fangs, that one had a beak clasped around the spine like a hinge, another was tied shut with a tentacle wrapped over it like a cord, twitching occasionally.

Everything he had ever wanted to learn about necromancy was here. Overwhelmed, he retreated, taking a moment to catch his breath. His feet carried him away from the bookshelves and back to the silver cloak, his mind turning to Elphame—and to Lupa, the hound he'd sent with Hazel.

In Elphame, there were spirits in the water and voices in the hills, and fairy courts that warred and reveled and spun illusions real enough to touch. It sounded like another world, but it wasn't; the human and fae realms lay side by side, and the places where they touched were borderlands, shared territory. A magical boundary separated the human realm from Elphame, but this boundary was a force of nature, not a wall. It had phases, like the moon; patterns, like the weather. It was porous. At a witching hour, like midnight, or days of power, like the solstice, the boundary thinned, and gaps opened up which allowed borderland fae to slip into the human realm or hapless, lost humans to stumble into Elphame. A wild, abandoned place in the human realm could disappear into Elphame over time, like an island sinking into the sea; and human encroachment into once-wild places could shrink the borderlands. Beyond the borderlands, there were places that belonged only to Elphame, and which a human could not reach unless they were either very determined or very unlucky.

Coven Blackthorn was both.

The last time he'd seen Hazel with his own eyes was the final night of the Midsummer Revels. Her ball gown was wilted like a crushed flower, her emerald-black hair had fallen into disarray, and dried tears had left tracks through the glittery makeup on her green skin. Hazel was Leo's little sister, and a changeling—a fairy child who, as a toddler, had switched places with a human girl. She had grown up believing that she was human. But she was really the illegitimate child of the Summer King, and Princess Narra had staged a coup in hopes of placing Hazel on the throne. Hazel had refused, and Leo had intervened when Narra had tried to force her hand. Now the Summer Court had no monarch at all and was sick with the jade rot. Hazel had set off with Beor the Huntsman to solicit aid from the Winter Court—the Summer Court's counterpart and the other half of the Court of the Seasons, the highest law in Elphame. The Winter Court was hidden somewhere in the mountains of the Pacific Northwest and ruled by the fearsome Queen Ceresia.

Hazel's journey had taken her through Elphame's unblemished wilderness, at times on foot and otherwise on the ghostly steeds that Beor summoned for them. But as Beor succumbed to the rot—his distant human ancestry providing him with a slight but ultimately inadequate resistance to it—his magic had grown harder to control. Nonetheless, after a few days, they had reached the mountain range that concealed the Winter Court's palace, and the gargoyles that guarded its entrances had found them. They were brought before the Winter Queen in her throne room.

"I heard the tale of King Ilanthus's long-lost heir," Queen Ceresia said. "I heard she would journey to the Winter Court to plead for our assistance. I confess I have been looking forward to this."

All fairies were beautiful, but Queen Ceresia was beautiful like the glare of the sun on a frozen lake, the mournful howl of a starving wolf, the stark white of bone showing through a wound—you couldn't look without flinching. She had arctic-gray skin and a pair of coal-black horns rising from her brow; in her hand, she held a crystal staff, and her shimmery dress—Tristan had realized with horror as he took in the scene through Lupa's eyes—was made of wings. Fairy wings.

"We beg you," Beor rasped.

They knelt, Beor practically collapsing to his knees, Hazel shivering as she followed his lead—whether from the cold or nerves, Tristan couldn't tell. Lupa sat beside her, head low in an imitation of a bow.

"While the Summer Court is vulnerable, any of our subjects might seize the chance to take its place and ascend to the high court of Elphame." Queen Ceresia's cold smile made Lupa flatten its ears and press closer to Hazel's side. "I have no intention of granting them that opportunity. For now, our interests are aligned."

So it was settled. Hazel was given a place to stay in the Winter Court as the queen's ward, while Beor was placed in quarantine. As for Lupa, the queen instructed Hazel to keep the hound out of sight. Beasts were not permitted to roam the halls of the Winter Court's palace.

This left Hazel worryingly alone. When Lupa was concealed in the shadow plane, Tristan couldn't hear or see what went on around it. In private, though, Hazel would whisper Lupa's name, and Lupa would materialize in an empty corridor or lavish bedchamber. She would feed Lupa a piece of goblin fruit or a chunk of venison and say, "Tris, if you're listening, tell everyone I'm okay."

In response, he bid Lupa bend its head so Hazel could reach up and ruffle the fur between its pricked ears.

Today, a glimpse of Lupa's surroundings yielded nothing but darkness. But Lupa would know if Hazel was ever in trouble; he tried to be satisfied with that.

CHAPTER 3
LEO

THE CLOSEST BOUNDARY to the Inkcap Court was a few miles south of Savannah, Georgia, in a long stretch of marshland divided into sodden islets by capillaries of tiny, nameless waterways.

"I ran into them when I was a teenager," Anne said. "They're used to me, so I can do most of the talking."

That worked fine for Leo. He had a lot of practice playing assistant hedgewitch. They left the rental car on the side of the road, hidden by a stand of oaks dripping with Spanish moss. The air was like steam, hot and damp, despite the dark storm clouds congregating overhead.

He'd been to Georgia before just once, on his own. Almost exactly a year ago. He had spent most of that summer on a crusade to break his curse, following the sketchy leads he got off the internet in search of anything occult, supernatural, or even vaguely mystical. And, from what he'd heard, Georgia had it all. Haunted graveyards, motels, theaters. Portals to hell. Lizard men and swamp monsters. Not that he ever found them. He got a job bussing tables at a roadside diner for a couple of weeks while he ran his amateur paranormal investigation in his time off.

Now he was returning as royalty.

Kind of.

They squeezed in sideways through a fissure in the trunk of a tree. Inside, an earthen passage sloped downhill and into the burrow-palace of the Inkcap Court. He heard them before he saw them—their singing and laughter breaking through the shapeshifting melodies of their warped string instruments, which were contoured for longer, stronger, quicker hands than any human's. He and Anne had caught them mid-banquet.

The grand hall at the end of the passage had a patchwork opulence to it, with long tables dressed in threadbare lace, scattered oval-back chairs in cream damask, and faded paintings in gilded frames—like something pilfered from Savannah's old mansion houses long ago. The Fair Folk wore velvet and silk, strings of pearls in every shade of lavender and gray, still-growing plants sewn into skirts and jackets, and ornate embroidery that turned liquid where the light touched it. Water dripped down the walls in shiny, viscous trails, and the gaudy clusters of toxic mushrooms he'd seen aboveground had popped up here as well, in the corners and under the seats. The eponymous inkcaps oozed little black puddles that caught the candlelight like drops of citrine held inside dark, toothless mouths. Lily wine poured into stout crystal goblets, and radiant lesser fairies flitted greedily around mountains of saccharine, overripe goblin fruit and whole roasted boars. Couples teetered and spun in ecstatic, uninhibited dances that bore little resemblance to the elegant displays he'd seen in the Summer Court's ballroom.

"Can we really just show up?" Leo had asked earlier, remembering the last time he had unwittingly crashed a party in Elphame.

"I have a standing invitation to the Inkcap Court," Anne had assured him. "Once they've heard what we have to say, word will get out to the others. They'll be curious. And then they'll extend invitations of their own."

By *the others*, she meant the low courts that had been loyal to the late King Ilanthus. The Summer and Winter Courts jointly ruled Elphame, but they were rivals, too; their territorial disputes ended in bloodshed, but they backed each other unequivocally when the low courts formed alliances that might have undermined their authority. They kept Elphame in balance. Now, unless they wanted Elphame to dissolve into full-fledged warfare, they needed King Ilanthus's followers to fall in line with Queen Ceresia until the Summer Court could be saved.

"The last great fairy war was in the 1930s," Anne had explained. "During that time, the human realm experienced widespread drought, dust storms in the Plains that turned the sky black as far as New York City, miles of farmland destroyed—"

Leo gave her a sideways look. "Are you talking about the Dust Bowl?"

"My mentor was an apprentice during that time," Anne said. "I should have paid more attention to the stories she told me."

So Anne needed a representative of the Summer Court to show solidarity with the Winter Queen. Hazel was too important to risk parading her around out in the open, where a well-timed arrow could end the Summer Court for good. But Leo, her brother, was also a Prince of Summer.

That was what he was here for. *Diplomacy.*

The thought of Hazel sequestered in the Winter Court and probably homesick gave him a sharp pang. He had feared that as Hazel spent more time among her own kind, becoming more fairylike, she would also become less recognizable to him. The next time they met, would she be a stranger? But she was still just Hazel, her letters—which Lupa brought to him—rambling and full of doodles in the margins. He wished he could see her through Lupa's eyes, the way Tristan could, but it was almost as good to read her long-winded descriptions of all the strange food she'd tried and her lessons with the other young fairies. He could practically hear her voice in her head as she complained, *Even fairies have to do math. But they call it "figures" and we don't have calculators.*

It still didn't feel real, that Hazel wouldn't be there when he went home, that they might never live under the same roof again. He would've given anything to have her bang on his door way too early in the morning, wheedling for a ride to the mall or asking him to pick up ice cream on his way back from work. He couldn't bring her home or give her back what was left of her childhood. But he could at least do this much for her. Do something to keep her safe, from afar.

They found the Inkcap King at a table in the back, surrounded by his courtiers and attendants. His coat was the deep purple color of ripe blackberries, with a vinous sheen where it caught the light and slits in the back for his double set of ochre hornet wings. A crown of red pokeweed stems and black pearls rested in his hair. His features were dusted with opalescent glitter, on the tips of his long ears and the calligraphic arch of his cheekbones.

"Anne! How long has it been, my dear? A few months?" he said, arms spread wide in welcome.

"Four years," Anne said.

"Truly?" he exclaimed in shock. "You have neglected us! And to think, once we were among your closest friends."

"I hope to make up for my lapse. I've brought a gift." She drew from her satchel a bundle of folded cloth. When the Inkcap King spread it open in his arms, it was a length of mottled darkness, which blended so well with the shadows that it was almost invisible except where it lay in contrast with his skin. "It's a cloak of my own making, spelled with shade mimicry."

"Lovely," the Inkcap King said, rubbing the edge of the cloak between his fingers. "But your craftsmanship always is."

"I've also brought company." She put a hand on Leo's shoulder. "Please allow me to introduce the new Prince of the Seasons."

His eyes found Leo, glimmering with dangerous interest. It had been barely a week since Narra's escape from the Summer Court, but news traveled fast in Elphame. The wood nymphs, who had witnessed nearly all of it, would have passed along the story of Leo's role in that ordeal to anyone who would listen. The Inkcap King probably knew everything.

"You seek a pledge of loyalty on Queen Ceresia's behalf," he said. "It is no surprise you came to me first. No doubt you felt us more inclined to listen to you, owing to the fond relationship we've always enjoyed. More suggestible, perhaps."

"It's more that I know others will follow your example," Anne parried. This piece of flattery was welcomed by the Inkcap King, who gave an airy laugh.

"But the following sort are not the ones Queen Ceresia must concern herself with," he said. "Those with the means and desire to take the Summer Court's place will not be deterred by either the young prince's gestures of friendship or the Winter Court's posturing."

"They can try if they like, but they'll need to act swiftly," Anne said.

"Not so very swiftly, I think. We have seven years."

"Perhaps."

"Perhaps?" The Inkcap King leaned forward. "Queen Ceresia has a plan, then, to save the Summer Court."

"Such matters are best discussed with the queen herself."

"I am not eager to receive an invitation to her banquet table." He relaxed in his seat, a smile playing over his features. "No, I shall wait and let the news reach me by other means. But I won't entertain any more talk of politics until you sit and have a drink with me!"

Someone produced a chalice full to the brim with wine; he stretched across the table to offer it to Anne, the liquid spilling over and dampening his long fingers. Another was pushed into Leo's hands. Anne had built up a resistance to fairy wine through years of microdosing, like secret agents did with poison. As for Leo, the amber eye protected him from fairy enchantment. But it wouldn't protect him from getting drunk, and he needed a clear head. He held the chalice but didn't drink.

They were ushered into seats near the Inkcap King. Anne leaned in to pick their conversation back up, too quietly for Leo to overhear. But Leo hardly went ignored—the others at the table began to pepper him with questions. They wanted to know what had really happened on the summer solstice, and also how he'd been tricked into joining the Wild Hunt, and was it true that he'd stolen Beor the Huntsman's silver sword?

"You may as well accuse the fox of stealing from the wolf," an Inkcap fairy said, hiding a giggle behind a jeweled glove. "The fault lies not in the fox's ingenuity, but the wolf's blunder."

"May we see it?" someone else asked eagerly.

"I gave it back to him," Leo said.

They were perplexed by this—the concept of the fox returning the wolf's teeth.

"There was a time when humans used to test their dueling skill against us," the first Inkcap fairy said. "Do you need a sparring partner?"

"He has no weapon," someone reminded her disdainfully.

"Borrow mine!" another one said, producing an ivory sword with an emerald pommel and a subtle, leaf-like curve to the blade.

Leo wasn't a huge fan of having swords pointed at him. He cast around for a change of subject; luckily, he had a perfect view of the rest of the banquet hall, where there was plenty of inspiration to be had. With the loss of his natural left eye, his field of vision had been halved. And he still felt a little jolt of surprise when he looked in a mirror and saw the thin scar that ran from his eyebrow to his cheekbone, where the nymphs had sliced him open. But that felt a small price to pay for his truesight. He could see through illusions and was immune to fairy charm, which clouded human minds. He was resistant to the intoxicating effects of lily wine, the blackout delirium that a single sip of it could induce in a human. If he concentrated, magical energy was visible to him—as a kind of light, or sparks, or a hazy glow that clung to the supernatural. He was in the best health he'd ever been, too; his reflexes were better and his stamina improved, which he had discovered when he'd gone for a run the other day, lost track of time, and came home three hours later having barely broken a sweat. So that was cool, if a little unnerving. He would never be able to weave illusions or cast enchantments—humans couldn't wield fairy magic—but he carried a fragment of Elphame inside him now.

He had hoped his truesight would allow him to "see" through his curse, and recall the memories that eluded him. No dice, though.

His enhanced gaze traveled over the party. A pair of moth-winged fairies spun together in the air, hands clasped as they danced, the eyespots on their wings blinking lazily. In a pond ringed by speckled mushrooms, a dark, whiskered head surfaced so that a golden-haired woman could hand-feed it raw fish. Elsewhere, a fight had broken out between two men with leathery green skin and long reptilian faces.

"Is the wine not to your liking, Your Highness?" one of the Inkcap King's courtiers asked. Her wings were a shiny dark bronze, and she had four mirror-black eyes.

His first instinct was to say *Please don't call me that*. His next reflex would have been to raise the chalice and take a big gulp of its contents, while assuring his hosts that it was very much to his liking and totally not going to give him a skull-shattering hangover tomorrow morning. But fairies didn't like a lie, and that would be a transparent one.

"I'm just a little distracted," he said instead, sidestepping; it was a clumsy but acceptable response, both truthful and polite. He nodded toward the corner of the room, where the brawl between the two reptilian men had attracted a handful of onlookers. "I was watching the chess match over there—uh, it was a chess match a few minutes ago. I guess someone cheated."

The fairy laughed. "That's not chess. It's High King of Finches."

Then he had an idea. Maybe a good one. Maybe a terrible one.

"I don't know that one," he said casually. "I don't know any fairy games."

"No? But that will never do," someone else said, leaning over the table. Others chimed in to agree.

If there was one thing he knew a fairy couldn't resist, it was a game. Once, he'd played a game of chance with Prince Tal himself, and even won. He couldn't talk to the Inkcap King with the ease that Anne did—but a game could be a kind of conversation, too.

"Maybe someone could teach me to play sometime," he suggested.

The results were even better than he had anticipated. Instantly, a space on the table was cleared away to make room for a circular, checkered game board with finch-shaped pieces carved from jade and quartz.

He laughed with surprise, as if he hadn't been hoping for exactly this response. "It doesn't have to be now. Don't let me interrupt the party."

"The little prince thinks he can manipulate us," the beetle-eyed fairy commented, the corner of her mouth curving up. "How cute."

He stiffened, sensing something predatory in that smile. But the fairies who were setting up the game board only snickered.

"High King of Finches is a strategy game," one of them said. "It's a game of deceit. And it's a game about getting what you want. If you're one of us now, you'll have to be good at all of those things, Princeling."

One of us? Leo thought. He wasn't one of them. Hazel was. But that seemed like the kind of thing he shouldn't say.

"Okay," he said, leaning over the board. "I'm listening."

THE INVITATIONS ANNE had anticipated from the low courts of Elphame were soon arriving in a steady stream. Silk moths deposited them in her coffee. Mountain lions crouched on her porch carrying them in their jaws, and would not leave until Fox lumbered toward them in bear form, giving a warning swipe of its claws. A cloak of gray-banded goshawk feathers landed on her shoulders, and when she reached up to take it off, the feathers blew apart and rearranged themselves in order so that the letter scrawled on their undersides in microscopic script could be read.

Although Leo was supposed to be the Summer Court's representative, the kings and queens of Elphame's low courts just didn't take him seriously, and honestly, who could blame them? But their subjects were delighted to have something as rare as a human Prince of Summer in their midst. Leo would have to take advantage of that for as long as he could before the novelty wore off. He taught Aziza and Tristan to play the fairy games he learned so that he could practice; he won maybe two-thirds of his matches against them, and about a fifth against Anne. He almost never won against the Fair Folk, but that was all right. Winning wasn't really the point.

While Anne conferred with the Queen of the Glen, a gaggle of young knights in training took turns playing against him. Some of them declared that they intended to leave the Court of the Glen and join the Gallowglass—the knights who served Summer and Winter.

"But I heard," one of them said, "that King Ilanthus's guards turned against him, in the end. They betrayed him on the princess's orders."

With a pang, Leo remembered the Gallowglass who had fought to the death to stop Princess Narra's coup from succeeding, many of whom Leo had cut down himself while under her thrall. He saw their faces in his dreams sometimes.

"No," he said firmly. "There was only one traitor—Viren. He was Prince Tal's lieutenant."

"We heard he was the one who slew Prince Talarix," his opponent said, as Leo scanned the board and deliberated over his next move.

"He did. And then he escaped with Princess Narra," Leo said. "They were both sick with the rot by then."

He kept his eyes on his game pieces, but he felt the chill that ran through the other Glen fairies; they all shuddered.

"The rot is a terrible fate," someone murmured.

"It looked like it. But Princess Narra was pretty sure someone could help them," he said. "A witch."

He made his move, setting down his finch piece with a confidence he didn't feel. The Folk always made conversation as they played, which was probably a calculated attempt to break his concentration. The things that distracted him most were news of the Winter Court, and of Princess Narra. He never asked for information directly; they'd only talk him in circles. But he let himself be distracted.

"Protect them from the rot?" his opponent said, not touching his own pieces yet. "Impossible."

"Maybe. But it's not the first time Narra ran away to the human realm, is it?" Leo said.

"Yes, yes," one of the spectators said, bored. To them, this was old news. "She had a human lover. But her father put a stop to that."

He didn't have to fake his surprise. "You're kidding."

"We do not lie," the boy said, narrow-eyed.

"I know you don't," he said quickly. "I just didn't realize. She had this scar on her neck—she said it was from a silver collar she had to wear for a year. I always thought it was kind of harsh punishment for running away. Was that really why? Or was it because she was seeing a human?"

His opponent had made his move and now gestured for Leo to proceed. Leo had missed it; he had to study the board to see what he'd done. He played up his uncertainty, touching the crown of first one piece and then another.

"It wasn't only that," his opponent said. Leo glanced up, his finger still resting on the top of his finch piece. "Such dalliances are not unheard of. But she took something with her and lost it there. All because of this lover of hers."

"What did she lose?" Leo asked.

They glanced up at the Queen of the Glen, who was staring Anne down over her wine glass. They were out of earshot. Still, the boy lowered his voice.

"She lost the summertide lord," he said. "He hasn't been seen since that day."

Leo didn't know what the summertide lord was; but he had met the springtide lord, a massive water elemental, and he couldn't fathom the thought of a magical creature of that scale lurking in the human realm. But was that really it? Had Narra refused the throne, killed her family, and tried to force the crown on Hazel just to run off and be with some human? With the infamous Castor Thorne, perhaps? But that didn't sound right.

A greater destiny awaits me, she had said.

The conversation shifted to the Winter Court, and which of the low courts whispered about moving against Queen Ceresia. Though none of their monarchs had yet made a play for power, many of the Folk expected war. And if that happened, where would that leave Hazel? The current Summer Court would be lost forever. Hazel would be a lone fairy, an outcast.

As long as he was here on Hazel's behalf, he would do whatever it took to make sure the Winter Court remained in control. He'd make friends and gather intel. He would be the Princess of Summer's advocate and spy.

No fairy was interested in a game without stakes. So he bet small things. Trivial things. When he won—which was rare—they gave him equally small, trivial tokens. A strand of braided kelpie mane he would give to Aziza for use in a spell; a pearl of crystallized cloud that looked like mist captured in a glass marble, which he thought she might trade to a sandman. His favorite of the prizes he won was a talisman of petrified bark with a tiny moth wing embedded in its surface, to guarantee safety in flight. He had been careful to specify that "flight" included the landing and takeoff. If it worked right, then his dad could travel on airplanes again, which he hadn't done in over a decade—not since he had been cursed with his poltergeist, Spot. Leo would triple-check his wording with Anne and Aziza before he gave it to him.

But he lost more often than not, so he never gambled with memories or body parts, and he didn't carry anything of sentimental value on him. He had to get creative. He got a lot of traction out of telling stories, and was prepared with a wealth of anecdotes about the Wild Hunt, the borderland fae, the hag, and the curse. The last was met with great enthusiasm from the Glen fairies; Hazel's mother, Lady Thula, had been a famous enchantress, and they were delighted to learn of the casting that had been her swan song—an intricate and inescapable knot of magic, tailor-made to each of its victims, as if woven from their own heartstrings.

He agreed to grant favors only when they were highly specific. One of his opponents asked him to recite a poem of her choosing. She wanted to catch it in a sea-glass bottle.

"Like a recording?" he asked.

"Yes, just like that," she said. "I'll weave it into enchantment, pluck the notes from it like feathers, and string them into a summer storm illusion."

"And I won't lose my voice? Or my ability to speak and communicate?" Leo asked. "Or my grasp of the English language, or—"

He couldn't think of what else. He turned her request over in his mind, examining it from every angle.

"I only ask for a single poem," she assured him.

So he read a poem she selected out of a slender, handwritten book, and after she capped the bottle, he didn't feel any different. He went home shortly after that with the tokens he'd won, unscathed and triumphant.

Only later, when he tried to tell Anne the name of the poem, his mouth opened and no sound came out. He couldn't write it down or say it out loud, or any of the lines he remembered. He could still use the individual words, and phrases of up to four words together, but no more than that in the specific order in which they appeared in the poem.

It could've been worse, but it definitely took the wind out of his sails a little bit. He'd thought he was being careful. But although truesight let him see through illusions and inoculated him against fairy allure, it was clearly going to take much more than that to protect him from all their tricks.

CHAPTER 4
AZIZA

THE FAIRIES OF the Summer Court were nomadic, sleeping under the stars and returning to their castle only a few times a year. But none of them had been seen since the jade rot had taken hold. Now it was the castle that moved, uprooted by their diseased, volatile magic. It had vanished from the birch forest and appeared miles away, in a fen teeming with echoes; they called the news out to each other until the wind sprites overheard and brought it to the Cattail Court. By the time anyone came looking for it, the castle had vanished again and materialized somewhere else. Sometimes it stayed put for days; sometimes only hours. A run-down Victorian mansion with enchantment upon enchantment layered around it, it had become less a castle and more a haunted house, restlessly roaming the countryside.

And when it crept into the borderlands where the fae and human realms overlapped, Elphame's boundary faltered. Thin, invisible fissures gasped open along its length like runs in nylon stockings.

"You've watched over Blackthorn by yourself for years," Anne had told her, that night in the other Bishop Library. "I've checked your work. You have a knack for mending the boundary. That's not something that comes naturally to every hedgewitch. Most of us learn by apprenticeship."

It wasn't a knack. It was practice, trial and error, and a little advice bartered from the pixies. That had been her apprenticeship.

"It's going to take all of us to keep the boundary intact until the Summer Court's predicament is resolved. I'll be relying on you," Anne had said.

By "all of us," Anne meant the other hedgewitches she knew—witches with decades of mastery over their craft, including former students of hers, though she hadn't had an apprentice in years. She'd made them aware of the situation in Elphame, and they would be her allies in mitigating its impact on the human realm. The worst of the damage happened where the castle traveled, so Anne had put an oracle—Nelle Osorio—in charge of tracking it, bending the full force of her gift to the task of predicting when and where it would appear. Her visions tended to feature places more than people, so Anne was playing to her strengths.

"But my readings won't be exact," Nelle had warned them. "And I might not be able to give you much time to prepare."

Her spells produced different results each time. She'd recite coordinates, or say the name of a nearby town, or describe a sprawling field of golden-bronze grasses bordered by a slow-moving greenish river. It wasn't precise. It was "around there, probably" or "somewhere in that general area." Visions about the fae were "slippery," she said. But she always managed to get them pretty close.

So Nelle would call Anne, and Anne would call her allies with instructions—where to go, when they would be needed. It usually took several hedgewitches to repair the damage; the affected parts of the boundary could span miles. In the month that had passed since the solstice, Aziza and Dion had been dispatched three times.

Today, as she had each time before, Aziza followed Dion into the other Bishop Library. Through the door at the end of the secret chamber, a stone passage stretched into darkness. Recesses in the walls held iron sconces with dusty bulbs that flared on at their approach, unimpeded by the conspicuous absence of wiring, switches, or any discernible source of electricity. Eventually, they reached a crossroads. To the right, the tiles stuttered into scuffed hardwood floors; to the left, navy carpet began to fill the growing spaces between them, so that the tiles were like stepping stones across a stretch of water.

Dion knelt in the crossroads and drew two connected circles on the floor with a stick of chalk—the beginnings of a magical array, a kind of advanced spell. The first ring he left blank; the second, he filled with a spiraling tracery of figures and equations, consulting his watch every now and then. The device was more than a simple timepiece; it was a chronometer and a compass, with sub-dials that showed the position of the sun and the phases of the moon.

"This kind of spell is numerological, which means any witch can use it. Math is a universal language, and that's true when it comes to magic, too," he had said when, on their second outing, she had been unable to resist asking about it. "This is a navigator spell; it will tell you which way to go, but you have to fill in certain variables to let it know where you started, your intended destination, and when you're making your journey."

"Does everyone use one of those to get around?" she had asked, indicating the watch. "How come Anne doesn't have one?"

"No. It was a gift from Emil for my sixteenth birthday," he said absently, brushing the chalk dust off his hands.

And then she regretted asking.

When he was done with his calculations, he drew an arrow in the center of the empty circle, struck a match, and touched it to the floor. The array burst into flames, except the arrow, which spun like the blade of a propeller. As the flames died, the arrow stopped, pointing to the left path.

Dion wiped the arrow away with his hand, reducing it to a smear of chalk; the rest of the array was already gone, leaving behind no mark, not even ash.

It was the first of several crossroads where mismatched halls split crookedly apart. They walked over marble and stone, past crumbling mortar and peeling paint, under coffered ceilings and timber beams. At one point, Aziza heard running water through layers of concrete and earth. Another hallway echoed with the roar of a train on a set of tracks somewhere over their heads. It was surreal, like moving through a collision of alternate universes, bits and pieces of them tumbling together in a haphazard subterranean dreamscape.

These were the Flight Paths, the labyrinthine network of passages connecting the secret libraries that housed the collective knowledge of the American witch community. Their creation was one of the greatest feats of collaborative enchantment in recorded history, woven by countless hearth witches working in concert. The project was led by the Legrand family coven, who had designed the necessary spells, like architects drafting the blueprints of a new world. The entirety of the Legrand line had perished in a catastrophic fire about ten years ago—of which Dion had been the sole survivor—but their notes were still referenced in the routine maintenance of the Flight Paths. Any witch could navigate the Flight Paths if they had the necessary understanding of numerology, but only a hearth witch could alter them. And only a very skilled one, at that.

The Flight Paths were the fastest mode of travel between any two magical libraries. But the hallways rearranged themselves by the minute. If Aziza and Dion had doubled back to the last crossroads they'd passed, they would have found a completely different configuration of paths to choose from. It was a kind of defensive measure. Many of the libraries contained dangerous texts—spell books brimming with deadly incantations; cursed scrolls locked in reliquaries; notebooks left behind by dead hags, detailing their corruptive transformations step by step. It took years of study to get a handle on the numerological arrays required to traverse the Flight Paths; this was by design. And it was why she needed Dion.

Using the Flight Paths, they traveled from Bishop Library to the University of South Carolina in under an hour. From there, they had to drive. You had to be twenty-one to rent a car, and Dion was nineteen, but he could wield a fake ID with all the confidence in the world. The final leg of their journey was a boat ride to one of the barrier islands on the coast.

Nelle had given them a few hours' head start, but even so, they almost missed it. They arrived just in time to catch a glimpse of the castle as it dwindled in clarity like a mirage, evaporating before their eyes. There wasn't much left of the roof; it had jettisoned most of its shingles like so much dead weight, and the rafters were visible in some places, white as a flash of exposed ribs. The windows were broken, the chipped frames lined with glittering glass teeth.

"It's just a house," Dion said beside her, surprised. The castle vanished before he finished speaking.

"It is now," she said. "I'm going. Wait here until I'm done."

"Don't be ridiculous. What am I supposed to do for the next few hours?" Dion said.

"Tetris?" she suggested.

He had made it clear he wanted nothing to do with her. He was only here as a favor to Anne. But he didn't have to come along for the next part. She was trying to give him an out, which she had thought he'd have the good sense to take.

Being honest, as much as he probably couldn't stand the sight of her, she felt the same way. For different reasons.

"I'm already here," Dion said waspishly. "I'm going with you."

"Fine! Do whatever you want."

"I intend to."

He could not have looked less like someone who was prepared to spend an evening trekking through a swamp. He was wearing a sport coat and argyle socks. She considered pointing this out and then decided against it. His imminent regrets weren't her problem. Her problem was mending the boundary.

This wasn't Blackthorn, and she had to learn the warp and weft of the magic here, feeling it out with her craft before she could do any work on it. They skirted the edge of the salt marshes, where a meandering line of pines and live oaks aligned with the fringes of Elphame. The marshes tripped into dense, unspoiled woodland, where the snaking contortions of moss-draped branches mirrored the bends of the ubiquitous streams. That was the heart of the borderland, the place that was both human and fae territory, separated only by the tattered boundary she slowly patched with her own magic. Hours had passed before she was satisfied; by then it was late evening.

"Done?" Dion said. It made her jump; she'd forgotten he was there. To his credit, he'd kept up and stayed out of her way, and hadn't complained once.

"Almost," she said, veering toward the sound of running water. There was something here that shouldn't be—something that had come through the boundary before she'd sewn it shut. She knew it in the same way you knew when you weren't alone in a room that should've been empty.

Through the trees, she caught sight of a woman perched on the far bank of a stream, the water lapping at her calves. She could have passed for human, if human women made a habit of lying around naked in the woods at night, humming dreamily to themselves.

Her suspicions confirmed, Aziza held a finger to her lips for silence and led Dion back in the other direction.

"What is she?" he asked under his breath, when they were safely out of earshot.

"Nixie. You have to stay here," she said. Predictably, he began to argue, but she cut him off. "I'm serious. If she gets you into the water, I won't be able to do anything for you."

His scowl became more pronounced. "Anne didn't send me with you just to leave you alone."

"She definitely didn't send you to be my chaperone, either. You could have waited in the boat," Aziza reminded him, digging her headphones out of her backpack and pulling up a playlist on her phone that Leo had sent her. She shoved both into Dion's hands. "You need to hide. And put those on. Volume all the way up."

She returned to the stream alone and stepped into the nixie's line of sight.

"Hello there," the nixie said. "I thought I sensed a gatewalker skittering about."

Though clouds blotted out the moon, her reflection in the dark water shone. Her bare skin was radiant beneath the tendrils of sleek black hair that twisted down her body and trailed into the stream.

"I didn't expect to find one of you this close to the sea," Aziza said. The sea was siren territory, and sirens were the nixie's natural enemy. "You must be anxious to return home. Allow me to assist you."

"Yes, of course," the nixie said. "But won't you indulge me first? Stay and listen to my song. It's been so long since I could perform for anyone."

This request was a trap. Nixie song lulled their listeners into a trance, allowing the nixie to lure them into the water and drown them. But outright refusal would enrage her, and then she would transform into a bloodthirsty river beast. The correct answer to the nixie's question was to offer to perform for her first. If you impressed her, she'd let you go. From experience, Aziza knew that fairy wine would also placate a nixie, but she didn't tend to keep any of that on hand.

Aziza couldn't sing or play any instruments, and a bad performance would only upset the nixie. But a hedgewitch was immune to fairy thrall, and the nixie's musical allure, too, would do her no harm.

"I would be honored to hear your song," Aziza said.

The nixie closed her eyes and began to sing in an airy, euphonious voice. Quietly, Aziza slipped a hand into her pocket and touched the charm she'd made the other night, which contained an incomplete spell.

A spell was magic given purpose and form. The magic came from the witch, an innate gift. From there, two additional elements were required to shape the spell—like the joining of spirit with body and mind, Anne said. First, the offering, the "body" of the spell. Usually, this was something physical, something to ground the spell in the natural world. Dion used fire, burning his arrays; Nelle poured liquor into her scrying bowl; Jiddo packed herbs into satchels and buried them to anchor his wards. Anne used wood from enchanted forests deep in Elphame, charms won off fairies in games of High King of Finches, natural materials like feathers or pieces of coral found at the boundary, or her own blood. Those were the kinds of things Aziza would use, too. Second, the language—the "mind" of the spell. Story was the language of hedgecraft. But that made a hedgewitch's spells slow and lengthy to cast.

Many witches never bothered learning spells. There was plenty that a witch could accomplish with clear, focused intentions and maybe a few words or a ritual action for good measure. This was how, for years, Aziza had maintained Blackthorn's boundary with Elphame by patrolling the length of it, and how Tristan could summon the hounds with a gesture. When magic was done without an offering, the body bore the cost; it would drain the witch's energy and could make them pass out if they weren't careful. But more complex or powerful workings required spells.

When casting on the spot wasn't an option, some spellwork could be done in advance. That was what the charm was for; it contained a sleeping spell Anne had taught her. Her charm was a vial of dream she'd gotten from a sandman in exchange for one of her own, and a story whispered over candlelight about a serving boy in Elphame trapped in an enchanted sleep. All she had to do was open the vial and focus her magic on the spell to trigger it.

She twisted the cap in her pocket. The nixie was still singing. Aziza couldn't understand the words, which were in an old language that belonged to the likes of water lilies and kingfishers. But it was pleasant enough. At least until the nixie stopped mid-sentence.

For a split second, Aziza felt a surge of triumph; the spell had worked.

"You don't like it," the nixie said, in wounded tones.

"What? No. It's great," Aziza tried. She clutched the charm more tightly, filling her mind with the soporific warmth of a sandman's voice and the glow of moonlight seen from the corner of one's eye.

"Your face," the nixie said. "You're supposed to fall in love when I sing. Everyone does. But you're not."

"It's not your fault," Aziza said. "I'm a—"

"A soulless philistine who wouldn't know good music if it bit you." Her teeth, bared in a twisted expression of rage, were sharper now than they had been a few seconds ago. Larger, too. Her jaw had widened to accommodate them, and her voice had gone jagged, as if it had cut itself on their points.

A cloud drifted away from the moon, and when the light fell over the stream, the nixie wasn't a beautiful girl anymore. She had scales; she was on all fours, with a reptilian body and a lashing tail—

Aziza turned on her heel and sprinted away.

In her beast form, a nixie was much faster in the water than on land. Though her raspy breathing and deep-throated, raptorial growls were loud and close—though the trees shuddered as her powerful tail slammed against them, leaves raining down—she tired faster than Aziza did. Soon, Aziza had lost her.

Once she was certain she was in the clear, she doubled back to check on Dion. She had been careful to lead the nixie away from him. In the distance, the nixie crashed around searching for her, all rapacious fury and no stealth. Listening hard in case the nixie came back, she forgot to watch where she was going and almost tripped over him.

"This is not bad," he said, waving the phone at her, where Leo's playlist was still going. And then: "Why are you out of breath?"

She set about making a trap spell. Her sleeping spell hadn't worked, but she was reliable with traps. A ring of salt; a few drops of blood; a story about a princess and a silver collar . . .

"Found something," Dion said, wading back across the stream, several strands of long black hair tangled around his fingers. Since he had insisted on accompanying her instead of hiding someplace safely out of the way, she had instructed him to make himself useful; she could use nixie hair as a charm component. She took it carefully from him, wiping it off where it stuck to his skin. It had a slippery-smooth texture, almost slimy, like pondweed.

"Are you sure you can do this?" Dion asked. When she looked up, his studious gaze was trained on her face, his expression opaque. After weeks of mutually avoiding each other's eyes, it somehow felt more personal than touching him.

"What do you mean?"

"We can get away while she's distracted. Anne will send one of the others to finish the job. You don't have to—"

Did he think so little of her that he doubted her ability to pull off one of the easiest spells in a hedge witch's arsenal? The spell he himself had taught her?

"I *know* this spell. It's going to be fine," she snapped.

But suddenly she wasn't as certain as she had been a few minutes ago.

It wasn't long before the nixie tracked Aziza back to the water. She came charging into view; her rage had not abated in the slightest. She was massive, her snout alone the size of Aziza's torso. The vertical slits of her pupils were trained on Aziza. She and Dion waited a few yards back from the trap spell, which they'd camouflaged under fallen leaves. The nixie would have to walk over it to get to them.

Aziza's heart rate picked up. Had she made the trap spell big enough?

They were about to find out.

Dion stood rigidly at her side. Out of some misplaced sense of obligation, or maybe pride, he'd refused to leave. She would have argued with him if they'd had more time. This was why she hadn't wanted Dion to come with her in the first place. Because it was dangerous—and because failing would feel ten times worse if he was around to see it.

And lately it seemed all she did was fail. She had indirectly caused Prince Tal's death. After promising to save Meryl, she had yet to uncover any clues as to her whereabouts. She had misjudged Dion, mistrusted him, deceived him, and he had repaid her by keeping her secrets and protecting her coven. Brilliant, poised, self-assured Dion Legrand, the youngest master hearth witch in the country, who always knew exactly what he was doing and never let his personal feelings cloud his judgment.

She had gotten by just fine as Blackthorn's sole hedgewitch all these years, and had never had reason to doubt her abilities, at least before the hag had come along. But now she was painfully aware of how little she really knew.

That was what she thought about whenever she looked at Dion.

The nixie picked up speed. Her body was heavy and low to the ground, gator-like, and moved sinuously from side to side as the distance between them shrank at an alarming rate. She lunged, mouth open as wide as it would go. Aziza could see her back teeth and straight down her red throat. For a second, she was certain she'd doomed herself and Dion both.

But then the nixie let out a roar. She had frozen where she stood, teeth snapping at the air, unable to get any closer. Her tail whipped against the invisible barrier of the trap spell.

Dion's breath rushed out of him. Aziza had to suppress her own sigh of relief.

"Change back," she said.

The nixie turned back, shaking with fury, her teeth still too large for her beautiful, delicate face.

"Gatewalkers are all the same. You don't have an ounce of poetry in your body," she said forlornly. "All you know is blood and debt."

Aziza stood at the edge of her trap circle and smiled as she said, "Would you like to make a deal?"

It was late enough that Tristan would be asleep when they returned to Bishop Library, but he'd left his door unlocked for her. She was looking forward to passing out on his couch.

"I wasn't expecting such a close call," Dion said, as they made their way back through the Flight Paths. "Is that . . . a common occurrence?"

"There's always danger when you're dealing with the fae," Aziza said defensively. "It would have been fine if my charm had worked."

"What charm?"

She showed him the vial. "It was supposed to be a sleeping spell."

"You just need more practice. Or maybe charms don't suit your craft. Not all witches can—" He stopped, squinting at it. "What did you use for the anchoring material?"

"A gift of dream from a sandman, braided dandelion stems, and some blækhound fur that Tristan trimmed off Lucky for me."

Dion gave her a scathing look. "You filled your charm with *weeds and hound fur*?"

"Most of my herb garden withered after the summer solstice. I just needed something to pad it out," she grumbled. It was a consequence of the Summer Court's fall—crops failing and plants shriveling to husks overnight, all up and down the East Coast. Gardens dying of drought while it rained nonstop; that was par for the course when the Court of the Seasons was broken. It would be seven more years of this, and worse, if they couldn't fix it.

"You'll get better results with better material, especially when you're just starting out," Dion said.

"Where am I supposed to get better material?" she said rhetorically. "I have to work with what I've got."

He was quiet for a moment before he said, "I know a place."

CHAPTER 5
TRISTAN

THE CAB DROPPED them off near an abandoned shopping mall, its walls streaked with faded graffiti and the flowerbeds by the entrance choked with weeds. Dion had led them through the Flight Paths and then sent them on alone; he had no interest in accompanying them where they were going. He said he didn't care for the crowds. Nelle met them outside.

"I knew you'd be late," she said with an enigmatic smile.

Her long hair hung loose to the middle of her back, a faded red with dark brown roots, and her headphones were pulled down around her neck. They were enchanted to suppress her Sight—her clairvoyance—and spare her from unwanted visions. Her gift was difficult to control, even when she guided it with spellwork. So sometimes when Nelle said *I knew that would happen* or *I saw that in a vision*, she meant it. And sometimes she was just messing with them.

She herded them through the automatic doors, which had frozen halfway open, and past vacant shops with desolate window displays populated by bare mannequins. Their reflections sailed through them like ghosts. Puddles of rainwater had collected under the broken skylights. A stalled escalator led down to a basement level. It was pitch-black, even when they pointed their flashlights into it.

"Just a few spells for privacy," Nelle said. "It won't hurt you. Go on."

With an uncertain glance at each other, they did.

Tristan's skin prickled as he descended, as if he'd walked into a spiderweb, delicate and clinging. He wanted to brush his hands over his hair and clothes to wipe away the feeling. But it lasted only a second; then they'd passed through the magical barrier and into an explosion of light and sound.

Downstairs, between a defunct food court and the husk of a Macy's, was a sprawling marketplace. Chipped laminate tables had been repurposed for shop displays, illuminated by candles and battery-powered camping lanterns on every surface. Colorful awnings and hand-painted signboards adorned the stalls. Some of the vendors had set up behind the counters of the empty restaurants; the escalator let out near what had once been a Wendy's, where a hearth witch sold pastries with cocoa-infused cantrips for luck and citrusy bursts of euphoria.

"No *way*," Leo said.

"Shh," Nelle said through a grin. "Be cool. Don't look like tourists."

"Where are we?" Aziza said, as wide-eyed as Leo.

"The Half Moon Market," Nelle said. "Once a month, sundown to sunrise, hosted at a different venue every time. Witches only. And plus-ones who can keep a secret. And the Folk, sometimes, if they can sneak in and don't cause enough trouble to get caught."

They passed booksellers with rare bestiaries and spell books locked in glass cases. At a closet-sized cantina, a bartender passed out shots. A woman held the glass to her lips, but didn't drink; instead, a plume of greenish smoke wafted from the glass and into her mouth. The stall next door had towers of mismatched ceramic tea sets, saucers stacked dozens high, cups piled precariously atop them and each other or hanging from hooks—all of them were spelled by a hearth witch so that your tea would never get cold or with shifting patterns that, at a touch, rearranged themselves into eerily specific words of advice. (Leo's said: *Fairy games are never fair. Proceed with caution.* Aziza's said: *Go upstairs. You'll know when it's time.* Tristan declined to participate. If he wanted questionable advice, all he had to do was look inward.) Down a narrow alley, someone was doing stick-and-poke tattoos. When the tattoo artist took away the needle and sat back, a newborn ink snake slithered up their client's wrist, over her elbow and into her sleeve, as if it was shy. A man played the cello for a small audience; Leo grabbed Tristan's hand and stopped them at the edge of the crowd to listen. Tristan held his breath, afraid to move in case it made Leo let go.

"He's an oracle," Nelle said, when she'd seen what had caught their attention. "When he wants to read someone's fortune, he composes a song for them. And over there? She's a telepath."

She indicated a tattooed apothecary with wire-rimmed glasses on a chain and a cardigan with the sleeves pushed up to her elbows, selling mason jars of potions to block intrusive thoughts, enhance daydreaming ability, improve focus, jog your memory—

"This one could come in handy," Nelle said, picking up the memory potion and showing it to Leo.

Leo shook his head regretfully. "The curse would probably knock me unconscious fighting it off."

Aziza took the potion from Nelle. "Do you think—"

"That's basically cheating. You don't need that when you have me," Leo said. "We already study together, so you'll be following my revision schedule like it or not. You think I can't get us both by without a magic potion?"

"What's cheating?" Nelle asked.

"She wants to use it for exams," Leo said.

Tristan was examining a row of vials. *Debate tinctures,* the sign above them said. *Cite sources from memory and win arguments!* "Isn't it also cheating when you copy each other's essays?" he asked, without looking up.

"That's just teamwork," Leo said.

"I don't know how you think we're going to keep up with class when Anne has us running halfway across the country every few days," Aziza said, putting the potion back. Tristan had wondered about that, too; their summer break was over in a couple of weeks. "We should drop out and take the GED with Tristan."

"I didn't claw my way back onto the honor roll just to drop out," Leo said indignantly. "And I'm not letting you leave me alone there."

They could've spent hours looking around and still not seen everything there was to see. Top priority for Leo was to try every kind of food available, splitting portions with the rest of them so that he wouldn't eat his own weight in enchanted pastries. With a mixture of interest and trepidation, Tristan perused a selection of blank grimoires; they came pre-charged with spiritual energy from the death offering used to make them, and were accompanied by small pots of blood-based ink for filling them with new spells. Nearby, Aziza inspected a display of healing poultices—to ward off infection, reduce scarring, numb pain. Abandoning the grimoires, Tristan pulled Leo to a shop that sold silver weapons.

"Isn't it about time you got one of these?" he said, indicating the knives. Both he and Aziza already had their own. Pure silver repelled the fae and could deflect or nullify dark magic, but it didn't hold an edge very well. Mundane weapons were usually steel, and most jewelry was sterling silver. But these were witch-made, and would be unalloyed and enchanted for durability.

"I don't think I'm a knife person," Leo said.

"It's for self-defense," Tristan argued. "Unless you'd prefer the jewelry? Maybe a nice piercing?"

"I think if I showed up in Elphame wearing silver, I'd lose whatever body part it was attached to." He shot a speculative glance at Tristan. "You think I should get a piercing?"

Tristan averted his eyes as he replied, firmly, "No, I think you should get a knife."

"What is it with you children and knives? The silver bullets are right there," Nelle said, appearing at Leo's side.

Nelle introduced Leo to the man who did her headphones to see if he could make contact lenses that would disguise the amber eye, to replace the patch he'd been wearing in public. Meanwhile, Aziza found a vendor who sold empty charm vials—many of them with flip-tops for easy opening, or etched with sigils to increase spell potency—and a selection of magical herbs to fill them with. A few spots down in the same row, a booth draped in black velvet was surrounded by a conspicuous bubble of empty space, as if people unconsciously gave it a berth. While the others were occupied, Tristan walked over and brushed aside the curtain entrance to peek curiously inside.

It was candlelit, with poppies in hanging planters and animal skulls on mounting stands. But most of the space was taken up by glass cases that contained pendants—orbs, lockets, iron knots. Tristan caught a chill when his eyes lingered on them.

"Are you coming in? You're messing up the mood lighting."

A boy sat with his head bent over a table in the back, looking up as Tristan stepped inside and let the entrance fall shut after him. His messy black hair stuck out in every direction, and he had creeping vines tattooed from the collar of his shirt up to his jaw. He wore blue feather earrings and cuffs of white beads on both wrists, which, upon closer inspection, weren't beads at all, but bone.

"This is a little theatrical, isn't it?" Tristan said.

"Theatre is what the people want," the boy said, his snakebite piercings glinting as he spoke. His voice had a dreamy, serene quality, as if he was talking half to himself. A glass pendant rested on the table between his hands; beside it was a grimoire, an ordinary yellow notepad, a ballpoint pen. He shifted, kicking his legs out as he leaned back in his seat. "But what is it *you* want? It's not every day a necromancer walks into some nobody medium's shop."

Tristan hesitated. "How did you know I was a necromancer?"

"The same way you knew I was a medium."

"Because you're in a black velvet tent surrounded by skeletons?" Tristan said, choosing not to admit that he *hadn't* known the boy was a medium until just then.

"Because your craft and mine are cousins." The boy scratched at a bit of stubble on his chin. "You sensed it. I mean, didn't you?"

Tristan's first instinct was to lie and say he had, but then he realized it *wasn't* a lie. It wasn't only curiosity that had drawn him here. When he concentrated, he did feel it—something familiar, like when he had met Theodore Serapion, but less . . . abrasive.

"I guess you're right," he said.

"You're new, aren't you?" the boy said. For a terrifying moment, Tristan was certain he'd been caught out as the imposter he was. But then the boy added, "It's your first time traveling to see the Market."

"Yeah," Tristan said. The boy kicked at the leg of the chair opposite his, indicating Tristan should sit. Warily, Tristan did. "I don't know many other witches. I'd never even met another necromancer until . . . recently."

"What about your family?"

"I don't have any family. Not by blood, anyway."

The boy held out a hand to shake, and Tristan took it.

"I'm Jun," he said, smiling warmly. He had the kind of eyes that struck Tristan as haunted, not like a graveyard, but like a well-loved old house. "Now you know one more necromancer. Sort of."

"Tristan," he replied. "What's the difference between a medium and a necromancer?"

"Power, mainly," Jun said. "Your craft can support much more complex spells than the average medium's. A necromancer can raise the dead, command spirits, create blækhounds. If you're a real fool, you could even perform a possession. In every generation, only a small handful of witches with an affinity for the infernal arts will manifest true necromancy. Most of us just get slivers of it." He propped his elbows on the table, nudging his grimoire aside. "It's like how some clairvoyants get the occasional premonition or maybe manage to scrape a few details about your fortune out of tarot cards or tea leaves, but an oracle Sees the future in HD. Full-fledged visions, prophecies, you name it."

"So if you're a medium, does that mean you can . . . talk to ghosts?" Tristan asked.

"Not exactly." Jun picked up the pendant, a glass sphere maybe an inch in diameter, with a metal closure at the top. "My specialty is reminiscence charms. People bring me objects that were important to the deceased, or a piece of their remains, like a lock of hair. I can capture the lingering anima attached to the object and imbue it into the charm, usually with something like sand to help it stick. Glass is popular—it's easy for me to work with, and it glows or shimmers sometimes when it's haunted. Lockets, too. Metal is sturdy and will hold a stronger haunting, as long as you avoid silver."

"Is there a big market for haunted jewelry?" Tristan asked.

"Sure. You touch the charm and feel the presence of your loved one. Who doesn't want that, when they're grieving?" Jun said, fiddling with the closure on the pendant. "It's harmless, of course. Their soul is gone, you're not keeping them from reaching the afterlife. Whichever afterlife you believe in. It's just a way of preserving a little piece of their energy. A wisp of them that you can hold in your hands."

"I guess it's no different from taking comfort in visiting a grave," Tristan said.

Jun shot him a knowing glance. "But you can't relate."

"No," he admitted.

"What would comfort you, then?" Jun asked.

"Nothing. I'll have to make sure the ones I love outlive me."

Jun laughed, as if he thought that was a joke.

"If you're interested, I can trade you a charm if you'll teach me a spell," he said. "Not a reminiscence charm—just something to help focus your craft or give your spellcasting a little boost."

"I thought you couldn't do a necromancer's spells?"

"I usually can't, but I like to test the limits of my craft. Sometimes, I manage to pull it off."

"Okay," Tristan said. "But I'm not very good at spells—I just started learning. And I'm mostly teaching myself."

From his backpack, he pulled out a slim tome bound in crimson snakeskin. The title was Latin in gold lettering on the front; it read *The Serpent Arts, Volume 1.*

"If you don't have a teacher, where'd you get that from?" Jun asked.

"I had one, but he passed away. This belonged to him," Tristan said. He picked a spell he'd already tried out a few times. It was only a few lines long, but it had taken him hours to translate the splotchy handwriting, and even longer to practice reciting it until the words felt comfortable in his mouth, and longer still to make the words *do* anything. Spellcasting required a state of deep focus that reminded him a little of sketching. He had to concentrate, but not so much that he stifled the subconscious workings of his mind. Magic, like art, required practice but eventually became muscle memory, at its best when it could be done without direct thought, when you had developed an intuition for it.

He read the spell aloud in his shaky Latin. When he finished, the laces binding the spine of the grimoire loosened; the page that contained the spell pulled itself free, shaking itself out with a little puff of sweet, dusty old-book smell. It began to curl in on itself as if in response to heat. But it wasn't burning. It folded itself up; it crinkled in some places and tore in others, bits of paper flying away and then reattaching themselves to the page in new configurations. The ink with which the incantation had been written traveled over the paper's surface, forming new markings: a pair of beady eyes, a mouth concealing twisted paper fangs and a dry flickering tongue, the delicate outline of scales. Soon, a paper snake sat before them, slithering in little exploratory circles under their rapt gazes.

"Who knew necromancy could be so adorable?" Jun said. He touched the tip of the snake's tail. When he picked it up, it coiled around his wrist.

"I think it's possessed by the spirit of the creature whose remains were used to make this grimoire," Tristan said, running a finger down the center of the book, which still lay open and unbound. "The snake is just a vessel for the spiritual energy. I haven't figured out how to control it yet, so it's . . . kind of useless."

"So niche! I love it," Jun said. "It's probably just a matter of adding commands into the spell before you cast it. Some spells are designed to be built on. It's good practice if you intend to compose your own one day."

Tristan ended the spell, and the paper snake sewed itself back into the grimoire. Jun copied the words off the slightly crumpled page into his own notepad. He'd have to transfer it into a suitable grimoire before he could use it. When he was finished, he dug around in a chest behind the table.

"Here—a spellcasting aid. Something I only sell or trade to other mediums, not the general public," he said. "It's a charm that will help you find dormant spirits and pull them under your control, even without a piece of their remains to anchor them."

An iron sigil swung at the end of a black cord, indecipherable at first glance, but when he looked more closely he thought there was something featherlike about it—a curved line bisecting an asymmetrical diamond shape.

"Thank you," Tristan said, surprised by how much it meant to him. He had stolen so much of what made him a witch—his magic, his hounds, the keepsakes from the Summer Court's graveyard hidden in his bag for emergency spirit summonings. But this was something he'd earned.

There was a tug in his mind—Aziza, on the other end of the bond, searching for him—and he realized abruptly how long he'd been gone. He shot to his feet. "Sorry—I just remembered my friends are waiting for me. I should go."

Jun waved him off. "Come see me next time you make it to the Market. I'm always here."

"I will," Tristan said, pausing at the entrance. "One more thing. Earlier, you said something about how . . . you'd be a fool to try a possession. Why is that?"

"There are three forbidden practices in necromancy." Jun counted them off on his fingers. "Human possession, hound possession, and resurrection. The first one's banned because of the obvious—it's a major human rights violation. Even if someone consents to the possession beforehand, they can't continue to give consent once the possession begins, and they can't revoke it if they change their mind. Second one's banned because of incidents where necromancers got stuck as hounds, or they kept some of the hound's temperament when they returned to their own bodies—they became aggressive, violent, or went completely mad. And resurrection is the most dangerous, because it's corruptive."

"Corruptive?"

"Corruptive magic can turn a witch into . . . something else. Something powerful, immortal, and parasitic. A hag, usually, or sometimes a striga or a lich."

Tristan's whole body went cold. He had to plant his feet against a wave of dizziness.

"I thought . . ." he said, and stopped. He had known that a witch could turn into a hag. It hadn't crossed his mind that *he*, a witch himself now, could—could turn into—

Jun's brow creased in a look of concern. "What?"

"Doesn't it take . . . a long time?" Tristan asked, clumsily formulating the first question that came to mind.

"Well, yeah, the transformation is more likely to happen if you use corruptive magic more than once," Jun said. "Sometimes it's a slow deterioration. But sometimes just once is all it takes."

"I see," Tristan said.

Jun's eyes narrowed, alarmingly perceptive. "Resurrection isn't the only form of corruptive magic, but it's certainly the most tempting for any necromancer who's capable of it. But anyone you cared enough about to bring back . . . like that teacher you mentioned . . . they wouldn't want you to take a risk like that."

"I get it," Tristan said, averting his eyes. "I was just curious. And I thought it would be nice if we could save people and not just steal their ghosts out of their graves after they're gone."

"There's salvation in death, too."

Not the kind of salvation that Tristan was looking for, though.

He almost collided with Aziza as he left. She had come looking for him; with the bond, he wasn't difficult to find. It allowed for an exchange of emotions and impressions as long as they weren't deliberately blocking each other out. The root of the bond, the underlying magic, was a contract that had shackled Tristan in service to the hag. When the hag died, the bond was supposed to take him with her. Aziza had adopted the hag's side of the bond to save his life, and in doing so, had turned it into a bond of equals—because a hedgewitch, unlike a hag, could not have a bondservant.

Was this, too, corruptive magic? Did it matter to him if it was? He wouldn't undo the bond even if he could. It had been uncomfortable at first, but he found it reassuring now, and he suspected Aziza did, too. The two of them sometimes plucked at it throughout the day for no real reason, like a loose thread on the hem of their sleeves, as if to say, *Are you there?* and *I'm here.* It was their bond now. But it had been the hag's first, the malevolent creation of a corrupted witch. Was corruption something that could be reclaimed—remade?

He didn't know, and that troubled him.

CHAPTER 6
AZIZA

After they caught up with Tristan, they made their way to the alley where most of the fortune tellers and seers congregated. They divined the future using crystal balls, tarot cards, runes, tea leaves, and she didn't know what else. Some of the booths had privacy screens, and clients disappeared behind them one by one. The stall next to Nelle's had a wall of mirrors as its backdrop. But Nelle's setup was no-frills, a collapsible utility table with a laminate surface. On it, the selenite scrying bowl that had been passed down from her grandmother sat beside a ten-dollar bottle of tequila; these were the implements of Nelle's witchcraft.

She scryed for tips, drinks, or IOUs. People came to her looking for lost things, family heirlooms, buried treasure; some of them asked for the locations of significant events in their future, though Nelle warned them that such knowledge could change the future and render her prediction null. In between clients, she maintained a running commentary about the things and people around them, and often friends of hers stopped by to say hello.

Just before midnight, the atmosphere in the Market began to change subtly. The crowd thinned out. A number of people milled around something on the edge of the Market floor.

Then a face flickered across the bottom of Nelle's scrying bowl. They jumped, but Nelle only rolled her eyes.

"I hate it when he does that," she said.

The face had also appeared on the mirrors in the neighboring stall, multiplied a dozen times; it was in the glass chambers of the camping lanterns on a few of the tables and on people's darkened cell phone screens, on potion bottles and on teakettles. The reflections belonged to a man in maybe his mid-forties, handsome like a seasoned movie star, clean-shaven with a square jaw and gray-streaked blond hair.

"Good evening!" he said, with a blinding smile. "Tonight's entertainment will begin shortly. Please make your way to the south end of the Market."

"Who's that?" Leo said.

"Castor Thorne," Nelle said. "I think he's running the duels tonight."

"*That's* Castor Thorne?" Leo said.

When the princess of the Summer Court had fled the castle the night of the solstice, already showing symptoms of the jade rot, she had told her knight: *"Thorne will help us."*

Thorne could have been anything or anyone, but Anne thought she meant Castor Thorne, one of the most famous witches in the country and a leader of the magical community. He was also an old friend of Aziza's parents. Aziza had never met him, but he was in the only picture she had of her parents' coven, both him and Emil.

What were Castor's ties to Elphame? Why did Princess Narra believe he would protect her? Even Anne didn't have those answers, but she said that Castor wasn't their concern, at least not yet. In the weeks since the solstice, Princess Narra had not reappeared; either she was lying low, or she'd succumbed to the jade rot after all. Either way, she had no reason to interfere with Queen Ceresia's efforts to save the Summer Court, as their salvation would mean that Narra and Viren, too, would be cured.

As for Castor, he would be far from the first person in the history of the world to have made highly questionable decisions when confronted with fairy allure. Maybe that was why he'd helped her escape. If it really had been him. More importantly, Castor was helping Anne counteract the effects of the Summer Court's ruin on the human realm. If not for him, the rainy days they'd had since the solstice would've been twisters and hurricanes and floods. For now, he was an ally they could not afford to lose.

"If you want to see him in his element, now's your chance," Nelle said.

The duels took place on a low wooden stage that had been erected a short distance away from the disordered grid of stalls. It stood underneath where the upper levels of the mall were open in the center, so that the audience could look up into the darkened balconies of the first and second floors. Through the skylights overhead, the clouds parted, allowing the moonlight entry into the Market. It was the first clear night she'd witnessed in weeks, and it had happened so suddenly Aziza could only assume a weather witch was responsible.

A cheer went up as Castor Thorne stepped up onto the stage. He bowed deeply, beaming with gratitude.

"Welcome!" he cried, to clamorous approval. "I'm honored to be your master of ceremonies for tonight's duels. It's been some time since I've had the pleasure. Most of you know the rules, but let's review them!"

He strutted about the stage, flinging smiles into the crowd. Gold cuff links glinted on his sleeves. His coat seemed a little warm for the season, and it had to be magical—it was dark and velvety, with an odd sheen where the light caught it.

"Challengers will be selected by random draw," he said. "To begin, the duelists will stand twenty paces apart. When the signal is given, each will cast their spell simultaneously. Only one spell per duelist, that's the way, because a good witch shouldn't need more than one!"

This declaration was met with vocal support. He laughed at the crowd's enthusiasm.

"In addition, duelists are allowed a silver blade, subject to approval by the master of—well, by *me*." His grin had a roguish edge to it, at odds with his tidy, respectable appearance. "First to draw blood wins, unless someone surrenders. If you can't fight anymore, you've surrendered. If you go out of bounds, you've surrendered. If no blood is spilled and no one yields, it's a draw and you both go home in shame! Just kidding. But do try to give us all a good show."

Aziza was morbidly fascinated. She didn't know what she'd expected Castor Thorne to be, but this charming showboat wasn't it. He relinquished the stage, and the first two duelists took his place.

According to Nelle, most witches dueled using charm vials, runestones, wands, grimoires, and the like—instruments that would allow them to quickly cast their one spell. Some of them had worked their spell into the silver knife that was their sole weapon, usually with sigils etched into the hilt or blade. That was what the first duelist had done; her knife rose from her hands and floated in midair, wobbling a little as it shot at her opponent. But the other witch summoned a dense mist that rolled in waves across the stage, engulfing both duelists and hiding them from view. When the mist cleared, the wind witch was on her back with a cut on her arm, the mist witch kneeling over her with both their knives in her hands.

"They're weather witches?" Aziza asked, over the applause.

"Most duelists are," Nelle said. Like all witchcraft, she explained, weather magic could be very small—the conjuring of a spark or a wisp of cooling breeze—or it could be very large, like the ability to call down blizzards and floods. But these large magics were as rare as they were destructive. Most weather witches fell somewhere in between those two extremes on the spectrum of power. But even a moderately powerful spell for, say, summoning a bolt of lightning was still deadlier—and more of a spectacle—than the moderately powerful spells of almost any other craft.

The next challenger blew into the side of an odd, crescent-shaped whistle and turned the surface of the stage to ice. As the mist witch struggled to keep her balance, her opponent skidded across the ice as gracefully as if she were on skates and plucked the knife from her hand. But the one who dueled the ice witch next was a medium who whispered a spell that brought her to her knees, weeping. She yielded without him ever having to lay a finger on her.

"He showed her visions of death," Nelle told them in an undertone. "Not the first time one of Professor Serapion's apprentices has used that spell."

"He has more than one apprentice?" Aziza asked.

"A flock of them."

"Is that common? How come Anne only has one?" Leo asked.

"Apprentices can be a kind of status symbol for master witches," Nelle said. "Most will take on two or three at a time, though Professor Serapion always has upward of five or six, so he's still an outlier. Anne doesn't care about looking good to the other masters, so she only accepts a student when she wants to."

Another duelist was stepping up to face the medium. She wiped her sweaty hands on her jeans before drawing her knife. But when the bell rang to start the duel, she summoned dust devils that manifested as literal ghouls—horned creatures with indistinct forms, the light passing through them. They leapt on the medium before he could finish his spell, overpowering and quickly divesting him of his grimoire and blade. She got the loudest cheers from the crowd yet.

"Some of them are wearing pins," Tristan said to Nelle as the next challenger stepped up. Aziza hadn't noticed, but he was right—the witch with the dust devils had a tiny pin on her lapel, a bird, she thought. It matched Castor Thorne's cuff links.

"Means they're jackdaws," Nelle said. "Some of them are on duty tonight."

By *jackdaws,* she meant they were members of AJA—the American Jackdaw Association. To outsiders, it was a very exclusive birding club with exorbitant membership fees and almost no online presence. In reality, it was a clandestine network of witches responsible for protecting the community's secrecy, training up young people with powerful gifts, and preserving magical artifacts, traditions, and landmarks. The last included Bishop Library, which had been entrusted to Professor Serapion's care primarily due to his position as a senior jackdaw.

"On duty?" Aziza asked.

"AJA runs the Half Moon Market. But, like, really just Castor," Nelle said. "He owns the properties that host the Market each month. Those weather witches, the ones wearing the pins, are handpicked by Castor to provide security."

Before there was AJA, Nelle explained, covens enforced their own laws in their own territories, kept oral histories, and took turns hosting gatherings. About a century ago, the Legrand family coven teamed up with several witches from the country's major universities to create the Flight Paths. They had also designed the enchantments that made large-scale gatherings like the Half Moon Market possible, by shrouding the locations of their meeting places so that no one could stumble upon them by accident—you had to be given directions or brought there by someone already in the know. That was the beginning of the centralization of power that gave rise to AJA as it was known today. The organization was run by a coven known as the Clattering, which consisted of one representative from each of the ten major branches of magic. Anne was a member of the Clattering, its hedgewitch representative; Professor Serapion was its necromancer; and Castor was its weather witch. It was primarily the weather witches, directed by Castor, who enforced AJA's laws.

"We don't have many laws that aren't covered by the mundane government," Nelle said. "But there are a few, like the Crow Mandate—that's what we call our rule of secrecy. It's basically our most important law. The Grimm Protocol—which says that in the event of a great fairy war, master hedgewitches can enlist the aid of any jackdaw they need to defend the border. The Virtue Act of 1951—which says that any witch found to have attempted corruptive magic can be imprisoned."

Onstage, the dust devils were obliterated by a whip of crackling blue-white electricity. Then a clairvoyant came forward, and Nelle broke off to cheer for him. His prescience spell allowed him to predict his opponent's moves; he dodged every blow and made her chase him across the stage, unable to land a hit. The duel ended when he took pity on her and surrendered, to raucous applause.

"Aziza?" a voice said, behind her. It was Castor Thorne. He had taken off his coat and carried it folded over his arm. As soon as their eyes met, his uncertain, searching look gave way to one of those megawatt smiles. "So it *is* you."

She glanced at Tristan and Leo. Without having to say it, she knew they were all thinking along the same lines. They'd wanted to know more about him. Here was their chance.

"You know who I am?" she asked Castor.

"Of course I do. Your parents were very dear to me," he said. His eyes were an odd, two-toned blue, like the eyespots on a peacock feather—dark around the pupil and then sapphire bright on the outer ring of the iris. "You look so much like Leila—it was just like seeing her in the crowd again. I don't know if anyone ever told you this, but your parents were marvelous duelists."

"No," she said. It was surreal, talking to someone other than Jiddo about her parents—talking to the man from the faded photo she had of their coven. Until this moment, he had felt as far away from her as the long-dead Leila. "No one ever did."

"Ahmed could trap his opponents in hollow runestones," he said. "And all Leila had to do was land a touch to her opponent's throat to close their windpipe. That usually got them to yield. That's how I met them, at the duels."

"Did you win?" she asked.

His unguarded laugh in that distinctive, expressive voice drew people's eyes. They were at the back of the audience, away from the press of the crowd around the stage, but it was far from secluded; she was aware of the furtive glances being cast in their direction, though no one tried to interrupt.

"Not as often as I would've liked," he said. "But, forgive me, I haven't introduced myself. I've spoken to you as if we were old friends, but you were only a baby when we met."

"I know who you are," she said.

"Most people do, but I try not to assume," he said, with a wink. "How is Khaled?"

"Good," she said awkwardly. Jiddo would not be pleased if he knew where she was, or who she was with.

Perhaps he'd deduced the turn her thoughts had taken, because he said, "I've wanted to meet you properly for a long time. Your grandfather made it clear he wanted nothing to do with me or Emil, so we respected his wishes. But I heard Anne had taken you on as her apprentice, and I'm pleased to see that you're claiming your rightful place in this community, among your own kind." He gave Leo and Tristan a cordial nod. "And with a coven of your own." His eyes shifted to Nelle and brightened with recognition. "Ah, Miss Osorio. Your aunt has been worried about you. Maybe you could give her a call sometime?"

"Sure," Nelle said, more coolly than Aziza had heard her speak to anyone.

"I must be going now—we're coming up on the final bracket, and they'll need their master of ceremonies," he said, returning his attention to Aziza. "But I'm sure this won't be the last time our paths cross."

He bid them farewell and was gone again as quickly as he'd come. By silent agreement, the rest of them didn't speak until the curious eyes around them had turned away.

"I thought he'd be . . . I don't know, more intimidating?" Leo said in an undertone after two more duels had passed.

"I thought he'd be more like Professor Serapion," Tristan said.

"He's the only member of the Clattering with a fan club for a reason," Nelle said. "I think you can buy T-shirts with his face on it somewhere around here . . ."

They declined the T-shirts, but stayed to watch the rest of the duels.

CHAPTER 7
TRISTAN

THEY RETURNED TO Bishop Library close enough to dawn that Aziza turned down his offer to stay over, wanting to be home in time to have breakfast with her grandfather. It was a short walk, but he sent Lucky with her just in case.

He wondered with a shade of embarrassment if she'd done that on purpose to give him time alone with Leo. If so, that was a gift and he had no intention of wasting it. Time was all he needed to rebuild their relationship—he had to believe that. After all, he had a tactical advantage here. He knew what Leo liked better than Leo did, knew what he responded to, had meticulously catalogued the empirical evidence gathered from years of research in the controlled environment of Leo's bedroom. It was probably unethical to use that data to his own benefit. But it had served them both so well the night after the solstice.

He locked the door after Aziza left and returned to where Leo had collapsed on the couch, an arm flung over his eyes.

"If they have privacy spells, then why does the Half Moon Market still have to happen in the middle of the night?" Leo said wearily. "The spells work the same during the day."

"Are you sleeping here?" Tristan asked.

Leo gave a hum of assent. "My bus doesn't start running for another hour."

"I know. What I meant was, are you planning to sleep on the couch?" He folded his arms on the backrest and leaned over to look down at Leo. Leo lowered his arm and blinked up at him, pupils blown wide, very much awake now. "You're welcome to it, if that's what you want. But you do have other options."

He held Leo's gaze in a silent challenge for a moment before he walked away. Leo knew where to find the blankets for the couch if he wanted them. He also knew where to find the bedroom.

Tristan wouldn't push him for anything he wasn't ready to give. There wouldn't be any excuses next time, if there was a next time. Falling into bed together once was a fluke. Twice was a choice. So Leo could take his time deciding and—

A hand caught his and reeled him back in. He had only taken a few steps away; Leo had moved with an almost predatory speed and silence to capture him, and Tristan was his willing captive, turning back and into Leo's open arms. Leo's other hand slid over the nape of Tristan's neck and into his hair. Tristan surrendered to the insistent touch without hesitation, and tugged him into a hard, close-mouthed kiss, the answer to an unvoiced question. Then a second, long and slow, lips parting to welcome the melting softness of Leo's mouth moving against his, Tristan snaking his arms under Leo's shirt to feel his skin heat up under his palms. Then a third, and this one had none of the desperation of the kisses they had traded the night after the solstice. It was almost chaste—tired and comfortable, with an unthinking, natural intimacy, so close to what he wanted and never thought he'd have again that it almost undid him. They parted, barely. He both heard and felt Leo inhale, as if he might be about to say something.

But he didn't, and maybe it was better not to talk. All that mattered was that Leo was looking at him. His mind was nowhere else; he wasn't thinking of some faceless lover from the memory of a memory. He was here, with Tristan. And Tristan wasn't going to let him forget it.

HE DIDN'T KNOW what woke him up. Leo slept peacefully beside him. The predawn light, shaded blue by the stained-glass clerestory window, fell over his bare shoulders and his messy hair on Tristan's pillow. Tristan rested his curled fingers in the dip between his shoulder blades, careful not to disturb him. Had he made a noise in his sleep?

No. Tristan had heard something, but it wasn't in this room.

Far away on the other side of Elphame's boundary, inside a hollow mountain, Hazel said, "Lupa, you can come out now."

Tristan closed his eyes and watched.

The hound was crawling from the shadows to stand before Hazel, stretching the corporeal form it hadn't been allowed to take in some days.

Hazel was dressed in what appeared to be the fashion of the Winter Court—a warm velvet gown in deep auburn, with a full skirt and a fur-trimmed cloak. They were in her room; Tristan recognized the ceiling inlaid with moonstone and the four-poster bed. Their first night at the Winter Court, Lupa had sprawled on the bed next to Hazel, but the shrieks of the maids who came in to wake her up had discouraged a repeat of that. To Lupa, the room smelled like spring water—a crisp, clean scent of mingled sunlight and snow.

"There's a banquet and Queen Ceresia said you can come with me," Hazel was saying, petting Lupa between its pricked ears. "An ambassador from the Court of Masks is visiting, plus the Autumn Prince, two princesses from the Cattail Court, a lord from the

Hollow Court, and, uh . . . I forgot. A lot of important people that we have to convince to help us. All you have to do is sit next to me so that they take me seriously, since I'm representing the Summer Court."

They set off right away. Hazel led Lupa down the halls of the palace, carrying herself with her head held high the way the queen herself had taught her; the other fairies they passed steered clear.

In the palatial banquet hall, lanterns floated like stars below a ceiling shrouded in darkness. Hazel's hand rested lightly on Lupa's flank as she made her way to a long table laden with platters of veal and boar, wild berries, and lily wine. Queen Ceresia sat at the head of the table. A few members of the Winter Court were present, but those seated nearest to Queen Ceresia appeared to be the diplomatic envoys from the low courts.

Hazel took her seat, perching on the edge of the high-backed chair. Lupa sat on its haunches next to her, and Tristan was gratified by the looks of unease and revulsion that crossed the fairies' beautiful faces at the sight of his hound.

They ate first, and once the feast had been cleared away and the wine had been poured, Queen Ceresia said, "The time for deliberation is past. Decisions must be made about the Summer Court, and quickly."

The man seated to her left smiled against the rim of his glass. He had a cascade of dark hair and pale gold eyes that were striking against his brown skin. Over his brow lay a wicker crown dotted with drops of topaz.

"I imagine you are not without your own ideas regarding how we might proceed," he said. "Don't be coy, my queen. It's not like you."

"Princess Narra must be found," Queen Ceresia said. "Traitor though she may be, she is King Ilanthus's heir. We will do what her soft-hearted father could not, and force her to accept her responsibility.

Once we capture her, she will complete the renewal ceremony at the winter solstice."

"The *winter* solstice?" someone echoed.

"We will bring her to a place where winter cannot reach her," Queen Ceresia said. "There, every solstice is a summer solstice, and will suffice for the renewal ceremony."

"And you're certain that will work?" the wicker lord asked.

"We must try," Queen Ceresia said gravely. "We can't afford to wait until the next summer solstice. By then, there won't be a Summer Court to save. Are you prepared for seven years of war to decide which of you will be the next to ascend to the Court of the Seasons? Even my own claim to the throne will be tested. Fortunately, the Winter Court can withstand any challenge, and my protection extends, as ever, to my faithful allies."

"Fortunate indeed," the wicker lord muttered, with a wry smile.

"Hush now," the queen said, giving him an affectionate pat on the cheek. "Your father would be quite lost without me, grand ambitions or no. But should some upstart set their sights on the Winter throne, I fear my attention and resources may become . . . limited."

In the brief silence that followed, Tristan supposed the representatives of the low courts were contemplating how soon they would lose *faithful ally* status if they didn't go along with Queen Ceresia's plans, and how their people would fare during wartime.

"But must we waste time searching for Princess Narra? We already have another heir." The speaker was one of two women with emerald-green skin and cicada wings. Every eye in the room turned to Hazel.

"Absolutely not," blustered a man with a multitude of arctic-blue braids and opalescent scales that started at his neck and disappeared into his collar. "A changeling princess cannot be queen. She doesn't know our ways, and she lies."

Tristan and Lupa both bristled at this, but Hazel was unconcerned, taking a demure sip of her wine and mirroring the queen's aloof expression.

"Might I propose an alternative?" the wicker lord said. "The late Summer King has one other heir. A cousin, Vetiver. We can infiltrate the Summer Court's castle and retrieve him. The autumn equinox will be our best chance—it is a day of power for my people."

There were murmurs around the table as the man that Tristan now supposed to be the Autumn Prince finished speaking.

"It will be difficult to rescue the boy," one of the cicada women said. "Or even to locate the castle. I hear it likes to hide in the mountains, on remote peaks across treacherous terrain. The infected Gallowglass will be hostile, and our knights will be at great risk of catching the rot themselves."

Since the jade rot could be transmitted through the blood, engaging the Summer Court in battle practically guaranteed that the disease would spread.

"Perhaps we might reconsider our options," said the piscine man. "It is high time we had a new Summer Court. King Ilanthus was weak. His own daughter conspired against him. The Queen of Masks would *never* have borne such impudence, and she fears no war."

His declaration was met with a ringing silence, and Tristan could almost pinpoint the moment he realized that he had made a mistake. Queen Ceresia didn't move, but two of her Gallowglass emerged from some corner of the hall, as if in response to a silent signal.

The piscine man shot to his feet.

"Wait," he said, voice quavering. "I meant no disrespect. I only—"

One of the Gallowglass caught him as he lurched away from the table, knocking his chair over with a bang; one gauntleted hand fisted in his blue braids while the other forced his wrists behind his back. The second Gallowglass drew a saber and decapitated him cleanly, blood pouring to the ground. The body collapsed while the head swung from its braids, its frozen-open eyes fixed on the impassive faces around the banquet table.

The brutality of it was so shocking that Tristan almost pulled away from Lupa's mind. Hazel was studying her reflection in her glass as if it were the most interesting thing in the room. Lupa pressed its nose against her shoulder, which made her jump, but then she reached back to touch her fingertips to the hound's snout, just for a moment.

"Take what's left of him back to the Court of Masks," Queen Ceresia told her Gallowglass. "Maybe the next one Queen Emryn sends will know when to hold their tongue."

The Autumn Prince held out a hand, and a servant hurried to give him a handkerchief so that he could wipe off a speck of blood that had landed on the back of his wrist.

"My sages can find the castle wherever it may appear," he said, as if nothing of note had happened. "The greater challenge will be finding the boy. All except the Gallowglass would have retreated into the heart of the castle's defenses, behind protective enchantments none of us are able to breach. None except . . ."

One of the cicada women—Tristan couldn't tell them apart—said, "None except a member of the royal family. In this, the changeling princess may be of use."

Once again, Hazel became the center of attention. She looked around in surprise. "You want me to come with you?"

"Would you?" the Autumn Prince asked lightly, as if merely curious about her response.

"No," Queen Ceresia said. "We can't afford to expose you to peril. Not until another heir is secured. Furthermore, I won't risk my Gallowglass in battle with the Summer Court. The rot would deplete my forces. In this time of uncertainty, as my subjects look to me for guidance, the Winter Court must stand strong."

"Then please allow the Autumn Court to take the risk on your behalf," he said, bowing his head. "It would be my honor to relieve you of this burden. Vetiver can be our fail-safe should Princess Narra elude us."

A beat of silence before Queen Ceresia smiled. "If anyone is equal to the task, it's you. Be my guest."

This put an end to the subject of Vetiver, and the meeting soon concluded. But as Hazel left the banquet hall, swift footsteps came in pursuit. Lupa spun back, ready to leap into action to protect her, but the voice that called her name belonged to the Autumn Prince.

"Good evening, Prince Senna," she said, with an awkward curtsy.

"Returning to your quarters, Princess?" he said. "I'm heading this way, too. Let us walk together."

Lupa growled, but Hazel patted the top of its head. "It's okay, Lupa. He's nice."

Gallantly, he offered her his arm, and she took it. They made their way through the palace together.

"If I might suggest a small detour, I don't believe you've had cause to admire the portrait gallery yet," Prince Senna said.

"I haven't," Hazel said, and allowed him to lead her in another direction. Lupa growled again, more insistently, and was ignored.

When they had reached a narrow, portrait-lined hall in a remote wing of the palace, and Prince Senna had looked discreetly around to make sure they were alone, he spoke.

"Earlier, when I said that there was someone who could get through the protective enchantments on the castle, I wasn't talking about you," he said. Despite the apparent need for secrecy, there was no particular urgency in his voice; it was cool and detached, if a little gentler than the tones with which he had spoken to the queen. "I meant your brother."

Tristan's heart sank.

"But he's human," Hazel said in a small voice. Her hand tightened on Prince Senna's arm. He tilted his head down to catch her gaze.

"He is a Prince of the Seasons, bound to the Summer Court through you," he said. "The castle's enchantments will recognize him. We need Vetiver. Hazel, even if Narra is found, how will you fare as a member of her court? This is about more than the Summer Court's survival. It's about the Summer Court's future."

Hazel hesitated. "I know, but . . ."

"You fear for his safety. I understand," Prince Senna said softly. "But you came here as the Summer Court's princess. You're the only one who can speak for them right now. At the very least, tell your brother he is needed, and let him decide."

"I can send him a message," she said reluctantly.

"And if he says no?" Prince Senna asked.

Despondently, Hazel replied, "He won't."

CHAPTER 8
LEO

ANNE WANTED HIM to say no.

"We don't fight fairy battles," she said when the three of them had relayed what Tristan had seen and heard through Lupa's eyes. "We only try to minimize their impact on the human realm. Prince Senna's mission is too dangerous."

"But I want to help," Leo said. It was short notice—the autumn equinox was only a couple of weeks away—but he couldn't bring himself to refuse.

"We barely escaped last time," Tristan argued. "I thought we all agreed to stay out of fairy business from now on."

He wasn't wrong; their meddling during the summer solstice had only made everything worse.

"It's different when they're asking us," Aziza said. It was no surprise that Aziza had landed squarely on Leo's side of the argument.

"You're only considering this because you feel responsible for what happened," Tristan bit out. "Instead of blaming yourselves, can we just blame Princess Narra?"

"It's not fairy business," Leo said. "It's for Hazel. That makes it *my* business. And there are humans trapped in the castle. They're in danger, too, the longer this goes on."

He was thinking of the servants—like Evan, who'd helped them during the solstice, and his friend May. And there was a chance that Leo's true love was among them, lured to the Summer Court by the enchantress who had cursed him and his family. Some humans entered into contracts with the Fair Folk willingly, but others were tricked. They were rewarded for their service with wealth and magical gifts, but their memories of their lives in the human realm faded over time. Now everyone who had been in the castle the night of the solstice was stuck there. He had always intended to go back for them.

Besides, he felt a discomfiting sense of responsibility to the Summer Court. He was, by a magical technicality, their prince; and while he didn't consider himself royalty by any stretch of the imagination, the least he could do for them was show up when he was needed, especially since their plight was partly his fault.

"You need to understand that the castle isn't unprotected," Anne said. "Fairies infected with the jade rot are aggressive. They won't know you're trying to help them. Prince Senna is going in prepared for a bloody fight. And you are very much mistaken if you think I'm sending you to a battlefield."

"I don't need to *fight*," Leo argued. "I know it's risky, but—"

Anne would not hear it.

"Prince Senna doesn't care about the danger he's putting you in," she said. "It's not his job to worry about you. But it is *mine*. None of you are getting involved."

HE AND ANNE visited the Dire Court a few days later. He took the opportunity to gather information from the fairies over game boards and cards, waiting for them to broach the subject of the Winter Court first. They always did, and he always contrived to mess up his next move, a little positive reinforcement for them. He didn't know if they could tell that it was on purpose; either way, the end result was that they got an advantage in the game and he got his intel.

"Do they play High King of Finches in the Winter Court, too?" he asked.

"Sometimes," his opponent said. "They prefer Shield and Capture, or Tall Bard Black Raven."

"King Ilanthus beat the Winter Queen in a Finch game once, and she had every game board in her court burned," someone else said. "It only fell out of fashion because no one there could play it anymore."

"That's only a rumor," another of the Dire fairies said.

"Because none among her people dare speak of it," the first insisted.

"Why is everyone so afraid of her?" Leo asked.

When they went quiet, he wondered if he'd gone too far.

"Many reasons," his opponent said at last.

"Like what?"

"When Queen Ceresia kills someone, she takes a trophy," someone else offered. "A length of hair, or their wings or horns."

Leo recalled Tristan saying that Ceresia wore a dress made from fairy wings, and suppressed a shudder.

"I heard she killed an ambassador from the Court of Masks the other day," Leo said. His opponent glanced sharply up at him, and a few of the others tensed. The news had not reached them here, it seemed. "Will she take a trophy from him, too?"

They all agreed she would.

"I guess Queen Emryn won't like that," Leo said.

"No," his opponent said. "The ambassador was her uncle. She will not be pleased."

"But the Court of Masks is small," someone else put in. "She won't retaliate."

"It sounds like the only one who isn't scared of Queen Ceresia is Prince Senna," Leo said. This was a stab in the dark, a guess with minimal evidence to support it, intended mainly to get a reaction. "Is it because the Autumn Court is strong enough to fight back?"

"They'd never," his opponent said.

"They would!" someone else shot back.

"Senna's father would have set his sights on the Summer Court's position if he could," someone else put in. "I hear whispers that he is rallying his closest allies. Perhaps he's found his spine."

"No," yet another Dire fairy argued. "The Autumn King may be a fool, but Senna is not. He knows a full-fledged war with Winter would decimate the Autumn Court. Besides, he likes his amusements and his leisure, and he will not wish to be a Prince of the Seasons."

Neither of them sounded like good news to Leo. Queen Ceresia was cruel, but Prince Senna was a mystery. Was Queen Ceresia protecting Hazel—or keeping her in a crystal cage? And why was Prince Senna sticking his neck out for the Summer Court, anyway?

If he helped Prince Senna now, was he taking sides in a brewing conflict between him and the Winter Queen?

"If he is gathering allies, it is to another end," his opponent said, as he took two of Leo's finch pieces in one move.

"It could be because . . ." He trailed off, pretending to hesitate.

All eyes were on him. He took his time working out his countermove.

"Because of what?" his opponent prompted when Leo looked up from the board.

"Because they're going to rescue the Summer King's cousin, Vetiver," Leo said. "That's the plan, anyway. Prince Senna asked for my help."

They hadn't known about that yet, either.

"Of course," someone commented. "You can unlock the safe room enchantments."

Tristan had heard something to that effect at the banquet, but having confirmation from the Summer Court's subjects silenced an inner doubt Leo hadn't even known he'd had.

"So you think I should go?" he asked.

"You have to ask?" someone snapped. "Prince Senna has summoned you."

"Hush," another fairy said. "No one has taught him his duty. He cannot know better."

"You think I should go," Leo repeated, "even though Queen Ceresia would rather focus on Princess Narra? It doesn't exactly sound like they're on the same page to me."

He'd gone too far. No one was willing to answer, except his opponent, who said, "If she has given Prince Senna her blessing to proceed, then that is all that matters."

"Even if they managed to find Princess Narra, how are they going to make her do anything?" Leo asked.

"Easily," one of the spectators said. "Queen Ceresia will break her in a way her indulgent father could not. She'll collar her if she must."

What was best for the Summer Court? Certainly not putting an unwilling Princess Narra on the throne. Chaining her there; collaring her. Despite everything she had done, he felt a tinge of pity for her.

Of all the things that could have made up Leo's mind, this was the one he would have least expected.

HE WOKE UP before his alarm. His mind fought it, his eyes screwed shut and his hands fisted in the blankets, as if he could cling to sleep a little longer—to the dream he had been having. But the details had already melted away into a familiar fog.

He made himself relax and opened his eyes. The other side of the mattress was still warm, but Tristan was gone. Leo got dressed, hoping he was just downstairs and not back at the library already. He didn't like the thought of Tristan slipping out before dawn like he was some stranger Leo had brought home on a whim—as if the now-empty guest room didn't still belong exclusively to him, at least in Leo's mind. But these days, when Tristan came over, he definitely wasn't sleeping down the hall.

The weirdest thing about what was going on between the two of them was how little had actually changed. By day, their friendship was the same as it had always been. It was only at night that the lines blurred. Leo didn't just stay up with Tristan when he couldn't sleep; he held him through his nightmares, the ones he had never been able to talk about. Tristan had done the same for him. And he always seemed to know when Leo needed to talk, and when he needed . . . to be distracted. Leo couldn't pretend sleeping with his best friend was only about comfort and not about pleasure, because that was laughably untrue. But it was freeing to not have to worry about what was okay for friends to do and what was okay for lovers to do. They didn't have to put a label on it. He didn't have to call it anything but being together.

Still, he couldn't shake the guilty voice in his head that said he was betraying someone. He had promised never to give up on his true love, no matter how long it took. Even if it took forever. And he intended to keep that promise. But by wanting someone else at all, let alone *acting* on that want, he felt he'd—failed some kind of test. Broken something that couldn't be replaced.

The worst part was the knowledge that he was allowing himself happiness when his true love could be suffering. His theory was that they were trapped in the Summer Court as a servant, their memory eroded by the enchantments that the fairies used to keep their servants complacent. If he was right, then his true love was in the ruined castle right now, adrift in Elphame.

The ache of being separated from that person had never grown easier to bear. He had just learned to function through it. He had this idea that they had met at school. Looking back, his memories of the private school he'd gone to before he transferred to Towne High were suspiciously fuzzy. The curse had smoothed those years to flatness, made them so dull and cloudy it was like they'd happened centuries ago. That was a past he'd shared with someone—a history that was gone now—and when he thought about it for too long, it felt like an insurmountable loss, like he'd never be a whole person again. Not until that beloved person in his dreams, always just out of reach, was beside him once more, and Leo could turn to them and not have their face dissolve in his mind the second he looked away.

The autumn equinox approached with increasing momentum, as if the slope of time grew steeper. He was counting down in days, not weeks. Leo's eighteenth birthday was coming up this month, too—the anniversary of the day the curse had wiped his memories. It had been two years. And when he found his true love, the first thing he'd have to do was apologize.

I'm sorry for what happened to you because of me, he would say. *I'm sorry for how long I took to fix it. I'm sorry that when you needed me, I was messing around with someone else.*

Outside, dawn was breaking. It wasn't raining yet, but the dense clouds on the horizon promised to change that soon. Tristan sat by the garden, his head bent over a grimoire.

"Morning," Leo said quietly, closing the door behind him. "What's that?"

Tristan's white-blond hair was still disheveled from sleep. *The Book of Fenrisúlfr* was open in front of him, and something was cupped in his hands. Upon closer inspection, it turned out to be a mouse, quivering with fear. Animals tended not to like Tristan.

"Lucky was hunting it," Tristan said. "The damn thing's bitten me three times—could you—"

"On it." Leo took the mouse from him, and it calmed down considerably. He stroked the top of its tiny head. It glowered at him with its beady black eyes, its nose twitching through the gap between his thumb and index finger. "Why are you rescuing mice from Lucky?"

"I wouldn't call it a rescue," Tristan muttered, turning a page in the book. "I found a spell that should let me bring passengers with me when I shadow-travel. But I don't want to test it on a person."

"Whoa," Leo said. "Are you going to try it out now? Can I help?"

"Please. Just keep holding on to it while I cast."

Tristan began to recite the spell from the grimoire. Leo loved listening to him read, all slow and serious, his voice softer and lower as it negotiated the sonorous vowels of Old Norse. His eyelashes fanned down; his graceful fingers turned the pages with a light, soundless touch. Leo got so distracted watching him that the mouse made a break for freedom and he had to clamp down on it before it could escape; Tristan flicked his eyes up at him once, amused, but his spellcasting never faltered.

When he had finished reading, he closed the book with a snap and took the mouse back from Leo. It squeaked, terrified. Leo felt bad for it. But the spell had taken; he could see the unobtrusive radiance of Tristan's magic on it. Tristan stood and Leo followed suit, watching with keen interest.

The sky had brightened by degrees; the elm tree past the garden cast a long shadow, from which Lucky emerged.

"Here goes," Tristan said, keeping a firm grip on the mouse with one hand and resting the other on the side of Lucky's neck as he walked with his hound into the shadow of the elm tree. Leo counted the seconds. One, two, three moments later, Tristan reappeared behind him.

The mouse was not squeaking anymore.

Tristan looked down at it and gasped in dismay. It wasn't only that the mouse was dead—though it very much was that—but also, it was . . . off. Its eyes were in the wrong place, too far up the top of its skull. Its tail was three times as long as it had been before, like a stretched-out rubber band. Its body was smaller, emaciated, as though in those few short seconds, it had starved to death.

Tristan shuddered, dropping it.

Then he said, "Lucky, *no*—"

But it was too late. The hound lapped up the mouse with its long tongue and snapped its jaws closed around it, swallowing it whole. Then it looked Tristan dead in the eye as if to say, *What are you going to do about it?*

Leo couldn't help it. He broke down laughing.

"I'm glad one of us is enjoying this," Tristan said.

"Two of us," Leo said, still snickering. "I think Lucky's enjoying it the most."

Tristan huffed. "Well, I won't be trying that on you anytime soon."

"I'll stick to the bus," Leo agreed. "The poor mouse didn't deserve that."

"It *bit* me," Tristan reminded him.

"Let me see." He took Tristan's hands and inspected them carefully, turning them over, and at last tangling their fingers together. His skin was a little colder than Leo's. He pulled their joined hands to his chest, warming him up. "It didn't even leave a mark. I think you'll live."

The clouds drew a milky pall across the sky. The half-light washed Tristan out, made the angles of his face into something brutal and fierce and cold; Leo could almost see the hound's growl hiding in his mouth and wanted to kiss it out of him, swallow it, until he was soft again the way he was when they were in his room. But he didn't, because they weren't in his room, were they, and Leo was already breaking their unspoken rules by doing this much, holding his hands outside in broad daylight, standing so close to him, staring at him the way he was probably staring.

"I won't be done with the spell before the equinox," Tristan said.

"No one's expecting you to master a brand-new, ridiculously advanced spell in less than a week," Leo assured him, but Tristan's eyes only tightened at the corners.

"Are you—sure you want to do this?" Tristan said.

Leo didn't have to ask what he meant.

"I can't say no when I'm the only one who can help. If it's me or Hazel, it has to be me."

Tristan sighed. "I know. You're right."

It didn't feel right. Leo was essentially asking Tristan to risk his life for the Summer Court—or to step aside while Leo and Aziza did it without him, which was so far outside the realm of possibility that it wasn't a real choice at all. If Leo tried to give him an out, Tristan would just dig his heels in; it was what Leo would do if their roles were reversed.

"Can you promise me something?" Leo said.

"Anything," Tristan said instantly.

"When it comes down to it, I have to do what I think is right," Leo said. "I want you to do the same, even if it's different from what *I* think is right."

Slowly, Tristan nodded. "I can do that."

CHAPTER 9
AZIZA

THEY WERE ON their way back from a corn farm in Ohio, where a wight had disguised itself as a slightly bloodstained scarecrow. It had dismembered at least two people in the days since it had limped through the broken boundary. Aziza and Dion had lured it back into Elphame, and then Aziza had used a spell to pull it apart like a jigsaw puzzle. Her charms were working a lot better ever since her trip to the Half Moon Market. Even Dion had approved of her handiwork this time.

He was still distant and guarded with her, and she couldn't fault him for it. Maybe, to him, she would always just be the person who had made one of the worst moments of his life a little more painful.

So when, during one of their first trips through the Flight Paths, she had asked, "How old were you the first time you came down here?" he had only shrugged and said, curtly, "Too young to remember."

"Alone?" she asked, undaunted.

"Of course not," he said. "My parents began teaching me the Flight Path enchantments as soon as I was old enough to start practicing basic hearthcraft."

"Then by now you must have been to every magic library in the country," she had said. "For the record, that doesn't mean you were qualified to be a librarian."

"I was *entirely* competent, and you were the *worst* patron ever." Then he'd added, grudgingly, like he didn't want to say any more but the urge to correct her was a force too powerful to combat, "And we call them the jackdaw collections. Unofficially."

"Because of AJA?"

"The jackdaw as a symbol of American witchcraft predates AJA," Dion had said. "Jackdaws are frequently mistaken for the common crow, and they're just as clever and resourceful. They can solve problems and learn skills. But jackdaws are more social. They form lifelong pair bonds and cohesive flocks that remain together throughout the year. In groups, they can drive away predators several times larger than they are."

The jackdaw collections contained texts on every form of magic and witchcraft imaginable, even the ones less common in the United States, like the brujería of Latin America. In mundane libraries, movable shelving units operated on a carriage-and-rail system; in the jackdaw collections, ten-foot-tall bookcases were known to shuffle around like geese, rearranging their aisles at will. In mundane libraries, the patrons went home eventually; in the jackdaw collections, she glimpsed the ghosts of dead academics drifting between the stacks, glimmering and insubstantial as the foam-flecked mist that forms over the ocean. In an astromancy library under the University of Chicago, which was furnished with the same cozy armchairs and long tables that could be found in the reading room aboveground, a star chart covered all four walls, its detailed illustrations moving to reflect the current positions of the stars. At the University of Wisconsin–Madison's augury archive, leaded windows looked out under the surface of the lake, where, occasionally, massive catfish, bass, and pike would swim past.

And what they all had in common was an entrance to the Flight

Paths: a web of ever-changing corridors that connected the secret archives of the magical world, a vascular system unfurling under the feet of the country's finest scholars, pumping arcane wisdom through its veins.

"Will you show me how your arrays work?" she asked today. "Before we go back?"

"Now?" he said.

She shrugged. "Unless you're in a hurry. I wanted to learn the one you use to get around this place."

"Are you that eager to get rid of me?" he said lightly. "I'm sorry to disappoint you, but you can't learn numerology overnight. It will be a while before you can navigate the Flight Paths on your own."

She didn't hear a *no*, which was encouraging.

"It sounds like you don't think you can teach me. Not up to the challenge? Am I too much of a novice for you?"

The next thing she knew, they were huddled over a table in a jackdaw collection about the same size as the one at Bishop Library. It was a circular room, the curved walls lined with books all the way up to the ceiling. The highest shelves could be reached with the help of a wheeled ladder, which rolled invitingly toward Dion when he entered.

"You already know the basics," he said, drawing a chalk circle directly on the table's surface. "A magical array is a configuration of numbers, words, sigils, and other symbols that, together, form a spell. A witch casts the spell by applying their magic to the completed array. Arrays can be very complex, or very simple. Even your trap circles are a kind of array."

She thought of her messy rings of salt, blood, and whatever else she had on hand; they bore little resemblance to Dion's clean, precise chalk markings. He was the scholar to her self-taught amateur, and she felt a now-familiar rush of mingled jealousy and admiration when she watched him draft his arrays with practiced efficiency.

"The first step is to define the boundaries of the array," Dion said. "Across history and cultures, arrays have taken countless forms. Alchemical circles, mandalas, pentagrams, Celtic knots, magic squares—these are all types of arrays. Circles are common. So are linked or interconnected rings. Within the rings, you'll then draw guiding lines. At points where your guiding lines meet, you might place additional materials, your offerings, usually in ceremonial bowls or dishes, though some witches choose to forego . . ."

She listened intently, though her attention wavered between his words and the fluid, unerring motion of his hand as it flew over the array, the lines of chalk fanning open underneath it like wings. Dion wasn't just naturally talented, though being born into a powerful bloodline and having access to the best education money could buy had certainly given him advantages. Still, he had worked at this. His skill had nothing to do with innate power; it was the product of endless hours of study. He had taken nothing for granted. He had bled for his craft. Though she'd never say it out loud, he was everything she'd ever thought a witch should be.

". . . and the offerings might be burned, buried, or drowned, though for minor spells the elemental component can serve as the offering itself. That's why I can use fire to cast my—" He broke off, looking up from his array and brushing chalk dust off his hands. A look of consternation crossed his features. "You're not even taking any *notes*?"

She shrugged. "Like you said, I can't learn this overnight."

"So what am I, free entertainment?"

"I just wanted to see it again," she said. She had only ever known the magic that existed in Elphame's borderlands and her grandfather's wards. She was learning a lot from Anne, but Anne only taught her hedgewitch spells—the things she could use right now. And that was what Aziza *wanted* to learn right now. But she had loved magic from the moment she was old enough to totter after the lesser fairies that snuck across the boundary at the winter solstice. She wanted to see every kind of magic there was.

She looked up to find he had been watching her study the array.

"You'll pick up on this quickly once Anne starts teaching you advanced spells," he said. "You're more than capable. I've seen that."

Had he? She hadn't even known he'd been looking.

Abruptly, he turned away, bending to wipe the table clean. "We should be getting back."

"What have you been doing since you left Bishop Library?" she asked as they slipped back out into the halls. "Shouldn't you be in college or something?"

It had suddenly occurred to her that Dion, about a year and a half older than her, had to be enrolled in university somewhere.

"I'm taking a gap year of sorts," he said. "I'm focusing on my apprenticeship right now."

"You're an apprentice?" she asked. "But you're already a master hearth witch."

"I'm studying advanced spell theory. My mentor isn't a hearth witch, but his spellwork is very innovative." His hands were in his pockets, his tone a little detached. He'd sounded more engaged a few minutes earlier going over an array he'd done possibly hundreds of times than he did talking about this apprenticeship. "He's offered before, but I always turned him down. Emil handled my magical education himself. And he knew plenty of hearth witches willing to teach me anything he couldn't."

"Is that why everyone we've seen in the jackdaw collections knows you?" she asked. "I assumed it was just the Legrand reputation."

Often when they passed through the libraries, there were other witches at work, academics conducting research. They greeted Dion by name, sparing only a curious glance toward Aziza, clearly assuming that if she was with Dion then she must belong there, even though she was younger than anyone else they saw in the Flight Paths. Nelle had told them that the Clattering's hearth witch representative had always been a Legrand, up until the tragedy that had wiped the whole family out; someone else held the seat now, but it was widely expected that Dion would take over once he was older. He had been marked for leadership essentially since the day he was born.

"It's partly that," he said. "But it's mostly because of Emil. He traveled for work—to present at universities, or abroad to consult with specialists in rare magics. He always took me with him. It was that or send me to boarding school, which he didn't want to do. Not unless I preferred that. I was nine when he adopted me—he felt that was old enough to have an opinion. And I wanted to stay with him. So he enrolled me in a private school with remote learning options, and I did most of my studying independently, or with the help of tutors."

"Was it hard for you to be on the road all the time?" she asked cautiously. She wouldn't have dared ask about Emil if he hadn't brought him up first.

"I liked traveling. Or I guess I just liked traveling with him," he said. "And I liked that Emil wanted to bring me along. That he trusted me to be good. And how he would proudly introduce me as his son to all his colleagues. He kept to himself, and he didn't have close friends. But he had me."

She thought of Jiddo and couldn't reply, her throat suddenly tight. She had visited Emil's study once, in a shared dream, and had seen the photos of him with a younger Dion. It was easy to imagine the boy from those photos as Emil's travel companion, and his quiet, dark-haired little shadow, and the son he'd brag about to anyone who would listen.

As they got closer to Bishop Library, she steeled herself to broach the subject that had been on her mind for the last few weeks. This would be her last chance to ask until after the equinox.

"I'm looking for Meryl, but I don't have any new leads," she said, forcing it out when the familiar arched doorway to the other Bishop Library came into view. "I think we dismissed Theodore Serapion too soon. Tristan thinks so, too."

"It's not him," Dion said, instantly and with such certainty it took her aback.

"How do you know?"

He hesitated, as if searching for the right words. "There's a certain kind of witch who thinks other magical beings are beneath them. Even the Fair Folk, they find distasteful at best. Professor Serapion is that kind of witch. To him, those beings are only worthwhile for . . . what they can provide. How they can be used."

"What do you mean?" she asked, dreading the answer.

Dion looked uncomfortable. "He would have used her sealskin to bind a grimoire. He would have harvested her teeth so that he might bend her ghost's will to his service, and brewed her blood into ink. If Professor Serapion had gotten hold of her, she wouldn't have lasted days, let alone years. She's not with him," he said firmly, "and that's a *good* thing."

"Then where is she?" she asked. It sounded childish even to herself; she wanted to cringe.

His voice was strained as he said, "I don't know."

CHAPTER 10

LEO

THE AUTUMN COURT'S sages had ruminated on the stars and the flight patterns of birds, had scried in freshwater pools and had cut open hares to read their entrails. They said the castle would materialize in a region they called "the Thrice-Shattered Bridge of the Heavens." On a map of the United States, that was in Arkansas. The region was a borderland, with a river as its boundary line. The three of them had studied it on a map that Prince Senna had sent to them, the sinuous curves of the river with its oxbow lakes scattered on either side like confetti scraps.

So there he was on the equinox, in the time and place that had been foretold by some of the finest sages in all of fairyland. Overhead, great slabs of storm cloud gathered in a sky that seemed to take up three times as much space as usual, plunging to meet the low horizon. A distant wink of light might have been the river. Beside him stood Prince Senna's second-in-command, Captain Vasilia of the Autumn Court's royal guard, and he had to admit he felt a little safer in her shadow. Fairy armor was usually trim and lightweight, but hers looked heavy, with thick shoulder pieces, gauntlets fashioned after bear claws, and a row of fangs in her helmet along the line of her jaw. Seven other knights stood with her, their armor sculpted in a mimicry of all the venomous and barbed things in nature, thorns and fangs and poison-tipped stingers. When the time came, Captain Vasilia would lead the charge to the castle while the others fell into formation around Leo, guarding him as they crossed the field.

The rest of the Autumn Court's forces were concealed nearby. As for the enchanters, they were stationed around the area in a wide circle, some in flight, others kneeling on the ground, prepared to bind the castle in place the moment it appeared, for as long as they could hold it. Leo just had to help them get Vetiver out before their strength failed. Midnight, the end of the equinox, was the absolute furthest they could likely push their powers, but chances were they wouldn't make it for even that long.

"It's starting," Captain Vasilia murmured to him. "We move the moment it appears. Just follow me and don't stop no matter what happens. Understood?"

"I got it," Leo said, though as far as he could tell the only thing that had started was the rain, a heavy downpour that liquefied the ground under his feet. Strangely, no chill accompanied the storm; if anything, Leo felt heat creeping over his skin, the air thick with it when he inhaled, almost like when you climbed into the car on a sunny day and it was baking inside. The warmth sank into his chest and spread slowly outward, to his fingertips, his stomach, and when he briefly closed his eyes, he *felt* the summer they'd lost this year—golden sunlight in a cloudless sky, afternoons that stretched on endlessly, the smell of sunscreen and citrus, the buzz of emerald June bugs.

He wiped rainwater out of his eyes, and when he opened them, the field wasn't empty anymore. The castle was there, huge and close; he felt a little jolt in his stomach like he'd looked up from his phone and realized he was about to walk into a wall. Its spires were starkly outlined against the heaving, thunderstruck sky. The Summer Court's Gallowglass paced unsteadily through the windswept grasses, as mindless as toy soldiers and bitter as spirits torn from their haunts. The rainwater slid into the gutters between the plates of their armor. The rot had ripped through their bodies. It grew where the ancient magic that was the privilege and burden of Elphame's highest court had left them hollow. From there, it devoured its host and flourished, spreading green trails of infection through their veins. It ate away at flesh and bone, leaving behind open sores in their skin and tiny craters in the antlers of the fairy men who had them. It made their translucent wings wilt, drag behind them on the ground, and eventually fall off. Some of their armor had been altered—deformed by their own magic—with ghastly results. Gauntleted fingers had fused together; horns atop helmets had elongated, twisting into cages around their wearer's necks.

Captain Vasilia moved forward. Leo bowed his head against the wind and followed.

Around his small troop of protectors, a battle had broken out already. The silhouettes of the Autumn and Summer knights collided and pulled apart, over and over, blades of glass and crystal flashing in the waning light. The field rang from end to end with the sound of clashing weapons. On the night of the summer solstice, the Gallowglass he and Aziza encountered had known they were infected. But since then, the rot had progressed. It traveled the branching pathways of the nervous system to sink its tendrils into the mind. The Summer Court's Gallowglass didn't know that the Autumn Court was here to save them. They only knew their castle was under siege, and defended it viciously.

A crackle of lightning sent hairline fractures through the sky. The accompanying boom of thunder made his teeth rattle. With the amber eye, Leo could see the gleaming paths carved by the enchanted arrows being volleyed across the battlefield. He could see which of the warriors fought with magic rather than weapons; they made beastly illusions from mud and wildflowers and wind, and set their fangs upon their enemies. With his truesight, the Summer fairies' illusions were easy to distinguish from the rest, black with the rot and feral. And the Autumn Court's forces were vastly outnumbered.

An arrow struck the guard on Leo's right, and he went down so fast Leo was several paces ahead of him before he'd processed it. A winged stranger loomed out of the rain-whipped darkness and fell upon the knight on Leo's left, but she spun around, sword flashing, to meet the challenge. He didn't know how many of his other guards were still there; he couldn't hear anything over the din of the battle.

Captain Vasilia stopped, her broadsword flying up as she swung around and beheaded an opponent Leo hadn't even seen coming at her. The next arrow flew at them—

—and struck a golden shield strapped to the arm of a rider on a winged steed, who had thrown himself in its path at the last moment. His mount had been shaped from frost and granite, its eyes smooth panes of ice, its snout purple. Its wings flexed as its rider pulled on the reins, urging it to turn, its hooves kicking at the air. The rider's long, dark hair, coarse and wild with curls, whipped over his shoulder.

"Go now!" Prince Senna called to him as his airborne cavalry streaked across the battlefield. Captain Vasilia whirled, grabbed Leo's arm, and shoved him forward.

He ran, but he wasn't alone for more than an instant. Two hounds rose from the earth like trout surfacing from a river. The unrelenting rain worked in Leo's favor, making it harder for the Gallowglass to see or hear him, especially now that he wasn't flanked by Captain Vasilia and the other knights in their conspicuous armor. *He* had trouble seeing, too; already half-blind, in this moment the amber eye's input was overwhelming rather than enlightening. But the hounds guided him around the worst of the battle, to the side of the castle, where Leo knew an entrance the servants used was hidden behind a curtain of ivy. He passed as many fallen knights as living ones, their blood running into the earth.

He grabbed the door knob but didn't open it, looking back for Captain Vasilia or Prince Senna. They were nowhere to be seen; they'd fallen too far behind.

He couldn't wait. He'd have to go on without them.

Something moved next to him on the castle wall, a flutter like the ivy leaves stirring in the wind. It was a third hound, sliding out of the darkness as if from an unseen passage, Tristan beside it. Almost at the same time, Aziza materialized on Leo's other side, raven feathers clutched in her hand, her curls plastered to her neck. She had used a shade mimicry spell Anne had taught her to follow him through the battlefield.

A bird called out overhead; it was a hawk flying circles directly above them. Not a real hawk, though. Just Fox, spying on him for Anne, and now it must have seen that Aziza and Tristan were with him, too. It circled once more before soaring away, vanishing into the rain, likely to rejoin Anne. She would be nearby, though not to fight; she'd be at the boundary with a cadre of hedgewitches, fortifying it against the disruption the battle would cause.

He checked the time. "We have about three hours until midnight. Ready?"

They were. Together, they slipped inside the castle and sealed the exit behind them, shutting out the howl of the wind and the thunder of battle.

CHAPTER 11
TRISTAN

HIS EARS WERE ringing, and he shivered as he wiped the rain out of his eyes. Beside him, Leo shook out his curls like a wet dog. Aziza took off her soaked jacket and knotted it one-handed around her waist.

Down the hall, a broken window let in the storm, the rain gusting across the corridor. Passing a cobwebbed cupboard door, slightly ajar, Tristan almost slipped. When he looked down, he found the floorboards had given way to serpentine green marble, gleaming even in the near darkness. The half-vanished tapestries in the next corridor didn't hang from the walls so much as grow from them, like tattered strips of colorful moss; and past that, they found the cavernous entrance hall, the ceiling soaring into shadow, the rain dripping inside through cracks in the walls. Deep in the castle, the illusion magic had been at its strongest, and some of it had held on; or maybe it was Leo's presence that had coaxed the enchantments briefly back to life.

"Where's the door?" Leo said. "Am I remembering wrong, or isn't it supposed to be over there?"

"You're not misremembering," Tristan said. In the place where the massive double doors had been, now there was only a blank wall between pillars that tapered into darkness.

"How do I . . . ?" Leo began.

"Magic relies on your intentions for guidance," Aziza reminded him as he floundered. "Focus on what you want. The castle will open for you."

Visibly uncertain, but trying to follow her advice, he turned away from them, brow creased in concentration. And Tristan could see the change come over him. It was a little like when Leo had put on the garments Princess Narra had gifted him upon his triumphant return from the Wild Hunt, which had made him look the part of the Summer Court's champion. This time nothing about his outward appearance changed; he was still in his muddied jeans with his wet shirt clinging to his shoulders, the ends of his damp curls scraping at his eyelashes, the scar across his left eye livid. But there was a new weight to his presence, a burgeoning from within.

"Okay," he said. "This way. I think."

The hall to the servants' entrance—which they'd just come out of—had vanished, and now ended at a moldering, outdated kitchen. The illusions were shifting. They doubled back and went up the sweeping staircase, which led to a corridor full of paintings of past monarchs, many of them bearing a resemblance to the late King Ilanthus. There was even a portrait of Ilanthus with a woman who must have been the last Summer Queen. Narra had inherited the fawn-like speckles on her skin and her radiant smile.

Uneven footsteps came toward them from up ahead. They didn't have a chance to hide. He let a hound emerge from the shadows at his feet, its chest rumbling with a low growl that Tristan half felt behind his own ribs.

"Don't," Leo breathed. "They're sick, I don't want to hurt them, it's not fair—"

A Gallowglass knight limped into the corridor. Under the helmet, which had pincers that put Tristan in mind of a scorpion, the jade rot had decayed most of his face. His skin, a waxy green, had gone black and leathery in patches as if charred.

"I won't hurt him," Tristan promised, the hound moving toward the fairy knight, who lifted his spear as it advanced. It darted forward, jaws snapping, to catch the spear in its teeth. But he was quick on his feet, spinning away—stumbling a little as he drew the spear back—and driving its tip into the side of the hound's throat. A sharp pain radiated from the same place on Tristan's neck, up to his jaw and down into his collar, and the hound snarled. It lunged again, knocking the spear from the knight's grip and bowling him over, its paws on his shoulders to keep him down.

Something flickered in the corner of his eye—no, the hound's eye. Ahead, at the end of the corridor, around the corner. He sent Lucky to look, but by the time it got there, there was nothing to see.

"Tris? You okay?" Leo asked. Aziza hovered at Tristan's other side, the bond open between them, the mental barriers they maintained for privacy discarded. A steadying warmth came through from her.

"Fine. Come on," Tristan said shakily, skirting around the knight as he struggled. The hound would hold him until they got away. The pain in his neck had already abated, but a new sensation made itself known; under his shirt, Jun's talisman had grown warm.

His hand rose to touch the cord from which it hung. *Restless spirits*, Jun had said. Of course—some of the Gallowglass were still standing, but many had died the night of the solstice, and others must have succumbed to the jade rot since then, too. The castle was thoroughly haunted. And as they progressed, haunted was what he felt—or, perhaps, stalked. Every now and then one of the hounds caught another flicker of white in its peripheral vision; they chased it to no avail. Whatever it was—if it was anything more than a ghost—it never showed itself. But Tristan would have felt better if it had.

The route they took made no logical sense. Corridors branched off from each other in directions that should not have been possible. A crooked staircase plunged down a narrow tower and let off onto a floor that held what appeared to be every mirror in the castle. And then it was like they breached some outer shell they hadn't even known was there, like they'd thought they were walking into a building but really they were breaking open a mollusk. In its center, a pair of colossal double doors waited in solemn silence. Leo froze when he saw them.

"Prince Senna was meant to take over from here," he said. "But I don't think he's going to catch up."

"So we do this ourselves," Aziza said. "Be fast."

The doors unlocked at Leo's touch to reveal a vast hall, the walls ribbed with live birch trees that grew half-embedded in the stone, their branches pushing up flat against the ceiling like white cranes with their necks bent. There were no windows or lanterns, but threads of light ran through their bark like silver wire. The effect was shimmery and disorienting, as if he were looking into a forest through a sheet of mist-fine rain.

All the surviving members of the Summer Court were there, fast asleep.

At first glance, Tristan feared the worst. But the ones who had passed were marked by the seedlings that wound diligently over their limbs. The rest were just unconscious. They were curled up on the floor with their wings shining against the tiles, or huddled together against the walls. Maybe this, too, was one of the magical protections worked into the castle's enchantments: something to induce a peaceful sleep in the event of disaster, so that the Folk could rest in stasis until they could be saved, like their human servants. Or maybe it was just what happened when the rot progressed past the aggression stage, and all that was left was to waste away.

A noise startled him—he didn't know what. In his mind, he riffled through the flashes of sensory input he got from each of the hounds, seeking that flicker of white again, that thing he was *sure* was following them. He found something else entirely.

Aziza spoke before he could form the words, feeling his alarm through the bond. "Find Vetiver!" she said, pushing Leo over the threshold.

"But—"

She closed the door on his protests, shutting him inside just as three Gallowglass came around the corner. All of them bore signs of the rot—the telltale green veins, sunken lesions on their skin, hollowed cheeks and clouded eyes. One had spotted lanternfly wings that had gone wilted and yellow at the edges, though they still kept him aloft. The woman beside him had an ink spill of purplish black hair, falling out in patches, and a transparent blur of whirring wings. The third came on foot, but wore a cloak of pure white swan feathers; it shifted as she walked, revealing a chestplate and gauntlets disfigured with lumpy brown growths.

But when they moved, it was too fast for him to think; all he could do was react. Everything that happened next was a blur. Lucky was with Leo, guarding him as he searched for Vetiver in the safe room. Tristan sent four of his remaining hounds to Aziza, keeping four on himself.

The lanternfly fairy drew a sword and launched himself at Aziza; one of the hounds shielded her from a lethal jab while another tackled him out of the air. They went rolling in a tangle of wings and fur. But he flung the hound away, gutted it before it could come back at him, swept high out of the other two hounds' reach—and when he turned back to Aziza, she was whispering into a lit match. It was a summoning spell, one Tristan had seen her practice before. Sparks flew from the match like miniature fireworks, and when she blew on it, a flurry of fire sprites swept from its tip and collided with the lanternfly fairy, catching his hair and wings on fire.

The one with the swan feathers came for Tristan; the hounds surrounded her, circling, teeth snapping, and kept her at bay. But the ink fairy ignored him and Aziza completely and went for the doors to the safe room.

The hounds couldn't get at a fairy in flight. He pulled Jun's feather-sigil talisman out from under his shirt; it was no longer warm, but insistently hot. He had done a spirit summoning once, in a lesson with Beor the Huntsman, and it had taken all his energy and concentration. Jun's charm made it easier. He baited the spirits of the Summer Court's recent dead with sorrow, and they materialized in picture-perfect clarity, drifting into the air on translucent wings, some of them in Gallowglass armor, others in the gowns and coats they'd died in. The ink fairy faltered as they converged on her, crying out in fear at the touch of their cold hands, which couldn't grab, but could bruise—couldn't tear her skin, but could lacerate her heart with fear, hopelessness, and an agony of despair. With a small army of spirits at his command, Tristan felt ablaze with power, the lightning rod to their deathly radiance.

Don't hurt her, he thought. The ghosts couldn't hear him, but he imbued his will into his craft. They dragged her down with what gentleness they were capable of.

"Tris!" Aziza said. "What . . . *is* that?"

He turned. Aziza and the hounds had dispatched the other two fairies. The lanternfly fairy was crumpled on the ground, moaning in pain, his wings charred, pinned by the tip of his own sword embedded in his shoulder. The swan-feather fairy was frozen where she stood with a loop of twisted cloth wrapped around her eyes—a sleep paralysis spell.

And something was looking back at him from the end of the

corridor. This was what had been stalking them; it wasn't a ghost, but it *was* death, the reanimated skeleton of some wolflike beast, down on all fours, eyeless and grinning.

Behind him, the ink fairy wailed. She had fallen to her knees, sobbing. His ghosts drifted above her, aimless as a school of glittering fish. Quickly, he banished them.

By the time he turned back, the dead thing that had been spying on them was gone.

LEO RETURNED FROM the safe room with Vetiver in his arms. The green veining in the boy's skin was vivid, and black bruises mottled his face and neck. His small antlers had fallen off. He was stringy and long-limbed, more a teenager than a kid and really too old to be carried, but Leo held him with little effort.

"Are you all right?" he asked, surveying the aftermath of their skirmish.

"Fine," Aziza said. "But someone was spying on us. I think—"

"It doesn't matter right now," Tristan said. The bone wolf was his problem, and he would be the one to deal with it. "We need to get Vetiver out of here before more of them show up."

"Not yet," Leo said. "I need to get to the basement first."

"The basement?" Tristan repeated, uncomprehending.

"It's where the servants are," Leo said.

"We don't have time for—" Tristan pleaded, hearing the desperation in his own voice and hating it.

Leo didn't back down. "My true love is here. I have to wake them up—I have to at least try."

"We came here for Vetiver!" Tristan said, his voice climbing. "For Hazel! If we're not out of here by midnight—"

"I can't leave without him!" Leo said, wild-eyed. "Not again!"

Him, he'd said, when he usually referred to his true love with a neutral *them*. But it didn't look like he had even heard himself. The same mindless impulse that had once almost driven him to jump off a boat into a storm-tossed, kraken-infested ocean was steering him now. That was the curse's deadliest power—not the way it suppressed Leo's memories, but the way it turned his own feelings, his own loyalty, against him.

He wasn't even wrong. His true love *was* in the castle. Leo just couldn't see him.

Tristan opened his mouth to argue again, but Aziza interrupted.

"I can take Vetiver alone," she said. The relief and gratitude on Leo's face nearly split Tristan's heart into pieces. "Tristan can stay and help you look for the basement."

Tristan turned to her, speechless at the betrayal. He felt her apology through the bond, and also her resignation. She hated this almost as much as he did. But it was something Leo had to do. There was no stopping him. Just like there would be no stopping Tristan from following him.

They helped her climb onto Lucky's back and then placed Vetiver in front of her so that he rested against her shoulder. She wrapped an arm around him and held on to Lucky's fur with her good hand. Lucky rose to its feet and carried them both away. He and Leo watched them disappear around a corner, a heavy silence falling in their absence.

"Tris, I . . ." Leo trailed off, uncomfortable, as if he wanted to apologize but knew he couldn't. Because he wasn't sorry. He thought he was doing the right thing.

"Do you know where it is?" Tristan asked, not wanting to hear it anyway.

He nodded. They set off without another word.

CHAPTER 12

LEO

In a room within the maze of passages that housed the servants' quarters, they found four cots occupied by several peacefully sleeping humans. They had fallen asleep in fearful little clusters on top of the covers or on the floor between the beds, where they'd settled in to wait out the chaos on the night of the solstice. And then the enchantment that kept them in stasis while the Summer Court traveled on their caravan route had set in.

Leo scanned their faces until he found one he recognized. "Evan!"

May was beside him, her head drooping against his shoulder. Neither of them stirred when Leo tried to shake them awake. He took a closer look at them with the amber eye. He could see the sleeping enchantment, like glimmery cobwebs covering their eyes, and tangled up in their hands and hair. He reached out tentatively. Costume illusions could sometimes be wiped off with a touch. But when he tried brushing away the points of glittering light on Evan's temple, nothing happened.

He looked at the sleeping faces around him, waiting for a spark of recognition. One of these people was his true love. He was sure of it. The person who had Leo's memories—Leo's summer nights and birthdays, and beach trips and bike rides, and secrets and firsts. Leo should know them like his own reflection. He should know them on sight. If he could only follow that ever-present pull in his heart back to them—if he could even make an educated guess—he could carry them out of here. His truesight couldn't bring his clouded memories into focus, but surely it could do this much. Right?

If this was true love, then shouldn't this be the part where destiny stepped in to clear the way for him? He had never believed that destiny was something that just happened to you while you waited passively for it to work its magic. You had to meet your fate halfway. But hadn't he done that? Hadn't he fought for his true love every way he could, every chance he got? He was *here*, wasn't he? He had met every condition and played by all the fairytale rules. He'd faced deadly trials, gained a magic power, even become a prince. And while the curse had been far from his mind when he'd done most of those things, that only made it feel even more likely that destiny had played a part, guiding him down the path that would bring him at last to his true love. That the choices he'd made then, in times of crisis, would be rewarded in unforeseen ways.

The only thing he hadn't tried was true love's kiss, and, uh, he really didn't think that was the right play here. He wasn't going to kiss all of these strangers hoping one of them would wake up and throw themselves into his arms. Fairytale logic or not, that was *too* creepy.

As he studied their features, though, he didn't feel a pull toward any of them. He only saw people who *all* deserved to be saved, whether or not one of them was special to him.

"Tris," Leo said, coming to a decision. "Go without me."

"No," Tristan said flatly.

He turned pleading eyes on Tristan, who was waiting in the doorway. "If I had a little more time, I might be able to figure out how to break the enchantment."

Even as he heard himself say it, he didn't actually believe it. How was he supposed to break an enchantment he didn't remotely understand? He just couldn't stand the thought of leaving. Again. Leaving the person he loved in here. In a *basement*.

"Leo, please," Tristan said, and Leo hated himself for making him beg.

"I'm so close," Leo said. "I can't leave without them."

"And *I* can't leave without *you*," Tristan said, swiftly losing his composure.

What if this was Leo's last chance to find them? What if he never came back here? What if being uprooted and dragged all over Elphame was too much abuse for the crumbling old house underneath the castle enchantments to bear, and the roof caved in and everyone inside died? The terror and urgency mounted in his chest. He closed his eyes and felt for the tattered edges of memories connected to the ones he'd lost—that face in his dreams, the fading echo of that voice, the name he had written down the night before he'd turned sixteen and willed himself to hold onto with every shred of resolve in his body.

"You don't get it," Leo said helplessly. His head was pounding. "I can't—"

He broke off as Tristan crossed the room, grabbed a fistful of Leo's shirt, and pulled him in so that they were nose-to-nose and Leo had nowhere to look but his furious glass-green eyes. He was angrier than Leo had ever seen him—it was maybe the first time he had *ever* seen Tristan truly angry.

"I don't care if you can't," Tristan seethed. "I don't *care* about your true love. I don't care about Vetiver or the Summer Court. I don't even care if the East Coast never sees the sun again! I came here for you and I'm not going back without you! So you can either waste time losing this argument, or you can accept it and *keep moving*!"

There was a weighty silence.

"Point taken," Leo said, placing his hand gently over Tristan's.

Tristan was beginning to look a little sheepish. "Sorry," he muttered, unwinding his fingers from Leo's collar.

"It's okay." Leo squeezed his hand lightly before letting go, pushing down mingled feelings of sadness and confusion and most of all an overpowering, guilty affection for Tristan. "You're right. I shouldn't have asked you to do that. It's just hard."

"I know," Tristan said, and Leo believed he really did.

It was the right decision—the rational decision—and the one he never would have made if he had been alone. What he couldn't do for himself, he could do for Tristan. But as they shut the door to the servants' quarters behind them and retraced their steps, his heart was heavy with a creeping certainty that he was going the wrong way.

CHAPTER 13

AZIZA

IT WAS NOT a comfortable journey through the castle.

Blækhounds weren't built to carry passengers. It wasn't like riding a horse, which had a skeletal and muscular structure designed for bearing loads and kept its spine straight as it ran. The hound lunged and loped, its back arching and lengthening, and it was all she could do to squeeze her knees into its sides, clutch a fistful of its fur, and hang on for dear life. Their weight was nothing to it; if it ran more slowly than it could have, that was only for her benefit, but even then it was nearly a full-tilt gallop.

She held Vetiver tightly. He was hardly warmer than the rain outside, his skin waxy where his brow pressed against the juncture of her neck and collar. He hadn't stirred once since Leo had passed him to her.

Only for his sake had she been willing to go ahead of Leo and Tristan. Vetiver had to be saved. After what she'd done to Prince Tal, she owed the Summer Court this much.

As Lucky bounded up a set of stairs, Aziza slid a couple of inches down its back—and almost went flying forward as it came to an abrupt halt. Someone was standing in their path, motionless with shock.

"*Dion?*" she said. "What are you doing here?"

"I should be asking *you* that." He had a silver penknife in one hand, a stick of chalk in the other, his dark hair in uncharacteristic disarray and his shirtsleeves pushed up. There was chalk dust on the ground where he must have just wiped out an array. His look of stunned disbelief was metamorphosing into one of silent judgment as he took in Aziza's bedraggled condition, her unlikely mount, and the future Summer King napping away in her arms.

"Forget it. We have to go," she said. "Did Anne send you?"

"She asked me to try and bind the castle in place," he said, waving the penknife. "I was etching sigils into the walls—"

"You can do that?" she asked, amazed. "Are you done? Did it work?"

He scowled. "It's a *house*. Whatever else they turned it into, it's still a house, and I'm a hearth witch. Of *course* I can do that. And yes, I'm done. I was just searching for the way out—"

Heavy footsteps echoed from somewhere too close for comfort, and a scraping sound, as of the tip of a broadsword being dragged across the floor.

"Climb on!" she said.

Dutifully, Lucky knelt. Dion looked a little ill. "You want me to . . ."

"Sorry, were you enjoying yourself here? Thought you'd take the scenic route?"

Swearing under his breath, he folded away the penknife and pocketed the chalk and climbed gingerly behind her.

"Is this safe?" he asked.

Lucky sprang into motion. Dion made a strangled noise of moderate terror that she found reassuring. He was always so composed, even when faced with rampaging nixies, she cherished the times when something rattled him. He flung an arm around her waist while his other hand caught hold of Lucky's fur.

"You're not supposed to be here," he said, teeth gritted with the effort it took to hang on. "Anne is furious."

"Why are you complaining? You're lucky I showed up."

"I would have found my own way out."

"If the Gallowglass didn't find you first."

"Do you really think I'd be so careless as to—"

He broke off as Lucky went careening around the corner and into a corridor where light spilled out of an open chamber.

"Wait," she said, tugging on its fur. The rest of the castle had been dark.

"Should we go the other way?" Dion asked in an undertone.

They'd never get out at this rate. She leaned over Vetiver to speak into Lucky's ear. "Go on, but quietly."

As they crept past the open door, Aziza looked inside and glimpsed an armored figure—a Gallowglass knight—bent over a lantern. It was only for a second, but her stomach swooped with a sudden nauseous familiarity. That silhouette, with the bow and arrows on his back and the corpse-pale hands lifting the lantern, reminded her strikingly of Viren. But it wasn't him; it couldn't be. Viren had fled the castle with Princess Narra on the summer solstice. He had no reason to return. Then they had passed through the slant of lantern-light spilling over the threshold, and the figure was gone from view as Lucky bounded away.

Outside, the rain turned the clashing knights into violent ghosts, hazy and indistinct. Lucky was forced to slow down as it skirted around the worst of the fighting. It dodged a pair of knights that grappled with their swords locked; one knocked the other to the ground and raised his battle-ax for a killing blow. They streaked past a volley of arrows, Aziza bending low until her face was practically buried in Lucky's fur. Vetiver was crushed into her chest, and Dion's grip on her waist was like iron. He was warm, but she shivered from the rain anyway, and the sight of the carnage unfolding around them.

A Gallowglass knight lurched into their path, his thorned armor warped in gruesome ways. Briar had grown out of his helmet and wrapped around his skull like a blindfold. Blood had crusted in the gaps where the plates of his armor met, as if more thorns had sprouted on the inside, skewering him. His mouth moved; she couldn't hear him over all the noise, but she could read his lips.

"Trespasser," he said. *"Kidnapper!"*

Even in his infected state, he recognized Vetiver. He drew his sword. Others were advancing on them now, surrounding Lucky. Thunder drowned out its warning growls. The rest of Tristan's pack leapt to their aid, billowing out of the darkness as if blown there by the wind, half shadow until their claws made contact. But the Gallowglass kept coming, outnumbering them, and Lucky turned in circles, searching for a breach in their ranks. It made her dizzy. And then its whole body jolted underneath her—it had been struck, an arrow in its neck—and it collapsed, its legs giving out. They slid sideways off its back, Aziza twisting to shield Vetiver from the landing.

The plain was flooded, the earth molten beneath them. She gasped for air, swallowing rain, as she fought to push herself upright. Vetiver's skin was frigid, his breathing shallow.

"Dion! Are you all right?" she asked, shouting to be heard.

He was getting to his knees, muddy and winded. "Fine! Are you?"

Before she could respond, movement in her peripheral vision stole the breath from her lungs. A dark silhouette was coming toward them through the rain and the chaos. The curve of a bow was visible in the stranger's hand.

"Take him!" she told Dion, shoving Vetiver into his arms and scrambling to her feet.

The Gallowglass took aim, drawing the arrow back.

"Aziza—" Dion said, his voice strained.

"Stay down!" she said. She'd used her only charms in the fight outside the safe room. She couldn't cast a new spell quickly enough. The other hounds were occupied; Lucky's body was twitching, the arrow slowly being pushed out of its neck as the wound healed itself, but it would need at least a couple more minutes to recover. Tristan may not have even seen what was happening, with his attention split between all nine hounds.

The last time she'd been in this position, it was Viren in front of her, poised to deliver a killing blow. But Prince Tal had been standing between them, and Aziza had been less than an afterthought to him. Now she was the target, and there was no getting out of this.

It seemed she was seeing Viren everywhere today.

Her hand closed around the hilt of her pocketknife. She would lunge at him. He would fire his arrow and probably hit her. But if she could get one good jab in, she'd buy Lucky time to recover. It was a long shot and her only hope.

Then the Gallowglass staggered as if he'd been struck from behind, releasing the arrow too soon and sending it wide. A scrap of gold sailed over their heads. It was the thing that had hit him, something shining and winged. It dove at her, and she flinched, arms going up to shield her face—but it only circled her and Dion without making contact. She could make out the shape of feathers and a beak. It was a bird made of pure light, the kind of light that burned and blistered and blinded, as radiant as an earthbound sun; the rain sizzled into steam around it.

All across the battlefield, a flock of spun-gold birds had descended like an army from heaven. They shot themselves at the Summer

Gallowglass, flying into their faces and briefly blinding them so that they could be disarmed by their opponents. They caught arrows mid-flight and orbited the Autumn knights who were too wounded to fight, intercepting enemies who came near. They struck onto the battlefield in precisely the places they were needed the most.

Dion got to his feet. Vetiver was limp in his arms, his curls sticking to his temples and his silken jacket dripping mud.

"Thank you," she said, reaching out to take him back.

Dion shook his head. "I have him." His eyes didn't quite meet hers. The cold had washed all the color from his face, and his clothes were soaked through, clinging to his lean frame. "You shouldn't have—What did you think you were going to—"

She recalled then that her idea of a plan had been something to the effect of *stab him and hope for the best*.

"I don't know," she said evasively. "I just couldn't let him get to Vetiver. What are those things?" She glanced up again at the birds streaking comet-like over the battlefield.

"It's a spell," he said woodenly. "We can follow them to safety. Come on."

Captain Vasilia intercepted them. Her helmet was gone, and so was her weapon, as if at some point she had resorted to fighting bare-handed. She took Vetiver, thanking them on the Autumn Court's behalf, and swept away. The battle had come to a bewilderingly swift end; Aziza's body still thrummed with adrenaline, not quite convinced the danger had passed. Above them, the birds—magical constructs, she thought—winged their way across the field, their work finished, to meet a figure who caught them in his outstretched hands. They dove at him and vanished. As she and Dion got closer, she recognized him: the graying blond hair, the striking blue eyes. It was Castor Thorne.

"Anne is coming over here," Dion said. "You should talk to her."

"What's the matter?" she demanded.

"Nothing. I'm not injured."

"That's not what I meant." But she wasn't sure what she *did* mean. All she knew was that one minute, she and Dion had been in this together—fleeing the castle, protecting Vetiver—and somewhere in between falling off of Lucky and narrowly escaping the Gallowglass, he had shut her out.

Anne was carrying an umbrella, which made her the only person within a mile radius who wasn't drenched. Despite that, her expression was thunderous.

"To say I'm disappointed in the reckless choices you made today is an *understatement*," Anne hissed, handing the umbrella to Aziza. "Where are the others?"

"They—" she began.

"Never mind," Anne said a moment before Leo crashed into Aziza, seizing her in an embrace that nearly knocked her off her feet. The umbrella swung in her lax grip, covering neither of them.

"Zee! Tris told me what happened," he said, distressed.

"I told him you were fine," Tristan objected as Leo released her. "And that Dion was with you."

It was only then that Aziza realized Dion was no longer beside her.

"Prince Senna is grateful to all of you. He didn't want to delay taking Vetiver to safety, but he thanks you for your assistance." Anne glared at the three of them in their sodden, shivering little cluster. "That doesn't mean you're off the hook. You could have died—you could have gotten Vetiver killed. You almost—"

"Come, now, Anne," someone else said. "They did us proud. Aren't you being a little harsh?"

Castor was strolling toward them. His gold cuff links shone as if with reflected sunlight. And there was Dion, trailing after him, a deferential half step behind.

"We meet again, Aziza," he said, with great cheer. Upon closer inspection, the cuff links were definitely glowing.

"Are those enchanted?" she asked, curious despite herself.

"These?" He turned his wrist over to show her. "Good eye. I use them as an anchor for my constructs. Allow me to demonstrate."

He opened his hands and held them out; at least a dozen of the winged constructs came down in a stream of light and, one by one, vanished into the cuff links. She should have known they belonged to him as soon as she'd seen them; they were the same ones that Leo had once seen whispering in Princess Narra's ear.

"Your parents and I used to collaborate on spells. This is the product of one such collaboration, between me and Leila," he said. "They absorb magic from their surroundings and allow me to release it in a new form. I based it off a kind of energy capture spell she showed me—she helped me adapt it into something I could use."

"Historically, that was the true purpose of a coven," Anne said. "To collaborate on shared magical goals. Not to drag each other on foolhardy adventures."

"But this is a learning opportunity! You used to love those, Professor Sterling," Castor said.

"I taught because it's what masters do, not because I loved it," she said. "I have just been *vividly* reminded of why I retired."

"But why—What are you doing here?" Aziza asked, addressing Castor, but it was Dion she looked at—she couldn't help it—as if she expected him to answer in his stead.

"Anne called me as soon as she got wind of how close to the boundary all of this would be happening. I brought a few others with me. There'll be tornadoes all over the state if we don't fix that." Castor gestured vaguely in the direction of the agitated sky. When he said *others,* he meant his weather witches. "I knew she'd asked for Dion's help, too, so I would have been here either way to keep an eye on him. I planned to steer clear of the battlefield—traditionally, we don't mix ourselves up in the affairs of the Folk."

The audacity of this statement, knowing what she knew about his connection to Princess Narra, was almost too much. It took all of her willpower to hold her tongue.

"But when one of my constructs saw our missing apprentices, and the peril they were in," he added, "I had no choice but to intervene."

Of all the things he'd said, it was the last that stopped her in her tracks.

"You have an apprentice?" Aziza said.

"Let me guess—he told you he's my intern," Castor said, resting a hand on Dion's shoulder. "And that's true. But he's also my apprentice, and one of the most exceptional witches I've ever had the pleasure of mentoring." He glanced between the two of them. "Were you already acquainted before today?"

"Anne introduced us," Dion said.

"Excellent. Escort them home, will you?"

"Yes, sir."

"I hope we'll run into each other at the next Market," Castor said to her. "For now, I leave you in my apprentice's capable hands."

He wished them a good night; Aziza didn't remember replying, but she must have. Her mind, still rattled from their near-miss during the battle and the whiplash of its conclusion, was working at the new mysteries this short conversation had presented, as if picking a lock with a touch both delicate and urgent.

Dion had lied by omission when he neglected to tell her that his mentor was Castor Thorne. They weren't friends and he didn't owe her any insight into his personal life. But he was aware of their suspicions about Castor's involvement with Princess Narra, chose to attach himself to Castor anyway, and then went out of his way to conceal that fact from her. Why keep it a secret? Was it that he didn't believe Castor had done anything wrong—or that he knew for certain he had?

But Dion knew little of Elphame and even less about Princess Narra. Why should he care about Castor's relationship with her, or whether or not Aziza took issue with his career choices? He wouldn't. Unless there was something else he was trying to hide. Something Aziza had a personal stake in. Something that was nagging at Aziza even now.

Where the Summer Court's castle was a spun-sugar confection of enchantment, Castor's spell-casting tasted metallic in the back of her mouth, as if she'd bitten her tongue. It was a magical energy so powerful, so domineering, any witch would have sensed it instantly. But there was something else, too—a tranquil magic she detected not because it was especially powerful, but because it was familiar. Frowning, she looked more closely at Castor. He had gone a few steps away, walking with Anne. They were deep in conversation. The drizzle seemed to bounce off his shoulders; she would have assumed it was some kind of weather-witch spell to shield him from the rain, but no—it dampened his hair, and a droplet ran down the side of his face. The only thing resisting the water was . . . his velvet coat.

It dawned on her with a wave of horror. That *wasn't* velvet. It was sealskin.

Meryl's skin.

The one who'd had her all this time was Castor.

PRINCE SENNA HAD sent knights on winged steeds to bring them to the site of the battle earlier that day; they were all relieved not to have to repeat the experience on their way back. Anne had stationed Nelle close by with a rented car to take them to the nearest jackdaw collection. From there, Dion took the lead, guiding them back to Bishop Library.

As the rest of their party made for the false wall that would transport them back to the reading room, Aziza said, "Dion, wait."

"Go ahead," he said when the others hesitated. "We'll be there in a minute."

Once they were alone, Dion faced her, hands in his pockets. With his damp hair falling in his eyes, he looked younger. The shoulders of his shirt were still spotted with rain.

"What is it?" he said.

She inhaled slowly. It felt like the first breath she'd taken in hours.

"That coat Castor wears. Did you know what . . . ?" She trailed off. "Never mind. Of course you do."

He nodded, just once, meeting her eyes squarely. "Yes. Not at first. But for a while now."

"Why didn't you tell me? When I asked about Professor Serapion, you knew even then, didn't you?" Her voice shook. "And I can't even be angry. I guess this is payback."

"It's not," he said. She almost wished he'd be spiteful or vindictive about it; his lack of expression was maddening, like trying to dig your fingernails into smooth marble—there was nothing to catch on to.

"No, you're right. Because it's not the same as what I did," she snarled. White hot anger flared in her, and the protective layer of ice around her heart cracked with a sharp finality. "Meryl is alive. She can be saved. I lied to you about Emil, but I never stood by and let someone hurt him!"

"Don't talk to me about Emil," Dion said, in that monotone that was, slowly but surely, driving her completely mad. He was pale and bruised under the eyes, but exhaustion did nothing to blunt his sharp edges: he wasn't like cloth, which went soft and threadbare once worn out, but more like clay—which only hardened when exposed to heat.

"Go fuck yourself!" She only realized she was shouting when her voice bounced off the walls.

She was sick with rage, dizzy with it. Castor Thorne was *wearing Meryl's skin*. He had taken her and imprisoned her and made her leave without saying goodbye, and then he stood in front of Aziza flaunting what he'd done, adorned in the evidence of his own cruelty. And there weren't words for what she felt. She had never wanted to hurt someone before just to hurt them, but she wanted to now. She could have killed Castor Thorne with her bare hands.

But even in the moment of realization, she had known there was nothing she could do. They had seen him single-handedly take possession of a battlefield. He was one of only ten witches who governed the entire magical community. When it came to witchcraft, there was no higher power than Castor, and having seen what weather witches could do, she was sure that taking the coat by force was impossible.

"So now you know," Dion said. "And there's nothing you can do about it. Do you feel better? Has this helped you?"

She stared at him in disbelief. "How the fuck do you think I feel?"

"Exactly," he said, as if she'd agreed with him. "Your lie didn't hurt Emil. It hurt *me*. It gave me false hope. I was better off after I knew the truth. But you—you're not better off now."

"So you were sparing me," she said, with a harsh laugh. "Thank you, Dion, for your compassion."

He had no reply, and she had nothing else to say. She left.

CHAPTER 14
TRISTAN

A COUPLE OF hours later, they had all gone to bed. Aziza was on the air mattress; Leo had nobly submitted himself to the ordeal of spending the night on the shabby tweed couch that creaked whenever its occupant so much as breathed. Tristan was in his room with the door cracked open, still awake, listening.

Before the curse—when they were kids, as young as twelve years old—Tristan was ready to follow Leo anywhere, anytime he called. They were never apart if they could help it, and the time they spent separated felt interstitial and meaningless, like the foam that filled the empty spaces in a package.

And today Leo had asked Tristan to leave him behind. He shouldn't have felt wounded by this, but he did. Was this it—the difference between being a friend that Leo loved, and being his true love? If Leo had known, would he have said such a thing to him?

And how had Tristan responded?

I don't care about your true love, he'd said.

Leo didn't know he was talking about himself. All he would have heard was Tristan's disregard for something—someone—that was important to Leo. No wonder Leo was out there on the couch instead of in here with Tristan.

His eyes were fixed on the window. As the sky brightened, it would drown the room in blue-tinged light.

His door eased open with a soft click.

It closed again a moment later, and Leo's footsteps crossed the room. Tristan felt himself unknot like a bowline as Leo's weight made the bed dip. His arm settled around Tristan's waist.

"Tris?" he said hoarsely.

"Yeah." Tristan let his palm skim over Leo's wrist. "I wasn't sure you were coming."

"Didn't know if I should," Leo breathed, relaxing against him as if he had just been waiting for Tristan's permission. Tristan's pulse jumped. He still lost his footing a little when present-day Leo diverged too drastically from the Leo he had known before the curse. Right now, in the dark, the dissonance made his head swim. Leo thought he needed *permission* to lie down next to Tristan. It would never make sense, no matter how much time he'd had to get used to it. It had to be a dream.

"Why not?" he asked, feeling as if he were talking to himself, interrogating a figment of his imagination.

"Thought you might be mad."

"No," Tristan said. "A little," he allowed, a moment later. "I'm sorry I yelled at you."

"Sorry for thinking it was kind of hot."

Tristan turned over so that he could level the full force of his glare at him. For a phantasm, he felt comfortingly solid. He couldn't see Leo's answering grin, but he felt it when Leo leaned in drowsily to kiss the corner of his mouth. Then he cupped Tristan's jaw in his hand and turned his face for a proper one, their dry lips catching and their teeth clicking together, clumsy but satisfying in a visceral way, like when you stretched until your back cracked. Tristan shifted, slotting them together and letting his tongue wet Leo's mouth, and then it was better. It almost didn't feel like a kiss—just answering a basic need, like he was thirsty and needed to drink, and he did, with unabashed greed.

"I shouldn't have let the three of us split up," Leo mumbled, his lips moving against Tristan's cheek. "That's what I'm sorry for. Should've just gone with you both from the start."

"Don't do it again," Tristan whispered, trying not to beg.

Leo would be chasing the ghost of his true love forever, but Tristan could live with that. As long as he could stay by his side, he'd be happy.

But would Leo be happy?

Leo's breathing evened out long before Tristan could dream up an answer to that question.

HE SHADOW-TRAVELED TO Emil's study early the next day. It was usually deserted, the rest of the house empty and silent—and it was a silence he could feel through the door, like the pressure of something leaning against it.

Once, on a prior visit, Tristan had opened the door to the study just to look outside. It wasn't that he wanted to snoop around. The study felt like an island suspended in time and space, and if he had never actually seen the rest of the house and if there wasn't ever any noise—not even the creak of the pipes, not even the wind in the eaves or the hum of electronics or *anything*—then could he be sure it existed?

Strange thoughts. Paranoid thoughts. But the pit in his stomach wasn't going away, so he had opened the door and verified that the study was connected to a hallway. There was a wide window at the end, the curtains drawn, and the curve of a railing to a staircase.

His skin prickled with goose bumps. The sense of foreboding was so powerful that he almost slammed the door shut.

He hadn't gone near it since then, preferring to retreat to the shelter of Emil's library as quickly as he could. Whatever affliction besieged the rest of the house, it couldn't reach him there.

After about three months of study, he was getting pretty good at Latin and Old Norse. The translation of spells was a slow process, made slower by the fact that he devoted hours every week to searching through the grimoires, puzzling out bits and pieces of a dozen different languages, in search of one particular spell. He hadn't found it yet; he wasn't even close. He knew it existed, but perhaps Emil didn't have it. That, or it was in the missing grimoire Dion had mentioned to him. *The Infernal Arts*. What had Dion said about it? Right—that Emil either kept it on his person or hid it someplace so secure even Dion had not known its location.

But he would just have to keep looking. The abstract drive he'd felt to master his craft—to not let this gift go to waste—had crystallized into sharp-edged urgency. Though the autumn equinox battle had been a decided victory for Coven Blackthorn, he could see the smoke on the horizon. The skeleton wolf that had spied on them; the discovery of Meryl's sealskin in Castor Thorne's possession; the fact that Leo kept getting pulled into Elphame's conflicts—all he could think was that their enemies were multiplying. They needed every advantage they could get. A contingency plan. So to speak.

In the meantime, he was focusing his efforts on *The Book of Fenrisúlfr*. It contained blækhound spells, like the one that would help him shadow-travel with a passenger—as well as a spell for creation. He had spent a long time translating it. Then he'd spent even longer agonizing over Old Norse pronunciation. Different sources disagreed about how it was meant to sound, so he had to make an educated guess and hope for the best.

Lucky watched him from under the table as he practiced reciting the incantation. When he paused to repeat one phrase three different ways, trying to work out the right inflection, it gave a disdainful huff.

"Unless *you* plan to teach me Old Norse, I don't want to hear it," Tristan said.

Another hound pulled their mental link taut, wanting his attention. It was Lupa. Hazel knelt in front of the hound, her arms around its neck. Tristan felt her thin frame shaking against the hound's body, its fur growing wet under her cheek, and realized with alarm that Hazel was crying.

He stood, prepared to shadow-travel to her side. Technically, he wasn't supposed to do that. Trespassing on the Winter Court's inner sanctum was a crime punishable by death. But Hazel was alone, and possibly in trouble. He had promised when he'd sent Lupa with her that he would be there if she needed him.

But then she pulled away, wiping the tears with her sleeve.

"Prince Senna is here," she told Lupa. "We're going to go see him and the queen."

Lupa nudged her cheek with its nose, gentle but insistent.

"I'm okay," she said, getting to her feet and checking her reflection in the mirror for stray tears. "But a lot of the Autumn Court's knights got hurt. Some of them are already coming down with the rot. And we can't fix it until the solstice in December. They'll keep getting worse. Some of them will die. Vetiver is safe, but he's not doing good. He isn't even conscious. He can't even . . ."

Hazel undid her hair with shaky fingers and braided it again. It was black with an emerald-green luster where it caught the light.

"I know it's good that the Summer Court has a chance of having a ruler other than Princess Narra," she said to her reflection. "If Vetiver can just survive until December, they can get him to drink the elixir of renewal, and then he'll be king, and he'll be healed. So will everyone else who's sick. But he won't know what's happening until it's over. We can't even ask him first."

Lupa cocked its head to the side in an un-houndlike gesture. Hazel met its expectant eyes in the mirror, but her gaze quickly dropped, her wings drooping.

"It's the same thing that Princess Narra tried to do to me," she said. "He'll just wake up one day and his—his whole life will be completely different. And it's not fair."

Her lip trembled, but she took a deep breath and strode to the doorway. Lupa followed. Together, they traversed the Winter Court's palace and arrived at the throne room.

Queen Ceresia was there; so was Prince Senna.

"I assure you, we are prepared to care for him. We would not have—" Prince Senna broke off as Hazel entered. Seeing who it was, he bowed to her. "Good morning, Princess. I was just updating Queen Ceresia on your cousin's condition."

"I will assess his condition myself," the Winter Queen said. "Bring him here."

Prince Senna bowed again, more deeply. "I do not wish to burden your healers."

"Nonsense. Yours will have their hands full tending to your wounded," she said, with a mirthless smile. "Don't take this as a slight against your capabilities. You've done well, Senna. I will admit—I didn't believe you would succeed. You have surprised me. Now, allow me to take it from here. It is my turn to relieve *you* of a burden."

To Lupa, the tension in the air was palpable. After a barely perceptible moment of hesitation, Prince Senna said, "Thank you, my queen."

"Can I visit him when he gets here?" Hazel asked.

"With the healers' supervision, and as long as you remain at a safe distance," Queen Ceresia said. "We can't risk exposing you to the rot. He will be placed in quarantine until the solstice. Fear not—he will have your other kinsman for company."

More conversation followed, but Tristan was no longer paying attention. Queen Ceresia had reminded him of something important—something he couldn't believe he hadn't thought about before. Without giving himself a chance to think better of it, he summoned Lucky and shadow-traveled to the Winter Court.

The infirmary was occupied by somber healers in dark gloves and robes, their hair braided behind their pointed ears. The patients were sequestered in glass chambers, like bubbles of isolation in a stream of light, which reflected off the walls from the lamps the healers carried. Watching from the shadows, through Lucky's eyes, Tristan waited until the coast was clear before he slipped inside one of the chambers. The entrance looked like gossamer, but it felt like peppermint tasted, sharp and clean.

Inside, Beor rested on a cot, his eyes closed. He had the greenish veins of all the jade rot's victims, and blotches of blackened skin down one side of his neck. The rot had darkened the old scars on his face, claw marks that Tristan suspected had been made by Beor's own hounds, back when he had been a less experienced summoner. Tristan had similar ones on his arms and torso. Only one of Beor's scars hadn't been affected; it was the slash mark on his cheek and the side of his nose where Tristan had cut him with a silver knife.

He had thought Beor was asleep, but his eyes flew open when Tristan entered. The rot had not dulled the intensity of their reddish-gold gaze. As they settled on Tristan, they narrowed with disbelief—and then laughter bubbled out of him. Once a deep, booming sound, now it was nothing more than a broken rasp.

"It's the little summoner whelp," Beor said, his head tilting toward him. His lips stretched in a grimace at the effort it took to move even that much. "Is it too much to hope that you would have brought some more wine? The blasted healers won't spare me a single drop, and the princess only brings me *books*. They'd all have me die of thirst."

"Not this time," Tristan said. "You're doing better than the others I saw in the castle."

"It's that tenacious human blood of mine," Beor said, with bitter resentment. "It can't save me from the rot, but it won't let me die, either. I'd reach back through time and wring my ancestor's neck if I could." He studied Tristan critically. "*You* are stronger, at least."

Was he? Tristan didn't feel it.

"I . . ." He rested a hand on the hound sitting tamely at his side. "This one. Its name is Lucky."

Beor laughed again, so hard it turned into a cough. "Is that a name, or a wish?"

"Where are your hounds?" Tristan asked hesitantly.

"Gone," he said. "I had to unmake them. I could no longer control them."

Tristan's fingers curled into Lucky's fur. The hounds had been a terrible burden at first. Now he didn't know what he'd do without them. He couldn't imagine what their loss was like for Beor, who'd had his for longer than Tristan had even been alive.

"When you get better, will you be able to make more?"

"If."

"*When*," Tristan insisted.

Beor scoffed. "Of course, but it will take time. Blækhound creation is a delicate process, and requires a great deal of power." He closed his eyes for a moment, opened them again, as if making a conscious effort not to doze off. "And to forge the bond of loyalty is an arduous task."

Tristan had told Jun that the teacher who'd given him his grimoires had died; and while that was true, he had another teacher, one who was still here. And he was the only person Tristan could talk to about the . . . independent study he had been pursuing.

"I have a question," he said. "It's important."

"Then you should have brought wine," Beor said. "Wine, you see, is also important."

"If you wanted to hide something," Tristan persisted, "where would you put it? Somewhere no one else would be able to find it."

"That's obvious," Beor said, with a wolfish grin. "You hide it in the dark."

Tristan understood immediately, and then felt foolish for not thinking of it himself. But it wasn't the answer he had wanted. Not even close.

The grimoire he needed was in the shadow plane. Tristan could travel through it with his hounds, but he couldn't linger there; he couldn't fold himself up and *become* shadow like they could. It was more like he used the shadows as a portal, or a bridge.

Shadows were everywhere, and that meant Emil's book of the infernal arts could be anywhere at all.

WHEN TRISTAN RETURNED to the library, Professor Serapion was waiting for him.

He stood behind the desk, his fingers resting proprietarily on the back of the chair. As Tristan came down the stairs, Serapion turned to him with eyes like a desert at night, colorless and barren.

"Professor," he said warily. "Can I help you?"

He had expected this visit as soon as he had seen the bone wolf in the castle. He just hadn't expected it so soon. He had hoped he'd have time to come up with a convincing lie.

"Come here," Serapion said.

There was no pretense of civility in his voice. There was no anger, either, but that wasn't reassuring, for much the same reason why it wasn't reassuring when the shark fin knifing its way toward you across the water vanished.

Tristan did as he was told; it seemed the most prudent course of action. He came around to the front of the desk.

"I have a task for you," Serapion said softly. He took a folded piece of paper from an inner pocket of his suit and passed it to Tristan. Confused and suspicious, Tristan opened it; a name he didn't recognize was written on it, and what appeared to be directions to a shop in the Half Moon Market. "Go and see him on the next Market night. Tell him I sent you. He'll be expecting you, and he'll know what to do."

The paper crumpled slightly in Tristan's grip. "I'm not going anywhere unless you tell me why."

Serapion's hand shot out and clamped down around his jaw. His bony fingers dug punitively into Tristan's skin, pressing against his teeth through his cheek. Tristan grabbed at his wrist, the paper with its cryptic instructions fluttering to the ground, but there was surprising strength in that deceptively thin frame.

"Watch your tone with me, thief," he snapped.

Tristan froze, his breath hissing through his gritted teeth, his nails embedded in Serapion's skin, leaving crescent-shaped indents. "What?"

"Does Anne Sterling know, I wonder?" Serapion said, his thin mouth twisted in a snarl of disgust. "No. She mustn't. If she had, she wouldn't have been so bold as to place you here, right under my nose."

Tristan held still, even as Serapion's fingers squeezed tighter, painfully. The bone rings on his fingers were cold and smooth against Tristan's skin, and it felt awful to touch them, like the darkest and most damned grimoires in Emil's collection.

"On the autumn equinox, I came here and found your post empty," he said coldly. "But we all knew what was to occur at the Summer Court that day, and I was aware that your coven was involved. I sent one of my constructs to watch you. You had nine hounds, when before you had claimed a pack of three. The only witch I've ever known to have more than that was Emil Wulfsige."

Tristan's tenth hound was Lupa, who had remained with Hazel throughout the battle.

"But I'm sure you know all about Emil's hounds," Serapion said. "He died here, in the same town where a young necromancer has gone undetected well into his teenage years, wielding power beyond his ken, known to no one in our community, and descended from a bloodline that has never, in any of the genealogy records I have been able to unearth, managed to produce a witch."

Tristan jerked away, trying to escape—but Serapion released him easily this time, so that Tristan staggered, colliding with the end of a bookcase. He'd known Serapion would be angry that Tristan had lied about how many hounds he had. But he hadn't realized that information was enough for Serapion to connect him to Emil.

Was it enough? It hadn't clicked for Dion until he learned of the hag's existence. Did Serapion know more than he was letting on? If he knew about the hag—how?

"You can stop trying to summon your hounds," Serapion said. He folded his hands together, his right absently stroking the bone rings on his left. "I set down countermeasures against shadow-travel before you came downstairs."

Tristan hadn't consciously tried to summon them; he'd just gotten so used to reaching for his hounds when faced with a threat that it had become instinct. Now that he was aware he was doing it, he was also aware that when his hounds tried to surface, they couldn't; it was as if they bumped up against a net wherever they tried to exit the shadow plane. It might even have been the same kind of enchantment that protected Emil's library.

"You're not going to kill me," Tristan said, realizing it even as he spoke the words aloud. He rubbed at his jaw, trying to erase the feeling of Serapion's touch. "You wouldn't have bothered talking to me if you were."

"No," Serapion said softly. "I see another path forward for you. You're going to be my apprentice." He picked up the note Tristan had dropped and pressed it into Tristan's hand, closing his fingers around it. "But I extract a price from my apprentices. A guarantee of loyalty, to ensure they don't betray the secrets I share with them."

"Your apprentice?" Tristan stared at him, not comprehending. *"Why?"*

"Rogue necromancers are like feral dogs. There are only two things to be done with them," Serapion said. "Either tame them, or put them down. Let's see if you can be tamed."

CHAPTER 15
LEO

He used to dream about his true love.

Not *dream* like *fantasize*. He would fall asleep and into a vision of a life that felt like a parallel universe, similar to his own but slightly askew. He was walking to school; he was digging his feet into the sand; he was slipping out the door in the middle of the night; he was falling into his bed, and he wasn't alone. There was someone—always the same someone—occupying the dream with him. Just out of sight. At his side, glimpsed in the corner of his eye, matching his pace as they walked. Taking his hand. The rhythm of their voice when they made a comment in an undertone meant just for Leo's ears, but not the sound of it; the way it made him feel when he looped his scarf around their neck and earned a smile in return, but not what it looked like. They were impressions, sense memories, nothing specific enough for the curse to wipe from his mind. But that other life, half dream and half memory, felt so real that the phantom touches lingered on him like invisible bruises after he woke. The person who had lived that life with him was real. And now they were just gone, and all Leo could do was miss them.

He couldn't say he was lonely, not when he had his parents and two best friends, and a sister who still needed him, even if he couldn't be there for her in person. Loneliness implied the absence of something that came from outside him, like companionship. This loss felt like part of himself was missing, excised like an organ. If he'd lost a lung, *lonely* wasn't the word he'd use to describe the experience. He just knew he couldn't breathe.

The dreams were proof that somewhere deep down, he still remembered, and what he'd lost could be won back. As long as he held on, didn't waver, didn't *give up*, he could wear away at the curse.

But he had wavered. And he hardly ever had the dreams anymore.

The guilt was intense. His true love had been collateral damage to *his* curse. He'd spent so much time thinking about what he'd say when he finally found them, and all the apologies he owed them. But the list kept getting longer. How could he explain himself? How was he supposed to get the words out? He tried to imagine it, how it would sound. *I'm sorry my heart misses a beat when Tristan walks into the room. I'm sorry that seeing him is the best part of my day. I'm sorry that when he and I agreed to keep things casual, I was already willing to do anything for him.*

Who had he been kidding?

He'd messed up. No two ways about it.

The morning after the first time they hooked up—an impulse decision made immediately upon their return from the Summer Court—Leo had stammered out something like, *Was that okay? Are we okay?* and Tristan had said, cheerful as anything, *I thought it was better than just okay. I'm getting coffee—do you want any?* and Leo had said something along the lines of *It's just that we're friends and—*

And Tristan had said, *Right, we're friends. So it's fine.*

As he spoke, he'd picked up the shirt that Leo had stripped off him last night and tugged it back on. There had been a faint indent on his cheek from a crease in Leo's pillow. He'd combed his fingers through his hair to tidy it and looked over his shoulder at Leo with a smile that had made him forget what he was about to say next.

That had been the one and only time Leo had tried to have the what-are-we conversation.

Tristan already knew that Leo had a true love he intended to win back. And Leo wasn't going to patronize him by forcing the discussion, as if he didn't trust that Tristan knew what he was doing.

He *did* know what he was doing, right?

He definitely had more experience in . . . uh, everything . . . than Leo did. So when he said it was fine, Leo had believed him. Leo was the conflicted one—the one who was fast becoming too invested.

That was what he'd thought, anyway.

Now, Tristan got up and carefully pulled the blanket back over him. It was a couple of days after the equinox. Leo had stayed over at the library the last two nights in a row.

"It's early, Tris," he mumbled.

"I know. I wanted to swap out some of Emil's grimoires before I have to open the library today," Tristan said, smoothing Leo's hair out of his face, a warm press of his hand on Leo's temple. Leo shut his eyes briefly, his chest tight.

"Aren't you tired?" he asked, squinting up at him. The first bluish glow of dawn stole inside through the window. It touched the pensive line of Tristan's mouth, the unerring slant of his jaw, the dizzying summit of a cheekbone where the color rose in his face when he was out of breath. His hair was getting a little long, a fall of white-blond silk. Leo's fingers tangled in it whenever he slid his hand over the back of his neck, in a move he had only now, retroactively and with a little electric shock of embarrassment, identified as the possessive gesture it was.

"I'll be fine," he said, Leo reading his lips more than listening to the words. He remembered suddenly how Tristan had kissed him back to sleep the night after the battle and had to swallow hard, his throat dry. It was silly to be flustered about a kiss considering everything else they'd done together, but sometimes—the way Tristan kissed him or looked at him when he thought Leo wasn't paying attention—

"They took Vetiver back to the Winter Court," Tristan added.

Leo propped himself up on his elbow. There were more important things to worry about than the wreck he'd made of his personal life. "Yeah?"

"Lupa saw them come in. He's in quarantine now," Tristan said. "Hazel's asleep—she hasn't seen them yet."

Leo sighed heavily. "I just hope this makes things easier for her."

"We got Vetiver out. What happens next is out of our hands." He stood to dig in his closet for a change of clothes. "I might not be back before you have to go. Don't fall asleep, or you're going to be late."

"Don't miss me too much," Leo returned, flopping down onto the pillow.

"I always miss you," Tristan said offhand. It could've passed for a joke if Tristan hadn't immediately frozen, as if he'd done something wrong. But he went on as if nothing had happened, and slipped out soon after that. Leo lay there, listening to his footsteps receding down the stairs, his mind replaying the last few moments.

I always miss you.

Did he really?

His heart sank as he thought back to Tristan's vehement refusal to leave him in the castle the other night. It wasn't the refusal itself that had struck Leo. It was the anger. The barely concealed hurt.

All along, Leo had thought he was the only one in danger of

getting his heart broken. But he was starting to have a feeling that he may have miscalculated.

HE HADN'T MISSED a day of class this week. His parents didn't think that rescuing the heir to the high court of Elphame was a legitimate excuse for skipping school. He didn't hold it against them; their summer had been almost as rough as his. Maybe worse, in some ways. On Hazel's fourteenth birthday, which was in late August, Mom had spent most of the day in tears. Then there were Leo's repeated visits to the low courts, which they tolerated firstly because Anne had come to speak to them in person, promising she would watch over him; secondly because they knew he was doing it all for Hazel's sake; and thirdly because they couldn't stop him. So when Mom glared daggers at him for suggesting he might cut school every now and then, he got that she was just trying to maintain some semblance of normalcy in his life. Meanwhile, according to Aziza, Khaled was making dire threats about boarding schools in icy, remote places with no Wi-Fi.

It was drizzling out, so lightly he hadn't bothered to put up the hood of his jacket. He sat under the shelter at the bus stop, watching the empty street while he waited. A layer of fallen leaves papered the sidewalk; a feeble wind stirred the rawboned elms that lined the road. Autumn had started too early, and now, when it should have been just beginning, it already felt dismal and endless. Summer was a distant memory.

The sound of soft footsteps on wet pavement brought him back to the present. Someone sat down on the other end of the bench.

"Good morning, Leo," the stranger said.

"Morning," he said automatically, thinking that it must be the

Man at the Bus Stop, one of Blackthorn's spirits. He only appeared when it was raining—which was almost always, these days—and he took a different form every time, so Leo wasn't troubled by the deep, unfamiliar timbre of his voice.

But the stranger wasn't carrying a notebook, the way the Man at the Bus Stop always did—just a coffee cup. And his eyes weren't a faded blue—the one thing about the Man at the Bus Stop that never changed—but a catlike yellowish gold. Topaz studs glittered in his ears. When he smiled, his incisors were just this side of too sharp.

"Your sister was right. This is quite good," he said, giving the coffee cup a little shake. He picked up another cup next to him on the bench and held it out to Leo.

Leo didn't take it. "What . . . is this?"

"They call it a *pumpkin spice latte*," the man said. "Your folk *are* clever when they want to be, aren't they?"

That wasn't what Leo had meant. He pushed up the patch that covered his amber eye so that he could see the stranger properly. Under the costume illusion, his hoodie was a finely embroidered coat, and a wicker circlet rested atop his head. The pointed tips of his ears were visible between strands of long, dark hair. His features were mostly the same, but the costume toned them down somehow, as if blunting the cruel edge of a blade. He was arrestingly beautiful, with the sort of compelling face that looked like it belonged on a stage or in front of a camera, but looking at him for too long without the dampening effect of the illusion was like being taken gently by the hand and led down a winding path into a snowy wood, growing colder and more lost by degrees.

Leo met that numbing gaze, reached out, and took the coffee.

"Prince Senna," he said. "Why are you here?"

"To thank you, of course. I didn't have the chance the other day,"

Prince Senna replied. "And to apologize. I couldn't keep up, and you had to rescue Vetiver alone. That wasn't the plan."

"It's all right," Leo said cautiously. "Is Vetiver okay?"

"For now," Prince Senna said. "For as long as the Winter Queen wills it."

"What do you mean?" Leo asked.

"I would have taken the boy back to the Autumn Court, but the queen insisted on assuming responsibility for his care." Prince Senna swirled the coffee around in his cup. "I could not refuse her."

"You think she's going to hurt him?" Leo asked, more sharply than he meant to.

"Not yet. Maybe not ever," Prince Senna said. "But her search for Princess Narra continues. She claims that securing Narra is necessary, as Vetiver's condition is precarious, and he may not survive until the solstice. Still, I have reason to believe that, of the candidates for the Summer Court's throne, Vetiver is her least preferred."

"She'd really rather have Narra?" Leo asked.

"Is that surprising? Princess Narra can be collared and controlled; without her people's loyalty and respect, which she will have lost after her actions on the solstice, few of them would object to the punishment or to Queen Ceresia's intercession. And yet, Princess Narra is not her first choice, either."

Leo's eyebrows rose as he followed his implications to the only possible conclusion. "I thought, since Hazel's a changeling . . ."

"Yes, some will take issue with that." Prince Senna took a sip of his latte, savoring it. "But I think it is not for nothing that Queen Ceresia has been giving your sister the education that she has. In politics, in history, in enchantment, in the arts. I imagine it will come as no shock to you that my most beloved Winter Queen does nothing unless she stands to profit three times over."

Leo had heard a little bit about Hazel's lessons from her letters.

Sure, it had crossed his mind to wonder why Queen Ceresia had taken Hazel under her wing the way she had, but he'd chalked it up to diplomacy, pity, and maybe the vague promise of being owed a favor from the Summer Court in the future. He had also guessed that if they couldn't find another heir, Hazel was probably the backup plan. Foolishly, he hadn't really stopped to consider that Queen Ceresia's motivations might be more—concrete. Or maybe he hadn't allowed himself to think about it, because there was nothing he could do either way.

"But how does she benefit from putting Hazel on the throne?" Leo asked. "Is she—planning to collar her, too?"

Prince Senna smiled, as if charmed by Leo's ignorance. "I doubt it will come to that. In this case, I believe she finds greater and more long-lasting value in a delicate approach. Should Hazel become the next ruler of the Summer Court, then Queen Ceresia, as her trusted mentor and protector, will have her ear and wield immeasurably more influence than she already enjoys. It must feel to her as if she has been given an opportunity to handpick her adversary, to make her troublesome rival and ally into her disciple. And perhaps it is no ill thing to have Queen Ceresia's support. She could silence those who would never otherwise accept a changeling queen. But I do not think such an arrangement is beneficial to the low courts. The Summer Court is meant to be her counterweight, not her puppet."

So she wanted to be the Summer Court's shadow queen. It made a sick kind of sense. Narra could be controlled by force; Hazel could be manipulated. Vetiver alone was the one Queen Ceresia had no power over. He had grown up in the Summer Court. His people and his subjects among the low courts would follow him without question. He would know what was expected of him as monarch, and he wouldn't need to rely on Queen Ceresia the way Hazel did.

"I thought you were loyal to the Winter Court," Leo said warily.

"My father is," he said. "But I was one of Prince Talarix's closest companions, now and again. Perhaps I am rather nostalgic for those times."

"You don't have the numbers to go against her," Leo said. The battle on the equinox had proved it. The Autumn knights had barely been a match for the Summer Gallowglass even at their weakest; they didn't stand a chance against Queen Ceresia's forces, especially now that so many of Senna's knights were sick with the rot.

"I can't oppose her openly," Prince Senna agreed. "At least not yet. But I will do what I can to advocate for Vetiver until I see another way forward. As for Hazel, I know that Queen Ceresia is not her only source of guidance. There is someone she trusts even more, whose word holds more sway with her than anyone else's."

There it was—the real reason the prince of the Autumn Court had stolen away into the human realm on what was almost certainly a clandestine visit, without any of his guards, to have a conversation that teetered dangerously on the edge of plotting against the Winter Queen.

Leo watched the steam rise out of the lid of his coffee cup. "I'll always be here if Hazel needs me, but I already screwed up everything by trying to make decisions for her. If she wants to follow Queen Ceresia's lead, how can I tell her not to? What right do I have?"

"You don't have to go that far. But sooner or later, she will need advisors and allies whose favor is not reliant on Queen Ceresia's approval," Prince Senna said. "There will be times when she and Queen Ceresia may not agree. When that happens, she will be glad to have other people around her whom she can trust. And perhaps her devoted older brother can help her discern who those trustworthy folk are."

"And how do I know we can trust you?"

"In the human realm, trust is earned. In Elphame, trust is traded," Prince Senna said.

"You mean bought," Leo replied.

"Exchanged," Prince Senna said. "To that end, I've brought you a gift from the Autumn Court."

From his satchel, he drew a carved length of frosty crystal and offered it to Leo. It was about the span of his hand from wrist to fingertip and flared on one end. The middle was subtly contoured, but as he moved to fit his fingers into the grooves—which matched the shape of his hand with disconcerting accuracy—Prince Senna halted him with a touch on his arm.

"Before you do that, take care not to point the end at anyone, including yourself," he advised.

Mystified, Leo obeyed, holding the object away from the body before he wrapped his fingers around the stem. Instantly, a blade materialized. It was another frost illusion, like the winged horses, as white and silken as scales of soft rime, and so sharp it seemed it could have sliced membrane-thin layers of moisture out of the air.

Leo's mouth fell open. "It's like a lightsaber," he blurted.

Prince Senna laughed. "Your sister said the same thing. What *is* a lightsaber?"

Leo was instantly struck by a vision of Prince Senna and a troop of armored Gallowglass warriors gathered around a television screen, pining over Leia Organa, which was what Leo usually did when *he* watched *Star Wars*. But the flicker of amusement was bittersweet. He had been the one to introduce Hazel to *Star Wars* in the first place. They'd marathoned all the movies over a few summer nights years ago. He didn't remember it clearly; he just knew it had happened. The scrap of childhood memory, just out of his reach, only made him miss her more.

"If I take this, what do you want in return?" Leo asked, uncurling his fingers so that the blade vanished.

"Only an open line of communication," he said. "Anne Sterling serves as something of an ambassador between her folk and ours, and the Winter Queen exchanges messages with her directly. But you may be in a position to discover things even she can't." Prince Senna's gaze was so piercing Leo had to wonder if he didn't have a dash of truesight himself. "Come to me first with what you know, and I will do the same in return. If ever you should find yourself in need of aid, send for me. And then tell your sister how, when you called, the Autumn Court was there for you."

Hesitantly, Leo tucked the gift into his pocket. "Thank you," he said.

Prince Senna rose gracefully to his feet. "Do you think I should bring one of these back to the Winter Court? The princess must be homesick. She might enjoy it."

"I don't think it'll still be warm by then," he said.

"Apparently, they make them iced. *Clever*, I told you!" He gave Leo a jaunty wave and strode off into the misting rain.

Leo sniffed at his own cup. Even if it was spiked with fairy wine, it couldn't do him any real damage. If it had any effect on him at all, that might honestly be an improvement on his day.

Please knock me the fuck out, he thought, and drank.

Disappointingly, it really was just pumpkin spice.

CHAPTER 16

AZIZA

During their lunch period, she and Leo went outside around the back of the main building on campus, where it smelled like spilled soda and contraband cigarettes, and napped sitting up against the wall. Aziza's alarm woke them for their next class. They ignored it and went back to sleep.

"Weirdly, I feel better now," he said around a yawn, as they walked to Bishop Library later. "Having a regular, boring school day and everything. Don't tell Mom I said that."

"We could've had a boring day sleeping in our own beds," Aziza groused, choosing not to remind him that a surprise visit from the Autumn Prince hardly classified as either "regular" or "boring." If and when Leo wanted to talk about it, he would.

They stopped at the crosswalk, waiting for the pedestrian light. He draped an arm over her shoulders and slouched against her. With his other hand, he scrolled through news articles on his phone, angling the screen so they could both see. He paused on a photo of Castor Thorne being interviewed by some talk show host, sitting back on a leather armchair with his legs crossed, the picture of relaxed elegance, genteel masculinity, and extravagant wealth.

"There. I knew I'd heard his name somewhere before we saw him at the Market. He's kind of famous."

"I thought he just ran a business."

"He's the CEO of a real estate agency called Luminous Horizons. They own millions of square feet of land and property spread out across a dozen states," Leo said, clicking through to another article. The light changed, and they crossed the street, Leo leaving his arm around her shoulders but lowering his phone so she could see where they were walking. "He's invested in a ton of start-ups . . . done some charity work . . . and he was on a few reality shows for a while? *Penthouse Pros. Listing L.A. Master of the House Hunt.*"

"Ugh."

"I *know*."

Castor Thorne's celebrity status wasn't surprising in itself. Some of the most wealthy and influential people in the country were witches—politicians, journalists, actors, judges. They received their magical training in private, first from family and then from elder jackdaws at the universities they attended. And when they went on to flourish in their chosen fields—sometimes honestly, but also sometimes by leaning on their magical gifts—they used their political and economic power to serve the interests of their community, especially when it came to maintaining its secrecy.

"That's just the work that's public," she said, as a clip from *Penthouse Pros* played on his screen. "Nelle says that he's known for buying up old magical buildings and saving them from redevelopment, putting them under AJA's care. When he can't buy, his legal team tries to get preservation orders from state agencies to make sure no one else can touch them. People say that almost no one else has done more for the conservation of magical history than he has."

Aziza had started doing her own research on Castor, though she had spent more time looking into his past than his present business endeavors. Castor Thorne had a rags-to-riches story that had been widely circulated in both the mundane and magical worlds. It went like this: Born in Sanctum, West Virginia, a small town plagued by poverty and devastating floods, he had worked hard and earned a full-ride scholarship to Yale. There, he met his closest friends and future colleagues. Castor, who would never return to his hometown, believed that a community's identity was tied to places, to land and to landmarks. He argued that every witch with the means to do so had a responsibility to protect their magical history from outside threats, which included everything from mundane capitalists to environmental disaster.

And all of that told her absolutely nothing about why someone like him would even *want* Meryl. There were countless stories of selkie women who had been stolen away from the sea by human men, usually to be their "wife." But she was disinclined to think that Castor had that kind of prurient interest in Meryl—if he had, then why leave her at Bishop Library for close to twenty years? In all that time, how often had he even seen her?

That was her biggest clue—the choice of the library as Meryl's prison. Something about Bishop Library, or maybe Blackthorn itself, held significance to Castor.

Her second biggest clue was the timing of Meryl's disappearance—the night the hag had died. And the fact that Meryl had been forbidden to speak of the hag. One of the few things Aziza knew about her parents' coven was that Emil and Castor had left her parents to fight the hag alone. But what if the whole truth was worse than that? What if Castor hadn't just refused to fight—what if he was the one who had woken the hag up in the first place? But if he had, then why?

When it came to Castor, there were no answers. Only questions that produced more questions.

"Apparently, he used to work closely with the Legrand family, too," she added absentmindedly.

"Is that why he, uh . . . ?" Leo trailed off.

"Why he wanted Dion as his apprentice?" Aziza said. "Maybe."

His name scalded her throat, like a match she'd struck and then swallowed. She wasn't mad at Dion anymore. Or maybe she was. And if she were only angry, that would have been fine. She understood anger. She was *comfortable* with anger. But the time she'd spent traversing the Flight Paths with Dion, chipping away at the wall of ice he'd built between them, watching him draw magic out of equations and concrete like it was nothing—it had changed things. He hadn't withheld the truth about Meryl out of malice. He had just decided that something else mattered more than rescuing Meryl as soon as possible.

Dion wasn't the only one, either.

"I didn't know for sure," Anne said, when Aziza went to her. "I could tell the coat was more than an ordinary garment, but not that it was sealskin, though I had wondered. You probably only recognized it because you know the selkie it belongs to."

"He could be hiding Meryl *anywhere*," Aziza said. "Where do I even start—"

"You *don't*," Anne said sharply. "Right now, we focus on keeping Elphame's boundary intact and helping Queen Ceresia avert a catastrophic war between the low courts, to what extent we safely can. As for Castor, I still don't know what he thought he was doing with Princess Narra, but he wouldn't be the first witch who lost his head over a fairy woman. For now, he and the other weather witches have provided essential support during this crisis. He will answer for the trouble he's caused in Elphame—and for abducting a selkie woman—*after* the Summer Court is restored. The law will hold him accountable."

"How?" Aziza said bitterly. "Castor *is* the law."

"I need proof," Anne said. "I don't have it yet. But everyone makes mistakes—even Castor Thorne—and when he does, I'll be ready. I can get the rest of the Clattering on board with removing him from the coven and, if necessary, putting him on trial for what he's done. To do that, I will need solid evidence, and a lot of it."

Witches who had committed magical crimes could be framed for mundane ones and sent to prison. They could be given magical bindings that prevented them from casting spells. In the most extreme cases, mainly those that compromised the community's secrecy, troublemakers had been quietly disappeared. But Castor had too much power. As a member of the Clattering, AJA's primary governing body, Castor made the rules—and as the leader of the weather witches, he also enforced them. Though the Clattering worked together to make decisions for AJA, each member was like the head of a faction, overseeing witches of their own kind—the hedgewitch, Anne, leading other hedgewitches; the rook leading other rooks; the oracle leading other oracles. If Anne or anyone else in the Clattering turned against Castor, they risked making enemies of every weather witch in the country.

He was respected in both the mundane and magical worlds; he had seemingly endless riches, a dragon's hoard of deeds and estates; he had a rare magical gift, too. Nelle had explained that he had an affinity for solar sorcery—he was a master of spellwork based on light, heat, and reflections. It was a power that occurred perhaps once every generation.

Aziza couldn't blame Anne, just as, deep down, she couldn't blame Dion—though his disregard felt more personal. Anne was being strategic. She wasn't callous enough to say it this way, but there were more important things to worry about than Meryl. A greater good. She was trying to save all of Elphame, and the human realm alongside it.

Aziza just wanted to save *one* selkie.

IT SNOWED AT the start of October, like the puzzled meteorologists had been saying it would. Then a heat wave rolled in like a belated summer, and then it was just rain, every hour, every day, for about two weeks straight.

The field where Dion had bound the Summer Court's castle vanished as if the storm had washed it away. The outpouring of wild magic produced during the battle had overwhelmed its tenuous borderland condition, until it could no longer *be* a borderland; it had to be one thing or the other. And so it had been subsumed into Elphame. In the human world, the land that used to be there had simply gone away, the edges of the field pinching shut, like a wound that had been stitched up. Now that the castle was stationary, there was no need to trek through the Flight Paths with Dion to clean up the damage it did to the boundary, which was convenient, because they hadn't spoken a word to each other since the equinox.

Since then, Coven Blackthorn was on their best behavior, devoting their time to their mundane and magical studies. Leo's mastery of his truesight was improving by the day. He was learning to focus the amber eye so that he could pick out individual strands of magic from a tangle, identifying the subtle differences between them. Fox took to hiding from him all over Bishop Library, and Leo would follow lingering traces of its magic until he found it. Then it started hiding all over the city, or in the woods, and Leo would lead them in a wandering route down alleys and onto rooftops or into some trash-strewn corner of St. Sithney's until he grinned, pointed at a pigeon or a cat or a garter snake, and said, "Gotcha." (These games of hide-and-seek also served as opportunities to help Fox practice its insect forms. Its damselflies had the right number of wings and its orb weavers had eyes in the right places these days, which was an improvement.)

But sometimes Leo gazed blankly out the window at the blurry rain-streaked world outside, and when she asked him what was wrong, he'd startle, guilty, as if he'd been caught doing something he shouldn't.

"Do you remember," he said, haltingly, "when Hazel kept sneaking out to the woods, and later, Ephira said that *the call* was leading her back to the Summer Court? I think—I feel it, too. I can ignore it, it's just like . . . every now and then, it's like someone's plucking a string and I can hear the music. And it's . . . sad."

As for Tristan, he still spent a lot of time learning languages. He mainly worked on Old English, Latin, and Old Norse, but he was determined to translate at least a little bit of as many of Emil's grimoires as he could, just so that he could get a sense of what was in them. This meant venturing into Sanskrit, Aramaic, Coptic, and more that she lost track of. He practiced his blækhound creation spell with little success; but he had finally gotten the mice he abducted from the Flight Paths and the frogs Maria donated to survive shadow travel, which they all viewed as a great victory.

And Aziza practiced the spells she learned from Anne. Spells that let her speak in the hissing language of steam sprites; find injured nymphs and scoop them from inside their host trees so that their wounds wouldn't mend poorly; borrow a wight's intuition for the finding of missing pieces. Countless boundary spells: to see the shape of a boundary around a city like a mental map, to track down fairy rings and nullify them, to siphon magic from the borderlands for use in the more complex enchantments Aziza hadn't started learning yet.

She and Tristan still shared her bestiary; it migrated back and forth between their backpacks freely. After the hound had crushed Aziza's right hand, Tristan had silently taken up the task of adding sketches to the notes Aziza wrote down about the fae they encountered. Now, on the empty pages in the back, he had started to leave notes on his spellwork, at first absent-mindedly, jotting down stray thoughts so that he wouldn't forget them. In response, she left fragments of her own spells. She noted down the turn of phrase that had let her temporarily steal the voice of a sick siren that had washed up under the pier, ensuring no passersby would be caught in her thrall until Aziza could nurse her back to health and send her away to deeper waters. Tristan borrowed those words from her story spell, translated them to Latin, and used them in an incantation he was modifying, inking it carefully into the pages of a blank grimoire; it gave voice to a spirit he summoned one night in the graveyard, which whispered its fragmented memories to him. He wrote the spirit's secrets to her, and she bargained them away to a sandman.

She worked with single-minded focus. Every moment of her time needed to be spent on this—on becoming the kind of witch who could save Meryl. She had told Anne she didn't know where to begin looking for Meryl, but she tried anyway. She sent wind sprites from coast to coast, paying them in scents by brewing the exotic teas she'd bought during their last visit to the Half Moon Market. Her kitchen was constantly filled with the aroma of honeyed, peppery chai and bittersweet matcha and delicate oolong. Even in her sleep, Aziza didn't rest. She wove a rope of valerian, skullcap, and lavender as she whispered a story-spell to an audience of taper candles, and tied it over her eyes when she was finished. Then she lay down to sleep, blindfolded, before the dying candles, inside a ring of chalk markings copied from a journal she'd found in Bishop Library's jackdaw collection. It was a spell to reach out to a sandman through her dreams—and soon she had a number of them aiding her, too, searching the realm of sleep the way the wind sprites searched the land, combing through the zephyrs of imagination, the turbulence of nightmare, and the flurries of memory.

If Anne had known of her efforts, Aziza was sure she would have been admonished, even though it had all amounted to nothing so far.

By the time the next Half Moon Market came around, they were all impatient for another visit. Aziza needed more charm components and tea for the wind sprites. Tristan needed blood ink for his personal grimoire, a blank one where he would copy in the most useful spells he found in Emil's library. And Leo needed to replenish his cache of tokens and treasures for wagering in games with the fairies of the low courts.

Aziza had dinner with Jiddo before she left that night, and they stood together at the sink to clean the dishes afterward. She did the washing, propping the plates in a draining rack on one side of the sink and using a scrubber wand with the dish soap in the handle to clean them off. Jiddo did the drying.

Usually, this task was done in comfortable silence. Today, Jiddo cleared his throat and said, "So. How are your college applications going?"

"What?" she said. "Fine, I guess."

Jiddo's expression was pained. "You *have* been working on those, right?"

"They're done. I think," she said, frowning a little. Leo had sat them down in front of the computer with all the necessary forms already pulled up and ready to be filled out, insisting that they would forget to do it if he didn't monitor them, which was insulting but true. They'd chipped away at them over the course of a few days. She didn't actually know which colleges they had collectively applied to, or how Leo had procured transcripts and letters of recommendation for them, or how he had access to her SAT scores . . .

"That's good," Jiddo said. "What's your top choice?"

"I . . . don't have one?" she said, mystified by this line of questioning. "I thought I'd just go to BCC."

"The community college?" Jiddo said, his brow crinkling.

"Or Blackthorn North. I could take your class," she said, turning back to the pot she was scrubbing, attacking it with vigor. She was kind of amused by the idea of taking one of Professor Khaled El-Amin's courses after years of listening to him grumble about lesson plans and despair over the quality of the essays his undergrads turned in. Then again, he would definitely grade her harder than any of his other students. Maybe she'd just sneak into his lectures instead and distract him by letting Fox turn into big, toothy felines and extinct birds in the back row.

"*Leo* is not going to community college."

This observation, delivered so emphatically, startled her into laughter. When had Leo become her grandfather's standard for academic excellence? But Jiddo's expression was grave.

"No," she said slowly. "He's not. Greg went to UMass, so he wants to send Leo there, too. Maria thinks he should try for a fancy private school in Boston. But he's leaning toward Bridgewater. It's close enough for him to live at home and commute."

Blackthorn North was even closer than Bridgewater, but it was a tiny liberal arts college with fewer options for majors. Leo didn't know what he wanted to study yet, and he didn't want his parents to pay a private school tuition while he figured it out.

"And Tristan?"

"He'll go wherever Leo goes, or as close as he can get."

"Don't you want to go with them?"

"Shouldn't you be telling me not to pick a college based on where my friends are going?" When he glared at her, she rolled her eyes. "Yes, okay, I might do that. But, honestly, Tristan and I can't get into the same schools Leo can, and I'll kick his ass if he even *thinks* about staying behind for us." Her grades were just fine, not amazing. Tristan was smart, but having a GED instead of a diploma would be a strike against him when it came to getting into some of the more selective universities. And their extracurricular activities were not exactly the kind that could be detailed on a college application. She turned back to the sink to finish washing up. "As long as they're on a campus with a jackdaw collection, I'll be able to see them whenever I want, so it doesn't really matter. I have a year to learn the arrays I'd need to use to get through the Flight Paths."

To get through the Flight Paths . . . without Dion.

The handle of the sponge slipped out of her grip and fell into the sink with a clatter. She scowled at it, as if it had done that just to spite her.

"You're missing the point," Jiddo said.

"What point?"

He threw down the dishrag and turned to her with his hands on his hips. "I should have had this conversation with you a long time ago, but your eyes glaze over when I try to make you think any farther than one week ahead!" he blustered.

She turned the water off. The plates left in the draining rack dripped quietly. "What's there to think about?"

"A *career*, maybe?" he said. She groaned, but he just raised his voice and kept going. "A *major*, at least! You'll have to pick one sooner or later!"

"I don't know. Maybe I'll take over at Bishop Library eventually. Tristan's not staying there forever. It's just a place to live for now. So—"

"*You?* A librarian?" Jiddo said so incredulously she was almost offended.

"Why not? I could be a librarian."

"Of course you could, but you would hate being cooped up inside all day! You don't even care about books!"

It was true. Historically, the thing she loved most about Bishop Library was the librarian.

"I don't need a career. I just need a job that isn't too demanding and gives me time to work on my craft," she said.

Jiddo took a deep, fortifying breath. "Hayati, if all you want is a quiet life in your hometown, then that's fine. But I don't believe that *is* what you want. You're too much like Leila."

He never talked about Aziza's mother. It was too painful for him. He had accused her of being *just like Leila* once before, and it hadn't been a good thing—he had been afraid she'd inherited a recklessness that would lead to her death. But this time his voice carried an unmistakable note of pride.

"You're hardworking and passionate, at least when it comes to things you're interested in. I *wish* you were interested in, say, AP Euro," he said, exasperated. "But if what matters to you the most is using your witchcraft to make the world a better place"—that was not the way she would have put it, but okay—"then you should pursue that. You can use your studies to improve your spellcasting. History, classics, or literature would give you a wealth of story material. Mathematics would help you master numerology. Plenty of witches study environmental sciences to better understand how magic fits into the natural world. There's only so much you can learn if you never leave Blackthorn. Universities are the center of American witchcraft. That's where you should go. Places where you can learn from other witches."

"I can't believe what I'm hearing," she said. "Last year, you *banned* me from witchcraft! You told me other witches couldn't be trusted and I should stay away from them!"

"And you didn't listen to me when I said it then, so I don't see how it's relevant now!" He sighed heavily, the wrinkles around his eyes deepening. "I'll always worry about you. But I tried too hard to instill a caution in you that I never did with Leila. And . . ." His voice became rough. "I used to think that if I had been more strict with her, if I had taught her to be less adventurous and more careful, then she might still be alive. But I understand now that it would never have worked. I would have only pushed her away, as I pushed *you* away."

"You didn't—"

"You have a brave heart. I couldn't change that if I tried. I shouldn't have tried."

Aziza was mortified to realize that her throat had gone tight. She glared at the trails of soap in the sink, twisting sylphlike into the drain, until the feeling subsided.

"Anne told me there are scholarships for young witches," Jiddo continued. "Disguised with mundane titles, obviously. You're not the most dedicated student, but you're an excellent witch. She's taken the liberty of submitting your name to some—"

"You talked to Anne about this?" she said, aghast.

"Someone had to!" he said. "Just think about it. What do you *want*? For your future? For your life?"

Her response was blank silence.

"You want to keep learning spells, right?" Jiddo suggested.

That was an easier question. "Yes," she said.

"And?"

"I want to hold my own with the Fair Folk the way Anne does," she said. "She goes wherever she wants in Elphame and doesn't have to be afraid of anything."

He nodded encouragingly, indicating that she should go on.

She didn't have to think as hard this time. "I want to make it so that no kelpie ever even thinks about hunting near Blackthorn again."

He squinted at her. "When did you see a kelpie?"

"And I want to be sure that no selkie under my protection will *ever* lose her freedom, not to anyone, but especially not another witch."

She didn't think these were quite the answers he had been looking for. But it must have been good enough. He wrapped an arm comfortingly around her, and that was the end of it.

CHAPTER 17

LEO

THERE WAS A rumor in the Salt-Scale Court. They said that Princess Narra was cured. They said the borderland fae had seen her in golden armor.

"Like the kind Prince Senna wears?" Leo asked.

"No. Not like that. It's something else," the Salt-Scale fairy said, touching a long black fingernail to the wingtip of one of his finch pieces. "What will you do the next time you meet her? Do you think she's still angry with you?"

He sat across from Leo over the board they'd set up on the stump of a cottonwood tree. It was his move, and he was still deliberating, barely glancing at Leo as he relayed the latest gossip. But there was a subtle leaning-in from the spectators—the tilt of a pair of twisted pronghorn antlers, the twitch of a rust-colored wing. The Salt-Scale Court lived beside a desert spring and wore golden-brown eagle-feather capes, diaphanous shrouds woven from thousands of glittering salt crystals, rings studded with large, glistening tarantula eyes. Leo's matches didn't draw the swarms of curious fairies they had in the beginning, but there was always an audience, and he had a steady stream of opponents.

"I don't care if she's angry," Leo said. "But I don't think she's worried about me. She's got bigger problems."

"You're not afraid of her, then?"

"Why should he be?" someone else said. "After he fought side by side with Prince Senna to rescue the next Summer King! We heard you were besieged by Gallowglass and battled through their ranks without receiving so much as a scratch."

His opponent had made his move, so Leo took his turn, shifting one of his pieces into a square he'd been eyeing. He'd gotten better at not letting the Folk distract him, no matter what they did or said or promised, or how many items of clothing they took off.

"I didn't do any fighting," he said. "But I'm not afraid of Princess Narra *or* Viren."

"Viren still lives, too," his opponent said, easily seeing through Leo's clumsy attempt to fish for information. "Clad in gold, the same as the princess."

"The borderland fae didn't happen to tell you where they saw them, did they?" he asked.

"Why?" someone said slyly. "Will you hunt them down?"

"Are you worried about her?" Leo returned. "She was almost your Summer Queen."

"No one is loyal to *almost*," one fairy said.

"What would you do if you found them, then?" another one asked.

"He'll cut her down with the sword Prince Senna gifted him, I imagine," the first one said. A clamor ensued; they all wanted to see what they referred to as *a token of the Autumn Prince's favor*.

"I'm not going to *cut her down*," Leo said, uncomfortable with being talked about like he was some sort of butcher. Still, he obliged, producing the crystal sword hilt, which he kept on him whenever he visited Elphame, though he hoped he wouldn't have to use it.

The frost blade sprang into existence, as pale as the full moon and trailing banners of steam; but it never got any smaller, so that the water that ran off it into the parched earth was less like melting and more like saliva dripping off a fang.

"He won't cut her down," someone else agreed, over murmurs of appreciation from the cluster of onlookers, "because he doesn't know *how*. He can't fight."

"We could teach him," another Salt-Scale fairy chimed in.

"We could *duel*," yet another added.

It wasn't the first time he had been challenged to a duel. He always said no. Though he'd accepted Prince Senna's gift, he had hated the thought of picking up a sword again, unable to forget what had happened the last time he'd held one. Princess Narra had put him under her thrall and forced him to slaughter the Gallowglass who had tried to protect the Summer Court from her.

But by refusing to learn a skill that could save his life, wasn't he just letting her control him in a different way?

He had agreed to play at royalty thinking it was like a mask he could put on and take off, and underneath he'd still be the same old Leo he'd always been. But in Elphame, an illusion was almost the same as the real thing. If he wanted to be convincing, he couldn't just pretend. He had to *be*.

And maybe the next time he returned to the castle, he would be able to lift that sleeping enchantment.

"I guess we *could* duel," he said. "But only if we all agree to some ground rules first."

They were delighted, and so eager to begin that he managed to secure more concessions from them than he might've otherwise. No lethal blows, no maiming, no permanent injuries. Each match would end when the first drop of blood was spilled, just like a witch's duel.

"Of course, accidents do happen," someone else remarked, sweetly sinister.

"Accidents?" Leo said, helping his opponent clear their finch pieces off the board and not bothering to look up. "But I thought I was going to be learning from experts, not amateurs."

The laughter that broke out around them was as good a guarantee of safety as he was going to get. Sure enough, his ground rules held up. Almost every fairy he went up against that day managed to cut him, but they knew what they were doing, and most of the wounds were so thin they barely bled. One fairy *did* land a deep slice to his bicep that hurt badly enough he dropped his sword. But his opponent sent for a healer immediately, and the wound was magically closed, leaving behind only a faint scar. The blow to his pride was worse than the physical damage he'd sustained.

They didn't go out of their way to teach him, exactly, but every now and then one of his opponents would glance pointedly at the positioning of his feet or the way he held his arms, and he would shift to mirror their pose, receiving a minuscule nod of approval in response. Or they would make an acerbic remark about his swing, and their own next attack would be a touch slower, so that, even as he parried, he could watch how they moved and copy it. It was actually nice, in an underhanded sort of way. When he wanted a break, he convinced some of the Salt-Scale fairies to duel each other, and watching them fight without holding back was intimidating but *really* cool.

"I promised your parents I would look after you," Anne said later. "Must you go out of your way to make it so difficult?"

"What did *your* parents think when you used to sneak out to parties at the Inkcap Court?" Leo asked. Anne, after all, had been a teenage hedgewitch like Aziza once.

Her eyes narrowed. "Who told you that?"

Leo shrugged, grinning unrepentantly. He got a little better at getting information he wanted from the Fair Folk every time he visited.

Dueling became his new favorite way of passing his time with the fairies of the low courts. He returned to the Salt-Scale Court more than once. He also dueled with the fairies of the Riven Court, the entrance to their fortress concealed behind a waterfall, and the Kestrel Court, who fought with daggers, knocking his blows away with swift and terrifying precision.

It was when they received their long-awaited invitation to the Spring Court that Anne came around on the dueling. They were nomadic, like the Summer Court, and had been among King Ilanthus's most loyal subjects. Some of them had been present at the solstice and were asleep in the castle's safe room even now. Ever since then, the Spring Court had gone into seclusion, rebuffing Anne's attempts to reach out to them.

They told Leo to bring the sword. To his surprise, he had only one opponent: Princess Kova, lacewinged and wearing emerald-green armor. She disarmed him so quickly it was embarrassing.

"Again," she said. She hadn't even introduced herself yet; he only knew who she was because Anne had briefed him before they'd arrived.

They dueled again.

"You accept defeat too easily," she said.

"It's my own skill level I accept," he said, with a respectful bow. "I'm no match for you."

She sheathed her sword. "I will go to war before I allow Princess Narra to become the Summer Queen."

It was an abrupt change in subject, and the first time one of the monarchs of the low courts had spoken to him beyond basic polite greetings, let alone to discuss Queen Ceresia and the future of the Summer Court with him. He resisted the urge to look at Anne for guidance. He had a feeling Princess Kova would not like that.

"They'd have to find her first," Leo said. "No one's come close. She's already shown she'll go to any lengths to avoid being queen. I doubt she'd be so careless as to get caught."

"Wouldn't she?" Princess Kova shot back. Her helmet covered the upper half of her face, the shine of her eyes showing through slits in the mask. "She has been careless often enough. I grew up with her. She would run away all the time, though she was only punished once. It's not that she disdains power; she merely wished to escape her father's control and Queen Ceresia's influence."

"Why's that?" Leo asked, seizing his opportunity to learn something more about Narra, something substantial. To him, she had been an enigma until their very last conversation. And the other fairies only had hearsay to offer him.

"King Ilanthus had three heirs by three different women. You know that much, correct?" she said. Leo nodded. Princess Narra had told him some of her family's grisly history last year. Her mother was the Summer Queen, while Prince Tal's was a royal consort—Lady Cirrine. And Hazel's mother, the enchantress, was Cirrine's sister. That made Hazel and Tal both half-siblings and cousins.

"Narra's mother was assassinated by her father's consort," Kova said. "She never forgave him for it. It changed her. She disdains our laws and customs, and she rebelled by running off to the human realm. King Ilanthus was indulgent, knowing her mother's loss was his own fault. He only punished her when she left him no choice; and then she resented him for it, even though she had all but dared him to do it. She is twisted. It may not be her fault, but she is. And if you see her again, you *must* kill her."

It wasn't that different from what the Salt-Scale fairies had said to him—but, coming from her, it carried more weight. Leo gaped at her. "I'm not an executioner. I'm not doing that."

He responded without thinking, knowing he meant it and hoping Narra didn't leave him without any other choice, like she'd left King Ilanthus no choice.

"Perhaps I should have expected that answer," Kova said, her lip curling in a sneer. He didn't know what to say to that, though he had the sense he'd been evaluated and found wanting.

"Would you support Vetiver's claim to the throne?" Leo asked.

"We would. Though Prince Senna may have sealed his fate when he turned him over to the Winter Queen," she said. "If that scapegrace had any sense, he would have told Ceresia the boy was dead and brought him straight here to me. Now it will be up to you and Prince Senna to make sure he survives the winter. And if he doesn't, I will hold you personally accountable."

WHEN HE ARRIVED at Bishop Library that night, he was only a little banged up, but very late to pick up Tristan and Aziza. They were going to the Half Moon Market, but since they couldn't take the Flight Paths on their own, Leo was borrowing his parents' car. Tonight's Market venue was a three-hour drive away, so they'd still make it there before midnight, which was when Nelle said the Market was at its best anyway.

He sent Tristan a text and waited with his arms folded over the steering wheel, his chin propped on top of them, still deep in thought.

The passenger side door swung open, Tristan dropping into the seat beside him. He tugged down the hood of his jacket and swept his hair back from his face in a move straight out of an ad for salon-quality conditioner, which, how did he do that? He used to steal Leo's three-in-one shampoo back when they shared a bathroom.

"Princess Kova went easy on you," Tristan said. A raindrop slid down the side of his neck, and Leo watched it disappear under his collar, transfixed. "She really *must* be loyal to the Summer Court."

"Huh?" Leo replied, distracted.

"You're usually in worse shape after you come back from dueling practice."

"But how did you know I—Tris! Has Lucky been spying on me this whole time?" Leo said, his face burning. He felt like he'd been caught posing in front of a mirror.

"I wasn't *spying*," Tristan said. "I thought it was a given that Lucky would be with you at all times. Did you think I was going to let you go to Elphame with no protection?"

"Uh . . . I didn't? Think about it, I mean."

Granted, he probably should have predicted this. And he had noticed every now and then that his shadow looked a little . . . furry . . . but the Fair Folk *loved* their weird lighting—floating orbs and sputtering candles and lesser fairies passed out drunk in little glass prisons—so his shadow never looked quite right when he was among them anyway.

Tristan looked into his eyes. "Are you going to ask me to stop?"

"Not if it makes you feel better," Leo said, knowing he was being puppeteered but helpless to combat it.

"It should make *you* feel better," Tristan said.

"I don't know if I can take all this concern seriously, coming from the guy who went to Beor the Huntsman for a private tutoring session," Leo reminded him, pulling out of the parking lot and driving carefully through the rain as it drummed against the hood of the car. "None of the Salt-Scale fairies ever tried to have me publicly executed."

"That's different," Tristan insisted.

"I'm only going to agree because I'd rather hear about your day instead."

"My day?" Tristan said. He tilted his face toward the window, away from Leo, though there was nothing to see outside but the gray blur of the rain. "It was the same as usual."

Something in his voice gave Leo pause.

"Are you sure you're up for an all-nighter?" Leo said. "If you need a break, just tell me what you want from the Market. I'll pick it up for you."

"Thanks, but it's all right," Tristan said, with a faint smile. "I was going to visit Jun."

"The medium?"

"Yeah. This came in handy on the equinox." He touched the talisman he always wore, with the feather sigil. "I think he'd like to hear about it."

"That's Jun's?" Leo asked. He'd assumed Tristan had found it with Emil's grimoires.

"He traded it to me in exchange for a spell I taught him. Didn't I tell you?"

"It must've slipped your mind. I bet you get jewelry from nice mediums all the time," he said lightly, and wanted to cringe as soon as it was out of his mouth. Was he jealous? *Really?* Wow. He was totally jealous, had absolutely no right to be, and could only hope and pray that Tristan hadn't noticed.

Tristan glanced at him, perplexed and maybe a little amused. He had definitely noticed.

"Only about as often as dashing princes buy you coffee," he said, startling Leo into laughter.

"Don't remind me. Uh, that . . . you know that wasn't anything," he felt the need to say, as he recalled the smirking way the Salt-Scale fairies had talked about him receiving gifts from the Autumn Prince.

"Neither was this." Tristan's hand closed around the necklace, and then let go. "Are we something?"

The gears stopped turning in Leo's brain. Somehow, he managed to keep driving. Heavy raindrops hammered at the windshield, filling the silence. It was a brave question. He was abruptly reminded that the first time he and Tristan had ever really talked was like this, alone in his car in the middle of the night, the light from the street lamps flickering past. Tristan had been brave then, too.

Leo must have let the moment stretch too long, because Tristan smiled in a quiet, knowing sort of way, as if he'd read the answer in Leo's face.

"We're—best friends," Leo said, because he had to say *something*, but he wished he could've come up with anything but that. Weakly, he added, "Right?"

"Always," Tristan said. "Can I ask you something?"

"Of course."

"It's kind of personal. And none of my business."

Leo could think of almost nothing in his life that he would consider *none of Tristan's business*. "It's okay," he said, meaning it.

"How can you be sure of how you feel about someone without . . . knowing who they are?" Tristan said, and it sounded like he had to force the end of that sentence out, like he'd changed his mind about saying it halfway through. "Do you ever wonder if it's real?"

"Yeah. But also no?" It was confusing even to him. "I doubt myself, but not them. It's kind of like when you walk into a room and then forget why you did? You know you were there for a reason, and you were *just* thinking about it a second ago, but suddenly your mind's blank," he said. "It feels like that, but worse. And all the time. I still see things that remind me of them, and my heart just—drops."

"It does?" Tristan said. There was something complicated in his voice, like a shadow under an ocean wave.

"It happens less now," Leo said, "but even that kind of hurts in a different way, like at least I had *something* to hold on to—like proof that they were real—and I might even lose that eventually." When he stopped to think about it, it was pretty messed up that he was clinging to the pain because that was better than not feeling it at all. Because when the loss didn't hurt anymore, that was when the person he loved would really be out of his reach. He was almost ashamed to let Tristan know this about him—know that he was devoted to the empty space where a person should have been, measuring his own love by the depth of the void it had left behind—sick with the hollowness, like his own personal jade rot. "But when I really let myself . . . not remember, but *feel* the way it felt to be with them, I'm . . . happy."

"You are?" Tristan asked.

Leo was telling the truth, though *happiness* felt like an oversimplification. That light inside him—that warm, anchoring presence from his dreams—had been his reason to keep going through the fog and the headaches and the curse's violent intrusions into the most intimate corners of his heart and mind. He had been lucky to have ever had a love like that. To have been changed by it, the way he knew he had been changed. And he could never, not under any circumstances, let go of that person.

He was *not* saying any of that.

"Yeah," he said, settling on something less revealing. "Because they made me feel like I was exactly where I was meant to be."

"I guess that's why you can't give up," Tristan said.

He sounded as if he understood, or was at least accepting of what he didn't understand. That should have made Leo feel better. But he only felt worse, and could not summon the buoyancy of true love that he had just described to Tristan. Maybe because, despite everything he'd just confessed, he hadn't really said what he needed to say.

They had never talked about what was going on between them, but that wasn't working anymore. He *had* to talk to Tristan before he messed things up between them irreparably. He just didn't know what to say, or what to ask for. Space? He had little hope it would make a difference to how he felt. Tristan had fit himself so seamlessly into Leo's life that Leo had no idea how he'd ever gotten by without him. He had gotten used to having Tristan around all the time. To watching him study his dead languages and practice his incantations, and how it felt when he got a new spell right and Leo was the first person he wanted to tell. To running errands together even though they lived apart, because Leo could borrow his parents' car and save Tristan from having to transport his groceries on the bus, and Tristan always reminded him which brand of coffee creamer Dad liked and which baking ingredients Mom was running low on. He couldn't fathom what he'd do with his nights if he had to go back to spending them alone—really alone, without even being able to text him, to call him and just hear his voice.

It no longer mattered to Leo's heart if they slept together or not. His feelings for Tristan grew when they were together or apart. And he didn't know what to do about it. He was so confused. He'd never thought of himself as someone who could have feelings this strong for more than one person at the same time. Other people could do it; Leo couldn't. He didn't want to. So what was it he felt for Tristan? A heady combination of friendship and lust? Was he using

Tristan as an emotional crutch? He needed someone, and Tristan was convenient and willing? He felt sick at the thought. Maybe his understanding of true love had a gaping, person-shaped hole in the middle, but he knew love wasn't about clinging to someone because they were the one stretch of dry land in the middle of a storm-tossed sea. Could he even call himself Tristan's friend if he was willing to let this go on, use Tristan in that way, knowing that Tristan might feel something that Leo didn't—couldn't—reciprocate?

He had to figure out what he was going to do next, and it had to be soon. Tristan deserved more than this unfair, half-hearted, wordless intimacy, and it was looking like that was all Leo had to give him. One day, he would have his true love back. And then what? Would he abandon Tristan then? Discard him like a jacket he'd outgrown? God. How could he have been so naïve as to think this wouldn't change anything between them?

"Listen—" Leo began.

"The light's green," Tristan said, softly interrupting.

"Huh? Oh." Leo had been stopped at an intersection. He accelerated too quickly, and they jolted into motion.

"What were you saying?" Tristan asked.

Leo didn't know what he had been about to say. Or maybe he did, but he didn't know how. And now wasn't the right time for this talk. They were almost at Aziza's, and then they had the Market and the drive back. And the conversation he needed to have with Tristan couldn't be rushed.

"Nothing important," he said.

CHAPTER 18
TRISTAN

THE HALF MOON Market had taken up residence for the night in an abandoned college campus in upstate New York. It had lived a past life as a failed luxury hotel, Nelle had told them; and then it was Susannah Martin College for a few decades, a failed attempt at an all-witch boarding school, before it was shuttered. The sprawling campus had long since fallen into disrepair, and wasn't safe to wander around, so the Market was restricted to the main building. It was lined with crumbling colonnades, and the roof was topped with a skeletal cupola that over the years had lost most of its domed siding and now admitted a cascade of moonlight and rain. The great hall on the first floor had probably hosted banquets and dances once, but now it bore the scars of neglect—water damage from burst pipes, eddies of dirt that had blown across the floor and obscured the pattern in the tiles, the branches of a tree thrusting inside through a broken window.

They had decided beforehand that they'd split up to do their shopping and reconvene when they were finished. They had a long drive back and couldn't risk running late, so "divide and conquer" was the plan tonight. That made things a lot easier for Tristan. They wouldn't know what he'd done until it was over.

He hadn't been lying to Leo; he really did want to see Jun. And he wanted to do it before fulfilling his promise to Professor Serapion. Somehow he didn't think he'd be in the mood to talk much afterward.

The configuration of the Market had changed entirely, and he had to ask someone for directions to Jun's shop. But when he ducked through the curtain opening of the black velvet booth, there was a girl sitting behind the table. Her head was down, the thin straps of her top clinging to her bony shoulders as she hunched over Jun's notes.

"Can I help you?" she asked, straightening. She bore a decidedly familial resemblance to Jun, with the same messy black hair, cropped even shorter than his, and the same penetrating dark eyes.

"I'm looking for Jun. I'm a . . . friend," he said uncertainly. "Sort of. We met at the last Market."

"Oh," she said, her eyes narrowing almost to slits. "*You're* the one who taught him that paper snake spell."

Before Tristan could ask what was so offensive about haunted origami, the flap of the tent rustled and Jun swept in.

"Hana! Lay off," he said. "I'm done, anyway. You're free for the rest of the night."

"I'm taking this," she said, snatching up his yellow notepad and clutching it possessively to her chest.

He rolled his eyes. "Fine, but only until morning."

With one more parting glare at Tristan, she flounced off.

"Was that your sister?" Tristan guessed.

Jun turned to him, starting to grin, but then he winced and rubbed at his jaw as if it hurt. "Sorry, she's a little protective. I'm really glad to see you! I wasn't sure if you'd be back."

"I wanted to thank you for this," Tristan said, touching the talisman that rested against his chest. Jun brightened when he saw it. "It got me out of some trouble a few weeks ago. But it sounds like I got the better end of our deal. Did something go wrong with the spell I gave you?"

"No! It was perfect. I was hoping I'd get the chance to thank you, too," Jun said. "After I got it to work for me, I landed an apprenticeship with a master necromancer. One of the best. I owe you big-time, seriously."

"Oh," Tristan said, his heart sinking. "Who . . . ?"

"Theodore Serapion. Have you heard of him?" Then he caught Tristan's expression, and his own became a little sheepish. "Ah. I guess you have."

"That's funny," Tristan said, even though it wasn't. "I just accepted an apprenticeship with Professor Serapion, too."

Jun gave a surprised laugh, and the laugh made him wince again, and Tristan *knew*.

"You already did it," Tristan said.

"Yeah," Jun said, with a little shrug, like it was a minor inconvenience and nothing more. "It's why I had Hana watch the shop for me. You?"

"I was going to go after this."

Jun nodded sympathetically. "It's not so bad. No pain or anything."

"I don't really have a choice," Tristan said. "But you—Wasn't there anyone else you could have—Did it *have* to be him?"

"Let's sit down," Jun said.

He passed Tristan a water bottle from a package behind his chair and took another for himself. The reminiscence charms hanging together on their display stands glimmered subtly, like rows of shining eyes.

"We're lucky we weren't born a hundred years ago," Jun said, picking at the label on his water bottle. "Master necromancers used to take a finger from each of their apprentices. But Professor Serapion says flesh spells don't appeal to him. Too messy."

"I'll bet," Tristan muttered.

"Blood is too simplistic, and shadow is for vermin and cowards," Jun went on. "According to him. Necromancy is an art, one which should be displayed with pride, not hidden away. He's a bone mage."

"I've seen one of his constructs," Tristan said. "And those rings he wears . . ."

"That's how he summons them. It's his signature—he composed that spell on the rings himself. There's nothing else like it in the world," Jun said. "Uh, but don't worry. He doesn't make those from his apprentice tithe or anything. Nothing he takes from us will be useable in his spells until we're dead. Out of every branch of magic, necromancy is the one with the highest death rate for young witches, ironically. I guess the tithe started as a kind of insurance for master necromancers. Something to make it worth their while to spend time on a student who might not live long enough to achieve mastery."

"How are you okay with this?" Tristan hissed. There was a loud crumpling sound as he squeezed the water bottle so tightly the plastic buckled. "Why did you tell him yes?"

With a sigh, Jun plucked the bottle from his hands and set it aside, along with his own.

"If I do well, I have a guaranteed full ride to any Ivy League university I want," he said. "That could change everything for me and my family. I'd be the first one of us to even go to college, let alone, like, Yale."

Tristan couldn't argue with that, much as he wished he could. He understood the things Jun wanted. Security. A future. To make sure the people he loved were taken care of.

"Are you sure he'll keep his promises?" Tristan asked.

"I'm not under any illusions that he's doing this because he wants to help me," Jun said. "I've met some of his apprentices before. They know they're only useful to him if they go on to be upstanding members of society. So I get an education. And a job. Something, y'know, respectable. Close the shop, because I won't have time for it. And when Professor Serapion calls in a favor someday, I pick up the phone on the first ring. Easy."

"And all you have to do is give him—"

"A fragment of bone. Something I'll barely miss."

Tristan's blood pounded in his ears. The rage he felt went so much deeper than emotion that it was like something that had always been part of him, like a second heartbeat. It had been building in him since he'd spoken to Serapion earlier. And before that. Since the first time he walked into the shadow of the hag's gateway tree.

"Let me do it for you," Tristan said. Part of him had known this would be his next move the moment Jun had said the word *apprenticeship*. Jun had had no such premonitions; his mouth fell open in wordless shock.

"You can't—" Jun began.

"I can," Tristan said. "He'll never know."

By the time he was finished explaining, Jun's eyes were very wide. "I don't know if another spellcasting aid will cover *this* debt."

"There's no debt to repay," Tristan said. "I just want to stop Professor Serapion from getting what he wants."

Somewhere in the bowels of every Half Moon Market, there was a crooked little alleyway where every kind of medical or cosmetic service imaginable could be purchased with magical favors, or at least at a significant discount. White screens for privacy; sterilizing enchantments;

the pervasive smell of disinfectant, not quite strong enough to cover the iron tang that could have been blood or witchcraft.

Following the directions he had been given, and retracing Jun's footsteps, Tristan pushed aside a curtain and stepped into a makeshift office, where a man on Theodore Serapion's payroll was expecting him.

He was a dentist. A few hours prior, he had extracted one of Jun's molars and replaced it with a fixed bridge. Jun was supposed to give the tooth to Serapion the next time they saw each other.

"Pull two of mine," Tristan said.

"The professor paid for one."

"I'll pay for the second."

"He only *needs* one from you," the dentist said, bored.

"And?" Tristan replied in his haughtiest tone of voice. "Do you want my money or not?"

Even if Tristan had arrived a few hours sooner, there would have been no saving Jun from this part. Serapion would have heard if Jun never showed up for his procedure. But Tristan could still save his afterlife.

Bone could be used to summon spirits. A ghost was only an echo, a memory; the soul would go on to wherever it was meant to go, no matter what was done with the lingering energy that clung to human remains and certain treasured possessions. But a ghost was also all that would be left of Jun after he was gone. And Serapion could hold it hostage. If Jun betrayed him, Serapion could kill him and weaponize his ghost. Use it to haunt his loved ones. Use it for anything he wanted.

Jun knew all of this and had decided it was worth the gamble. The apprentice tithe was an old tradition; apparently it was only natural for master witches to treat their subordinates this way. Maybe Serapion would never make any real use of it. But no one should be able to exert that kind of control over another person. Tristan didn't care who they were or what they were offering. It was barely any different from what the hag had done to Tristan. She'd held the fate of his loved ones over his head; she'd trapped him in a magical contract designed to give her all the power and none to him, to make him subservient and wring him for all he was worth. She'd used what he wanted and what made him vulnerable against him. But the hag had died before Tristan could *really* hate her. He had spent that year being afraid of the hag and hating only himself. The fury he never had a chance to direct at her had now found a new target in Professor Serapion. And Tristan wasn't afraid of him at all.

For once he wasn't thinking of the shameful and unforgivable things he had done for the hag. He was remembering how, in the end, his position as her bondservant had granted him knowledge about her that no one else had. His betrayal had left her vulnerable. His fall from grace had been crucial to the hag's defeat.

Maybe he couldn't overpower Serapion in a fight, but he could make sure no one else ended up in the same position he had once put himself in. So he lost two molars and got two silver bridges, and the whole thing only took a couple of hours. Serapion would get one; Jun would get the other, to give to Serapion and pass off as his own.

Toward the end of the procedure, Tristan's phone started vibrating nonstop.

That was his first sign that something was wrong.

CHAPTER 19

LEO

SHOPPING FOR THE Fair Folk was easy at the Half Moon Market. Quality witchcraft like Anne's cloak of shadow was out of his budget, but he grabbed a couple of bottles of absinthe—no one asked for his ID—and a few magical trinkets to bring with him on his next visits to the low courts of Elphame. He found an enchanted handheld mirror that showed you the reflections of long-dead ancestors; a music box that played a lullaby imbued with a mild sleeping spell and bit your fingers if you tried to touch the tiny rotating ballerina inside; and a semi-telepathic deck of cards that always pulled the card you were thinking of, and also attracted stray cats for some reason. It wouldn't impress a fairy, but it would probably amuse them, which was all he really needed.

The contact lenses he'd commissioned last time to disguise his amber eye were ready, so he picked those up, too. They blocked his truesight, so he'd really only use them when he had to, like at school. He didn't think he could get away with wearing the patch much longer. He'd told everyone that he'd been in a car crash, hurt his eye, and had to get surgery—which was sort of true—but at some point he would have to fake-heal from his fake operation.

But no one at the Market gave the amber eye a second glance, so he put the contact lenses away. He had time to kill before he had to meet back up with the others, and he wanted to get a closer look at the protective enchantments on Martin College.

The vendors had set up their stalls around the broken windows and gaping holes in the walls that let in the rain, a barely audible drizzle. The lamplight scorched the clammy air and dug deep trenches of shadow. The Market spilled through the main hall and into the empty classrooms; the tattoo artist had commandeered the little attached chapel for their studio, and the cellist played for an audience clustered between a pair of pillars.

He brought the enchantments into focus with his amber eye, the trails of magic etched into the walls and ceiling. An individual magical signature had its own distinct tone, something arcane, like the phosphorescence found in deep, sunless places, under the sea or in mineral-rich caves. He couldn't have described it as a color; he couldn't even truly describe it as light. That was just the easiest way for him to conceptualize it. It wasn't light, but it was the furthest thing from darkness.

He wandered along the edge of the Market, reaching out here and there to trace an invisible script—carefully, as the scrawl of enchantment led his fingers over jagged glass and splintered wood. There, a cursive stroke of a spell gave him a shiver of warning analogous to Khaled El-Amin's wards; and over there, he singled out a shade of magic he'd seen all over the Flight Paths and identified it as hearthcraft. It gave him a little thrill of accomplishment, like when you remembered a tricky vocabulary word in a language you were still learning.

Toward the back of the great hall, the enchantments sort of—*warped*, like glass that had softened under extreme heat. Curiously, he followed the twist of molten spellwork outside, onto what must have once been the quad but now was a rambling stretch of ankle-high grass divided by cracked stone walking paths. The light from the Market overflowed into the night, but the chatter of the crowd was muffled. The patter of the sluggish rainfall and the chirping of crickets filled the air.

The spellwork led him to a greenhouse on the edge of campus. It was like a little palace, with its bell-shaped roof and curls of iron cresting. Spidery clusters of green vegetation dotted the outside, and the cobbled footpath vanished through the open door. Inside, a light was on, glowing weakly through the clouded glass.

This wasn't part of the Market. It was so out of the way he couldn't even see the light from the main hall anymore, and dead quiet. But it was plugged into the Market enchantments. Chewing on his lip, he pulled out his phone, took a picture of the greenhouse, and texted it to Nelle.

hey what's in here? he asked. *it's got market spells but no market?*

She didn't reply, probably busy with a client.

Inside, off to the corner, a rusted staircase twisted up to a raised walkway. Tangled vines spilled between the balusters and dangled like streamers. The footpath continued down the middle of the greenhouse, almost swallowed by what had, over the years, become a small jungle of leafy plants taller than Leo was and thorny flowering shrubs. He could just make out the dark shape of a fountain in the back.

That was the source of the light—the fountain, or rather, the lantern perched on top of it as if someone had come by, set it down for a moment, and then forgotten about it.

The back of his neck prickled with foreboding. He didn't know which was more unsettling: the thought that someone might come back for the lantern at any moment—or the possibility that they had never left.

Okay, he thought. *No more found footage horror movies before bedtime for you.*

He could have turned back then; maybe he should have. But that was no ordinary lantern. Cautiously, he went closer, wanting a better look. The trails of magic that had brought him here fed into a star chart of spellwork that covered the fountain, diamantine threads beaded with bright points of intensity, woven together so tightly that Leo couldn't pick them apart.

He couldn't decipher the spellwork. But he recognized that light. He'd seen it on the autumn equinox. If it had sprouted wings, it would've been identical to the light of Castor Thorne's constructs.

Behind the fountain, in the deep shadows cast by the lantern, something moved.

He backed away, but it didn't come out—it had retreated out of his sight. He could hear it, though. A rattling, like something metallic. It snaked across the room so that it came as if from every direction. Then a lapping noise, like when a cat drank out of a bowl of water. The crunch of broken glass. Twigs snapping. A rustle—directly behind him—and he didn't think. He whipped out the hilt of the frost sword; he'd kept it in his pocket after his visit to the Spring Court earlier that day. The blade materialized with a little burst of cold that stung his face and hands, its shimmer catching the lantern light with a wintry malice.

He spun around, using the momentum to slash with the sword. The edge of its blade met tattered cloth and tough flesh; it was like trying to use a butter knife to saw through gristle. His sword stuck in what turned out to be a torso, so that he and the *thing* on the other end were connected by the bridge of the frost blade. The light of the lantern revealed a cloaked, humanoid figure; beneath the hood, its face was shriveled, like all the moisture had been siphoned from its skin. Its eyes were shadowy slits, and its crooked mouth was smeared with blood. There were manacles on its wrists, connected to chains that trailed on the ground, so long he couldn't see where they ended. That was the source of the rattling he'd heard before.

He only got a glimpse before it lunged, using the sword embedded in its body to unbalance him. It knocked him back; he held on to the hilt with all his strength and kept the sword between them. As it strained toward him, its neck stretching, he almost gagged on the stench of death and rot. It reminded him horribly and vividly of the place underneath the hag's gateway tree, where she had kept the vile, oozing black thing that had been her heart. The creature scrabbled at him with clawed fingers, tearing at his sleeves, ripping the fabric and drawing blood. It contorted its spine, twisting to reach, and—and *licked* the blood on his shoulder.

No way in hell, he thought.

He heaved the sword across his body, completing his swing and dragging the blade through the creature's torso. It made a noise, a shapeless sound of agony—and then the blade came out the other side, cutting it in half, and the two pieces of it fell heavily to the ground at his feet. They were still *twitching*. He probably needed silver to kill it properly.

His first thought was that he was going to bring the Salt-Scale fairies all the absinthe he could carry as thanks for their dueling lessons.

His second was that Tristan had been right. It was about time he started carrying a silver knife.

CHAPTER 20

AZIZA

THE DUELS WERE on, but Castor wasn't hosting tonight. She had seen him in the Market crowd, surrounded by a flock of admirers, with Dion at his side.

She recalled how Dion had brought them through the Flight Paths last time but declined to join them at the Market, claiming an aversion to the crowds. Even then she'd known that was only an excuse, but she'd assumed his refusal was motivated by a desire not to spend more time around her and Tristan than absolutely necessary. It was only in hindsight that she realized he must have known Castor would be there, and couldn't chance revealing his secret apprenticeship. The pains he'd taken to withhold the truth from her made her fume even now, weeks later.

Nelle was alone at her table when Aziza turned up.

"Done already?" she asked.

"Almost," Aziza said, and sat across from her in the chair reserved for her clients. From her backpack, she produced a bottle of fairy wine and a note in Meryl's handwriting. She placed both on the table.

Leo had brought the bottle back from the Salt-Scale Court for this purpose. The note belonged to Meryl's father. Aziza had delivered it to him; later, Marinus had given the note back to Aziza before he had taken his pod and left Blackthorn for good. Until recently, she had forgotten she even had it.

"Don't actually drink that," Aziza said.

"I'll save it for a special occasion." Nelle pulled her headphones down around her neck, unfolded the paper, and trailed her fingertips over the words, eyes closed. "The spell will ruin the note."

"That's fine." A small price to pay if it would get her closer to Meryl.

The note went into the bottom of the bowl. Nelle picked a bottle of vermouth from under her table, uncapped it, and drank a few mouthfuls. Aziza still didn't know if that was part of the spell or not. Then she poured the rest of it into the bowl, the paper turning dark and translucent as it soaked through. Soon the ink had blurred until it was illegible.

Nelle rested her hands on either side of the bowl, holding it lightly. Her expression emptied. The impish tilt to her smile; the half-here, half-there flicker in her eyes, as if there was always something in her peripheral vision trying to capture her attention; the minuscule motions of a quirked eyebrow or a flutter of eyelashes—all the things that were Nelle—were gone.

She spoke, and it was like Aziza had called her and someone else had picked up the phone, though her voice sounded the same. It had made her shiver, as if suddenly she'd realized she was speaking to her doppelganger.

"I'm standing in front of a big black house with purple flowers outside," Nelle murmured. "It's summer. No one is home, but the house isn't empty—the light is on, and I can hear voices. You have to leave. In the end, you were hardly any trouble. Sleep now."

Then silence. Nelle pulled her hands away from the bowl and blinked away the reverie.

"Did you get anything out of that?" she asked in her normal voice.

"You have to be kidding," Aziza said. "You tracked Emil to a city and state. When Dion was keeping tabs on me, you pinpointed my location down to the street corner and the hour I'd be there. But you can't even tell me if Meryl is still on this continent?"

"Come on! You know this isn't an exact science," Nelle said. "Especially when I'm scrying for the fae. It's also possible that Meryl's future is more in flux than your average person's. There are many potential futures—for some people more than others."

"You said it was summer," Aziza said. "Does that mean I won't find her until next year?"

Nelle's gaze slid back toward the bowl, where the ink had run entirely out of the note and left it blank. "I don't know. I can't even say for sure that you'll find her. All I know is that, wherever that place is, she *will* be there. At . . . some point."

Aziza sighed. "That's still more than I had before. Thank you."

"Not my best work, I'll admit," Nelle said, with a grimace. "But my craft has never been very dependable. I can't produce consistent results. It's why I dropped my apprenticeship. I have power, but control is what defines mastery."

"You were an apprentice?" Aziza asked.

"Yeah. With my aunt Penelope. I'm even named after her," Nelle said. "But the difference between her and me is that she'd never set foot here."

"Didn't Castor mention her?" Aziza asked. "When we met him at the last Market. They know each other?"

"She's a member of the Clattering," Nelle said. "The country's top oracle. So they're technically covenmates. That's how I know Dion, too—his dad and my aunt worked together."

"And you don't get along with her."

"No." Nelle tapped the side of her headphones, which she hadn't put back on yet. "My gift . . . hurts. Unless I keep it in check with these. My aunt said I'd learn to bear it over the years and that pain is a consequence of power. But I hated it. The constant headaches. The vertigo. The dissociative episodes. The horrible things I'd see sometimes. I like my small spells best. And I like scrying for whoever I want to scry for, and turning away anyone for any reason I want. Not selling my gift to the highest bidder like she does. But when I dropped my apprenticeship, my family sided with my aunt and cut me off. I'm on my own unless I go back. And I'm not ever going back."

Aziza had learned enough about the inner workings of AJA to understand what this meant. The completion of an apprenticeship was a requirement for joining AJA; without that, the connections and opportunities it afforded would be inaccessible to Nelle. Aziza wondered now if that was why she'd dropped out of college—did Nelle have an AJA-funded scholarship that got pulled once she cut ties with her family?

"So what will you do instead?" Aziza asked.

Nelle shrugged. "For now, I support myself bartending. Eventually I might go to the West Coast, where AJA has a little less influence, or abroad. I may not be part of the in-group anymore, but a witch is an outsider by definition and by design. Witchcraft is about finding your own path. Or making one. I don't need my aunt to pave the way for me."

Someone came up to the table, and Aziza rose from her seat, thinking it was a client. Instead, she came face-to-face with Dion.

"What do you want?" she snapped.

"Nothing from you. I came to talk to Nelle," he said dismissively. His eyes flicked down to the scrying bowl. "Were you getting your fortune read?"

"Maybe. But I'm surprised you're here," she said, matching his icy tone. "I thought you were on the clock."

"I was helping Castor oversee some routine maintenance on the Market enchantments," he said. "We've finished for the night."

"So you decided you'd get your fortune read, too."

"No. I think I'm done searching for things that can't be found," he said pointedly. "Or shouldn't be."

They glared at each other. Nelle cleared her throat. "Okay! Well, let me pack up, and we can go grab some food."

Aziza's phone buzzed. She glanced down at a text from Leo. It took a concerted effort not to react.

"You two go on," she said. "I'll see you later, Nelle."

It wasn't how she would have chosen to leave—fleeing as if Dion's mere presence had the power to chase her away. But she was in no frame of mind to come up with a believable excuse.

She followed Leo's directions to the greenhouse and found him standing over a corpse—though *corpse* was maybe not the right word, as it wasn't all the way dead. Beside him, an old-fashioned iron lantern stood atop a fountain; an eerie light pulsed behind its glass walls.

She knew who it belonged to even before Leo said, "It's Castor's. I'm pretty sure of it. He—Uh, never mind, can you help me with this first?"

"Are you okay?"

"Yeah! A few cuts, nothing bad—I think I need—"

"Silver," Aziza said, flipping open her pocketknife. The thing on the ground looked like the stage of decomposition when most of the body's soft parts had liquefied, and all that was left was skin clinging to bone. But the wrinkled, lipless gash of its mouth opened and closed; its hands did, too, grasping at nothing, touching at the floor as if it might push itself up. Leo had missed its heart when he'd cut it in half. The two raw edges of its split torso were frosted over, the ice marbled with dark blood.

Aziza knelt over it, ignoring the way it hissed it at her, its mouth opening wide, hungrily, a dry black tongue moving grublike in its cavity. She ended it swiftly, the silver blade buried to the handle in its chest. The creature convulsed, but it couldn't move enough to fight. The last of its breath escaped it in a rattle. And then it was still.

Leo met her eyes with queasy horror.

"I found—It's been feeding on people," Leo said. "I looked around the greenhouse—There are bodies, they're hidden in the bushes—"

She wrenched her knife free and stood to clean it off in the stagnant water in the fountain. The carved birds on the side were worn down so that the once-fine details in their feathers had all but vanished. The inside was stained with mildew. The lantern stood on the upper tier, in front of the dry spout where the water would've once cascaded out and into the wide bowl below.

Her foot nudged something underneath the fountain. She bent to investigate. It was the end of the creature's chain—it had been shackled there.

"The lantern's connected to the Market enchantments. I followed the spellwork here," Leo said, hushed. "You saw a lantern in the castle, right? Do you think this is the same one?"

"I didn't get a good look, and I was paying more attention to the person holding it. I thought it was Viren . . . or that it looked like Viren, but it couldn't be him . . . but now I don't know." She shook off the memory. She couldn't puzzle this out right now; it was hard to focus on anything but the dead body next to them. "If the lantern is Castor's, then he's the one responsible for . . . that."

Leo had knelt beside the creature and gingerly lifted its cloak. Slowly, he said: "Why is it wearing a Yale sweater?"

She had been afraid of exactly this.

"It's human," she said. "Or it was."

"A hag?" Leo asked, standing and backing away from the corpse.

"I don't know. I think if it was a hag, that wouldn't have been so easy." She folded away the knife and turned to examine the lantern. "We need to figure out what this is for."

He came over and hovered at her shoulder. Tentatively, she tapped the glass with a fingertip. It wasn't hot. But it brimmed with such power that the air pulsed, her skull throbbing with it. It was too bright to look at directly.

She flipped the latch open.

"Don't!" someone shouted, too late; a shock wave blasted from the lantern, knocking both her and Leo flat. She hit the ground, dazed, as the fountain split down the middle, the stone cracking—the plants rippled as if a gust of wind had rolled over them—and the greenhouse shattered. The walls blew open; the ceiling crashed down in a million shards of glass.

Her arms flew up to cover her face. She braced herself for the pain.

But nothing happened. Leo was next to her, breathing hard. She hadn't imagined it; the greenhouse was in pieces around them. The ceiling had broken—but it hadn't fallen. A starscape of broken shards hovered in midair, glinting dangerously.

"Aziza."

She thought it was Tristan for a split second. Something about the ashen face, the pale eyes wide with a cornered animal's fear, was so much like her first glimpse of Tristan in the woods that she was struck with an intense feeling of déjà vu. But then his shadowed features resolved into Dion's. He stood where the entrance to the greenhouse used to be, his eyes fixed on the broken ceiling, his expression frozen in concentration.

"*Move,*" he said, without looking away from the glass. "*Now.*"

They scrambled to their feet and ran. The moment they were clear, there was an explosive crash behind them. They turned back. Dion had sunk to his knees, panting with exhaustion, and the greenhouse plants were covered in glass. The lantern's glass chamber had shattered, too. It was nothing but an empty iron skeleton now.

"Dion?" she said, approaching cautiously. "Are you all right?"

He looked up with a glare. "You shouldn't have come here."

"There was something in there, it wasn't—"

"We have to go," he said, cutting her off. "This way."

"Were you following me?" she asked, as he led them across the lawn, off the paved walking paths.

"I was, and you're welcome," he said acerbically. "For god's sake, *hurry*. We need to get you out of here before you're seen."

He shouldered through the door of a nearby structure that turned out to be the shell of a library. The shelves were bare except for a coat of dust, and the window glass so cloudy it was nearly opaque. Their damp footsteps slapped quietly over the musty carpet.

"We can get to the Flight Paths from here?"

"Yes," Dion whispered. "The jackdaw collection was moved when the college shut down, but the room is still connected to the rest of the system."

"We have to get Tris first," Leo said.

"I'm trying to get his attention, but he's shutting me out," she said.

"Shutting you out?" Dion asked.

Aziza froze guiltily, appalled at her own lack of discretion. Other than herself and Tristan, no one but Leo knew about their bond. She and Tristan preferred it that way. But Dion was too distracted to pursue this line of questioning. He was studying a blank patch of wall, searching for something. Finally, he wrapped his hands around the stem of a candle holder and pulled hard, as if to snap it off. Instead, a door sprang into existence with the guttural scraping sound of an old enchantment coughing itself awake. It was wide enough for the three of them to walk through side by side, flanked with pilasters, its handle shining despite years of disuse.

He opened the door to reveal an empty room that was a mirror to the one they were in, except that it was windowless, and the bookcases were empty. At the end, a pitch-dark open doorway led not outside, but into the Flight Paths.

"In," Dion ordered.

"We can't—" she began.

"He can shadow-travel," Dion said impatiently. "He'll catch up with us. He's in much less danger in the Market than you are waiting here for him."

"I took my parents' car here," Leo objected weakly. "I can't leave it."

"I'll give the keys to Nelle. She'll bring it to you in the morning," Dion said. His voice was strained with an emotion she slowly identified as fear. He was frightened of something.

He was frightened *for* them.

As they filed through the door, Aziza looked back. Outside one of the dusty windows, she caught a flash—like lightning—but there was no thunderstorm tonight, only a muted rainfall. She thought, for an instant, she'd glimpsed a pair of fluttering wings.

THE MOOD AT Bishop Library was dismal.

Tristan had finally responded to their texts and was waiting for them when they got there, to her and Leo's relief. It had taken less than half an hour to return, and the journey had been completed mostly in silence, at a brisk walk, Dion checking around corners to make sure the halls were empty before they proceeded. The first time he stopped to draw the arrays for his navigation spell, consulting his chronometer for the numerical elements he needed to complete it, he scowled down at the partially finished spell as if unhappy with what the numbers told him. Then he said, irritably, "No. That won't work," erased the array, and scrawled a new one. He set it ablaze, the fire springing up so high it nearly brushed the ceiling. When the flames died, the branches of the crossroads were different; they couldn't go right anymore, only left or straight ahead, and the wide path with the terrazzo floor to their left had been replaced by a cramped hallway with board-and-batten walls and a slightly musty carpet. He had *forced* the Flight Paths to shift, to get them away faster.

Upon arrival, Dion had listened to their side of the story. But he had yet to offer any explanations of his own.

"What was that thing?" Leo asked. He was sitting on top of the desk while Tristan tended to his cuts with the first aid kit, wincing occasionally at the sting of the antiseptic.

"A striga," Dion said.

Tristan made a small movement, like he had stopped himself from turning to look at Dion. She wouldn't have noticed if she hadn't been paying attention, and she wouldn't have been paying attention if Tristan wasn't still keeping himself suspiciously remote from their bond.

"It's what a witch sometimes becomes if they perform corruptive magic," Dion continued. "That one couldn't have turned more than a few years ago. You're lucky it was so young. Older strigas can sometimes control their victim's mind, teleport, shapeshift . . ."

"So it's like a hag," Aziza said.

"A hag feeds on life energy. A lich feeds on souls. And the striga feeds on blood," Dion said. "That's what corruptive magic is—untold power, in exchange for your humanity. It turns you into a parasite."

"When you say it was young," Leo said, "do you mean—"

"I just mean recently turned," Dion said.

"But it *was* young. Before it turned. Right?" Leo said. "It was wearing a university sweater."

"Probably. I can't be sure." He was pacing, agitated, and it seemed the striga was far from his chief concern. "I should have known you would see Castor's spellwork. And you had no choice but to kill the striga. You'd never have escaped otherwise. But why did you have to open the lantern?" He answered his own question. "No, why wouldn't you? You had no reason to think . . ."

He pressed the heels of his hands into his eyes. Lowering them, his weary gaze landed on Aziza.

"You need to leave this alone," he said, in a tone of finality.

"You want us to just . . . pretend we didn't see anything?" she said.

"Yes," he said. "That's exactly what I want. If he finds out what you've done, he'll retaliate. You have to stay out of his way."

"You knew that thing was there," Aziza said. "Did he tell you? Are you covering for him?"

She was filled with a righteous anger, which she welcomed. Her vendetta against Castor Thorne had been entirely personal up to this point. He had hurt her friend, so Aziza wanted him punished. But now she had proof that there were bigger things at stake—a greater good. A transgression big enough, that had affected enough people, to justify Aziza's almost fanatical desire to see him *ruined*.

"Why would I need to cover for him?" Dion said. "He has everything he needs to cover his own tracks. No, I found the striga myself."

She waited with rising incredulity for him to say something else. He didn't.

"And then you didn't tell anyone?" she demanded.

"Who would I tell?" he said. "What would they do about it except report it to the Clattering, which, if you've forgotten, is Castor's coven? The striga would have been killed, but there's nothing connecting it to Castor. I checked. I have access to his personal records, his correspondence, his schedule, his ledgers—everything. If there was anything to incriminate him, I would have found it by now."

"Fine!" Aziza said. "So Castor gets away with it, but at least some of the striga's victims might still be *alive*!"

"Didn't you see that it was *chained up*?" Dion said, his tight grip on his temper slipping at last. "Its victims didn't stumble across it like Leo did. It was being *fed*."

He paused a moment as they digested the terrible implications of that. Instinctively, she looked at Tristan, who had frozen with a roll of gauze in his hands. Leo took it from him and tugged him by the elbow to sit next to him on the desk.

"So this striga is gone," Dion said. "And so is the lantern. But that's nothing but a minor inconvenience to Castor. He and the person or people who are helping him are free to continue—"

He broke off.

"Continue what?" she asked.

"None of you need to be involved. You've killed the monster. You've done your good deed," he said cuttingly. "Next time I need something broken into a million pieces or cut in half with a sword, you'll be my first call. Happy?"

"Go to *hell*, Dion," she snarled.

"The lantern looked like it was pulling magic from the Market enchantments," Leo said, interrupting them before the argument could really hit its stride. "Didn't Castor say he had a spell like that?"

"On his cuff links," Aziza said. "He can take in magic from the environment and use it to power his spells. I think the lantern is just a bigger version of that."

"Like a magical battery," Leo said.

"And if we're right that the one in the castle was also his," Aziza said, "then that one could have been pulling magic from the Summer Court."

Tristan glanced at Dion. "Would you like to fill in some blanks, or are you going to let them keep piecing it together themselves?"

"He must have sent Viren to move it," Leo said, continuing Aziza's train of thought. "When the castle got uprooted, he couldn't get to the lantern anymore. So as soon as the castle held still for a few hours, he had Viren pick it up for him. Because . . . it's kind of fragile, isn't it?"

"Opening the lantern is all it takes to release the energy inside. Assuming they're two separate lanterns, Narra must have been hiding the one in the castle, up until the solstice. And he left the striga in the greenhouse to protect the other one," Aziza said. "We wanted to know who woke Blackthorn's hag. Is this the answer? Was the hag protecting a lantern?"

"No," Tristan said. "I would have known."

Then he seemed to remember Dion was still in the room, and looked over at him again, this time with apprehension.

"The hag wasn't the lantern's guardian," Dion said grudgingly. "She was only a source of magic for the lantern to feed on. Its guardian was . . ."

He trailed off.

"It was Meryl," Aziza finished. "And the lantern was here, in the library. Is it still here?"

"No. Once I made the connection between Meryl and Castor, I looked for it," he said. "But she must have taken it with her."

At last Aziza had her answer to the question of what Castor wanted with Meryl. It was the first Aziza had heard of a selkie being taken for her power instead of her beauty. The knowledge offered no solace, but then, she hadn't expected it to.

"*This* is the reason Meryl was stuck here," Aziza said, her temper skyrocketing. "And the reason she's gone. Castor made her his prisoner. He sabotaged the Summer Court and apparently he keeps strigas as *pets*. And you won't *do* anything?"

"I'm doing something. But I'm doing it my way. I'm sorry it's not fast enough for you," he said. "You can't solve every problem by *stabbing* it."

"It looked pretty solved to me. The striga is dead and the lantern is broken—"

"And as soon as Castor notices, he'll just make another one," Dion said. "He's going to use them to cast a spell—one so massive it would take *hundreds* of witches to power it—and no one has a chance at stopping him unless we know what the spell will do. That's why I've tried to get close to him. All *you've* done is make yourself a target. *And* them." He nodded toward Leo and Tristan, who watched this back-and-forth in uncomfortable silence. "If you keep looking for trouble, they might be the ones to face the consequences. Will you be happy then? Can you live with that?"

"Back off," Leo said, his voice uncharacteristically hard. "She's not responsible for us."

Dion didn't acknowledge this, not even to glance at him. His eyes were on Aziza, and she hated it. She hated how he looked at her, and she hated that it felt worse when he looked away. A hot, angry flush rose to her face. The thing she hated most of all was that he was right.

"Why are you so scared of Castor Thorne?" she asked.

"Do you need a reason to be scared of a powerful witch who will sacrifice anything and anyone to get what he wants? Most people would call that common sense, but I realize that's a foreign concept to you," he said. It was such a transparent attempt to get a rise out of her, to distract her from this line of questioning, that it only confirmed to her that she was onto something.

"Did Emil know, too?" she said, following a trail of speculation she'd wandered down in the past with little success. But she had more information now—confirmation of Castor's connection to the hag. She forced her tired mind to push past the dead end she'd hit before. "They used to be covenmates. Maybe Emil figured out what he was up to. So Castor somehow—lured Emil here, to the hag. To get rid of him."

Dion's jaw clenched. "This has *nothing* to do with Emil."

That didn't feel true—not completely—but she thought there was a partial truth to it. That what drove him now went deeper than the loss of Emil Wulfsige.

"Never mind," she said abruptly. "You do what you have to do. And so will I."

"Fine," he said, turning on his heel and storming away. "Goodbye, Aziza. And good luck."

She waited, listening until his footsteps had ceased. He had returned to the Flight Paths.

"Is he gone?" she asked Tristan. He was quiet, a pensive, inward look on his face, as he sent Lucky to check. A moment later, he nodded. They were alone.

Dion had warned them to expect retaliation if Castor ever discovered what they'd done tonight. She thought of the flash of light through the window at Martin College's abandoned library. The wings. Unless she'd imagined that, they had been seen, and Castor already knew everything.

So they had made an enemy of Castor Thorne. Fine. He had been her enemy since before she'd ever heard his name, when she'd only known him as Meryl's captor.

Castor had seemed untouchable in every way, but the lanterns weren't. She didn't know what they were for, but she knew they were important to him. They were a weak spot—a vulnerability that she could exploit. And it was Meryl's job to guard at least one of them.

If she found the other lanterns, she would find Meryl, too.

CHAPTER 21
TRISTAN

Lucky nosed its way out of the shadows, which piled deep as snowdrifts around the single lamp he had turned on in Emil's library. Tristan opened his eyes as it emerged. He didn't know when he had closed them.

"Let's look again," he said. "It has to be here."

Lucky responded with a disgruntled *whuff*.

"Yeah, well, I'm tired of it, too," he said.

He sank into Lucky's mind as it retreated into the darkness again. It wasn't a possession, but it was so close he sometimes had trouble disentangling his own consciousness from the hound's. When it was a shadow, Tristan was a shadow. He—it—*he* sailed through an airless vacuum, as if through space. He had no body, had no thoughts; something like instinct guided him. Shadows were deeper than they looked, concealing infinite layers of darkness, like when you put two mirrors facing each other and created an endless loop of reflections. And that was where Emil had hidden his most powerful grimoire.

As an experiment, Tristan had had Lucky hide one of his beginner grimoires in the shadows under the desk in Emil's study, and then he rode along in Lucky's mind to fish it back out, so that he knew how it felt to find something there. When Lucky dove into the shadow plane with the book held between its teeth, the book became a part of the hound—in the same way that, when two objects touched, their shadows merged. Then Lucky could leave the shadow essence of the grimoire there, like a drop of gray ink deposited with a syringe into a pool of black. Lucky could—not taste, not feel, but—*sense* the difference.

Theoretically. Lucky hadn't yet found anything in the shadows that Tristan hadn't put there himself.

Since Leo's run-in with the striga, Tristan had redoubled his efforts to find Emil's grimoire. He had already sent Lucky back to the Summer Court's castle to confirm that the lantern there was gone. Aziza had the borderland fae searching for it now, in case Viren had hidden it somewhere else in Elphame.

Sooner or later, they'd find it. And then . . . well. Coven Blackthorn's team meeting in the aftermath of their trip to the Half Moon Market had been a mess; they had all disagreed with each other and yet, somehow, still came to a unanimous decision. Leo felt that Aziza had a severe case of tunnel vision when it came to Meryl, and that they should consider heeding Dion's warnings no matter how obnoxious his delivery had been. Aziza had countered that Dion's good judgment was compromised. Furthermore, if Castor's construct had seen them—then it had seen Dion with them, too. But how *much* had it seen? Would Dion be blamed for the destruction of the lantern and the striga? If not, would Dion be punished for helping the culprits escape?

"Then we should warn him," Tristan said.

"No," Aziza said, "because he'll just say something like, *I can handle Castor Thorne. I can take care of myself. I'm the youngest master hearth witch on this side of the globe, and I know everything and I'm always right.*"

Tristan had conceded that Aziza was the resident expert on Dion

Legrand. This had started a new argument entirely. Then Leo had said, "If we do look for the other lanterns and Castor finds out, that probably takes the heat off Dion. As long as we leave him out of it."

"But if you don't think we should do it—" Aziza began reluctantly.

"I didn't say that," Tristan said. "I think we have to."

The Half Moon Market was probably the most amazing place he'd ever been. And while he wasn't a trueborn witch, he had almost instantly found things about it—found people there—that made him feel like he could belong. Like anyone could. But the Market and the common ground it represented stood in stark contrast to the places where real power lay—the Flight Paths, the jackdaw collections and universities, and the master witches and their apprentices who made up AJA, the secret society that was the closest thing to government they had. AJA used the wealth and connections of its membership to protect the secrecy of the magical world and to make large-scale undertakings like the Market possible. But there was an unmistakable elitism and carefully guarded exclusivity to the way AJA functioned, too. Most advanced spellwork, like arrays, required study and the mentorship of a master witch; most master witches were part of AJA, and highly selective about the apprentices they took on. Often, landing an apprenticeship had as much to do with your family name as it did with merit. That was why Jun had been desperate enough to take his chances with the likes of Professor Serapion; meanwhile, when Nelle had been disowned by her family, she had ceded her place among the elites. It was AJA's closed ranks, its insular culture, that had enabled Castor Thorne and the destruction he had wrought already.

That university sweater Leo had seen on the striga—Tristan couldn't stop thinking about it. A young striga, Dion had said, recently turned. What had driven that witch to pursue corruptive magic? How had they ended up in chains, being fed victims by

Castor or his allies? Blackthorn's hag had felt like . . . almost like a deity, so ancient and with such total control over him. It was strange to now encounter a creature like the hag and think of it as—maybe not as a *victim*, but as a tool being wielded by a far more fearsome predator. Tristan didn't think he could sleep knowing Castor was out there, possibly prepared to inflict another hag on some other town.

He didn't know what dangers awaited them when they found the next lantern. Another striga? Meryl, under orders to kill them on sight? Castor himself?

Before that happened, he *needed* Emil's grimoire.

So he searched. The hounds had sifted through the dusty corners of Emil's deserted study; they had combed through the serene darkness in the library of grimoires; they had crept through the rest of the suffocatingly empty house. He had even checked around the hag's graveyard and in the tunnel where Emil's body had been found, in case Emil might have tucked it someplace there for safekeeping before he confronted the hag; perhaps in a rocky nook where its shadow would have the ants and earthworms for company.

What was he missing? Where hadn't he looked?

One problem was solved, at least: Professor Serapion had accepted Tristan's bone tithe—and the one Tristan had given to Jun to replace his own. Aziza and Leo had been predictably furious when they'd learned what Serapion had demanded of him. And they didn't understand why Tristan had complied instead of trying to find another way. But what he'd done was the easiest, cleanest way of dealing with the situation, and he had no regrets.

The dentist Serapion had sent him to had done good work; the bridge he'd put in was a close match for the teeth it replaced, and Tristan could barely tell the difference when he examined it in a mirror. There was a little pain after, but it was nothing some Tylenol and Maria's lemon ginger chicken soup couldn't fix. Frankly, Tristan thought Leo was in no position to criticize, since he had done basically the same thing when he had given his left eye to the wood nymphs.

"That was different," Leo said.

"Yes. It was worse. Especially since you didn't know they would replace it for you."

It was Sunday morning, so Greg and Maria were at church, Aziza was sleeping in, and Leo had come by Bishop Library with food and coffee. They were camped out at one of the study tables, empty take-out bags crumpled off to the side. Tristan pored over one of his grimoires. Leo had his laptop open in front of him, the sleeves of his sweatshirt pushed up and his chin propped in his hand.

"Look at this," he said, turning his screen so that Tristan could see.

It was a clip of Castor Thorne at a press conference. From the date under the video, it had taken place just last night. He nodded along to a question someone asked and then spoke into a microphone, saying things like "My heart goes out to the families of the victims," and "Luminous Horizons is working closely with the authorities to get to the bottom of this horrific tragedy," and "As the police investigation is ongoing, I'm not at liberty to discuss the details."

They were talking about the bodies in the greenhouse at Martin College. The morning after the Half Moon Market, Aziza and Leo had told Anne what had happened. In response, she had told them more or less the same thing as Dion: to stay out of Castor's way and let her handle it. She had reported the dead striga to the rest of the Clattering, claiming to have found it herself. It turned out most of its victims weren't witches. A debate had ensued about whether to dispose of the remains in secret, but they had concluded that, due to the sheer number of bodies they'd found, the risk was too great that one of the missing people would eventually be traced back to

Martin College. The last thing anyone wanted was for the campus to become the subject of some true crime podcast, for amateur detectives to come snooping around, rendering it ineligible to host the Half Moon Market ever again. Better to get ahead of it and control what information reached the public.

Castor had feigned ignorance, as expected, and had jumped into action, volunteering to reach out to a few well-connected jackdaws who could deal with the cleanup, liaise with mundane law enforcement, and conduct an investigation into the striga's origins. After all, it was only natural that Castor would take charge of resolving the situation—making it disappear—since he owned Martin College.

"It says here that he bought the place with plans to turn it back into a hotel, but then they got hit with an environmental protection order and couldn't get the permits they needed to start construction," Leo said, skimming the article attached to the video of the press conference. "That's just the public story. Castor was never really going to knock it down. Nelle says it's part of some kind of national register of magical places with historical significance."

The discovery of the striga had accelerated Anne's timeline for ousting Castor from the Clattering. They had told her about the lantern and their ensuing argument with Dion, particularly what he'd let slip about his theory that Castor was preparing to cast a spell of monumental proportions. By the time she and the rest of the Clattering were on the scene, the broken lantern was already gone. But she believed them. Now she was testing the waters with some of her covenmates, trying to determine which of them would help her build a case against Castor—and which of them would go running to him with the news that Anne was attempting such a thing.

Nelle was the only reason they knew any of that. She had become something like Anne's unofficial assistant. It was unofficial because if her aunt Penelope, the Clattering's oracle, found out that Anne had taken her disgraced niece under her wing, it would ruin any chance Anne had of getting Penelope on her side. She would view it as Anne interceding in a family affair.

"But it doesn't matter either way," Nelle had said. "My aunt will side with whoever she thinks is going to come out on top."

Leo gave up on the news and switched to the essay he was supposed to be writing. They worked in silence for a little bit. Rather, Tristan worked, and Leo glanced up at him every few minutes. He couldn't possibly be getting anything done when he was this distracted.

Finally, Tristan looked up, eyebrows raised inquisitively, catching Leo before he could pretend not to have been looking. Leo opened his mouth to say something and then seemed to think better of it.

"What's in that one?" he asked, nodding at the grimoire. "More hound spells?"

"Shadow magic," Tristan said. "Are you going to tell me what's on your mind, or do you want me to guess?"

From the look on Leo's face, the answer to the first part of that question might actually be *no*, and the answer to the second part was probably *please don't*. He shut his laptop with visible reluctance.

"Um. Yeah, okay," he said. "I've been meaning to talk to you. Tristan, I—"

Tristan flinched. "What did you just call me?"

"What?" Leo went a little pale. "I—I didn't mean it like—"

"I get it. You're breaking up with me." A hysterical laugh bubbled out of him. "We're not even together, and you're breaking up with me."

"Tris."

"Am I wrong?"

"Just—let me start over."

That wasn't a *yes, you're wrong*, which told him everything he needed to know. But he didn't resist when Leo took his hands. He blinked furiously, feeling his eyes sting and hating himself for it.

"I know we said that . . . this . . . between us, it wasn't going to be serious," Leo began.

"And it's not," Tristan said. "It doesn't have to be."

Leo swallowed audibly. "Yeah, but I, uh . . . caught feelings."

"Caught feelings," Tristan repeated hollowly.

"And I think . . . maybe . . . you did, too?" he said, his tone rising at the end, turning it into a question.

After an agonizing moment, Tristan made himself nod incrementally. He heard Leo's breath hitch, felt his grip tighten, and finally raised his burning eyes to meet his gaze. It didn't make him feel any better to see the longing on Leo's face, mirroring his own.

"What we're doing can't go on forever," Leo said. "And I need us to be forever. I can't lose you."

"Is this a breakup or a marriage proposal?" Tristan said, with a brittle laugh.

"More like a covenant," Leo said, smiling faintly back. "If we kept going like we were, I'd be lying to myself—to both of us—if I pretended it didn't mean anything to me. But I don't think I can really be with anyone until the curse is broken and I have the answers I need. Otherwise, I'll always wonder. And you deserve someone who doesn't have any doubts. I'm—I'm so sorry. I never should've . . . I never wanted to hurt you."

A sudden stab of shame pierced through the heartbreak. How could he let Leo apologize to him when Tristan was the one who had misled him? Hidden how he really felt, used the shared history Leo didn't remember to his own advantage, pretended he had no ulterior motives. Leo was genuinely confused about his feelings; Tristan had lied outright about his own. He'd thought he could, what—seduce Leo into falling in love with him? Make everything the way it had been before? And all he'd done was make Leo blame himself for something that wasn't his fault. Tristan was the one who needed to beg for forgiveness.

"I'm sorry, too," Tristan said, because he needed to, even if Leo couldn't fully understand. He cast about for the right words. "I don't want you to be afraid when you're with me. Afraid you're . . . doing something wrong, something you shouldn't."

Leo's breath hitched; and then he looked a little perplexed, as if he didn't know why that had gotten under his skin. His voice was hoarse as he said, "I don't feel like that."

"You thought you were betraying someone. You felt guilty, you . . . had reservations, and I knew that and I still—"

"You're *not* something I feel guilty about."

"I don't want to lose you, either," Tristan said. "You gave me a place to come home to when I didn't have anything else."

It was the kind of pain so intense there was nothing to be done but brace himself and wait for the wave to crash over him. He had thought once that he would be selfish—that he would hold on to Leo no matter what. Curse or no curse, Leo was *his*. But he knew now that he couldn't. He'd fought the curse, and it was tearing Leo apart. He had clung to a promise he'd made to a fifteen-year-old Leo who hadn't had the faintest notion of what was coming for him—of the insurmountable force that would pull them apart—when he'd asked Tristan to stay and remind him of what he'd forgotten. He hadn't known what he was asking, and Tristan hadn't known what he was vowing to do. Hadn't known that it was impossible.

The curse had won. And it was okay.

Maybe Tristan would never measure up to a version of himself that had died years ago. But he could still be with Leo. He could be what Leo needed—a friend. And Leo's friendship wasn't something he was just settling for; it was everything to him. He had fucked up—a lot—and he had been a coward, and he had been weak. But he'd learned bravery mostly because Leo, without even knowing it, had given him a reason. And that had nothing to do with whether or not Leo felt the same way.

Even if you never love me back again, he'd thought once. It was still true. He had made his choice a long time ago, and he wouldn't change it, even now.

HE SLEPT ALONE that night, and his dreams were restless.

They had to be careful as they descended into the valley, a steep and zigzagging route that took them gradually downhill. The soil was loose under their feet, soft and powdery and dark gray from the ash mixed into it. The acrid scent of it burned his—*its* nose. Lupa bared its teeth with distaste. Hazel held on to its side for balance, her hand an almost imperceptible pressure on its neck, though she didn't really need the support; she simply took to the air whenever she started to slip, her wings fluttering and her feet lifting an inch or two off the ground.

A small envoy of Gallowglass flanked them. The setting sun brought a lifelike flush to the animal features of their armor, carved scales gleaming, talons on gauntlets and fangs on helmets polished by its fiery light. Below, the sparsely wooded bowl of the valley had been plunged into a dark twilight, but an ominous, reddish light could be glimpsed from the trees.

Aware that its summoner was paying attention, Lupa looked at Hazel so that he could see she was healthy and unharmed, that Lupa had done its job well. They had given her a warm tunic, pants, and boots for the journey. Her silvery eyes were very wide in her pale green face as she looked down into the valley. Ahead of them, the

Autumn Prince led the way, his armor golden and sculpted so close to his frame it appeared almost liquid. He had removed the helmet and left behind his wicker crown. His hair was tied back in a low tail, spilling down the backplate of his armor.

"What do you think?" the Autumn Prince said over his shoulder, as they reached level ground. "Does it feel like summer yet?"

"Not really," Hazel said uneasily. "It feels . . . empty."

"The summertide lord hasn't been seen in over ten years," Prince Senna said. "But this is its territory, and its magic lingers here. Look."

They had reached the forest. The strange light that Lupa had seen before came from *within* the trees. They were long dead, their trunks cracked open, and rivers of flame burned inside them like everlasting torches.

"That the woods still burn is a sign that the summertide lord lives on, but where it has gone, we cannot say," Prince Senna said.

"So this is where we'll do the renewal ceremony?" Hazel asked. "The *place where winter cannot reach us*?"

"Yes. Queen Ceresia was correct; it is never winter in the summertide lord's domain."

"And—what if the summertide lord comes back?"

"You would have nothing to fear," Prince Senna said. "The legends say that it obeys the Summer Court's royal family. That's why Queen Ceresia asked you to accompany us, even though this is only a scouting mission."

They walked through the forest and reached the cliffs on the far side of the valley. A cavern gaped open there, pitch-dark. They lit torches and went inside. The walls glinted as if with embedded minerals. Prince Senna ran the palm of his hand over one of the shimmering spots, brushing aside the dirt and digging something out of the wall. He presented it to Hazel. It was a black scale that must have belonged to something massive; it barely fit in her hand. Lupa nudged it with its nose. It was warm.

"How will we get Vetiver here?" Hazel said. "It's a long trip."

Prince Senna gave a thoughtful hum. "I suppose we might carry him. I believe he can withstand the journey. He is strong. He will have to be, if he is to rule."

Hazel's fingers closed around the scale.

In the morning, Tristan got the text from Aziza, the one he'd been waiting for.

She said: *I found it.*

CHAPTER 22
AZIZA

IF THE OTHER lantern was still in Elphame, Aziza had been sure the pixies would find it. But it was a sandman who tracked it down in the end.

She went to sleep one night and woke up outside a blackened husk of an old mansion house. It was scorched, with deep fissures in the walls where the wood had split and the paint had melted away. The hellebore plants outside had run wild, spreading in patches. Their leaves were open flat like outstretched hands, and their stems were two feet tall, drooping with blooms in every shade of purple from lavender-gray to wine-dark mulberry.

She knew she was dreaming because the sandman stood beside her, tall as a plume of smoke and grave as nightfall.

"From what I have been able to discern, the nearest town is perhaps a mile away," the sandman said, as if in answer to a question she'd asked. "Some of the locals still remember the night this building burned down."

The house burst into flame; Aziza jumped at the sudden roar of the inferno, and the blast of heat and light that rolled over them. The fire surged through the windows and leapt at the sky.

"Others sometimes think of it as it once was, before the catastrophe," the sandman said.

The fire vanished, along with any sign that it had ever happened. The mansion was returned to its former grandeur. All the lights were on, and it was full of people, visible behind the windows. Festive music spilled outside.

"But, to the young ones, it is only the subject of scary stories and nightmares. Especially as of late," the sandman said. The cheerful picture melted away, and the building was a wreck again—silent and disfigured beyond repair. But the light still glowed from inside, as if, despite all evidence to the contrary, someone still lived there.

"Before the equinox," the sandman said, "this dreamscape was always dark."

A black house with purple flowers, just like the one Nelle had described in her vision. It wasn't summertime, but still—Aziza had to go there. She had to check. Just in case.

Lucky could not shadow-travel to it. There were enchantments to obfuscate its location, so that you couldn't find it without being told where it was by someone who already knew. It was similar to the protective spells on the Half Moon Market host sites. Which made sense, considering who the house belonged to. Or used to belong to.

But the dreamers who still remembered told the sandman where it was, in conversations they would forget having by morning, and the sandman told Aziza.

So they took a train out of Massachusetts after class on Thursday, and then a few buses, and then they walked the last couple of miles. This put their arrival time after midnight. Leo and Aziza had told their parents they were going to have a late-night study session at Bishop Library; they would crash there with Tristan and go straight to school in the morning, which was pretty routine for them. They'd be back before anyone missed them.

It was around two a.m. when they hiked up the winding back-country road, watching the ruin from a dozen stolen dreams appear over the crest of a hill. In real life, there was a chain-link fence around it. A placard on the gate said the building was condemned. But, as in the dreams, a light was on inside. It burned through the dark with an incongruous heat, like captive sunlight.

That struck her as odd. It hadn't been hot in the greenhouse.

But Leo could see Castor's magical signature, same as before. And when Tristan sent Lucky inside to check—the lantern wasn't even hidden.

They jumped the fence. The front door had survived the inferno, but the hinges had melted out of shape, and they had to break it down. Inside, parts of the roof had caved in, littering the floor with debris. The furniture was gone, or maybe it had all burned to cinders. The high-ceilinged foyer ended in a wide, curved staircase that no longer looked like it could have supported her weight.

The lantern had been set down at the foot of the stairs, its light reflecting off a puddle of rainwater beneath a gaping hole in the ceiling. And Meryl sat beside it with her arms around her knees. Her head was bowed, her sleek dark hair shading her face.

It didn't feel real. Maybe Aziza was asleep, walking into another dream the sandman had brought her. All the time she'd spent searching for her, wondering if she was all right, practicing her spells until she was too exhausted to do anything but fall into bed fully clothed—and now Meryl was *here*, alive and in one piece.

She flinched when Aziza said her name.

"You shouldn't have come," Meryl said, her voice thin and broken. She had barely finished speaking before Aziza was moving, and Aziza didn't recall making the decision to do it. All she knew was that one moment she was in the threshold with Leo and Tristan, and the next, she was practically sprinting across the dark cavern of the entrance hall and falling to her knees at the base of the stairs, throwing her arms around Meryl. Tendrils of black hair stuck to her cheeks, which were tacky with dried tears where her face pressed against Aziza's neck. Already thin, especially for a selkie, she had, impossibly, lost weight in the time since Aziza had seen her last; Aziza could feel the ridges of her bones through the material of her cardigan.

Meryl's arms came up to return the embrace, though her grip was weak. "You have to leave," she said. When Aziza pulled away to look at her, Meryl's eyes were dark, her pupils huge with fear, the hadal blue-black of her irises reduced to a narrow ring.

"Is he here?" Aziza asked. "Castor."

Meryl shook her head. "He knew you were looking for me. He wanted to see what you'd do if—And I can't let you take the lantern. If you try, I'll have to . . . stop you."

"It's okay," Aziza said. "We'll go."

She glanced at the others, who had hung back—Leo watching the landing at the top of the staircase and the dark doorways that led into the entrance hall, Tristan and Lucky at the front door, making sure they weren't followed.

This was what she'd wanted—to find Castor's lanterns, but especially to find the one in Meryl's care. She hadn't expected it to happen so soon, to be so easy. Meryl's confirmation that Castor had been a step ahead of them the whole time—had maybe even lured them here somehow, to enact his revenge for the destruction of the lantern at Martin College—was almost reassuring. A trap was something she understood.

But what *was* the trap? Not Meryl herself. Something else, then. Something in the house.

She had to end this conversation and get out of here. But first, she had to make sure that she could find Meryl again. Wherever Castor sent her next. She hadn't thought she'd see Meryl today, but she was ready to make the most of it. And so, while they spoke, something crept out from under her jacket sleeve and onto Meryl's collar, unnoticed. It could have flown, and would have if necessary; but this was better. This way, it wouldn't be heard.

"Are you alone?" Aziza asked. "How long have you been here?"

"I can't—" Meryl said, breaking off as if her throat had sealed shut around the words, strangling them. She was fighting against her orders with all her might, but Castor's control over her was complete.

"It's all right," Aziza said. "But I want you to know that I'm not giving up. I'm going to come back for you. No matter where he hides you—I'll find you again."

Meryl squeezed her good hand. The lenses of her glasses were flecked with tears where her eyelashes had brushed them.

"I know that," she said, with a tremulous smile.

She drew back, but Meryl's hand clamped down on hers, holding her in place.

"What is it?" Aziza asked.

Meryl was silent, her mouth opening and no words coming out. Her grip on Aziza's hand was crushing. Before Aziza could make another move, a blaze of light erupted from the front door.

Tristan leapt away from the threshold, flinging an arm over his eyes to shield them. They all reacted before they knew what was happening—Lucky surging forward with a growl like a chainsaw, Leo drawing the frost sword, and Aziza planting herself in front of Meryl. There was a hard impact on her chest, like she'd been shoved; she took a half step back, winded, but didn't fall.

A tall, luminous figure filled the entrance like an avenging angel. As her eyes adjusted to the light—which burned like a flare of sunshine—she saw the bow in the intruder's hands. An arrow was nocked and aimed at them already. It released with a *twang* of the bowstring. Leo dodged, his truesight saving his life as the bolt missed his skull by inches; it whooshed past Aziza's face.

"Viren," he said furiously.

"Your Highness," Viren returned, with a mocking smile. He was unmistakable, even though his spider-fang helmet was gone. He had four eyes, two on each side, like curls of ink against his skin, which was a cadaverous purple-white. One eye had gone cloudy, an effect of the rot. The light that had momentarily blinded them was coming from his armor, which was like sunshine made solid. It was around him and in him, too, that radiance. His face was webbed with gold, running over his skin in branching patterns like a Lichtenberg scar. It started under his collar, covered his neck and jaw, and stretched across his cheek to his clouded fourth eye. It was the light of Castor's sorcery, burning away the jade rot.

She had maybe half a second to take it in before Lucky leapt at Viren, intent on ripping out his throat. Two more hounds had materialized so quickly Aziza didn't see it happen. But they crashed into a wave of smoke, which billowed from the walls. The smoke coalesced into a pack of magical beasts, an easy match for the hounds in size, with rippling manes and wide, fanged mouths—lions, an illusion crafted from soot.

Before she could finish the thought and follow it to the obvious conclusion, a familiar voice rang out behind them.

"Good work. Now come here," Princess Narra said, and Aziza felt Meryl release her hand and move to obey. Aziza turned dizzily to see her—why was she dizzy? Her shirt felt damp, warm, as though she had sweated through it. Strange. It was hot inside this place, but not *that* hot. Princess Narra was hard to look at, so brilliant was the armor that Castor had given her—a matched set with Viren's—but Aziza could make out the curve of her sudden smile as their eyes met.

"Thorne was right," Narra said. "In the end, you were hardly any trouble at all."

"Aziza," Meryl said, her voice choked with tears. She could barely get the words out. "I'm so sorry."

Aziza heard it without comprehending. The dizziness was getting worse, not better. She touched the warm, wet patch on her shirt, and her fingers came away red.

Oh, she thought. That was when she looked down and saw the arrow in her ribs.

It was as if seeing it confirmed to her body that it was real, and she suddenly registered the pain radiating through her chest, making it hard to breathe. She remembered how she'd felt something hit her in the chest earlier—how Meryl had held her still with a look of agony on her face. She wrapped her hand around the arrow where it stuck out of her torso, but didn't pull. Prince Tal's face flashed before her eyes. Was this how it had felt for him, too?

The next few moments were chaos, made even more difficult to parse by the fog that had descended on her mind. She was on her knees with her hand on the shaft of the arrow; she didn't know when her legs had given out. Around her, Tristan's hounds and Narra's lions tore at each other, but in the dark, by the pulsing glow of the lantern—which intensified gradually, like a star drifting nearer—they were like ocean waves crashing over the floor, their silhouettes fluid and changeable, the flash of claws and teeth as distorted as the spots in her vision. Leo was beside her, holding her shoulders, saying, "Zee? Fuck—" And then he was gone and Tristan was there, pulling her to her feet and bracing an arm around her back as he guided her to the door.

She was bleeding out, she realized. Possibly dying.

But she was a witch of borders and boundaries, and no boundary held more power than the one between life and death, where she stood now. She felt her innate magic, the gift she had been born with, dying, too—dying like a star did, an internal collapse triggering an explosive release of energy. She could use it. She had time for maybe one or two more spells, the strongest she'd ever cast.

"My bag—" she croaked, speaking to Tristan, plucking insistently at the fraying bond between them.

"What?" he said, his voice suffused with panic, the bond choked with it. Her backpack slid off her shoulder and touched down on the ground, as if a wind sprite had carried it; the top tore open, burned, as if from the bite of a fire sprite. She reached down with her good hand and what she needed leapt from her bag and into her open palm, a tiny vial containing a ring made of nixie hair, braided and knotted intricately together, waiting to be used in a spell or turned into a charm. The vial opened itself, and her fingers curled around the rim, dripping blood onto the silky black ring inside. She didn't have to come up with a story, not now; the final hour of Prince Tal's life played in her mind with perfect clarity, and she heard her own voice in her memory, telling him the tale she'd used to cast her trap spell. There was no need to say it aloud. She grasped that memory and turned the vial counterclockwise between her fingers as she said, "*Viren, come here.*"

She had lost sight of him in the battle. Locked in combat with the hounds, he moved so swiftly she could not have tracked him even if she'd had all her wits about her. But she didn't need to see him. Her voice was harmonic with borrowed nixie allure, or something like it, and carried across the room. Beside her, Tristan stiffened, throwing an arm protectively in front of her—because Viren had staggered into view, his bow exchanged for a sword that dripped with hound blood, his face slack with confusion.

"Viren," she said. *"Stay."*

He did.

And then the hounds were on him, and he didn't even fight.

CHAPTER 23
LEO

By the time he had gotten to her, she was covered in blood from her ribs to the tops of her thighs. It spilled onto the floorboards and mingled with the ash. She had leaned heavily against him, not responding when he said her name. Leo had moved her hand away from the wound to get a proper look at it. The arrow was lodged between her ribs.

"Get her out of here," he told Tristan, whose hands shook as he took Leo's place. "I'm right behind you."

None of the hounds could get at Princess Narra; her prowling coal-black lions caught them mid-leap and flung them away. Their fur was soft flakes of ash layered together like curling strips of fine paper. Wisps of smoke shook out of their long manes with every motion. Their eyes were red-hot embers.

Some illusions were costumes, and when the amber eye saw through them, it was a little like holding up an envelope to sunlight so that you could faintly read the words inside. Others, like these soot illusions, were more complex; they were more like true creation. He couldn't see the soot. He just knew it was there. Their roars had the timbre of inferno, full of heat and rage. There was something sick about them—something skeletal, thin, and ragged—but even so they were strong as they grappled with the hounds.

Princess Narra advanced on the three of them as Tristan walked Aziza to the door. Viren stood between them and escape, and when he moved to fend off a hound's attack, one of Narra's beasts was always there to take his place, roaring like hellfire. No one was getting out until they dealt with Narra. And there was no time to waste.

"Wait outside," Narra said. Meryl cast one more stricken look toward Aziza before she obeyed, picking up the lantern and retreating to the back hall, her movements stiff, as if she was fighting every step.

Narra laughed her beautiful, chiming laugh as he faced her, his sword held ready. Everywhere the rot had eaten away at her was marked with gold. It wrapped around her, probably concealing wounds where her body had started to putrefy from the inside out. His amber eye could see the blight in Narra's magic, even through the celestial light of Castor's.

"I hear you've had dueling lessons recently, but do remember that *I* was your first teacher." She drew a rapier not unlike the crystal spike he'd once seen her brother wield.

"What are you doing here?" he asked. Would distraction work? Could he buy Tristan and Aziza time to slip out? He gritted his teeth, wanting nothing more than to turn around and see how far they'd gotten, but not daring to take his eyes off Narra.

"Castor sent me. He really should have listened to me months ago, when I warned him the three of you were too dangerous to be left alive," she said. "You destroyed almost a decade's work when you broke the other lantern. You are a problem he can no longer delay solving."

She darted forward, her golden hair flying. Her rapier came

down on him, but she was better with illusions than sword fighting; he blocked, though he was still no expert himself, relying on the sharper reflexes the amber eye granted him. He could see the tiny muscle movements that told him how she'd strike next. Their swords clashed once, twice, a ringing sound; then a hound was knocking her away, but before she'd finished hitting the ground, she was spearing it through the stomach and heaving it off her.

She was back on her feet in a flash and lunging at Leo again. He parried; and then she *screamed*, as if he had struck her, and for a confused moment he thought maybe he had—but she wasn't looking at him. Her gaze was directed over his shoulder, at the door. Heart pounding, he chanced a look backward and saw Aziza and Tristan—and Viren, or what was left of him. Lucky was ripping out a chunk of his throat, jaws dripping with gore; two of the other hounds had torn pieces off him. As Narra's lions converged on them, wild with vengeance, their teeth elongating and sparks flying from the ends of their manes, Tristan half pulled, half carried Aziza away. Cornered, they fled up the stairs.

Narra lunged, going after them, and Leo didn't hesitate. He swung the sword wildly and with all his might, and felt it connect with sick satisfaction. It severed her arm at the elbow. The limb fell, her crystal sword with it.

She gave a howl that sounded more like rage than pain. Behind him, the slam of heavy paws striking the floor was his only warning before the soot lions descended on him. Lucky intercepted the first; Leo was ready for the second one, thrusting his sword between its eyes. Steam erupted from the place where the frozen blade met the illusion's terrible heat, and he turned his face away from the blast as he wrenched his sword free. The others were disintegrating as Narra fell to her knees, cradling the bleeding stump of her arm. Her eyes were wide and filled with hate as she looked up at him. He kicked the rapier away for good measure.

He could kill her right now. Aziza's blood was on the ground just there; he only had to look at it to know that whatever he did next would be justified.

"Just get out," he told Narra roughly.

"Mercy?" she sneered. "You'll come to regret that."

He was already regretting it as she staggered to her feet and ran, following Meryl. Her lions dissolved into smoke, one by one. As the battle ceased, a deafening silence took its place. His ears rang with it.

"Zee? Tris?" he shouted, taking the dilapidated stairs three at a time, still clutching the sword, which dripped gray-tinged water. If they threw caution to the wind, put Aziza with Tristan on the back of a hound, and let it tear into that town they'd passed earlier, they could get to a hospital in time, and everything would be fine.

It didn't take long to find them; they had stopped halfway down the upstairs hall. Aziza sat against the wall with her hand on the place where the arrow protruded from her chest, Tristan kneeling in front of her, saying, "It's over—We can go back now—Aziza, can you hear me?"

A witch's magic was a kind of glow, Aziza's and Tristan's similar but different in a way Leo couldn't express in words. The greatest difference between them just now was that Tristan's was bright, and Aziza's was swiftly fading.

No, Leo thought. *This isn't happening.*

The hall ended in a darkness so complete it seemed to go on for miles, like a mine shaft. There, in the shadows, something moved. He thought at first it was one of Tristan's hounds; then he feared he'd been followed by Narra's soot illusions, that she had pretended to leave only to chase them up here. But as he focused on the slow, erratic movement with his amber eye and deciphered its meaning, he knew this was no illusion. It was real.

"Tris, watch out!" he said, and ran toward him, as fast as he had ever run in his entire life.

Tristan shot to his feet as flames surged, swallowing the end of the hallway. In the middle of it was a dark shape like the eye of a firestorm. The house wasn't on fire—that thing was. It uncoiled, slithered up the walls and through gaps in the ceiling, into the third floor and back down to the second, sewing its burning body through the upper stories of the house. Tristan hauled Aziza to her feet, though she made a noise of pain as the motion jolted the arrow in her chest. They weren't going to be fast enough to get away. Leo planted himself between them and the thing slithering in their direction, bringing the inferno with it, its gaping maw almost spanning the width of the hallway. It struck at him open-mouthed as if it meant to swallow him, but he twisted aside and stabbed—and his aim was true. His blade sank into a great reptilian eye, with a gush of steam and a sharp crack, ice fracturing, as the weapon was engulfed by its sudden immense heat.

The serpent thrashed, the blade breaking off in its eye like a splinter and leaving him holding the hilt and a few inches of jagged ice. Its huge body wound away in coils that seemed endless. The flames coming off its dark scales caught onto the rotted old walls and began to spread. Leo's hand was burned where it had brushed against its scales, an agony of blistered red skin. Smoke filled the air, making him choke.

"Don't—" Tristan said; but he wasn't talking to Leo.

Aziza had pulled away from him, stepped past Leo, wobbling but upright. Her hair hung down her shoulders, the ends damp with blood. The color had drained from her face, but her eyes had regained some clarity. The serpent was retreating, sliding away, but the fire was only spreading farther. Aziza followed the serpent, heedless of the growing inferno.

Something creaked overhead. This house had taken far too much abuse. Leo had just enough time to push Tristan forcefully away before, with a groan, the smoldering ceiling came down, and pain erupted across Leo's skull, and then there wasn't anything else.

CHAPTER 24

AZIZA

SHE'D LOST HER backpack somewhere downstairs, but Viren had generously provided all she needed for a final spell. The shaft of the arrow was birch, the fletching made of black feathers. She broke the end off, ignoring the way it made the rest of the arrow jolt in her chest and send fresh waves of pain through her. Her hand was soaked in blood and the end of the arrow was, too, where drops of it had trickled down the shaft. As she followed the salamander into the blazing hallway and waves of heat rolled over her, she let the arrow's tail graze the wall and catch fire.

She had already tried to get its attention by reaching out with her own magic, a thread of it that she might have woven into the boundary, something meant to synchronize with what was already there. But the salamander was too angry. It had been so angry, for so long, that Aziza felt it, too, and it hurt like needles stabbed under her fingernails or boiling water poured down her throat—a kind of pain that bypassed your defenses and tore you apart from inside.

So she whispered the words of a sleeping spell—a meandering story about a dream she'd had once, with a door to a lamplit study and lessons in trap spells and watchful red-haired ghosts. It helped, a little, that she was also feeling kind of sleepy. It would be nice to sit back down against the wall and close her eyes for a little.

The arrow was nothing but a lump of coal by now, and she dropped it before it could burn her hand. Around her, the sounds of slithering and thrashing ceased. A reptilian head armored in black scales rested in the middle of the floor, the coils of its body vanishing down the hall. Its slitted eye was level with her face, Leo's sword sticking out of it. But it was nearly unconscious now, and only hissed when she slid the broken blade free—the edges cutting into her palm—and let it drop.

Its good eye rolled in her direction as the flames died. The salamander was like the undine they'd met once—an ancient fire elemental, made of living ember and coal, like something that had squirmed out of a crack in the earth's core. The pattern of its black scales was limned in the pulsing red-gold light of an inner burning. Everything it touched burned, too. It must have been trapped here. There were no boundaries nearby for it to escape through and return to Elphame. No wonder it was angry, gnawing away at what was left of this dead place.

Narra had known it was here. She had used her conjured lions to herd Aziza and Tristan toward the stairs. Maybe she had been the one to bring it here in the first place. It couldn't—wouldn't—have come on its own.

She'd found what had really killed the Legrand family. She wished she could tell Dion.

"Sleep now," Aziza said. "I'm sorry I can't send you home. If I could come back for you, I would."

As her spell took, the salamander slipped into a deep and peaceful sleep, dissolving in a rain of powder-fine black sediment. In rest, it looked like a pattern of ash, a streak of soot, ripples of scale etched into the wooden boards and winding over the walls and ceiling. She bent and touched it; it was still warm.

Satisfied, she staggered back down the hall to where Tristan knelt, clutching Leo to his chest. Blood trickled down Leo's face from under his hair, and his eyes were shut.

CHAPTER 25
TRISTAN

Aziza braced herself against the wall and slid down beside them. The serpent was gone, and the flames had gone with it, but the house groaned around them, destabilized by the ordeal. Some of the ceiling had fallen down, exposing an upstairs hall. He'd had to drag Leo out of the debris. Everything was still too hot; he was sweating under his clothes, and his throat and lungs felt raw from all the smoke he'd inhaled.

"Leo," he whispered, squeezing his arms tightly around his shoulders. His head lolled. "Come on. Wake up. We have to get out of here."

Aziza touched the back of Tristan's hand, her fingers bloody.

"The hounds can get you out," she said, her voice ragged. She coughed into her arm; when she lowered it, her lips were bloody. "You can get help. Go to Anne. Or . . . Dion."

She didn't mean that, about him getting help. She just wanted him to leave so that he'd be safe. But he couldn't leave until Leo woke up. He touched his messy brown hair, his freckled cheek, unable to grasp what was happening. His Leo, the warmest person he knew, growing cold in Tristan's useless hands.

"Go," she said, very gently. She sent a wave of soothing emotion through the bond. "I'll wait here with him until you come back."

"Stop." He pried one hand off Leo to clutch at hers. His chest burned as if he had been struck by an arrow himself.

Leo wasn't breathing. Rationally, he knew this. But he still felt an unshakable certainty that Leo would wake up if he just waited here long enough. It was the only fathomable outcome. The last few minutes played on repeat in his mind; he thought they might forever. As long as he didn't move past this moment, he would never have to accept it.

Aziza's head nodded like she couldn't keep it upright, as if she was tired at the end of an afternoon study session and now she was dozing off over their table in the library. She slumped against the wall, pulling their connected hands with her, though it was really only Tristan still holding on. Her grip was weak. Through the bond, he felt her fading. The pain in his chest mounted, until he felt like he was being crushed by its weight, his body unable to carry it.

"It's . . . going to . . . be okay," she said haltingly. "Please . . . go."

"I can't leave," he said. "I can't. I *can't*."

"I wouldn't . . . ask if I . . . didn't know . . . that you could."

She had to catch her breath between every other word. Her eyelashes fluttered as she fought to stay awake.

"Don't say that. I can fix this," he told her.

It was why he had been looking for Emil's grimoire. He could still find it. He'd go and find it right now. Or he'd find another grimoire with the spell he needed.

But he couldn't do it—He couldn't bring himself to leave yet—He couldn't *move*—

"Aziza, please," he said. He released her long enough to set Leo down next to her—just the way he would nudge Leo off his shoulder and back onto his pillow when he wanted to get out of bed without waking him. He shuffled closer to Aziza on his knees and took her hand again, clinging hard, in a grotesque reprise of the way they had clasped hands when she had taken over the hag's bond. "I need you to hold on. I—I don't think I can do the next part alone."

Her eyes were open, but she didn't say anything.

Something was building in him; he'd thought it was a scream. Something *burned*, but he'd thought it was the smoke. The pain radiated in his chest, in his skull. It intensified so vividly he couldn't believe it was coming from inside him; it felt like the nerve endings were being flensed from his skin.

He'd felt something like this only once before—once, when the hag had died. Through the agony, understanding dawned on him. The hag's contract had a trap built into it—something that made it so that if the hag died, Tristan would have died, too. She could dispose of him anytime she wanted, but he couldn't abandon her and survive. That was the whole reason Aziza had to take up the bond in the first place, to save him.

When she'd done that, slotting herself into the hag's end of the bond, she had remade it as a bond of equals. And they had both assumed that the worst of the hag's magic was gone from it. But they had been wrong. The bond tied their fates together.

So his nightmares had been true all along: His freedom was an illusion. He had never really escaped the hag.

I can't. I can't yet, Tristan thought desperately. Everything in him resisted what he knew, deep down, to be inevitable. He had to survive so he could fix this. Undo it. Set it right. He was the only one who could.

He gasped for air; his vision went black around the edges. The bond was dragging him after Aziza, incinerating him from the inside out, and he was slipping beneath the surface of a darkness vaster than the deepest of shadows—

He held on with every last drop of willpower in him.

Despite everything, he *wanted* to live.

But there was no fighting this. It was the hag's final punishment, but it felt bigger than her—it felt cosmic, a divine wrath falling upon him. As certain as the stroke of midnight and as irreversible as history already come to pass, the bond death he had always been destined for—

—finally caught up with him.

CHAPTER 26

LUCKY

IT HAD BEEN sitting in the empty house for most of the day, but it was patient. The passage of time meant nothing to its kind. It—he—*it* was good at waiting.

When the lock clicked, it stood with a languid stretch. The witch crossed over the threshold and, seeing Lucky, froze. Then he shut the door and cautiously approached. He smelled of chalk, smoke, ink, and the cleansing substances humans used—soap and antiperspirant and laundry detergent.

Lucky couldn't go to him until he was alone. Its summoner had long ago commanded Lucky to conceal itself from most humans, all but a select few. Although its summoner had perished, Lucky was still driven to obedience.

"Tristan?" The witch looked around for Lucky's summoner and then, not finding him, turned back to Lucky. "Did he send you?"

Lucky understood the inquisitive tone in his voice, but had neither the inclination nor the means to respond.

"Are they in trouble?"

Its tail swished idly over the floor. It couldn't remember why it had come here, except that it wanted something from this human.

Or perhaps its summoner had wanted something. But as for what that was, such knowledge was beyond Lucky's grasp.

The witch consulted his phone as he climbed the stairs, Lucky following, its claws clicking on the floor. He went down the hall and entered the study where Lucky had brought its summoner many times.

"Anne says Aziza and Leo never came home after class. Bishop Library is closed and there's no sign of Tristan. She's searching for them," he murmured. He unlocked the door behind the bookcase and took the stairs down in a hurry. Moments later, he returned. He stood in front of Lucky and looked intently into its face. "Something is wrong. Come on, hound. You need something from me, right? Something for your summoner? Can you show me where he went?"

A thought stirred within Lucky. An image: that smoke-filled place where its summoner lay, and the big snake that was too hot for Lucky to eat, burning its mouth when it had tried biting into its scales. It wasn't a hound thought, because hound thoughts were never images. Lucky had never been able to *see* what wasn't in front of it.

It had investigated the bodies before it left, nudging its summoner experimentally with its snout. He was certainly dead. Their bond was broken, and Lucky was untethered. Already its packmates had scattered; it did not seem as if their summoner's commands had lingered in their minds. Yet his will still guided Lucky.

Dion's phone rang. He glanced at the screen and quickly answered.

"Nelle? Yes, I just heard from Anne." He paused to listen. His eyes flicked warily toward Lucky as he responded, "No, I haven't seen them. Did you try—"

He stopped talking. His face slowly drained of color. Lucky

sniffed at the air and pricked an ear. The potent smell of his fear made Lucky salivate.

"I have no idea," Dion said, and then, "Yes," and then, "Of course. I will."

He hung up and looked at Lucky.

"Nelle has been scrying for them," he said. "She saw a black building with purple flowers outside. She said she saw it in a vision about Meryl, too. Is that really where they are?"

Lucky was silent.

"The spells that shield its location are interfering with her visions, of course. She'll never be able to pin it down," Dion said, calm in spite of the galloping heartbeat that Lucky could hear. He shut the door to the study and took out a nub of chalk, which he used to write all over its surface, the lines of his script clean even though his hands shook. "He was right to send you to me. If they're in trouble, I can get there the fastest."

He used a match to set the door on fire. When the flames went out, he flung it open. Now it led to the burned place. There was another body there, not far from the door; it was the fairy that Lucky and its packmates had killed. So rare for their summoner to let them kill anything but animals. They had relished it. Dion paused with horror to study the fairy's remains. Lucky followed him as he ventured deeper into the ruins, fists clenched at his sides and trembling faintly.

"Tristan? Leo?" he called, and then coughed into his sleeve. The smell of blood lingered, but it was probably too faint for a human to detect under the much stronger scent of smoke. He hesitated before calling out one more time. "Aziza?"

Lucky nudged him toward the stairs. Dion glanced at Lucky with a wild look, the whites of his eyes gleaming in the paltry light. It nudged him again, growing impatient. Finally, he moved, taking the steps at a run.

Lucky's summoner was where it had left him, next to the other two bodies. Insects buzzed nearby, creeping toward the stench of death, but none had approached the corpses yet; living things didn't like the smell of a summoner. Lucky bared its teeth at the sight as if to ward it off. Something hurt, but it wasn't hunger, nor did it stem from a wound. It was like the snake thought from before, inside of Lucky but not belonging to it.

Perplexingly, as soon as Dion saw the bodies, he stopped.

"Aziza," he said. He walked forward, step by step, and finally dropped to his knees before the bodies. He reached for her, saying quietly, "No, no, no—"

He picked up her wrist, pressing his fingers searchingly into the skin, and then touched the other two bodies the same way. Then he bent close, in a gesture which Lucky, after a moment of study, interpreted to mean he was listening for their breathing. This was foolish, as they were unmistakably dead. But this witch wasn't a summoner. Maybe he couldn't tell.

Lucky's tail flicked, making brushstrokes over the sooty floor. The impulse that had brought it to Dion hadn't been satisfied yet. There was something else, still. But it didn't know what. It—he—*it* waited for Dion to stand up again. He sat on his knees for a long time, his fingers still curled around the gatewalker's wrist. His face was wet—a faint sheen on his skin, the smell of salt.

Lucky prowled closer to him and bit delicately at the elbow of his sleeve.

"Leave me alone," Dion snapped, without looking up. His voice was ragged, almost a growl.

Lucky growled back and was ignored.

But Lucky had no commands to follow, and it still wasn't hungry, so there was no need to hunt. And so it stayed, too. It . . . He . . . ? *It* was good at waiting.

LATER, DION WAS in the study again. He'd had something to drink from a clear bottle and was slumped in the chair behind the desk, head tipped back, eyes glassy. He reeked of whatever was in the bottle; Lucky did not care for it.

"I can't do this," he mumbled. "Castor always wins."

The phone in Dion's pocket vibrated until he threw it across the room, hard. Then it stopped.

MUCH LATER, THE sun had risen and the acrid scent from the bottle had worn off. Dion circled the study wrathfully, like a caged lion working itself into a frenzy.

"Of course she's dead!" he ranted. "I told her to be careful. I *told* her to stay out of Castor's way. She doesn't listen to a damn thing anyone tells her. Died of stubbornness. Died of always having to be right! I can't *stand* her! Why does she have to be so—"

The window shattered. The door to the study blew off its hinges. Books went flying as if swept from their shelves by a violent wind. Dion did not appear to notice.

STILL LATER, DION had fallen asleep at the desk. Lucky watched the shadows slink across the room as the sun set. It grew restless. Why had its summoner wanted it to come here? How did Lucky know what its summoner wanted, when he was not alive to give it commands?

Such questions were not for hounds to ask. Such thoughts were not hound thoughts.

Perhaps Lucky was meant to search in the shadows the way it had done before. He had wanted a book that smelled of summoner magic. Lucky had thoroughly explored all of the shadows in this house. But it would check one last time.

DION HAD ACQUIRED another bottle and was a third of the way through it. It stood at his elbow as he drowsed with his head resting on his folded arms.

"How are you still here?" he asked Lucky. "Tristan is dead. Don't you get it? You can go."

A long silence.

Dion sat bolt upright.

"How *are* you here? You should be feral." He scrubbed a hand over his eyes. Thinking seemed to require an enormous effort. "He *is* dead, isn't he? I *checked*. Unless . . ."

He pushed himself out of his seat and warily approached Lucky. When Lucky gave no reaction other than to look back at him, he reached for its face, holding its snout between his hands, as if he could peer through its eyes and inside its skull. Lucky allowed this, though it did not know why. It—he—*it* only tolerated being touched when its summoner wanted it to.

"Hound possession," Dion muttered under his breath. "Good lord."

Lucky grumbled discontentedly. That unsettled feeling in his stomach had come back. Maybe it was hunger after all, and he should hunt, even if he didn't feel like it.

"You didn't use a spell. Must have botched it," Dion said, releasing Lucky and standing back. He ran both hands through his hair, breathing fast. "You're mostly hound at the moment."

He left the room, but returned shortly with a glass of water and a couple of small white tablets, which he consumed.

"Okay," he said. "You possessed your hound. You came to me. You . . . need something from me. But what?"

Lucky sat on its haunches, comprehending none of this. Those thoughts that weren't hound thoughts and feelings that weren't hunger had left it confused and disoriented. He—*it* wanted to retreat into the shadows. It wanted to bite at its own skin as if it itched. It wanted to go after its former packmates, and hunt with them, or fight them, or possibly devour them. But it remained in the study where Dion paced back and forth, muttering to himself.

"You must have done it by accident. If you came here because you need help undoing it, you might be stuck for a while. You don't have a body to go back to, so the only way out is to destroy the hound you've possessed so that you can . . . move on." He stopped walking, a hand over his mouth as if he didn't want to hear his own words. When he spoke again, his voice was unsteady. "I haven't . . . I haven't told anyone what happened to you yet. I have to tell . . . Anne, Nelle. Your families."

At this, Lucky growled.

"Don't tell?" Dion said. "All right, fine. I'll figure out a way to communicate with you. And I won't do anything until then. God, how much of you is even left?"

He pressed the heels of his hands into his eyes and took several shaky breaths.

"I should have—I knew she wasn't going to leave it alone, and I still—And I can't go back and fix that now. But I won't leave you like this. I promise."

LUCKY FOLLOWED A pull like the one that had sent it to Dion and shadow-traveled without thinking about it, almost unintentionally. It did not manifest its true form, but remained in the shadow plane, allowing one eye to surface disembodied in a dark corner.

Its eye beheld a small room lit by a fireplace. The room was occupied by two men, one of them the white-haired witch that Lucky's summoner had loathed.

Lucky's summoner was there, too.

He was an apparition—a glimmer of light and air that faintly resembled a person—and Lucky couldn't smell summoner magic on it. It didn't smell like anything. But it could . . . sense him, and a flutter of the bond that Lucky had thought eradicated.

"This confirms it," the elder witch said. "I couldn't summon his spirit if he weren't dead. Shall I retrieve the bodies?"

"No," the other man said. "Disposing of them will be more trouble than leaving them there. They won't be found. And even if they are, it won't matter."

As the spirit wavered in the air, hazy, Lucky's vision wavered, too. The white-haired summoner's thrall was like a collar around the spirit's neck, eradicating its will, its self. Lucky could see the faces of the two witches as if it stood in front of them, and he could also see the backs of their chairs from the dark one-eyed corner where the rest of him lurked, and—

Overwhelmed and confused, his mouth suddenly tasting of ash, Lucky could do nothing but flee.

DION SCOURED THE room and finally found his phone behind a potted plant, swearing under his breath as he inspected the damage. He had showered and changed. While his eyes were still bloodshot and his face sallow, he no longer looked like someone who had spent much of the last day crumpled in a heap over the desk.

"I have to behave normally. Stick to my routine. He'll notice if I don't," he told Lucky. "Just stay here until I come back."

Lucky only took orders from its summoner. But the strange new impulses that had plagued Lucky since its summoner's death came from someplace deep inside of it, and felt like instinct. They compelled Lucky to obey. So Lucky stayed.

DION HAD BROUGHT a stack of grimoires upstairs and was paging through them.

"I assume these are the ones you were studying last. You'd set them aside," Dion said. "I can only read the Latin ones. Translating the others will take a while."

He gave Lucky an assessing look. Then he uncapped a pen and held it out. "Couldn't you—hold this between your teeth and write me a note? Or something?"

Lucky sniffed his outstretched hand.

"No? Right," Dion said, sitting back. "I guess you would have found a way to speak to me already if you were that . . . lucid."

Lucky stood and came closer, sniffing at his hair and collar.

"What?" Dion leaned away, perturbed.

As Lucky spent more time in Dion's company, it had learned the complexities of his scent, the nuances that made it uniquely his own. But there was something familiar in it. Something that shouldn't have been there. Lucky pressed its nose into Dion's collar. Summoner magic. Dion leaned back farther, but Lucky followed. The scent wasn't coming from his body. It was coming . . . from his shadow.

Lucky chased that scent into the dark. Dion called after it—called it by its summoner's name, as he had been doing the entire time—but his voice became muffled as Lucky dove deeper into the shadow plane. It flowed through the cool nothingness the way a snake flowed through water, buoyant and free. The summoner-scent was nestled among layers of shadow like a pearl; it pulled the scent into itself and slithered back to the surface, and when it emerged, it had a grimoire clutched between its teeth.

Dion gasped and reached out to take it reverently into his hands.

"This—this is Emil's," he said, hushed. "The one I couldn't find. He left it with *me*."

Lucky poked its snout over Dion's shoulder as he leafed through the book.

"While I'm glad to see this again, I don't know what you want me to do with it," Dion said. "Even if there's a hound possession spell in here, I'm not sure we *can* fix an incomplete possession without starting over. And I certainly can't perform necromancy."

Lucky growled almost directly into his ear. This was not intended as a threat, and Dion, not an easily frightened sort of human, did not take it as one.

"Fine, so there's something else," Dion said, still flipping slowly through the grimoire.

Suddenly, and without consciously deciding to do it, Lucky thrust its nose at the page before Dion could turn it. Lucky was as startled by this move as Dion was. But Dion quickly rallied.

"Here?" he said. "This page? This is what you want?"

The answer to this question was yes. Lucky could not tell him so, but Dion proceeded as if he had heard.

"Whatever this spell is, it's long," he muttered, turning the pages while using his finger to mark the one Lucky found so compelling. "It just goes on and on. It's at least a quarter of the book, this one spell. Give me a minute—I have to translate the title."

Soon, he was holding the grimoire in his lap while he tapped at a computer. He inhaled sharply.

"*This* is what you . . ." He stared aghast at Lucky for a long moment. "That's corruptive magic of the most dangerous kind. Do you know what could happen to you if you do this?"

These protests meant nothing to Lucky, not even to the part of Lucky that truly comprehended them. The part of Lucky that had grown more and more insistent as the days passed—but which was now oddly subdued.

Quietly, and with a sort of dread, Dion asked: "All three of you?"

Lucky growled. He . . . it? . . . *He* was offended that Dion even had to ask.

"Right. Then I guess I had better get started," Dion said.

IT TOOK DION weeks to translate the whole spell. He left during the day and spent most of his nights in the study, periodically emptying it of coffee mugs and take-out containers. Lucky's desire to hunt had not returned. Feeling the absence of its summoner and its packmates acutely, Lucky preferred it when Dion was present. When Lucky was alone, it often retreated into the shadows, where it was less likely to . . . *think*.

But Dion proved frustrating in his own way. When he wasn't absorbed in the grimoire, he talked to Lucky as if Lucky could understand. And the more Dion talked, the more Lucky *could* understand.

"I went back to the house and renewed some of the old protective enchantments," Dion said. "Added some new ones, too. Nothing is going to touch the . . . the . . . nothing is going to touch the three of you. Scavengers, or anything. There will still be some . . . decomposition . . ."

He closed his eyes, breathing slowly, as if suddenly dizzy. After a moment, he bent over his work again, with an air of determination.

"There will be some decay, but I've done what I can to slow it down. Of course, if this spell works properly, all of that can be reversed," Dion said. "Anne asked me if I knew anything. I told her I didn't. But she must suspect the truth, because there's been news of feral blækhounds popping up all over the place. Yours, I presume. Every master necromancer in the country has been working to capture and unmake them, but I hear they're having trouble."

He waited as if to see whether Lucky would react to this, even though Lucky never reacted to anything he said. The news came as no surprise. Before their summoner had died, they had been allowed to kill something larger than a deer for the first time in months. That fairy knight, with the armor that crunched between Lucky's teeth and the sour taint of disease in his blood. They had wanted more. And Lucky's summoner was not there to stop them.

"I searched your pockets, and you weren't even carrying your phone when you died," he went on, managing to sound both indignant and queasy. "I ended up breaking into your apartment to look for it. Sorry," he added, without remorse. "You keep getting texts from someone called Jun. He's worried. I don't know what to tell him."

He glanced at Lucky, who had no suggestions to offer.

"Nelle is filling in for you at Bishop Library, by the way. She's still having visions about my . . . about the place where you . . ." He shook his head and gave up on finishing that sentence. "But she doesn't know that she's looking at the old Legrand house. If she figures it out, I might have to tell her what we're doing. As for your families, they . . . I only know what Nelle's told me. They are, obviously, beside themselves with worry."

Memories that weren't hound memories. Thoughts that weren't hound thoughts. It ignored them as best it could, but when Dion was gone, it was harder.

It was still linked to its former packmates, but their connection had been stretched almost beyond its limits, until all that remained was the thinnest membrane of awareness clinging to the edge of Lucky's consciousness. It ignored that, too.

Until it couldn't.

It was late in the night, and Dion was asleep. Lucky usually spent those hours prowling the house. He—*it* knew these shadows, knew their canyons of darkness and their crevices, and knew when anything, even an insect, moved through them. Now he caught a scent that did not belong here: the earthy, sweet smell of fairy magic. He spun in the middle of the upstairs hall, trying to identify which direction it had come from, and then he understood that the scent wasn't *here*. It had come from one of his packmates.

Suddenly he knew he had to *go*.

Go. Right now. GO!

It dove into the shadows, knowing where it needed to be in the same way that it had known to find Dion. It emerged into a cold and cavernous place. In the middle of the room stood a long table, a throne, and a gathering of fairies, some in armor and others in soft and vibrant finery. None of them noticed Lucky as it hid behind a pillar. Lupa was there, too, not hidden—and surrounded by a ring of warriors with weapons drawn. It was growling incessantly. Its eyes were locked on the smallest of the fairies.

"Lupa!" Hazel was saying. "Where have you been? What happened?"

"Stay back, Princess," one of the warriors said. He nodded at one of the others, an archer, who nocked an arrow and drew it back.

Hazel waved them away frantically. "Don't! You can't!"

The moment she took her eyes off of Lupa, the hound pounced. But Lucky did, too, diving into the shadows, emerging behind Lupa a fraction of a second later, and leaping onto its back. Then they were tearing into each other. There was an uproar around them, screams and wingbeats and footsteps. Lupa rolled them over, clawing at Lucky's chest, but Lucky snapped up at its throat, grazing its skin and tasting blood. Twisting, Lupa pulled away, but Lucky followed, refusing to let the other hound get its bearings. Lupa caught Lucky's left foreleg in its jaws, shattering the joint; but Lucky gouged out its eye with a swipe of his claws. When it vanished into the shadows, Lucky followed; he could feel the way the other hound moved, a rise and fall like when an object passed in front of a torch and interrupted its light with a wave of darkness. An oscillation. Lucky tracked the movement and reappeared almost exactly where Lupa did. Lupa lunged again, but this time, Lucky came out on top. He tore into Lupa's chest with teeth and claws until he had dug out Lupa's heart and swallowed it.

Breathing hard over Lupa's broken-open carcass, Lucky became conscious again of being observed. Back hunched, head low, he peered at Hazel over his shoulder. Her hands were clapped over her mouth in horror.

Lupa's body twitched, already healing. As its flesh knitted back together and its bones snapped into place, it looked balefully up at Lucky and fled. It would not return. Lucky had made his point. His tongue flicked out, lapping up the blood on his snout. Approaching footsteps made his hackles rise until he caught Hazel's scent again.

"What just happened?" she asked, in a small, shivery voice. "Why did Lupa do that?"

Lucky watched her in silence.

She glanced down at the scars on his belly. "You're Lucky. Did Tristan send you?"

Lucky sat up straighter, pleased to finally be addressed by its name.

"But why did Lupa do that?" Hazel said quietly. "It's never tried to hurt me before. Tris would never let it . . ."

Another fairy appeared behind Hazel. This one was very tall, and very pale, and her scent was so crisp and sharp and dry that Lucky's fur stood on end, a chill running from its ears to the tip of its tail.

"I hope there is a good reason for this disturbance," the frost fairy said.

Hazel's eyes were filling slowly with tears. "Something's wrong."

ALL THE WOUNDS from its fight with Lupa had healed as cleanly as ever, but still it hurt, constantly. Its chest, and its stomach, and its head. Even its name, *Lucky*, had become like an ill-fitting collar, something it wanted to scratch at. Dion addressed it by its summoner's name, and that was even worse.

Thoughts that weren't hound thoughts and didn't belong in hound skulls rattled around inside and made it want to howl. It couldn't sleep to escape them, because hounds didn't sleep; and it missed being able to sleep, but hounds didn't miss things, either, let alone things they had never known. Hounds didn't dread or grieve or yearn or regret. Those were for summoners, and sometimes for spirits. Lucky shouldn't even have known the words for those feelings. He saw the bodies in the burned house every time he closed his eyes, and even when he flattened himself into a shadow and should have been able to see nothing at all. He saw Leo push him out of the way of the crumbling ceiling, protecting him until the very end. And when Aziza had walked through fire to calm the serpent and had still found the strength to stagger back to his side after, to lie to him in the hopes that she could spare him what would happen next. Rain on a windshield and a bestiary filling up with two different sets of handwriting. How Aziza had given him the next nine years of her life and how Leo had brought him back home. And now it was over. And he understood it no better as a hound than he had as a human. He couldn't move past it.

The pain built inside him like boiling water, pressure with nowhere to go, seething endlessly and eating him away to nothing.

Jun stopped dead in the doorway when Dion led him into the study, where Lucky sprawled on the floor in front of the desk, gnawing listlessly at half of a deer carcass. Lucky had resumed hunting mainly out of boredom. Burying his teeth in the warm, wet hide of a felled deer was an effective distraction from the thoughts he couldn't shake. Now there was not much left but bone. He sharpened his teeth on it.

"Are you *sure* that's Tristan?" Jun was saying, hiding behind Dion and studying the hound from over his shoulder. "Couldn't it just be a weirdly tame blækhound?"

"No. I'm not sure," Dion said. "I might be losing my mind."

The ensuing silence was broken only by the scratch of Lucky's fangs as he dug for marrow.

"It's not that I don't want to help," Jun said uncomfortably. "But this is . . . so, so taboo. Even if I'm only a go-between and not the one actually . . ." He made a vague gesture at Dion's head. "You will have no autonomy whatsoever. You may have some level of awareness about what's happening, but you'll be a prisoner in your own mind. And if you want out—too bad. I won't have a say. Once it takes, it won't be over until he lets you go. And if you're *wrong*, and Tristan's not in there—I don't even know what—"

A flash of blue swung at Jun's ears—feathers—which Lucky's eyes followed with great interest. The fluttery little movement made Lucky's mouth water. It was like a taunt. He wanted to pounce on it. It was satisfying to rip apart squirming things.

No, something inside the hound said.

Lucky bared his teeth, growling resentfully. At this, Jun ducked behind Dion again.

"I'm willing to take the risk," Dion said. "Neither of us can perform this spell. We need a necromancer, and he's our only option."

They both looked at the hound.

"I'm only doing this because I owe him," Jun said. "One good turn, and all."

"Now?" Dion asked.

"Now?" Jun parroted. "Well, I . . . I mean . . . don't you need to, I don't know, mentally prepare yourself or get your affairs in order or—"

"I did that *before* I called you."

"Ah. Well," Jun said, wilting. "In that case, I guess . . . there's no need to delay."

He and Dion sat across from each other. Jun had set a votive candle by his knee, burning with a tall yellow flame, and a grimoire open in his lap. He was reading and rereading a passage, his finger moving down the page as he mouthed the words to himself.

"You don't look well," Dion said. "If you're ill, we can postpone this."

"No, I'm fine. Just a little behind on sleep lately," he muttered.

"In that case, get on with it, please," Dion said.

"This is a *little* more complicated than a paper snake," Jun said. "Forgive me if I need a few minutes to psyche myself up." He sighed, fiddling with the corner of the page he had been studying. "I borrowed the family grimoire. It's written in Baekje. I'm . . . a *little* rusty . . . but it should be fine."

"I believe in you," Dion said, in a monotone.

"Great," Jun said under his breath. He cleared his throat and started to read aloud.

Lucky's ears pricked as he listened. And then he felt, amazingly, that the pain that had replaced everything else inside him—his hunger, his drive to hunt, his defiance, his name—had finally begun to fade. He felt weightless. The ground dropped away, but it was a gentle separation, like when you picked apart two pages in a book that were stuck together. He couldn't see, hear, or smell anything, but that didn't bother him, because fear didn't exist in this place, wherever or whatever it was. There was a light; he knew it was there without having to see it, and it guided him. He was a shadow. He was a ghost. He was tethered, and he followed the line of it, a bright yellow strand of magic. It wasn't a bond he knew, but it *was* a bond, and he took hold of it and it pulled him in.

And the world came slamming down on him.

CHAPTER 27
TRISTAN

HE WOKE UP on the floor. He must have dozed off studying Old Norse again. His head was pounding, his mouth dry, and his muscles stiff and weak. It was as if he had been sick for a long time, drifting in and out of muddled dreams, and the fever had only just broken.

"Tristan?" someone said.

He opened his eyes. Jun leaned over him. Lucky was beside them with its head up and ears perked, watching him with rapt attention.

"What are you doing here?" Tristan mumbled, and then he frowned. His voice sounded strange—too deep—and sitting up only made him more disoriented. His shoulders were too broad, and his hands—

Looking down at them, his stomach flipped. His scars were gone, and his fingers were dusted with chalk. A smattering of dark hair disappeared into the cuffs of his shirt. Those weren't his hands.

"Did it work?" Jun asked. "You passed out at the end of the spell. It's been, like, ten minutes and the hound keeps *staring* at me—"

It all came back to him at once. A reunion in the charred ruins of an old mansion house; the ambush that had awaited them; the princess, the knight, the serpent. And all three of them had—

He was suffocating. He was suffocating, even though he could feel his lungs gasping for air. There were spots in his vision. His hand—not his hand—flew to his chest.

"Hey—hey, deep breaths," Jun said.

Tristan barely heard him. He remembered being on the brink of death. Desperate to live, he had fled instinctively to the only place he could: his connection to his hound. Beor had once said, *When you have power over the boundary between life and death, you can't unravel yourself. You must remain grounded, and keep a tight hold on your humanity. Summoners who are careless with their magic go mad, soon enough, or worse.*

That was what had happened. Tristan had unraveled himself. He had been more hound than human, with no body to go back to. The things he'd seen and done in that time were like half-remembered dreams, both reassuring in some ways—there had been enough of him left to find Emil's grimoire and protect Hazel—and horrifying in others. He hadn't been himself. He hadn't been human. And—for weeks, he had existed in a world that didn't have Leo in it.

He was alone now. Again. They had *left him here.*

"Tristan," Jun said, his voice calm and steady. "You're having a panic attack. Can you look at me?"

After a long moment, Tristan did. He couldn't meet Jun's eyes. He focused on the earrings instead, the feathers that had fascinated him so much as a hound.

"Good," Jun said. "I'm going to count to three. When you're ready, repeat after me, okay? One . . . Two . . . Three."

Tristan's foggy memories of the last few weeks were replaying in his mind. He had *eaten an entire raw deer* today.

"One . . . Two . . . Three," Jun said, between slow, even breaths.

"One," Tristan managed.

The room came into focus around him. His back was against the desk in Emil's study. A black, rain-streaked night was framed in the window. The candle Jun had brought was the only source of light.

"I—I'm sorry," Tristan said. "That you—got involved in this."

One of the first things Jun had ever said to him was that human possession was a deeply forbidden practice. It was a terrible thing he had been asked to do.

"Dion was very transparent about what I was getting myself into," Jun said dryly. "No one forced me. I'm here because I wanted to help."

Unsteadily, Tristan reached up and touched his own face, which was wet. It felt like a stranger's touch, the pressure of his fingertips as wrong as the shape of his jawline and nose.

"I can't—sense Dion at all," Tristan whispered.

"That's okay," Jun said. "He's there, just . . . not in the driver's seat."

Tristan had no choice but to believe him. Searching his mind for Dion revealed his bond with the hounds was still there—his magic had traveled with his spirit. Otherwise there would be no point to this whole exercise. Remembering Lucky and Lupa's fight, his heart sank. His hounds had gone feral when he'd died. Other necromancers were out there, trying to hunt them down, but mostly they had failed. All but two of them ran free.

His eyes closed, his throat going tight with a new wave of grief. Emil had made those hounds. They were all that was left of him. Tristan had never even finished naming them. He had no right to do what he was about to do.

With some effort, he summoned one of the remaining hounds. Jun jumped when it materialized next to Lucky. Tristan lifted his hand and crooked his fingers at the hound, as if to beckon it nearer. It growled and backed away, ears flat, reading his intent through their bond. But he was its summoner; it couldn't run from him, not even as he peeled apart the shadow magic that made the hound what it was.

The last thing he felt from the hound was a ripping hatred that tore apart their bond as it dissipated, permanently, into the darkness.

"What did you . . . Where did it go?" Jun asked, hushed.

"I destroyed it. A precaution," Tristan said. He called the other hounds one by one, trying to make quick work of it. His magic was slow to respond at first, Tristan feeling out of place in this form. But it got a little easier each time, at least until it was Lupa's turn. He wished he could send it back to Hazel, but that wasn't an option, not after what had happened before. He had made protecting and obeying Hazel the center of Lupa's existence. After he'd died, the command had been lost, and only the fixation on Hazel remained. It was harder to unmake a hound he'd named—Lupa resisted it so fiercely he almost faltered, afraid it would lash out at him and injure Dion's body—but he steeled himself and cleaved it apart in one final, definitive stroke.

When Lupa was gone, he looked over at Lucky, the sole remaining member of his pack. Lucky looked back at him, calm, contemptuous. It had been an indifferent spectator to the annihilation of its pack. It knew that its time had come. Its only reaction was a kind of bored and vaguely hungry disdain.

It was a monster. If Tristan wasn't around to control it, Lucky would become an indescribable terror, more violent and more elusive than his other nine hounds put together. Getting rid of it was the right thing to do.

But he just couldn't.

With a wave of his hand, he sent Lucky away—far away. To a densely wooded and unpopulated place. Plenty to hunt, but no people. It was the best he could do.

He didn't have the strength to kill it. If he did, he would be alone in his own mind. And then he might not be able to hold it together long enough to finish this.

"Maybe you should rest," Jun said. "You'll need your strength if you want to pull this off, and I don't think Dion has been taking the best care of himself, so—"

"No," Tristan said. "I don't want this to go on longer than necessary. Dion needs his body back." He took a proper look at Jun for the first time, noting the bags under his eyes and dull complexion. "You're the one who looks like you need rest. That spell, did it take a lot out of you?"

Jun smiled shakily. "No, it was fine. It was worth it. But . . . listen, about the next part . . . corruptive magic, it's . . . terrible. You want no part of it."

"Is it worse than death?" he asked. Standing, he found Emil's grimoire on the desk. It felt familiar, maybe because of how often Dion's hands had held it. It was bound with black leather so old that it had gone soft as silk; the pages were made of a heavy vellum, with a bittersweet scent, like smoke and honey. The title on the cover read, in Old Norse: *The Infernal Arts*. Beside it lay a notebook where Dion had translated the spell, but Tristan found he already knew what it said. Dion had read it aloud to him a number of times.

This body's hearthcraft was dormant now. But Dion had already altered the entrance to the study with his door spell—the spell that could take Dion home no matter where he was. The polished mahogany door with the brass handle had transformed; now the wood was gouged with burn marks, the hinges partially melted. Tristan had to pry it open.

"Wait," Jun said, following him into the ruins.

"I've waited long enough."

In the middle of the room, a birch sapling grew from Viren's remains. Tristan climbed the staircase that had haunted his and Lucky's waking nightmares. Outside, dusk had given way to night, and a subdued storm rumbled overhead, a dreary rainfall dampening the air and dripping inside through the cracks in the walls.

"It *is* worse than death, what you're risking," Jun said, still trailing after him. "And I know—I know you're in pain and that you'd do anything to change what happened. Most people in your position would. But corruptive magic can—"

"I've seen what it can do," Tristan said softly. "I'm not changing my mind."

"But you—Oh god." They had made it to the second-floor landing, and the bodies were just there, strewn together against the wall like discarded furniture. Dion had mentioned doing something to preserve them. The hall was frigid—markedly colder than the rest of the house. No insects or scavengers had come near them, from the looks of it, despite the gaps in the roof and the broken windows. Not even the rain was making it inside. Dried blood had crusted in their clothes and on the ground. His own body had slumped against the wall with its neck awkwardly bent, its eyes slitted open and unseeing.

A summoner cannot be squeamish. It won't do, he told himself chidingly. He almost wanted to laugh. There was no humor in it, only a kind of clear-eyed madness.

"You should go back," he told Jun. "Thank you for everything."

If Jun responded, he didn't hear it. He was walking what felt a very long way, though it wasn't really, until he could lower himself to his knees before the bodies. It was surreal to look at his own face from the outside, its pallor even more pronounced in death, his eyes glassy, his lips gray and bloodless. His hand was frozen in Aziza's.

On her other side, Leo's head rested against her shoulder. Tristan gathered him into his arms. He was beautiful even now. Months of cloudy days had done nothing to discourage his summer freckles. His skin was cold when Tristan stroked his cheek, but the amber eye—a sliver of it visible through his lashes—shone as golden as ever. When Tristan brushed his thumb down the scar that cut across it, he thought he could detect its warmth under the surface of his skin. He bent and kissed his indifferent mouth, allowing himself this liberty. It could be the last time.

He set the body down and picked up *The Infernal Arts*. He brushed the dust and soot off its cover, flipped it open, and found the first page of the spell.

This was the first thing he had ever tried to do with his necromancy gift of his own free will—not something the hag had ordered him to do. He had tried to resurrect someone that had been killed by the hounds. It hadn't worked. He hadn't known it at the time, but such a complex and powerful feat of magic required a spell. When he had begun his search for it months ago, he'd thought he might use it to bring Emil back. That would never happen now. If it didn't work, he would have to go willingly into his death, knowing he had failed.

If it did work—he didn't know what would happen to him. But this was worth any cost.

He began to read out loud, haltingly at first. But as his magic joined with the words, the Old Norse flowed from his tongue as if he had it memorized. It was as if the spell possessed him, the way he had possessed Dion, and his only purpose was to channel it into the world.

Necromancy could mend a corpse, of course. It could stitch up torn skin and bind muscle to bone, flood the veins with new blood. It couldn't heal the living, but it could *perfect* a corpse. His magic found the place where Leo's skull had broken and where Aziza's lung had caved in, and repaired them. It felt where the decay had started inside them and cleansed it. Where their hearts had gone cold and stiff and had to be worked back into beating. Where their brains had shut down, starved of oxygen, and had to be shocked back to life.

That wasn't the hard part. The hard part was bringing back what made them who they were. Traces of spiritual energy lingered on them—their anima, with which he could have conjured faint spirits. He pictured it, their ghostly faces looking down at him without recognition. Or he could have used it to animate their remains and speak to an echo of their personalities. But their anima served a different purpose for him now. Through the spell, he breathed it in, reminded it of what life felt like, and exhaled it; it passed through his borrowed body and made him shiver. He gathered up a bit of it, and then there was more and more, like a tiny loose thread that, when pulled, lengthened indefinitely. The way that Jun's candle had led his spirit from Lucky's body into Dion's, now it was Tristan's turn to guide the dead back home from wherever it was they had gone. He felt them settling in—heard Aziza sigh, saw Leo's hand twitch. He didn't react; he couldn't. He had to finish the spell.

Her hand couldn't be fixed; it was a blækhound injury. And Tristan wouldn't remove the amber eye to regrow the natural one without Leo's permission, even if he was sure he could do it safely, which he wasn't. It was magically affixed to the socket. So he left these old wounds of theirs alone. His own body was uninjured, except for the scars it wasn't worth the energy to try and erase. Soon, the other two were breathing on their own, and there were only a few lines left in the spell. His hands felt stiff; his whole body felt stiff. He must have been sitting there for two hours or more.

His body was alive. He could return to it. But he hesitated. A peculiar instinct whispered in him that he would be happier if he left his body for good and slipped into Leo's; and then they would never be apart. The whisper didn't sound like his own voice. It sounded like the rustle of brittle paper, the swish of ink in a bottle, the scratch of a quill. It was a comforting suggestion, like a fantasy you used to lull yourself to sleep, but he shook the impulse off.

Once his body had come back to life, it had been hard to hang on to Dion's; his spirit knew where it belonged. He spoke the final word of the spell and it left something of itself in the air, an after-image as if from a bright light. The grimoire turned to dust in his hands, dispersing into the air and trickling through his fingers in a gritty stream. The spell had drained it completely. And Tristan was dust, too, floating away. There was no candle to guide him to his destination, but he was used to traveling through shadow.

The next thing he knew was an impact—a crash. Or maybe an eruption, a sudden sensory overload after a period of deprivation. Nerves lighting up and neurons firing and his heart racing so fast it felt dangerous, like it might give out again.

It was abrupt and violent and final. His body hurt all over. He was confused until he realized it was because he hadn't moved in weeks. He felt disgusting, his skin clammy, his hair lank and itchy. And he was so cold, except for his hand. That was because, he remembered, he was still hanging on to Aziza's.

He tugged on it weakly and felt an answering pull in return.

CHAPTER 28

LEO

IT WAS HALF an hour into a scalding shower before Leo began to feel more like himself again and less like roadkill.

He took a mental inventory as he worked shampoo aggressively into his scalp. *Any cravings for human flesh?* he thought. *Uncontrollable urge to bite things?*

As far as he could tell, he was fine, and no surprise there. If there was anyone he could trust to pull all three of them through a resurrection unscathed, it was Tristan. But he couldn't think about that yet. He was going to focus on manageable things first. Like washing the blood out of his hair. It came off in flakes, turning the water pink. He scrubbed until it ran clear again.

His muscles felt sore; his brain felt like a clump of dough that had been stretched until it went transparent in the middle. But it was no worse than if he'd slept poorly. That was all it had been for him—a deep sleep. As far as he was concerned, he had dozed off in October and woken up in November. They'd missed Thanksgiving; his parents must have spent it alone, wondering where he was. He didn't remember anything between closing his eyes and opening them. There hadn't been a bright light, or his life flashing before his eyes. Just that blast of pain in his skull, and then, upon regaining consciousness, a freezing cold that turned out to be an effect of the spells Dion had put on the hallway to stop them from, uh. Decomposing.

Gingerly, he touched the place where he had been hit in the head. His fingers pushed aside his wet hair carefully as he felt at his scalp. He didn't really remember that part, either. For once, he was glad to be missing a memory.

Experimentally, he probed at the limits of the curse, as he'd done countless times before. Was dying enough to sever its hold on him? He closed his eyes and tried to conjure those memories that he knew contained gaps. Being fourteen volunteering to take Hazel trick-or-treating with the neighborhood kids instead of going to a Halloween party with his friends, just so he could trail behind them and hold hands with the one he loved when no one was looking. Fifteen and sneaking that person into the house, nearly keeling over with fright as Spot knocked a photograph off the wall, and choking down giddy laughter when no one came out into the hallway to investigate. A few hours short of sixteen, filling out a notebook with everything he knew he'd forget at the stroke of midnight, etching a treasured name into the pages. But it was no use. His mind still glitched over that name, that face, even as his heart ached, issuing its usual demands.

It didn't register as a disappointment; he hadn't really believed he'd be rid of the curse just like that. After all, he was the only one who could break it.

He pressed his forehead against the cool tile of the shower wall. No one else got second chances like this. It was *amazing*. Miraculous. And he was going to make the most of it.

He got dressed in the button-up shirt and slacks he'd borrowed from Dion. They had gone with him through the door of the burnt house to the study in Emil Wulfsige's secluded country manor, which he'd inherited from some great-grandfather and then left to Dion. Wulfsige necromancers apparently were specialists in shadow magic, and kept blækhounds the way other people kept horses. They had always lived in remote places where there was no risk of a young summoner's out-of-control hound running into some poor unsuspecting stranger on the street. The nearest neighbor was miles away, and there were enough spare bedrooms for all three of them plus Jun, had he wanted to stay. But Jun had been happy to duck out at the first opportunity.

Leo had wanted to go home, too—he needed his parents to know he was okay—but Dion had advised against it. They couldn't just go back to their old lives. They were only safe as long as Castor thought they were dead. If word got back to him that they had survived, he would come after them again. It wasn't a sustainable long-term plan—they couldn't hide forever. But Leo had reluctantly agreed to lie low until they figured out their next move.

He went out into the hallway, peeking into the other rooms. It was so quiet—even Bishop Library was never this quiet. In the Merritt household, there was always someone else in the other room, or Spot banging around downstairs. And in the Summer Court, the bustle of servants could be heard in the halls while the fairies slept away the days in between their all-night revels. But only a timid patter of rain broke the somber silence here.

They hadn't really had a chance to talk yet, though Dion had given him and Aziza the CliffsNotes of what had happened. They had all died, except Tristan, who had been—both dead and alive at the same time? And it had fallen on him to save them all. Tristan hadn't spoken much. None of them had; they had been too disoriented to do more than stumble after each other and let Dion order them around. Leo thought of what it would have been like to be the last surviving member of Coven Blackthorn, or to be trapped in a hound's body and barely even remember who or what he really was, and shuddered.

Once he had ascertained that there was no one on the second floor, he crept downstairs. A partly open door led to a parlor with wall-to-wall bookshelves. It wasn't a library, but it was probably close enough, if Aziza needed a place to retreat and lick her metaphorical wounds.

He poked his head inside and found her by the window. On a clear night, the moonlight would've fallen across a wooded countryside. Now the light from the house ran up against a solid wall of darkness, the slow rain dripping down the glass in wobbly streaks.

"I was wondering where everyone went," he said, coming in and leaving the door cracked behind him. "Have you seen the others?"

"No," she said shortly, not returning his smile. Actually, she didn't look at him at all.

"Someone woke up on the wrong side of the deathbed." He sidled up next to her by the window, bumping his shoulder against hers. "You okay?"

She glared at the window in silence. Her hair was still wet from her own shower, gathered over one shoulder in a spill of dark curls and leaving damp splotches on the front of her shirt—another donation from Dion. It hung off her. She'd rolled up one sleeve and pushed the other messily over her elbow.

"I'm sorry," she said.

"What for?" he asked, taken aback.

She turned her face away from him, but not before he caught her rubbing angrily at her eyes with the back of her hand. Leo stared at the side of her head, dumbfounded. He had literally never seen her cry. She hadn't even cried when Lucky had crushed her right hand. He remembered packing her into the passenger seat of his car and praying she wouldn't bleed out as he floored it to the hospital, tires screeching, and *he* had been on the verge of tears. But Aziza had just looked sort of annoyed at the inconvenience of it all.

"I—" Her breathing was a shaky staccato. "I let Castor Thorne bait me. Dion and Anne both warned me, but I wouldn't listen. We never should've been there—you and Tristan shouldn't have, anyway. And you wouldn't have been, if it wasn't for me."

"You didn't make us do anything. We all agreed."

"I got you killed," she said. "And Tristan had to—He had to—"

This was the crux of the issue, the part that pained both of them the most—that *Tristan had to.*

"We didn't have to go with you," he insisted.

"Do you remember the first time I told you—that you didn't have to follow me—and you said, *Of course I do*?" she said, her breath catching as she tried in vain to staunch the flow of tears. The part of her face he could see was wet, and reddened where she kept swiping her too-long sleeve roughly over it. "To you, it's not a real choice. Because we're friends. At first—I was so sure you'd hold me back—because everything was just simpler when I was by myself. And I thought that was the same thing as being better off alone. But it was the other way around. You're the one who was better off without—"

She broke off, crying silently with her head still turned away. Carefully, Leo gathered her into a hug, so that at least she could hide her face against his shoulder and preserve her dignity.

"Listen," he said. "We've never really talked about this, but you probably guessed some of it. Before we met, I was in a really, really bad place." His eyes were fastened on the blurred window, a reminder of the nights he had spent on the road, watching the world through his windshield for hours on end. "And I don't know how long I would have lasted if something hadn't changed. I think I would've gotten myself killed driving across the country because of a rumor I heard from some dodgy stranger on the internet. And I honestly didn't care." The cold from Aziza's wet hair leached into his shirt, but her cheek was fever-hot against his neck. "I don't know what would've happened to me if I hadn't met you. Chasing shades in the woods with a flashlight, and rounding people up when they got lost following the wills-o'-the-wisp, and watching shitty sci-fi movies while we patched ourselves up in my car in the middle of the night . . . saved me. Even if I'd known what was going to happen to us, I still would have followed you to that house. And it's not because I didn't have a choice. It's because I really fucking love you. In case that wasn't obvious."

"I—Me too," she mumbled, sounding embarrassed even through her sniffles.

He laughed. "Yeah, yeah, I know. I'm the light of your life. You don't have to say it."

"Shut up." She drew back and scrubbed viciously at her eyes, as if she was tired of this breakdown and had decided it was going to be done now. "It's not over. Castor still wants us dead. And I still . . . want to make him pay for everything he's done. As if I even could. He's one of the most powerful people in this entire country, and I'm an *okay* witch when all I have to worry about is myself and Blackthorn. But I don't think I could back down now even if I wanted to." Her eyes were puffy and bloodshot, but no more tears fell. "You were right. I do have tunnel vision about Meryl. I can't trust my own judgment."

Aziza wasn't an *okay* witch. She was a scary powerful one. The more he learned about witchcraft, the more it became apparent to him that Aziza's was exceptional—the things she could do with and without spells, and how quickly she picked up new ones when she really put her mind to it. But she didn't measure her magical competence by sheer power or how many spells she could do. In the ways that mattered to her, she had fallen short.

"If you can't trust yourself, then trust me," he said. "All I know is that we can't hide and wait for Castor to catch up with us. We have to strike first."

"Are you sure?"

"At this point, I think it's personal," he said. "For all of us."

THEY SEARCHED FOR the others together. The lamp that Aziza had turned on in the parlor was the only source of light on the first floor, and that stifling silence still pervaded the rest of the house. Aziza kept rubbing at the spot on her ribs where the arrow had pierced her.

"Does it hurt?" he asked.

"No," she said. They were both whispering, though he couldn't have said why. "There's not even a scar. I just can't stop thinking about it. And I can't . . ."

"What?" he prompted, as she fell into a troubled silence.

"The bond is gone," she said. "I haven't seen Tristan since we got here, and now I can't even tell if he's in the house."

"He probably just needed some space," Leo said, uncertain.

"Fuck that," Aziza said, to which he nodded vigorously. They went upstairs to check the spare rooms again. At the top of the steps, Leo hesitated, suddenly overcome with panic. Just, like, a minor case of panic. Maybe guilt. Maybe he was weirdly embarrassed, too? Aziza got a couple of paces away before she realized he wasn't with her.

"What?" she whispered.

"I broke up with him, and then he brought me back from the dead," Leo said. "What the hell do I say to him? 'That was rad, thanks'?"

Her hand flew to her mouth, trying unsuccessfully to cover a laugh. "No. I don't think that would be good."

Then he was stifling laughter, too, and saying, "It's so not funny. What are *you* going to say to Dion?"

"What does that have to do with anything?" she asked, sounding totally chill and not at all evasive. She tried the first door, which turned out to be a linen closet. They went on to the next.

"Come on," Leo said. "He didn't spend a month translating his dead dad's grimoire and let a ghost hijack his body to perform the most forbidden kind of magic *ever* . . . to save *me*."

"I think he would have done it for anyone," Aziza said, even sounding like she actually believed it, which in Leo's opinion was the very pinnacle of absurdity. "He's . . . a good person."

"Whoa, slow down! How can you talk like that about a man you're not even married to?"

She pushed open another door to reveal another empty room. Turning back to him, she gasped in horror.

"What?" he said, alarmed.

"It's . . . it can't be . . ."

"What?"

"No . . . I'm sure of it . . . You were . . . definitely funnier before you died."

His surprised laugh felt much too loud in the hollow quiet.

"Yeah, I left all my best jokes in the afterlife to keep your sense of humor company." He wiped a fake tear off his cheek. "They're in a better place now."

She was reaching for the next door down, looking back at him to respond, when her eyes focused on something over his shoulder. Her hand dropped. Leo followed her gaze, turning in time to see a kind of tremor work its way through the darkness. Lucky materialized with its usual grace, gliding out of the shadows as smoothly as a knife being drawn from a sheath. Tristan appeared beside it, a hand resting on its flank.

Leo's heart gave a fierce pang at the sight of him. In his memory, they had only been apart for a few hours. But it was as if part of him had somehow felt their separation—had felt that Leo had gone on to someplace else while Tristan . . . hadn't.

His hair was windswept, as if he'd been outdoors. He had left the top few buttons of his shirt open, and Leo's eyes traced the stark white column of his neck to a triangle of exposed collar. The deadly glint of his eyes was like something glimpsed on a cold night between a pair of snow-laden trees—a ravenous and searching look, meant to observe but not be seen.

"How . . . how are you two feeling?" Tristan asked hoarsely.

"We're fine," Aziza said. "Where were you?"

His lips parted in surprise, as if, until she'd spoken, he hadn't been entirely sure he wasn't hallucinating. It took him a moment to respond. "I was with Hazel."

"You were?" Leo said quickly. A surge of emotion twisted his heart into knots. Fear of what might have happened to Hazel in the weeks they'd been gone. Envy, because Leo would've done pretty much anything to give his little sister a hug right now. Gratitude that visiting her was the first thing Tristan had thought to do.

The urge to grab Tristan by that open collar, pull him close, and never let him go again was almost overwhelming.

"I know what Dion said about staying hidden," Tristan said, a little defensively, as if he somehow thought they were going to tell him off. "But she knew something was wrong because—because Lupa left her. I had to tell her we were okay. She was alone. I told her she shouldn't let anyone know she'd seen me."

"Thank you for checking on her. But you should rest," Leo said. He wanted to move closer, but he felt rooted to the spot. "Have you even sat down yet?"

"I can't rest," Tristan said. "We can't. We're still in danger. And Emil's grimoire is gone. We won't get another do-over."

Privately, Leo was thankful for that. He didn't want another do-over—didn't want Tristan to be the one responsible for giving it to them.

"How much do you remember?" Aziza asked.

"Bits and pieces," he said. "It was . . . I'm glad it's over. That's all."

His gaze had dropped, so he didn't see Aziza cross the room until she had thrown her arms around him in a tight hug. Tristan sagged against her, as if she was the only thing keeping him upright. And Leo just stood there uselessly.

Downstairs, a lock clicked; they heard the front door swing open.

"That's Dion. I should go talk to him," Aziza said, releasing Tristan. She shot Leo a meaningful look over her shoulder as she abandoned him, pitilessly, to a conversation she knew he wasn't prepared for. Then she was gone.

"So," Leo began. He had no idea how he was going to finish that sentence.

"I have to tell you something," Tristan said at the exact same moment. He paused. "Sorry. You first."

"No! I didn't . . . It wasn't important. What's up?" Leo said.

Tristan opened one of those empty rooms and pulled Leo inside.

"I have to say this, just once," Tristan said, spinning to face him, his back against the closed door. "And then I'll never bring it up again. Leo, I love you."

"What?" Leo choked out.

"I never should have said that we could mess around and it wouldn't be serious. It was always serious for me," Tristan said. "I lied so I could be with you. Then I let us break up and pretended I was fine with it. You *died* not knowing how important you are to me. The truth is, I've always loved you. I loved you from the moment we met."

Somehow, though this confession shook him to the core, Leo wasn't surprised by it. Not as surprised as he should have been.

Deep down, he found he had already known that Tristan loved him. Because Leo had always felt loved when they were together.

"I don't . . . know what to say," Leo said, caught in a stalemate between the wild impulse to ask Tristan to say it again, and the crushing knowledge that he couldn't, and that this would be the only time he would ever hear it. Part of him marveled at how he could feel both elated and heartbroken at the same time.

He'd also never felt like more of an asshole in his entire life.

"It's okay." Tristan smiled, and it looked like poetry sounded, like something a fairy could bottle and turn into magic. "I just needed you to know. If there's ever a time I can get away with being uncomfortably honest, it's probably now."

"Tris, you can always be honest with me," Leo said, hating that Tristan had ever doubted it. His voice was rough; he barely got the words out.

"Really? Even if it's hard to hear?"

"Of course."

"Because if I was being *really* honest, I'd tell you to give up on your true love," Tristan said. "I can't be the person you lost. But I'm *here*. And I'm yours. If you want me to be."

Leo took his hand. He didn't have the right words, but the one thing he was certain of was that he couldn't stand the rift that had opened between them. For a second, he was afraid Tristan would pull away—afraid he would enforce the boundaries that Leo had stupidly placed on their closeness. But Tristan held on just as tightly.

"I'm glad you're not the person I lost," Leo said.

Because he'd rather die again than give up even one memory with Tristan in it.

"I am, too," Tristan said.

CHAPTER 29
AZIZA

DION HAD COME back with enough takeout to feed twice as many people as were present. Leo borrowed a phone charger so that he could catch up on the news while they ate, reading a few headlines aloud for them. She had a feeling he just wanted to break the silence, so she assisted, responding absentmindedly to his commentary in between forkfuls of lo mein. Tristan hardly ate a bite, and Dion hardly spoke a word.

"It's late," Dion said, as they cleaned up after. "You should all get some sleep."

"Shouldn't we—figure out our next move?" Leo said awkwardly.

"Your next move is staying put until it's safe," Dion said.

"And when will it be safe?" Aziza said. "When Castor passes away peacefully in his sleep at age ninety?"

She didn't mean for it to sound argumentative, but it probably did. It was *true*, though. Dion drew in a furious breath and opened his mouth to respond, but Tristan put a quelling hand on his shoulder. Odd, the way they suddenly seemed so close; to Aziza, it was as if it had happened overnight.

"We can talk about it in the morning," Tristan said. It was directed at Aziza and Leo. She didn't need the bond to know what that look meant. *Let it go.*

They went up to bed, Aziza feeling obscurely as if she had taken the easy way out. She had failed to say anything of substance at all to Dion. She'd tried to thank him earlier, before Leo and Tristan had followed her downstairs—but he had looked so horrified by the attempt that she'd barely gotten a sentence out before she lost her nerve and changed the subject.

Sleep was a lost cause. She'd never been prone to insomnia the way Leo and Tristan were; she kept strange hours sometimes, but when she decided it was time to sleep, she generally did. But tonight she couldn't keep her eyes shut. She climbed out of bed and crept into the hall, unsurprised to find a light was on behind the door to the study.

Before she could second guess herself, she padded over to it and knocked.

"Come in," Dion's muffled voice said.

She did, easing the door shut behind her. Dion's eyes flicked up at her, but he said nothing. He sat at the desk with a laptop open in front of him. The glare from its screen was harsh on his features—the adamant slash of his black brows, the uncompromising set of his mouth, the bruises under eyes that were a darker gray in this light, closer to coal than ash. He had cast little spells on the room—something to keep the snake plant in the corner happy, something to warm the hours-old coffee in the mug next to him, something to vaporize the dust that wanted to settle atop the books on the shelves, in the gutters between their front and back covers. She had become accustomed to the feeling of his magic, the way you did when you were very familiar with someone. His had a clean, piercing quality, like a knife so sharp you didn't feel it when it cut you, so that it went straight through her chest, painlessly.

She wandered to the framed photographs of Emil with a younger Dion, looking at them so that she wouldn't have to look at him. It was cowardly. She didn't care.

"If you can just magic a place clean, why did you dust and mop the entire library almost every single day?" she asked.

"I *can't* just magic a place clean," he said. "Not always. And definitely not a place that doesn't know me. Household spells don't work if you don't *care*. They don't do anything that I can't or won't do with my own hands every now and then."

Did he mean that the *building* had a resistance to hearthcraft that had to be overcome? Did that only apply to places with a magical history, or mundane buildings too? She imagined a supermarket throwing a black-mold tantrum in the stockroom in response to a strange hearth witch trying to tame it with cleaning charms, or a graffiti-covered apartment complex on the bad side of town flushing its elevator shaft with rust. Or maybe it was the hearth witch's magic that had to adapt to an unfamiliar place. Maybe it was a kind of ritual that had to be done, like her years of walking along Blackthorn's boundaries with Elphame, learning them. But she hadn't come here for lessons in hearthcraft.

She sank into the chair across from his. "Working overtime?"

"Playing catch-up," Dion said. "I've been doing the bare minimum for weeks. If I don't pull it together, Castor will notice I'm not performing up to my usual standard."

"Should I leave you alone?"

"If I was just going to tell you to go away, I would have ignored you when you knocked."

"You're ignoring me now," she said, reaching over and snapping the laptop screen closed, forcing him to whip his fingers out of the way. "Are you going to let me thank you for saving our lives?"

He got that look on his face again like someone had kicked him in the stomach and he was trying not to react. "Please don't."

"Fine. But you should know I'm going to find the rest of Castor's lanterns. Tomorrow. Leo and Tristan are coming with me."

He glared at her. "Actually, I changed my mind. Feel free to keep talking about your undying gratitude."

"I don't know if *undying* is the word I'd use."

"It's not funny," he snapped, for all the world as if *he* had been the one who'd spent last month rotting in a dark corner.

"I *know* that," she said, more harshly than she meant it. She used to try so hard to get a rise out of him, and never succeeded. When she did, it was usually by accident, and it never felt good. Deciding that blunt honesty was the only way forward, she said, "I'm terrified it's going to happen again. I'll get them both killed."

"Not if you stay here," he said, with an air of futility, like he knew he wasn't going to convince her but still had to try.

She hadn't come here to argue. She'd only wanted to talk to him. It always felt like she had unfinished business with Dion. It bothered her; she didn't like loose ends. She returned to her old game instead, the one where she asked Dion questions he couldn't resist answering, like tiny projectiles seeking the cracks in his defenses. "You took that apprenticeship to gather more information about Castor, right? You basically told me that much the last time we spoke."

Dion stubbornly avoided her gaze, which was starting to truly piss her off. It would probably be immature of her to grab him by the collar and shake him, but she gave it a moment of serious consideration.

"I did," he said finally.

"But before, you said he's been trying to bring you on as an apprentice for years," she said. "Was that true?"

"Yes," he admitted. He leaned back in his chair and rubbed his eyes tiredly. "But it goes back further than that. After the fire, he offered to take me in. As a favor to my parents, since they'd worked together. But Emil got there minutes before he did, and had already volunteered to adopt me. So Castor gracefully stepped aside."

"You weren't meant to survive, were you?" she asked.

"No. I'm sure if Castor had managed to appoint himself as my guardian, I would have met with some tragic accident of my own in a year or two," Dion said. "Emil protected me. But I'm old enough to protect myself now."

"The thing that caused the fire," Aziza began, unsure of how to say it. "It—In the house, it—"

The burnt house they'd died in belonged to the Legrand family; it was the place where Dion had grown up. She had suspected it as soon as she'd seen it in person, and even more when she encountered the creature that slept upstairs. But Dion using his door spell on the entrance had confirmed it. He could only use that spell to go home.

The Legrand family coven were the architects who had made the jackdaw collections, the Flight Paths, and the Half Moon Market possible. And who knew what else. The story of how they'd died had always struck her as mysterious and tragic, but it was more than that—it was absurd. How was it possible that a group of spectacularly powerful hearth witches had died in a *house fire*?

"You found something," Dion guessed.

"It's a salamander," she said. "Not like the amphibian. The fae being we call a salamander is more like a snake. It's a kind of ancient elemental spirit, like an undine or a sylph. When it's dormant, it disguises itself as ash and soot. It's almost undetectable. I used a sleeping spell on it, but it's still there."

"Yes. I saw the strange patterns in the ash when I went back to do the preservation spells on . . . on your resting place," he said, a flicker of pain appearing in his expression before he suppressed it. "I always knew what happened to my family wasn't an accident. I just didn't know why or how. No one would have thought to send a hedgewitch to investigate a house fire."

"It was Castor. Wasn't it?" she asked. She was still just piecing it together, but she was sure Dion had reached the same conclusion long ago. "He hides his lanterns in magical places, or close by, so that they can absorb power. Eventually, a Legrand witch would have noticed, just like *you* noticed. So he had to get rid of them, to make sure they wouldn't interfere."

"That's what I suspected, but I couldn't figure out how he dragged a creature from the depths of Elphame to the human realm and got it to the house undetected." He grimaced. "It all made sense after the summer solstice."

"Princess Narra did it on his orders. Then she was punished for running away to the human realm," Aziza said, remembering something Leo had told her.

It was alarming to think that Castor had had such a hold on Princess Narra even a decade ago. Had she already felt stifled by her responsibilities as heir to the crown, or had Castor been the one to plant those seeds of discontent in her? And then, when she'd been collared for her transgression, that had probably pushed her closer to Castor—even though it was his fault it had happened in the first place.

"Once I had that piece of the puzzle, I decided I'd do whatever it took to make Castor pay for what he'd done," Dion said, sounding more weary than vengeful. "But I couldn't. The more I uncovered, the more I began to act defensively and second-guess myself. You were right. I *am* afraid of him, and—worse than that—I started to think he couldn't be beaten."

Dion thought he hadn't done enough. But she could never have done what he'd done—swallowed her own grief and hatred, acted with patience and restraint, and maneuvered her way into her enemy's inner circle.

"No one could blame you for that," she said. And then she winced, remembering the last conversation they'd had before Coven Blackthorn's demise. "Except me. And I was wrong."

"You *weren't*. I thought I was getting close enough to Castor to do him real damage, and to make sure no one else who mattered to me got hurt because of him. But he always held me at a slight distance." He pressed his knuckles against his temple as if to push down a migraine. "Of course he must have suspected what I was really doing, and he took the opportunity to keep an eye on me, which I guess is what he always wanted, if he couldn't get rid of me."

"But I took the gamble you didn't, and I lost," she said. "Catastrophically. You still managed to learn things that no one else knows about his plans. Didn't you?"

Reluctantly, he nodded.

"I think I've pieced together his past and present," Dion said. "But I don't have a clear picture of the future he envisions. And that's the part that worries me the most."

Some of what he told her next, she already knew from the research she'd done with Leo. She had already studied the biographical details of Castor's life: his upbringing in a poor West Virginia town, which was ultimately destroyed by a storm; his time at Yale pursuing an advanced degree in theology; his early business ventures. He'd built a following around the promise of securing land and property for their community's use—something to pass down to future generations of witches. That was the whole purpose of Luminous Horizons.

He met Emil Wulfsige as an undergrad, and they became fast

friends. They attended the Half Moon Market together nearly every month, to make connections outside their on-campus social circles and participate in the duels. There, they'd met Leila and Ahmed El-Amin.

Then came the part of the story that only Dion could tell her.

"I learned some of it by looking through Emil's old planners and correspondence," Dion said. "And by speaking with people who knew him at the time. They were happy to share fond memories with his grieving son."

The four of them—Castor, Emil, Leila, and Ahmed—eventually formed a coven. Covenhood was defined by its collaborative nature—the pursuit of the same magical goals, the sharing of spell-work. Castor and Leila had worked together to refine the energy-capture spell he used on his cuff links, giving him a way to heighten his casting by absorbing magic from outside sources and trapping it. The lanterns were an extension of that—magical energy banks.

This was where Dion began to speculate. Very advanced spells needed greater offerings, more complex arrays, and more magic to cast; Dion believed that Castor was working on a spell that required more power than he could supply on his own. So he had planted his lanterns in places that he could guard, usually by having Luminous Horizons purchase them. Ideally, they would be located near major sources of magical energy, like the one in Martin College, which was fed by the magic of the Half Moon Market, and the one in the Summer Court's castle, which drank in fairy enchantment.

"I think the lantern that used to be in Bishop Library is the first one he ever made," Dion said. "And I think it's why he woke the hag."

In the absence of a convenient energy source for his lanterns, Castor would create one: a large-scale magical event or disaster that could funnel power into them. The hag was one of those disasters—a creature bloated with magic, even able to steal it from others and repurpose it. Dion didn't know how Castor had learned of her existence when she had lain dormant for centuries, but he had clearly seen it as an opportunity he couldn't pass up.

"Do you think . . . ?" She didn't really want to ask. But she had to. "Did our parents know what he'd done?"

"Most likely," Dion said. "I think that Castor would have shared his plans with his coven and tried to get them on board."

But he'd failed. When Leila had chosen to fight the hag, had she done it in part because she felt responsible? Because Castor was their covenmate, and they hadn't realized how deadly his ambitions had grown—hadn't been able to keep him in check?

"After your parents passed away, Emil stopped visiting Blackthorn. By the time he adopted me, he and Castor were more like distant acquaintances," Dion said. "I assume the loss of their covenmates was the reason they fell out. Especially if it was Castor's fault. The few times I tried to ask about his years as the famous Castor Thorne's best friend, he always managed to deflect. But I believe he felt guilty about his part in what happened in Blackthorn for the rest of his life. And that would explain why he felt he had to do something, when he learned the hag had returned."

"How did he find that out?"

"I think he was checking on you," Dion said, startling her.

"Me? Why?"

She riffled through her memory for any hint of Emil Wulfsige. Had she ever seen a red-haired stranger glancing over at her from the other end of the train car or across the street? Had he been among the crowds at St. Sithney's holiday fair one year or another, observing from afar as she surreptitiously rescued lesser fairies who had gotten tangled in the string lights? But if he was there, concealed somewhere on the fringes of her recollections, she could not find him.

"Is that so strange?" Dion said. "He probably felt it was the least he could do for his old friends. But, yes, I'm sure. I found a stack of yearbooks in the attic over the summer. One for every year of your education." Against all odds, a touch of humor found its way into his eyes. "You didn't smile even once on picture day, your whole life. I was impressed. So consistent and dependable for a small child."

Though Aziza's parents had imprisoned the hag and put her back to sleep, Castor had left his lantern in Blackthorn and later placed a selkie in charge of guarding it. There, it had received a trickle of magic over the years—because Blackthorn was an uncommonly magical place, where the veil was thin and every holiday, solstice, equinox, sunrise, and sunset was a time of heightened power. But the lantern needed more. It wasn't complete. And its first, best power source was right there, temptingly close and with no meddlesome covenmates left to interfere when Castor woke her up the second time.

When Emil discovered that the hag was hunting in Blackthorn again, he would have known that it was Castor's doing. Regretting his inaction in the fight that had led to Leila's and Ahmed's deaths, he came forward to deal with the hag himself this time. And he perished in the attempt.

Aziza felt a pang of—something. Could she call it grief? She hadn't known Emil. But he had cared about her parents, and maybe her, too. And maybe she did know him, a little, through Dion.

"Then you, Leo, and Tristan came along and finished the job," Dion said. "But that wasn't a setback for Castor. Because he still got what he wanted."

Every battle with the hag had generated an excess of magical energy, which the lantern would have pulled in. Even her death had been a boon to Castor, maybe the greatest one of all. Aziza remembered the moment she had taken on the bond that tied Tristan to the hag. Through him, she had been linked temporarily to the hag; she'd felt her die and the hoarded magic in her territory disperse. And Castor's lantern had been waiting to take it all in. That was the genius of Castor's design: the outcome of the disasters he created didn't really matter. It didn't matter if someone intervened and saved the day. He profited from the chaos regardless. Dion suspected Castor's alliance with Princess Narra had similar motivations. He'd wanted to place a lantern at the Summer Court, so he found someone who would help him do it. If Narra's rebellion eventually led to a fairy war, all the better; that would only boost the lantern's power.

Castor, monitoring his lanterns, would have realized that the hag had been killed; he would have come to investigate and learned that Meryl's loyalty was compromised. He could have gotten rid of her then, but why give up a servant whose obedience was guaranteed? Especially when he could use her to gain information and as leverage against Aziza and her coven, whose involvement with both the hag and the Summer Court had caught his attention and flagged them as a potential enemy.

As the lanterns could be replaced—and Dion thought Castor had already replaced the one that Aziza had destroyed—he hadn't wanted to show his hand by tampering with them until he had more information. If he had acted too soon, Castor would have killed him, as he'd killed the rest of the Legrand family, Emil Wulfsige, Coven Blackthorn, and likely anyone else who had gotten in his way over the years.

"How many lanterns are there?" she asked.

"Just three. I think." He counted them off. "The one you found at Martin College, which has traveled with the Market for years. The one in the Summer Court's castle. And the one in Bishop Library. All of them have been moved now."

"Moved where?" she asked. "Don't be modest. I'm sure you've got ideas. Probably good ones, too."

Dion sat back in his chair, arms crossed. "Maybe."

He had proved repeatedly that he would withhold information from her if he believed ignorance would keep her safe. She would really prefer it if that pattern didn't continue.

"The spell must be close to finished," Aziza pressed. "That's why he used the hag again. He's getting impatient."

"I've considered that possibility," Dion said, not meeting her gaze. She couldn't tolerate it when he did that. She didn't even know why it got on her nerves so much, but it did.

"*Look at me*," she snapped, more transparent than she wanted to be.

"I *am*," Dion said, and he did, his gray eyes visible under dark lashes, his jaw tense, his shoulders rigid. He was like a windup clock that couldn't unwind; she wanted to pull him apart.

"He already decided he wants us dead," she said. "If I'm a target, I want to take out those lanterns before he catches up with us. Maybe I can't stop him completely. But it took him decades to get this far with his lanterns, to fill them with as much magic as he has. If I can delay him another ten or twenty years, someone else eventually *will* stop him."

"I knew you'd say that, and I don't like it." He hesitated before adding, "But I don't think you're wrong, either."

The silence was heavier now than it had been before. He reached over the desk; his hand settled on her wrist, cautiously, and then more firmly when she didn't pull away, the palm of his hand sliding over her pulse point. Her heart was in her throat.

"I *want* to tell you to change your mind," he said. "But I don't have the right. You destroyed the hag that killed Emil. You found the salamander that annihilated my entire family, and put it to sleep. You go around vanquishing my demons one by one. Who am I to tell you to stay put?"

She slid her wrist from his grasp only to turn her hand over and take his. "I don't want to ask for more help after everything you've already done for—for all of us."

He said, "This time, you don't have to ask."

CHAPTER 30
LEO

HE WOKE UP in the middle of the night to the sound of his door opening and then closing again, softly, with a click. Someone had come into the room. Leo twisted in the blankets, squinting at the pale, blurry figure who had just entered.

"Tris?" he asked, his voice hoarse with sleep, as he pushed himself up on his elbow.

In the hall, a muffled scratching told him Spot was restless, probably gouging nail marks into the wall again. The noise covered Tristan's footsteps, and Leo felt almost as if he glided across the room. He sat on the edge of the bed, the mattress dipping slightly with his weight.

Blearily, Leo thought that there was something about this that wasn't right. They were broken up, they weren't supposed to . . . But his mind was so fuzzy he couldn't think what could possibly be wrong about this. Tristan was pressing his fingertips to Leo's cheek, turning his face toward him. Leo's eyes fluttered closed; he had to force them open before he dozed off again.

"C'mere, Tris," he slurred.

Obligingly, Tristan bent closer, as if to kiss him. His eyes were pitch-black with a needle's point of white pupil, and his touch on Leo's cheek felt like nothing at all.

"The Autumn Prince requests an audience," Tristan said. His voice was low and a little staticky. Listening to it made Leo's stomach swoop with vertigo.

"The . . . Autumn Prince," Leo repeated sluggishly.

"Indeed," Tristan said, in the voice that wasn't his own. "He has been waiting for some time, but I was unable to find you."

It was starting to occur to Leo that other things were not as they should be, either. He was in his bedroom at home, but he knew he hadn't fallen asleep there. And Tristan's face—those eyes like a light at the end of a long, dark tunnel—

Leo sat bolt upright, and the thing wearing Tristan's skin drew back to gaze at him with blank indifference.

"Am I dreaming?" Leo asked.

The buzzing in Leo's head that had started as soon as Tristan had spoken was growing louder. His lips moved. He couldn't hear what he said, but he still somehow understood.

Will you grant the Autumn Prince's request?

"Yes," Leo said out loud. He closed his eyes to shut out the buzzing, and, illogically, it worked. His mind cleared. A flash of light turned the inside of his eyelids red; when he slowly peeled them open, he was standing in a kind of courtyard surrounded by sheer rock walls. A frosty light poured down from above. A verdant garden of flowering bushes and lazily drooping trees sprawled across most of the space, so perfect it was like a painted scene from the inside of a snow globe. The imposter stood beside him.

"You're a sandman," Leo said accusingly. "Why do you look like that?"

"I have taken a form better suited for your dreams, thus enabling me to infiltrate them more easily," the sandman said.

Leo had the distinct feeling he was being mocked. He glared at the imposter. "Change, please."

The sandman blinked at him thoughtfully. Then Tristan wasn't standing next to him anymore; Lucky was, and the switch had happened in the indistinct way that two dreams tended to merge, where you couldn't tell when one had ended and the other had begun. It felt like Lucky had been there the entire time.

Lucky's fanged mouth dropped open, and it spoke. "Better?"

"Sure," Leo said. He rubbed at his cheek as if he could get the memory of the false touch out of his head. "Where are we? Another dream?"

"Yes," Lucky said, a flash of its tongue visible behind its teeth. "It is a shared dream I constructed at the behest of the Autumn Prince. I have kept it safe while I waited to hear of your whereabouts from the wild fae. The soot sprites noticed your return first. They told the wind, who told the pixies, who told the nymphs. The sycamore crone beside the lake to the north of the place where you now sleep whispered the rumor to one of my brothers. That is how I was able to find you."

Before he could respond, the dream sort of . . . *rustled,* like a garment Leo was wearing, and all of a sudden they weren't alone.

Prince Senna stood nearby, looking into a pond where tiny, jewel-toned fish darted back and forth. Before Leo could call out to him, he lifted his head sharply. His feline gaze found Leo and the sandman.

"I was certain you must have perished," Prince Senna said. "I was disappointed. A shame I traveled all that way to the human realm just to visit a careless boy who would vanish before he could be of any use." He came closer, and there was something of a cat's prowl in his gait, too, the calculated movement of a hunter. "But now I see that you were only avoiding me. Was our agreement so insignificant to you?"

When Leo had seen Prince Senna last, he had worn a costume illusion to pass for a human. The illusion was gone now. He was dressed in regalia befitting a prince, a tunic trimmed with gold and a thick fur-lined cloak. The hilt of a sword glittered at his hip. Leo felt a November chill creep into the dream, as if through a drafty window.

Prince Senna was angry. Even though it was only a dream, and Leo—probably—was in no danger, he felt a prickle of alarm, a primal instinct that told him to back away. With effort, he ignored it.

"I wasn't avoiding you," Leo said. "Something happened. I can't explain it, but it wasn't on purpose."

The sandman laughed through Lucky's teeth. "He is telling the truth. Such rumors I have heard from the soot sprites and the pixies. Such things I've seen in his dreams."

Prince Senna's eyes narrowed in a speculative look.

"You can check with Hazel. She didn't hear from us until today. But I *am* sorry," Leo said. "Did something happen? The sandman said you've been trying to contact me."

"I have been attempting to keep you apprised of recent events here in the Winter Court," Prince Senna said. He relaxed, the hard edge in his tone melting away. "A few weeks ago, they finally captured Princess Narra. She was found hiding in the borderlands, badly wounded. She'd lost a hand and was trying to treat the injury herself. We still haven't tracked down Viren."

"*Lost* isn't totally accurate," Leo said. "I may have cut it off? I did, I mean. I did cut it off. With the sword you gave me, so, uh, thanks for that. Also, Viren is dead. I didn't do that one, though."

"I see," Prince Senna said, with a microscopic quirk of an eyebrow. "She didn't tell us that."

"Did she tell you . . . anything?"

"No. She hasn't spoken a word since we brought her in," Prince

Senna said. "Narra's presence in the Winter palace is a secret to all except those in the queen's inner circle. If Ceresia gets her way, no one else will know until after the solstice—after Narra is crowned the new Summer Queen. Princess Kova of Spring will declare war, but Winter will crush her."

"Isn't there anything we can do?" Leo asked.

"Technically, you outrank me. You should be the one giving me orders."

Leo had a feeling this was a joke, but he didn't want to risk laughing in case it wasn't.

"I think Hazel outranks us both," he said.

"Hazel's chief concern is for her cousin's wellbeing. She is afraid to disobey Queen Ceresia while Vetiver is a hostage in the Winter Court," Prince Senna said. "But with what you've told me, new paths may yet open for us."

"What have I told you?" Leo said, feeling very much as if he had contributed nothing of value to this discussion.

"That *you* were the one who fought and wounded Narra, of course," Prince Senna said. "And Kova was so sure you were conspiring to help Ceresia put her on the throne. I do so enjoy proving her wrong."

"She thinks *I* want Narra to be queen?" Leo said, astonished.

"We all know the lengths you'd go to ensure the responsibility doesn't fall on Hazel's shoulders," Senna said. "And if Vetiver doesn't survive the rot, then that is exactly what will happen, without Narra to take her place. Why *wouldn't* anyone think you had delivered Narra into Ceresia's hands in order to protect Hazel—again?"

Leo winced. "You're right. I know I helped make this mess. If I can help you fix it, then I'll do whatever it takes."

"Are you giving me your word?" Prince Senna asked.

"Tell me what you have in mind first," Leo said. By now, he knew better than to hand out blank checks in Elphame.

Prince Senna laughed. "Very well. I ask only for one of your memories—the memory of your duel with Narra. Let me show Kova that you are Narra's enemy, and whoever else among the gentry that might doubt it. I am going to need their aid if I am to succeed."

"A memory?" Leo said. "How do I do that?"

"I will facilitate the exchange," the sandman growled, cleaning his paw with a long black tongue. "For dream is the keeper of memory, even those memories one may have otherwise forgotten."

"Does that mean I'll forget what happened?"

"You will," the sandman said.

"Is that a problem?" Prince Senna asked.

Once, a similar request from a sandman had made him freeze up with dread. Now he didn't even hesitate. He didn't feel like he'd become a braver person. Maybe just a more decisive one. Or maybe one who valued the future more than the past.

"No," Leo said. "Do it."

The sandman approached him, and Leo closed his eyes as Lucky's snout touched his brow. He braced himself for the feelings he associated with the curse—the headache accompanied by a vague sense of missing time, confusion, and loss—but nothing of the sort happened. It was more like he felt something lift away from him, a momentary lightness. It was almost a relief.

That's it? Leo thought, as the sandman moved back. That was what he'd been so afraid of?

Before he could speak, a sudden banging resounded across the cliff walls, making him jump.

"What is that?" he asked.

"You are waking up," the sandman said. Around them, the

courtyard began to grow a little . . . dull. As if all its edges had been sanded down and its colors washed out. It was fading away.

"I will speak with you again soon," Prince Senna said, but his face was blurring, and his voice was barely audible.

Leo's eyes flew open. He was in a guest room at Emil Wulfsige's house. The pounding noise had come from downstairs—someone was banging on the front door, loud enough to be heard through the whole building. It sounded like cannon fire. Whoever was out there really wanted Dion's attention.

It was the middle of the night, the window black through the gap in the curtains. He fought his way out of the tangled covers and sat up, disoriented by the sudden end of the dream.

The banging stopped as he climbed out of bed. He got dressed in a hurry, but before he could reach for his phone and hopefully find out what the hell was going on, the bedroom door was being thrown open.

"Good, you're up," Aziza said breathlessly. "We're leaving. Right now."

CHAPTER 31
TRISTAN

He was standing in a close, dark, fire-lit room. His mouth hurt; there was an ache in one of his molars as if someone was pulling on it, trying to pry it out with dry, hard fingers. It was the only thing he could feel.

Two people sat in plush armchairs, glasses of some dark amber liquid in hand, speaking calmly to each other, as if he wasn't there—*was* he there? He couldn't think. He wanted to touch that hurt place in his jaw, but he couldn't lift his hand. He wanted to look around; he couldn't turn his head. One of the men rolled something between his fingertips—something—that belonged to Tristan.

Tristan watched him and felt the wrenching pain and felt the hatred—felt that his summoner hated him—and the hate was the only thing standing between him and oblivion, and Tristan would stay there for as long as he commanded him to—

He woke up and knew instantly that it hadn't been a dream. But Lucky stood over him on the bed, its huge paws digging into the mattress on either side of him, its breath suffocatingly hot as it growled in his face.

"I'm up," he said, shoving Lucky's snout out of his way so he could sit up. It had seen something and wanted to show him.

It dove into the shadows, and he kept part of his attention on its progress as he got dressed. He had shadow-traveled home before they all went to sleep to grab clothing for the three of them, careful not to be heard when he snuck into Leo's and Aziza's rooms. As he yanked on a T-shirt, the hound was materializing in the woods behind the Wulfsige house; it was skulking through the darkness, sniffing at the ground, following a scent it didn't like—dusty, bitter, medicinal.

Then someone tried to break down the front door. That was what it sounded like, anyway. He yanked his shoes on as Lucky gave up the chase to go bounding toward the source of the noise. When Tristan saw who it was, he ran down the hallway.

Nelle shouted a strangled expletive as Lucky lunged out of the bushes and almost pounced on her; Tristan heard it twice, through the closed door and through Lucky's ears.

"You!" Nelle said indignantly, relaxing as she recognized Lucky. "You better tell Tristan to get out here right now or I'll—"

He opened the front door.

"Hi, Nelle," he said. "This is kind of a bad time."

Satisfied that there was no threat here, Lucky slinked away into the woods to continue its search.

"Tristan?" she said, eyes going wide and—to his dismay—shiny with tears. "You three scared the crap out of everyone! Where were you? I've been scrying for *weeks* looking for you. It didn't work until this morning and Dion's not answering his *damn* phone—I've been driving all day because I didn't want to say anything to Anne until I was sure—"

Her headphones were around her neck, her eyes bloodshot as if from lack of sleep, or a hangover, or both. A rental car was parked a short way down the drive, still running, its high beams pointed at the house and making Tristan feel as if they were standing in a spotlight.

Lucky was close to its target, its rising thirst for violence distracting Tristan from what Nelle was saying. It squirmed under a tangle of brambles, the thorns raking through its fur, the bitter scent in its nose getting stronger. Then Lucky saw it—the white lupine shape creeping around the edge of the house.

The dead, hungry thing searching for them.

"Nelle?" Dion said, coming downstairs with Aziza.

Nelle rounded on him. "You better have dropped your phone off a cliff or something!"

"Serapion found us," Tristan said, silencing the argument before it could begin.

"Professor Serapion? Why—"

"I'll get Leo," Aziza said, pivoting back to the stairs.

"I'm going with the three of you," Dion told him. "Nelle—can we take your car?"

Dion ushered her inside, shutting the door, as he fielded her panicked questions. Tristan ran ahead of them—he needed to grab his backpack and a few of his grimoires from Emil's library. He took *The Book of Fenrisúlfr*; he was down to one hound and needed to rebuild his pack. He also chose a book of spirits, though he didn't look forward to using it. He was getting decent at spirit summonings, but now that he had firsthand experience on the other side of it—felt the lack of free will, the lack of *self*—he didn't know if he could stomach it anymore. He probably would've left it if not for Beor's scolding voice in his head. And then he had room for one more. Best to travel light. *The Serpent Arts*? He had mastered its easier spells, and he had high hopes he could pull off the more advanced ones it contained. Or maybe *Liber Os*, a book of bone magic, which he'd just started dabbling in. But he doubted he could best Professor Serapion in that arena.

He was in and out of the library in minutes. He locked it and shut the door to the study for good measure. Somewhere, a window shattered, and Tristan launched into a sprint, his backpack full of grimoires banging against his side. The others were scattered part of the way down the stairs, Dion in the lead but pausing at the front door to look back, stricken—

"Get to the car!" Tristan called. "There's only one, Lucky can hold it off—"

It had broken inside through the kitchen, which was off the hallway, out of sight from the entrance. Lucky leapt inside after it and clamped its teeth down on its tail, affording Tristan his first up-close view of Professor Serapion's bone constructs.

Compared to Lucky, it was small, maybe half the size of a blækhound. It rattled when it moved—like a pouch of dice being shaken about. Its tail ripped out of Lucky's jaws with frightening strength, almost breaking his hound's teeth in the process. Lucky stared it down, growling; the bone wolf's jaws opened, but it had no voice, and its answering snarl was silent.

A real wolf had a lithe grace that the bone construct could not mimic. Lacking muscle, its movements were jerky, rigid, and uncoordinated; almost obscene, like a postmortem spasm in a cold body. Lacking fur, its teeth looked twice as large. The ridges of its skull curved around its nasal cavity and empty eye sockets. He couldn't tell if its proportions were right; its neck seemed too long, the taper of its silhouette too abrupt, from the barrel of its rib cage to the chain of its spine, ending in the triangle of its sacrum and the narrow bowl of its pelvis.

It leapt at Lucky, and they grappled, Tristan getting flashes of pain from his hound. Lucky tried to catch its teeth on the construct's neck, spine, and ribs, but it couldn't snap the bones, could do nothing more than use its grip to thrash it against the walls and floor. In return, the construct tore into Lucky with its claws, neither of them able to die. The fight could go on forever.

Or until more of Serapion's wolves showed up. And then Lucky would be outnumbered.

Nelle unlocked the car, dove in, and forced the key into the ignition. They piled inside, Dion in the passenger seat, the rest of them squeezing into the back, half on top of each other. Leo practically knocked Aziza into Tristan's lap as he fell in after them. Nelle floored it before Leo even got the door fully closed, and then they were speeding away into the night.

THEY DROVE TO a small city a couple of hours away, arriving around dawn. There, they camped out at a Denny's until the local Rent-A-Car opened so they could swap out their ride for a new one. Then they kept driving.

Dion thought that Serapion must have been watching him on Castor's orders. His bone constructs shouldn't have been able to get into the house; Dion was annoyed but not surprised about it.

"My spells on the place have . . . frayed . . . since Emil died," Dion said, sounding faintly embarrassed. Tristan remembered the oppressive, almost sinister feeling he'd had when he opened the study door and peeked down the upstairs hall that first time. That was what a hearth witch's grief felt like, tainting their craft.

It wasn't safe for Nelle to go home; the construct easily could have seen her outside the house, which meant that Castor and Serapion would be searching for her, too. Nelle said, firstly, that she had no intention of going home until they told her what was going on, and secondly, that they should call their parents, which proved to be a highly controversial suggestion.

"It's bad enough that we dragged *you* into this," Aziza said. "The less they know about what we're doing, the better."

"What *are* we doing?" Tristan asked.

The bone construct was proof that Castor had no intention of letting them go, but they'd known that already. So, as they drove nonstop through the rest of the day, Aziza and Dion shared the knowledge they'd pooled about Castor Thorne and his lanterns, and they planned their counterattack.

By evening they were the only car on a desolate stretch of I-90 where there was nothing to see but open pasture and the occasional silo or wind farm. They'd meant to find someplace to sleep, but they had taken a twisting route across state borders in an effort to make sure they weren't followed, which had delayed them; the next town was probably another hour or so away.

"Should we just park out here for the night?" Leo asked, over the rain drumming against the windows. "It'll be harder for them to find us in the middle of nowhere."

They had shuffled around and swapped drivers a couple of times; it was Dion's turn now, with Leo in the passenger seat and Nelle in the back with Aziza and Tristan.

"Not if we can avoid it," Dion said. "We're safer in a larger city where Professor Serapion can't let his constructs be seen. Whatever else he and Castor will do, they won't violate the Crow Mandate."

"Safety in numbers," Leo muttered.

"Safety in secrecy," Dion said. "It's all we have."

Outside, there was a clatter like hailstones on the roof of the car. Then a *clack-clack-clack*. Like footsteps. Leo swore under his breath;

Dion accelerated until he was going as fast as he safely could on the flooded road.

"Leo, open the glove compartment," Nelle said.

He did, and swore again at what he found. Dion looked at her in the rearview mirror, appalled. "Why do you have that?"

"I'll show you why if you hand it to me."

Leo obliged, passing the revolver back to her. Another *clack-clack-clack* overhead, and then the bone wolf dropped into view through the windshield—standing on the roof, it craned its neck down and turned its head a full 180 degrees to observe them with its hollow eye sockets.

Dion slammed on the brakes. Claws screeched against metal as the bone wolf tried to hang on, but it was flung off the roof and into the street. It rolled across the slick road and through the beam of the headlights. Lucky materialized in time to strike at it before it could find its feet, and they grappled, tumbling off the asphalt in a tangle of bone and fur.

"There's another one," Aziza said.

It was a flash of white through the rain, the only thing moving in the dark. In the open fields around them, it couldn't have hidden and didn't try. It came toward them with a terrible swiftness. The car lurched forward, but Nelle said, "Wait!"

"Are you sure?" Dion said, but he braked without waiting for her to answer.

She opened the door and stepped out halfway, gun raised, taking aim. Tristan was flipping through *The Serpent Arts*—just in case—but as he scanned its pages desperately for a spell that might help them now, he knew he'd never have time to read the incantation. Not if Nelle missed.

He looked up. The bone wolf was close—yards away—lunging from the field.

Nelle fired twice, striking the construct between the eyes. It collapsed mid-leap in a cascade of bone shards, like a jigsaw puzzle that had been flung into the air crashing down.

Tristan slowly lowered *The Serpent Arts* into his lap.

"Silver bullets?" Aziza asked.

Nelle grinned. "Never leave home without them. Leo, there's also an umbrella in the glove compartment."

He passed it to her in silent awe.

Umbrella in one hand and revolver in the other, Nelle went to the other side of the road, where Lucky and the second bone wolf were half-buried in the long grass, still locked in battle. One more gunshot rang out. Then Nelle and Lucky were both returning to the car, Lucky disappearing into the shadows underneath it.

Tristan climbed out and took the umbrella from her, trading places. "Give me a minute," he told the others. He approached the scattered remains of the bone wolf.

At first, he'd thought these creatures were something similar to his hounds, only made of bone instead of shadow. But when he had looked into its hollow eyes through the windshield, he'd known instantly that he had been wrong. They were nothing like his hounds at all. They were haunted; and the spirit that had possessed this construct still lingered on its remains. Shivering—only in part because he had left his jacket in the car, draped over Aziza's lap—he knelt and sifted through the pieces. Some of them were intact bones—a femur, several vertebra, a mostly complete paw—and others were broken fragments.

At last, he found it: a human molar. The other bones may or may not have belonged to a person, and they may or may not have belonged to the *same* person. Serapion might have simply used animal bones for the construct, reshaping them until they took the form he required. But the spirit within the construct was no animal.

He knew now what Serapion did with his dead apprentices' teeth.

He searched the other set of bones and found another molar. Pocketing them both, he turned back to the car. He'd bury the teeth someplace when he had a chance and make sure they never fell into Serapion's hands again.

THEY CHECKED INTO a motel, where they sprawled across the floor of their room with a take-out feast spread between them: half a dozen paper pails of rice, plastic containers of soup with bubbles of oil shining in clear broth, noodles and chicken and tofu glistening with sauce. Tristan was starving, even though they had picked up snacks when they'd stopped to fuel up. But the food never seemed to satisfy him. The last time he had felt this famished, he had been living on the streets. He had to restrain himself from scooping up rice with his bare hands like an animal.

Maybe, he told himself, the stress of being on the run was making him burn through the calories faster than usual. He tried to savor the burst of heat on his tongue from the chili oil and the crunch of bok choy. But even when he was full, he still felt like—a hound. Like he could've eaten forever and not been satisfied. It disgusted him; it even scared him a little.

"Since you disappeared, Anne went on the offensive," Nelle said, pushing away her empty container of fried rice. "She knows Castor had something to do with it, and she's pissed. Most of her covenmates are still skeptical, but she did get Irma Olin on her side—"

"Really?" Dion said, perking up.

"She's the Clattering's telepath," Nelle told the rest of them, at their mystified looks. "So she's tapping into her network—the master telepaths who studied under her, and their apprentices—and getting them to spy on the weather witches. It turns out they've been holding secret gatherings in Luminous Horizons properties—we don't know how long it's been happening—and word has been spreading that when Castor gives the signal, they all have to go to the Flight Paths and convince as many other witches as they can to come with them."

"The Flight Paths?" Dion said. "Why?"

"No clue," Nelle said. "We're still working on that part."

Nelle wanted to tell Anne they were alive. To their surprise, Aziza agreed with her, at least until Dion pointed out that Anne would talk to their parents. None of them wanted to involve Khaled, Greg, or Maria in the trouble they were about to walk into. Or to have to say *no* to a tearful request to come home. Besides, Anne was making the kind of progress against Castor that they could not. They didn't want to distract her from that—or for her to try and stop them from doing what they were going to do.

As they went to bed, Tristan volunteered for first watch. He retreated onto the balcony, where he rested his elbows on the railing, buried his face in his hands, and breathed in the cold air. The rain from earlier had frozen into a mellow snowfall, and a few wispy flurries blew past now and again. A snowflake landed on the back of his neck, making him shiver. He looked down at the streetlights in the parking lot, the tire tracks through muddy frost, the filigree of ice on the cars.

The glass door slid open behind him and then shut very quietly. He knew it was Aziza by the sound of her footsteps.

"Can't sleep?" he asked, as she leaned on the railing next to him.

"Yeah. It's almost like the Hunt all over again."

"I wish it was only Beor chasing us this time."

"Last time, I wouldn't have had to ask if you were okay. I'd just know."

Her eyes were following the path his own had taken earlier, over the barren view below. Her hair hung in a rope over her shoulder; Leo had braided it for her.

"I thought you'd be relieved the bond was gone," he said.

"I guess I got used to it."

"I did, too," he admitted. "Did—did it hurt?"

She didn't have to ask what he meant. "No."

"Are you lying to me?"

The corner of her mouth turned up in a small, secretive smile. "Do I usually lie to you?"

"Never," he said. "But I think you'd make an exception if you felt like it was necessary."

She gave a thoughtful hum. "Maybe. And when you were tearing through Emil's whole library, making excuses so we wouldn't find out what you were really looking for, I guess that was necessary, too."

He fidgeted with his sleeve. "I didn't want to speak my fears into existence."

"How long were you planning on learning that spell?" she asked.

"I think part of me wanted to be able to do it as soon as I knew it was possible," he said.

She nodded, as if this made perfect sense to her.

"I didn't think I would feel so normal," she said, after a moment. "You'd think something would be different, once you've come back from the dead."

And she gave him a sidelong look that felt uncomfortably perceptive. Even though the bond wasn't there anymore, he was almost convinced she knew exactly what was going on in his head. But he couldn't make himself answer her unspoken question.

"I miss Maria's cooking," he said instead. "I'm already sick of fast food."

"I miss my bed," she said.

"I think I even miss the library's patrons."

She laughed. "We're all high school dropouts now. Leo's going to be so annoyed when he realizes."

"I must be a bad influence."

"The worst," she said fondly.

And he knew that he could tell her. If there was anyone he could talk to about this, it was her. But he didn't think he could say the words out loud. Right now, it was only a slight discomfort, like the beginnings of a cold—when you sensed you were coming down with something but didn't yet feel badly enough that you couldn't brush it off and pretend you were fine. Maybe he was imagining things, and it would go away on its own if he just ignored it.

He didn't want anything to be wrong. He didn't want to be different. To have changed again, against his will, and probably for the worse.

But it wasn't against his will, was it? He had chosen this. He had done it to himself. That had been true every time, even the times when he'd felt like he had no choice. He always had.

He had been afraid that he would screw up the resurrection. It was the most complicated spell he had ever even attempted, and the stakes were so high. If he'd failed, he could've turned his friends into shells of what they'd been, empty vessels, mindless and violent. Or they could have come back different, like Aziza had said—come back wrong. But Aziza and Leo were perfect. They were exactly as they'd been before.

The one who'd come back wrong was Tristan.

CHAPTER 32

LEO

THERE WERE THREE lanterns in total. Dion thought they could ignore one of them for now—the replacement for the lantern Aziza and Leo had broken in the greenhouse. Castor would need to refill it. It would be of little use to him until then. So they were going to prioritize the other two.

The second lantern was the one he'd kept in Bishop Library; the third had been placed in the Summer Court's castle. Both of them, Dion speculated, were complete—or close to it.

"Castor will have hidden them in places that he knows well and can control," Dion said. "One of them will be in Sanctum, West Virginia—his hometown. The other one is at Yale University, where he has many allies, including Professor Serapion, who appears to be part of Castor's inner circle—though what he gets out of the arrangement, I'm not sure yet."

New Haven was easier to reach, so they started there. It was blanketed in a thin layer of snow. Downtown was quiet; it was exam time at Yale, and most of the students were hunkered down in libraries and study rooms. Leo tugged at the collar of the button-down Oxford shirt under the cable-knit cashmere sweater he'd borrowed from Dion and adjusted the strap of the laptop bag on his shoulder, feeling ridiculous beyond belief. Also, half-blind. Which he *was*, but his truesight usually made it easier to ignore that, even if it didn't give him the other half of his vision back. But today he'd put on one of the disguise contacts he'd commissioned during his first trip to the Half Moon Market to cover the amber eye, matching his natural one perfectly. He hardly ever used them because they blocked his truesight. At least when he wore an eye patch, he could take it off and put it back on as he pleased.

"Stop fidgeting," Tristan muttered. "You blend right in."

Leo glanced at him. They were supposed to be freshmen today, and Dion had insisted that a slight wardrobe adjustment would help them look less like lost high schoolers. But somehow Dion's preppy attire looked a lot better on Tristan than it did on Leo. Nelle had put some kind of product into Tristan's hair to smooth it into glossy perfection; it looked exactly as soft as Leo knew it felt. Despite the cold, he'd left his collar open, and he had adopted a haughty tilt to his chin and an air of cool superiority that suggested he'd step over you if you were on the ground and probably not even notice.

"I don't know," Leo said, tearing his eyes away. "I think I'd need Legrand genes to have a chance at pulling off this getup."

The two of them had set off alone. New Haven had one of the largest witch populations in the country, so Dion couldn't risk being seen here. He had been indignant when Aziza had pointed it out, but she was sure—and Nelle agreed—that the witches who attended and taught at the university, masters and apprentices alike, would recognize him on sight. He'd tried to argue, but the rest of them had quickly outvoted him. So he was their Q today, or maybe their Giles. Coven Blackthorn had to be split up, too. Together, the three of them were too recognizable. Leo and Aziza both had distinctive scars, Tristan had his uncommonly pale coloring, and anyone in the magical community who knew them—either because they were Anne's apprentice coven, or from seeing them around the Half Moon Market—would know them as a unit. So Tristan and Leo went together while Aziza had gone with Nelle.

Yale was Castor Thorne's alma mater. He'd double-majored in religious studies and environmental science, and then he'd gone on to complete a graduate program. That meant he had spent almost ten of the most formative years of his magical career on this campus, and Dion was positive they'd find a lantern here.

But it was a big place, and Dion had a list of potential hiding spots. Aziza and Nelle were searching two of them. First, Sterling Memorial Library—it was the main campus library, the oldest, and the one that used to house Yale's jackdaw collection, though it didn't any longer. Second, they would check the Divinity School, where Castor had gotten his master's in theology.

Leo and Tristan had two other spots to investigate. The first was an imposing sandstone building that served as the meeting place for one of Yale's infamous secret societies. They weren't much of a secret anymore. The oldest and most highly regarded ones used to be student covens, but were ultimately abandoned by their magical founders once they gained too much notoriety. Now they pretty much existed for wealthy, popular, or otherwise influential upperclassmen to network with each other and a legion of alumni.

"All the Ivies have their secret societies, but Yale's in particular once drew some of the most legendary necromancers in the world," Dion had said. "And Professor Serapion still usually has an apprentice or two among them."

Tristan shadow-traveled inside and unlocked a basement passage, allowing Leo to sneak in and give it a scan with his truesight. It was morning, and the society met a few evenings a week, so no one was around. The interior was comfortable, if a little macabre.

There was a lot of skull imagery, and a couple of actual skulls, but also couches, scattered candles, and an open trunk with blankets piled messily inside. In one room, they came across a human skeleton in a glass case and a grandfather clock. Other chambers had glass-fronted cabinets filled with books and manuscripts. But there was no trace of magic in the place, not even necromancy, and definitely no sign of the lantern.

"Jun would have felt right at home in there," Tristan muttered as they came back down the stairs and returned to the basement passage. "It looks a lot like his shop. But with more human remains."

"Have you talked to him since . . . the other day?" Leo asked, which he knew was an absurd way to euphemize the event of their resurrection.

"Yes. I don't think Castor knows he's connected to us. No one's come after him," Tristan said. "I told him he has a spot in our getaway car if he needs to make a run for it, though."

Leo hadn't spoken much to Jun, only vaguely registering him as a gentle, solicitous presence welcoming the three of them back to the land of the living. Before he left, he used one of his talismans to make sure Tristan's ghostly possession of Dion had been fully ended with no lingering aftereffects. He had paused to talk quietly to Tristan on his way out, and while Leo hadn't really paid attention at the time, he couldn't quite shake the image of the two of them crowded together at the door to Emil's study. As Leo had suspected and feared, Jun was good-looking in this scruffy, punk-rock sort of way, with his piercings and boots and messy black hair, a perfect contrast to Tristan's delicate beauty. They looked good together. And Jun clearly cared a lot about Tristan. Which was great. Really. Tristan deserved to be surrounded by people who cared for him. Especially cute mediums who weren't in love with anyone else.

They sealed the basement passage behind them. It was a comparatively bright day outside, with a gray-white pall of sunlight filtering through the clouds. Tristan hooked an arm around his elbow and tugged him to the side so they could pass a group of students coming the other way. Leo hadn't even noticed them. Guilty that he'd let his mind wander—and that his thoughts were so petty—he forced his attention back to the present. It was getting colder as the sky darkened, and Tristan was warm, which was why Leo didn't pull away after the other group had passed them.

"What do you think?" Tristan asked.

"Of what?" Leo said, a flush creeping up his neck. Had Tristan sensed how distracted he was? Had he guessed why?

"Of Jun joining our scavenger hunt, if necessary."

"We need all the help we can get," Leo said. "You could teach him more spells."

"I could. Though I think he's better off staying out of all this."

"Probably, but I bet he'd still do it if you asked."

"You think so?" Tristan said, his tone deceptively innocent. "Why's that?"

"I mean," Leo said stoically, refusing to be flustered. "You've got a whole thing going on."

"A *thing*? What thing?"

"You know. You teach him a spell . . . he gives you jewelry . . . you give him one of your teeth . . ."

"Would you like a tooth, too?" Tristan inquired. "Maybe you can have one if you ask nicely."

"Stop, I'm swooning," Leo said, a smile twitching at the corners of his lips. He tried to suppress it. Were they flirting? Was it okay to talk like this when you were ex-friends-with-benefits?

It was a twenty-minute walk to the building that housed the

anthropology department. They passed the clocktower and cut through the courtyard, which was populated by a few scattered trees, bare and tipped with frost. The Gothic edifices of old campus loomed over it.

"Aziza and Nelle finished checking the library. No luck," Tristan said, tucking his phone away.

That meant they would be headed to the Divinity School next.

"What about Dion?" Leo asked.

"He's finding a halfway point to wait for all of us."

"I don't like splitting up."

"Me neither."

Dion had wanted them to rule out the other locations, but he thought the Divinity School was the most likely hiding place for the lantern. So if anyone was going to run into trouble, it would probably be Aziza and Nelle.

There would be no monsters guarding the lantern this time. Castor was relying on his allies and followers to keep it safe. As Dion couldn't be seen here, he was waiting nearby with their ride, ready to swoop in should they need to make a quick escape. The Divinity School and the anthropology department were both on the north side of campus, no more than a few minutes apart by car.

Still. Leo didn't like it.

"Lucky is with them, too. I'll know if something goes wrong," Tristan said. Absently, he added, "It would have been nice to still have the bond right now."

"Do you miss it?" Leo asked.

"More than I thought I would. Less now than I did before," Tristan said, his voice detached, as if he were speaking without hearing himself. "When I was . . . a hound, or thought I was . . . Well, hounds are supposed to have a pack, and I was alone."

Tristan had told them very little of his time as a prisoner in Lucky's mind. He and Dion had bonded over it in odd ways, even though *they* didn't talk about it, either. But every now and then, Dion would say something offhand to Lucky and look surprised when Tristan was the one who answered. And sometimes, Tristan seemed to lose all concept of personal space around Dion, practically hanging off his shoulder to read a notebook or map he was holding.

"Do you wanna talk about it?" he asked.

"Not yet," Tristan said.

Wordlessly, he took Tristan's hand. It was the only thing he could do. Tristan clung to it.

"Tell me about the snake spells," he said, changing the subject. "That's the grimoire you were reading last night, right?"

Tristan smiled. It was a little bit of a sinister smile; it probably said nothing good about Leo that he was instantly charmed by it. "They're mostly for spying on people and sneaking into places. There's one that creates a spiritual construct that takes the form of a python and devours human ghosts. And there's another one that's supposed to make your enemy feel like there are worms crawling under their skin. There's a warning on it that says it's driven its past victims to madness."

Leo wrinkled his nose, disgusted and fascinated in equal measure. "Maybe save that one for Castor."

"Maybe." Tristan's gaze wandered over the courtyard, taking note of every person who passed by. "Did you apply here?"

"We applied to all the same schools."

"Did we apply here?"

Leo laughed. "No."

"Why not?"

"I don't want to go out of state," he said. "I'm even more sure of that now. I think I'd just . . . really like to go home after this."

They were talking as if there would definitely be an *after*, even though it was looking like they could not coexist with Castor Thorne. He tried not to dwell on it.

At the intersection where College Street met Grove, they could see the corner of the cemetery. The inscription on its stately rust-colored gate read *The Dead Shall Be Raised*, which was both a biblical reference and an inside joke. But they turned the other way, toward Hillhouse Avenue. It was a one-way road lined with oak trees and old mansion houses that had been converted into university buildings. He didn't let go of Tristan's hand, and none of the people passing them on the sidewalk spared them a glance. They'd decided to strike in broad daylight because the jackdaw need for secrecy would protect them to some degree, at least from the most conspicuous magical attacks. Serapion couldn't let his bone wolves be seen running around the streets of New Haven. But anyone around them could be a witch, and with the amber eye covered, he wouldn't even know it.

If it wasn't for those persistent, paranoid thoughts, it would have been nice, though. Walking around a college campus hand in hand with Tristan. As if they were a real couple.

They found the department of anthropology and loitered near the entrance until someone else tapped in with their student ID. Dion had procured Serapion's schedule and the location of his office. The professor was supposed to be away overseeing a lab session for the next hour. Tristan vanished into a restroom so that he could shadow-travel to the inside of the office and let Leo in. Then Leo removed the contact lens from his amber eye and inspected the small room.

He found what they were looking for right away—not the lantern, not yet, but the protective enchantments that revealed to him the invisible shape of a concealed door. It was the entrance to Serapion's library of grimoires. Dion had told them that Serapion was the one who'd taught Emil how to secure his own collection.

"Emil was never his apprentice, but he learned a few tricks from him," he'd said. "I'm sure every necromancer who passes through Yale does."

The trouble was the key—a quick sweep of his desk, cabinets, and the other bookcases turned up nothing. Serapion probably kept it on his person. So they had to resort to old-fashioned breaking and entering. When they pushed the bookcase out of the way, there was nothing behind it but a blank wall. This, too, Dion had prepared them for.

"The entrance to his *real* office won't reveal itself until you've already unlocked it," he said. "The lock is a magical mechanism. Leo, you can probably shatter it with that fairy weapon of yours."

They cleared the books off the shelves until they uncovered a tiny keyhole in the back of the bookcase. Leo took the hilt of the frost sword from his backpack and drew the blade; he aimed the tip at the keyhole, where the protective enchantments were concentrated, and thrust the blade into it with all his strength. The sword cleaved straight through the back of the bookcase. There was a sharp *crack* and a flash of light, and the blank wall in the corner of the office transformed. The hidden door had materialized, visible even to Leo's natural eye now. They turned the handle, and it opened without resistance.

As they entered, a row of candles on the wall burst into flame, illuminating a long, book-lined corridor that ended at another unlit doorway. An incomprehensible whispering followed them through the passage. Leo turned back sharply, but no one was there. The whispers were coming from the grimoires. Tristan folded an arm over his stomach and clung to Lucky's fur with his other hand, looking a little ill.

"You all right?" Leo said under his breath.

"Fine." Tristan's jaw was tense, as if with suppressed pain. "It's his books of spirits. Some of them have human ghosts bound to them. I can . . . sense them."

He looked as if he might have said more, but then, from the end of the hall, they heard something else. A groan, like something in pain.

They froze, except for Lucky, who growled.

"Go," Tristan whispered to his hound, and Lucky did, its claws clicking against tile. He looked fixedly into the middle distance, seeing through Lucky's eyes. Then—without warning—Tristan lurched forward, taking off after Lucky into the next chamber.

"What's wrong?" Leo hissed, but Tristan didn't answer; all Leo could do was follow him.

As they crossed the next threshold, more candles flared to life. The wavering light filled a large, circular room with a set of tables in the center that held the components of unbound grimoires—ink and paper and lengths of sinewy thread, bone samples in wooden trays, and glass containers that, to Leo's amber eye, were aglow with spiritual energy. A curving staircase led up to a loft space. There was another groan, louder, and the shadows behind the balustrade shifted with movement. Someone was up there.

They had more than ascertained that the lantern was not here. But Tristan ran for the stairs anyway, stopping so suddenly at the top that Leo almost collided with him. He was breathing hard, as if the short run had winded him. In the dark, something rattled—chains. And then a figure crawled into the candlelight.

It was a girl—kind of. Long brown hair hung around a face that was so gaunt, its features so sunken, that it was impossible to tell its age. The chains were connected to the silver collar around her neck and the manacles that hung on her wrists, which were striped with burn marks from contact with the metal. The wounds had healed badly into thick, discolored scar tissue. Her eyes were all pupil, ink-black wells that narrowed on them. Lucky had lowered itself into a predatory crouch so that it was almost at eye level with her, its fangs bared. But the chained girl's gaze never left Leo and Tristan.

"*Stay back*," she growled, a split second before she lunged at them, teeth snapping. The chains pulled taut, the collar almost strangling her, and the girl slammed against the ground, snarling.

Tristan had to grab two fistfuls of Lucky's fur to hold it back. "Don't!" he commanded.

Through curtains of tangled hair, the girl looked up at them.

"Kill me," she rasped.

"What the hell is this?" Leo asked, in a horrified whisper.

"I think," Tristan said slowly, "this is one of Professor Serapion's apprentices."

"Yes," the girl said, her eyes shut now, her hands flexing open and closed. "He said . . . if I turned . . . he could reverse it."

"Are you a striga?" Tristan asked. "A . . . hag?"

"I don't know," she said. "It depends."

"On what?"

Her eyelashes flickered. Her lips, colorless, peeled back from her broken teeth. "On what part of you I would devour, if I could break these chains."

Leo took a cautious step closer, but she cringed, hiding her face and breathing hard.

"*Don't*," she hissed. "I can—Your *scent*—"

He stopped. "You're hurt. We want to help you—just tell us how."

"Kill me," she said again, her eyes shut.

"We're not going to—"

"*Please.* While I'm still myself," she gasped. "Or he'll make me keep going."

"What does she mean?" Leo asked Tristan quietly.

"He forced her to corrupt her magic," Tristan said, his face blank.

He inched closer, though the girl still wouldn't look at him. "Are you sure there's no other way?"

She nodded, brow pressed to the floor. "I'm already dead."

"No," Leo said firmly. "No, there has to be something else we can do."

Tristan took two steps forward. The change in her was immediate. She whipped off the ground, her body twisting, her face contorted with feral hunger, and struck at Tristan. Lucky knocked her down and pinned her with a paw on her chest, just below the silver collar. It must have hurt—should have hurt—but her response was a wordless sound of rage, an animal roar, as she clawed at Lucky.

Tristan knelt beside her. She swiped at his face with her long nails, but he batted her flailing hands away. He had drawn his silver knife. Leo didn't catch on to what he was doing until it was almost too late, and then he couldn't think of any way to stop it except for tackling him. Pure instinct, nothing more, a simple knee-jerk reaction. He crashed into Tristan, grabbing at his wrist and immobilizing his knife hand a moment before he would have plunged the blade into her chest.

They fell, Leo on top of him and Tristan hissing with pain as his wrist slammed against the floor. The chains rattled as the girl bucked under Lucky's weight, straining to reach them. Leo hauled himself and Tristan upright, pulling them both farther away at the same time, if only so that she might calm down.

"Sorry," Leo said, releasing him, sickened by the faint whiteish imprints circling Tristan's wrist where his fingers had been. "I didn't mean to—But why did you—What are you *doing*?"

He wanted to take the knife, but Tristan's white-knuckled grip stopped him from trying; he would have had to pry it out of his hand. Tristan put his free hand on Leo's chest and pushed him lightly back so he had space to get up.

"She asked to die," Tristan said without inflection.

"She's desperate and afraid and traumatized!" Leo said, scrambling to his feet. "Chained up in someone's office for who knows how long—No wonder she doesn't see another way out, that doesn't mean you just—"

"*You* killed a striga recently," Tristan said, his eyes hard. "How is this different?"

"She's still a—a *person*!"

"Barely," Tristan said with icy apathy. "And if we leave her here, she won't be for much longer. I'm not going to stand by and let another hag loose when I could have stopped it."

Leo had no argument for this. He turned away so he wouldn't have to look at the struggling girl—or at Tristan, who was suddenly as closed off and remote as a stranger. Maybe he was right; maybe Leo was being a hypocrite. It wasn't like they could take her with them.

"If it were me in her place," Tristan said, "I would—"

"*Don't* finish that sentence," Leo said, abruptly furious as he spun back to face Tristan—only to find that Tristan was much closer than he had been before. There was a flash of winter's night in his eyes again, a kind of economical ruthlessness.

"Or what?" Tristan said.

Or you'll break my heart, Leo thought, but he couldn't say it—not because he was worried about the lines he could or couldn't cross, but because he couldn't speak at all when Tristan looked at him like that.

His phone vibrated, so loud in the tense silence that he actually jumped.

"It's Dion," Leo said, reading his message. "We have to go."

"We'll go in a minute," Tristan said, turning back to the girl. She had stopped trying to fight the hound and was watching Tristan with huge, hopeful eyes.

Leo couldn't stop him from doing this. He was afraid to find out if Tristan would physically fight him over it, and either way Leo wouldn't lift a hand against Tristan even to save someone's life. A terrifying realization.

And wasn't he the one who had once made Tristan promise to do what he thought was right? Even if it was different from what was right to Leo.

"Wait," Leo said hoarsely. "I'll do it."

Tristan swung back around to him. *"What?"*

Leo had the distinct feeling that nothing else he could have said in that moment would have given him pause. He felt a kind of sick satisfaction, like he'd chipped the stranger's mask and caught a glimpse of Tristan's true face underneath it. It propelled him, kept the words coming even when he wasn't sure they were the right ones.

"You've killed enough hags," he said. "I'm not making you do this alone."

"You don't even want to do it."

"You don't, either. What, it's okay for you to get your hands dirty, but not me?"

"Are you sure that you can?" Tristan parried. It was almost challenging, like he was baiting him. Another chip came off the mask.

"Do you really think she's better off dead?" Leo asked, though he knew the answer already. He was just buying himself time to decode the things Tristan *wasn't* saying. "What if we could save her?"

Somehow, out of all the reckless things he had done and said during this conversation, that question was his first unequivocally wrong move. Tristan's expression froze over. Stiffly, he said, "Not everyone can be saved. We should respect her wishes."

"How can you say that when we haven't even *tried* to save her?" Leo said. "Tris, I'm worried about you. Zee is, too—we were talking about it earlier."

"Conspiring against me?" Tristan asked.

"Do we need to?"

He flipped the knife over, held it by the blade and offered the hilt to Leo. "We can talk later. If you're doing this, go ahead. If not, then I will."

Leo took it like a dare. He'd held this knife more times than he could count; it had never felt heavier. Could he go through with this? Could he afford *not* to?

A noise from downstairs made them both start. It was a *clack-clack-clack* like scattering ice cubes, chilling and hollow. Lucky snarled, its hackles rising. The chained girl gave a low moan of utter despair.

"It's too late now," she whispered, tears leaking from the corners of her eyes.

Tristan dove down the stairs; Leo was a half-step behind. They reached the lower level in time to see six bone wolves prowl into the room. Their snouts opened and closed with a *snap* like a bear trap.

Professor Serapion was the last to enter. The hidden door from the office swung closed, locking them all inside.

CHAPTER 33
TRISTAN

"I HAD WONDERED if someone had merely reanimated your bodies," Professor Serapion said, with a kind of studious curiosity, as if mentally vivisecting them. "But that's obviously not the case. Who was it, then?" A bone wolf crouched under a table, the vertebral chain of its tail curving around one of the legs. Another crept close to the edge of the room where the candlelight didn't quite reach. The rest of the pack stayed close to him. "Who brought you back?"

The memory-dream of his short time as a ghost was foggy at best. Tristan was aware of what had happened, not in the part of him that was flesh and blood, but in his . . . spirit. It was his spirit, not his body, that shivered at the sight of the necromancer who had held him in the palm of his hand, trapped him there, made him helpless, made him submit.

His jaw clenched, his teeth grinding. The missing one ached. "What did you do to that girl upstairs?"

Leo was beside him, silent and tense, doubtless doing the same mental arithmetic Tristan was reckoning with. Eight against three. Serapion's decades of experience against Tristan's months of scattershot self-study. Zero silver bullets and one silver knife between them, the hilt sliding into Tristan's palm as Leo discreetly returned it to him. They were standing close enough that their coats concealed the motion.

"Her condition is self-inflicted. She cast those corruptive spells herself," Serapion said, his voice all smug condescension. The bone wolves were slinking closer, inch by inch. "Now, tell me. I want to know which of my colleagues would dare to do what they've done."

Lucky answered for him, leaping over the rail of the loft space and landing in the middle of the workroom, almost on top of Serapion's head.

The bone wolves flew into action. One slammed into Lucky, but Lucky rolled it over and gnawed at it while it struggled. The others descended on him and Leo.

In one swift motion, Leo drew the frost sword and swung, hitting the first construct directly in the face. The fairy weapon couldn't kill it, not like silver could—but the blow knocked it back, and his next swing caught the second construct in midair as it sprang up at him. The touch of the enchanted blade froze their joints and spines, and a follow-up blow shattered what was frozen, forcing them to reassemble themselves. One he stabbed through the ribs, used the blade like a lever to pick it up, and heaved it away so that it crashed into the wall, its bones snapping in several places.

Another one of the bone wolves came at Tristan. He held up the silver knife, ready to fend it off. It lunged under his guard and bit at his arm, but he moved just in time, and it only caught his sleeve. He slid out of his jacket while it pulled with its teeth, and the sudden release of tension sent it reeling backward. That gave Tristan an opening to jab the knife into the place where its spine met the base of its skull. The construct buckled underneath him; he dug the knife in, prying the skull off its body, and it collapsed to the ground in pieces.

On his knees in a pile of bone shards, he pulled out *The Serpent*

Arts, flipped to the page he wanted, and read the incantation aloud, so quickly the words ran together. As he spoke, a shiver disturbed the pieces of discarded bone, almost like a gentle wind. The fragments moved as if of their own accord, drawing together and recombining. Not into a wolf, though. With the serpent art of twisting and turning and transforming, Tristan reshaped it into something new.

When he was done, a bone python as thick across as Tristan's torso was slithering into the fray. It caught one of the wolves as it danced away from Leo, wrapped around it, and held it immobile; Leo took the opportunity and beheaded it. Tristan followed up by slamming the edge of his knife against its spine, cracking the vertebra. It fell to pieces and merged with the bone python, which lengthened. All at once, Serapion was down to four constructs.

When Tristan looked up at Serapion, the professor was reading from a pocket-sized grimoire, his voice too low for Tristan to hear. The remaining wolves backed up, as if to retreat—and then they were fusing and changing, not unlike the way the other two had transformed for Tristan's spell. But these weren't the simple contortions of a serpent art. The bone shards *grew*, expanding; plates of cartilage built up layer by layer and ossified. Soon the constructs had merged into a three-headed wolf, thrice Lucky's size and towering over Tristan and Leo. When its jaws snapped shut, it was like the smash of ocean waves on Blackthorn's cliffs. The rattle of its tail was a rockslide, calamitous; as it whipped from side to side, it hit the tables, splintering them and sending half-finished grimoires sliding to the ground.

"Fuck," Leo said, the tip of the sword dipping as his grip slackened with shock.

Tristan grabbed his arm and dragged him to the stairs. The girl—the half hag or striga or lich—was lying on the floor in mute despair, rolling her head to look listlessly at them as they reappeared, though this time she didn't speak. He thought of breaking her chains—if he set her free, would she be rational enough to go for Serapion? Or would her ravenous instincts set her upon whoever was closest? Behind them, two of the bone wolf's heads squeezed into the staircase, one on top of the other. Both sets of teeth snapped at them, and its claws screeched against the floor. It was too large to climb up after them.

"Trade?" Tristan said. He offered Leo the silver knife again. Leo passed over the hilt of the frost sword.

"Be careful," Leo whispered.

Tristan shadow-traveled downstairs with Lucky, reappearing silently behind Serapion. Then he sent Lucky back to Leo's side. His bone python came to him instead, weaving around the three-headed construct's paws and tail. Serapion spotted it right away, and as he watched it approach, Tristan crept up behind him and drove the frost blade at his back.

Serapion spun so fast he must have known all along that Tristan was there, dodging the blow with shocking agility for his age. His hard, cold fingers clamped down on Tristan's wrist, squeezing into a nerve point. The hilt slipped from his hand, blade vanishing, and rolled away. His bone python reared up and struck at Serapion—but Serapion flung out his free hand, whispering a Latin incantation, and it froze with its open mouth millimeters from his palm.

Tristan clawed at Serapion's face with his free hand—he had no weapon, fine, he'd gouge his eyes out if that was what it took. He broke the skin, leaving deep, bleeding scratch marks, and Serapion hissed with pain. But he didn't let go. He made a gesture with his outstretched hand, a snap of his wrist, and a spray of bone shards tore off the python and shot at Tristan like bullets. He dove out of the way not a moment too soon, finally ripping out of the professor's grasp. The pointed shards embedded themselves in the wall like long, crooked nails. They would have pierced him straight through.

"If Emil Wulfsige were still alive, he would have been my first guess," Serapion said conversationally. Blood dripped down his jaw. He picked up the hilt of the frost sword, turning it over in his thin, veiny hands as if to figure out the trick of it. "But if it wasn't him, then who?"

"Why would I tell you?" Tristan said.

Serapion's fingers closed around the hilt. The blade appeared. Tristan imagined Serapion killing him with that sword—with Leo's sword. He couldn't let that happen. But Serapion didn't lift the weapon, just let it hang from one hand.

"Perhaps some encouragement will help," he said instead. He took something from his pocket. It must have been the size of a bead, too small for Tristan to see what it was. But as Serapion murmured into his curled fingers, and Tristan felt the magic come over him, he knew—it was another tooth from a dead apprentice. He had commanded their ghost to possess Tristan.

Tristan couldn't help it; he laughed. He laughed even as that dreadful hunger gaped open inside him again, like a wound he had been holding shut with a few messy stitches; it ached so badly his knees buckled, and he had to brace himself against the wall. His mouth watered. He swallowed hard on nothing. He couldn't see the spirit, but he felt its presence nudging at him—couldn't feel it, but knew it was there. But it was like mist against the windshield of a car. No sooner did it make contact than was it split apart and blown away.

Serapion watched him intently, not yet afraid. "How are you resisting it?"

Tristan couldn't speak. He feared if he opened his mouth, he'd be sick, or . . . he didn't know what.

The three-headed wolf construct made a strange noise, a howl like the wind, the first howl he'd heard from it. It made both him and Serapion look up. Tristan's heart nearly stopped. Leo was on *top* of the construct, his feet braced behind its neck, his hand hooked into the ridge where an ear would have been. The middle head tried to buck him off; Lucky kept the one on the right distracted, but the left head pivoted toward Leo, snapping at him, unable to reach. Leo raised the silver knife and stabbed it down into the top of the middle skull, cracking through bone and burying it to the hilt. The broken skull crashed to the ground with a *boom*, pulling the other heads down with it. But now Leo was in reach of the left head, almost directly underneath it. It struck at him; he dove out of its way, slipped to the ground, and was nearly trampled by its giant paws. Lucky snatched the hood of his coat and dragged him to safety, but both remaining heads followed, necks stretching toward them.

Sensing his construct's imminent defeat, Serapion sneered. He murmured an incantation that made ghostly shackles appear on Tristan's ankles, immobilizing him. "I'll be back for you in a moment," he said. "One way or another, you *will* answer my questions."

He lifted the frost blade and turned to Leo. One of the remaining heads had its teeth in Lucky's middle, slowly chewing through it. Leo was moving around to the back of the construct as if looking for a way up again, careful to stay out of the other head's reach. He didn't see Serapion coming toward him.

"Stop!" Tristan shouted. But Serapion paid him no attention, and Leo didn't hear.

The ghostly shackles kept Tristan rooted to the spot. But as he strained against them, the cold magic seeping into his skin while the distance between him and Serapion grew, there was no pain, or even any fear. He felt only that insatiable hunger drilling a hole in his stomach and flooding his mouth with saliva.

Tristan knew what starving felt like, but this was different; this starving didn't make him weak. It made him strong. Not like the wretch he'd been once. Like a *devourer*. He didn't know where the feeling was coming from. But he wanted more of whatever it was.

"Don't touch him. Don't even look at him," Tristan said wrathfully. He hardly sounded like himself. *"I will kill you."*

The ghostly shackles broke, coming apart easily all of a sudden. Breaking them felt good. But he didn't take a step, though he could have.

He didn't need to. His prey would come to him.

Serapion froze. He turned slowly back. At the other end of the room, Leo brought the second skull crashing down. One remained. Lucky was mostly dead, twitching as it healed from bite marks that had nearly cut it in half. Any moment now, the two of them would finish off the last of the three heads. If Tristan only stalled for a little longer, they would come and help him overpower Serapion before he had a chance to make another construct. But Tristan couldn't have stopped. He didn't know what he was about to do, but he *had* to do it.

"It was *you*," Serapion said, and his tone was complicated. Astonishment, disgust, envy.

Tristan reached out instinctively, with the same gesture he had always used to summon his hounds, and curled his fingers as if to beckon Serapion closer. It was not his hounds he was calling for. It was something else. He didn't know how he knew to do it; the knowledge was just a part of him now. It came from that hollow, voracious thing inside him. This time, he didn't fight it. He let it take control.

In the back of the room, a *crash*, and then silence. The bone construct was dead. Tristan didn't even look up.

There was a visible change in Serapion, so subtle at first he thought he was imagining it. His eyes went dull, their color fading; his skin gained a papery quality. Something was leaving him, a vibrancy or presence—and then something was *physically* leaving him, too. It was a mist of spiritual energy, drifting from him in coils, winding through the air until it found Tristan's extended hand. As more of it rose from Serapion, he grew gaunt and haggard—as though, before Tristan's eyes, he was rapidly aging. He clutched his chest, gasping for air.

"You . . ." he rasped. "You . . . were the one who . . ."

His spirit curled around Tristan's fingers. He pet at it, fascinated, almost lovingly. Death didn't need to be violent. It could be a gentle release. An escape, like falling asleep in the woods midwinter and not feeling the cold anymore. He understood with the suddenly-there knowledge one had in dreams that the persistent hunger—that was assuaged by none of the things Tristan usually craved, like food or touch—could be sated in only one way.

He breathed in. The spirit didn't have a scent, exactly, and it wasn't quite tangible, but he felt a frigid touch on his lips, and his lungs burned a little the way it did when you inhaled dry winter air.

Serapion fell over, drained—and he wasn't dead, but it didn't matter anymore either way.

The clouds in Tristan's mind cleared as soon as it was done. He looked down at his hand, at Serapion's unresponsive body, and finally, at Leo, his mismatched eyes wide as he stared back at Tristan. The sudden realization was written on his face, the same that had dawned on Serapion much too late.

Tristan didn't consciously call for Lucky—but still Lucky was there, pulled to him by the sheer desperate force of Tristan's want, still bloody as it rose limping from the shadows at his side.

"Wait!" Leo said, but Tristan couldn't. He didn't dare. He grabbed on to his hound, tucking himself close to its side, and fled into the dark.

CHAPTER 34

AZIZA

The Yale Divinity School was a gated brick complex surrounding a narrow, snow-glazed quad with intersecting footpaths. A chapel stood at the end, its white steeple framed by bare trees and shrouded by a low-hanging mist.

The bell tolled the hour as she and Nelle crossed the quad. It felt smaller than it had looked in the pictures, and was enclosed on all sides by tall brick walls. On a warmer day, there would have been people out here, studying in the grass or on one of the wooden benches, but just then there was no one to see them skulking around near the chapel's entrance, waiting for someone to tap into one of the doors on either side of the steps. Someone did in short order, a custodian with a rolling trash can who hit the button for the automatic door opener. After he disappeared through it, the door hung open for several seconds, and they slipped inside unimpeded.

It let them into a busy hallway; they looked like any other pair of students, and no one gave them a second glance. Aziza kept her phone pressed to her ear, with Dion on the line giving them step-by-step instructions. Nelle leaned in occasionally to listen or comment, Aziza tilting the phone so they could both hear. He had accompanied Emil on research trips to the Divinity Library, and had also managed to dig up a few campus floor plans. He guided them past the entrance to the library, which was situated directly under the chapel, into a stairwell, and up to the next level.

She tried to picture a younger Castor here and found it difficult. It felt so peaceful and subdued, which were words she could never have associated with Castor Thorne.

"Why did he pick theology?" Aziza asked as they climbed the steps. "He doesn't strike me as very . . . spiritual."

"He's not," Dion said. "He has no religious affiliation, as far as I know. But he is very good at understanding people. He says understanding someone is the first step to controlling them. Turn left at the landing."

"Lovely," Nelle said. "But he's right. There's, like, a disproportionately high concentration of witches in the field of theology. It was on the list of approved majors my aunt gave me to choose from. Not a long list, by the way."

"So that you could control people?"

"So that I could understand how they think and guide them the way they expect an oracle to be able to guide them," Nelle said.

"That's what theology essentially is," Dion added. "It's a study of belief systems and how they influenced history, science, the arts. How people across time grappled with questions of morality, and why they made the choices they made. And it's woven inextricably with the history of the occult."

The chapel was full of muted sunlight from the arched windows. Rows of wooden chairs were arranged between tall white columns, facing the elevated chancel. Overhead, a pair of tiered chandeliers glittered. A balcony held the organ, its pipes positioned above the main entrance.

"I don't see anything out of the ordinary," Nelle said. Dion had enchanted Nelle's sunglasses last night so that they would reveal hidden aspects of magical buildings—secret doors, false dead ends, trick stairs. A little bit of portable hearthcraft to ease the way for them.

"Then try the balcony," Dion said. "If that doesn't work, you'll have to find a way into the steeple."

He was so sure the lantern would be here, Aziza would almost be disappointed *for* him if it wasn't. Following his directions, they backed out into the hall and went up another set of steps, to the organ loft.

"If you didn't pick theology, what did you do instead?" she asked Nelle.

"Poli sci with a geography minor."

"Really?"

"You don't need to sound so shocked," Nelle said. "I could be a politician. If I stopped dyeing my hair, scrubbed all my socials, and woke up before noon."

"Nelle, you're an inspiration," Dion said.

"Maybe I'll take over as librarian for good once Tristan leaves," Nelle mused. "I kind of liked it there."

Aziza remembered saying something similar to her grandfather, and he had been right that it wouldn't have suited her at all. But she thought, actually, that Bishop Library would be in good hands with Nelle. She would always be able to help you find the book you were looking for. She would come up with her own obscure shelving system, coherent to no one but her. She'd turn the empty office into an extension of her booth at the Half Moon Market, reading people's fortunes in the back during business hours.

"Careful," Dion was saying. "Aziza is picky about her librarians."

"I'm not," Aziza said absently. "I just didn't like you."

"Then why did you come to see me so often?"

"I thought you were suspicious."

"No other reason?"

"Like what?"

If he replied, Nelle was laughing too hard for Aziza to hear it.

The door at the top of the stairs was locked and required an ID to tap in. Aziza was sure they had been thwarted at last by campus security, but Nelle said, "Wait here," and vanished downstairs against Dion's vehement protests. Aziza waited for several agonizing minutes. Somewhere below her feet, there was a *crash*, followed by a minor commotion of confused voices. At last, Nelle reappeared, jogging up the steps with an ID card clutched in her hand.

"Had to steal this from one of the offices down there," Nelle whispered. "Let's hope it works."

"You stole it? From a faculty member?" Dion said, scandalized.

"Sorry, next time I'll ask politely," Nelle said.

The ID was accepted by the scanner with a chirp, and she pulled the door open. It led directly into the organ loft. Most of the space was taken up by the casework, though a narrow passage behind it led to a door that Aziza assumed went into the steeple. It was pitch-dark in there, though the dim light from the loft illuminated a ladder in the corner.

But Nelle had gone around the front of the organ to the console, which was situated at the balcony, overlooking the nave. She studied the keyboard through her tinted lenses.

"Dion, I need the solution for a musical lock," she said.

The key to a musical lock involved playing a specific series of notes; it wasn't difficult for Dion and Nelle to break, but it *was* loud. Loud enough, even, to likely be heard from outside the chapel. They were going to have to hurry.

To the left of the console when facing the balcony rail, there was an arched recess in the wall, as if a space to hang a painting. As the final note rang out, a door appeared in the empty recess. They wasted no time opening it, revealing a narrow hallway to a windowless room. The lantern was the only thing inside.

Like the one in the greenhouse, it had a glass chamber in an iron frame. Inside, an ethereal light shone so brightly it filled the secret room and spilled out into the organ loft. It was sunlight; it was liquid gold, bottled summer, and if Dion was correct in assuming that this was the lantern Viren had retrieved from the castle—then much of the magic it contained was Elphame's. It was the late King Ilanthus and his subjects, the dazzling costume illusions and otherworldly music of the Midsummer Revels, the nixies lounging in the springs of the birch forest, the jade rot ripping through the castle, the servants caught in their enchanted sleep.

"Found it," Aziza said into the phone, when she knew she'd been silent too long.

"Good. Now get out of there," he said.

They couldn't open it here. The magical backlash could bring the building down on their heads. They had to take it off campus, somewhere they could destroy it safely.

She picked it up by the ring at the top and eased it into her backpack. Then she and Nelle fled, down the stairs from the loft, through the chapel's front entrance, and onto the steps that led to the quad. It was the fastest way out. Dion stayed on the line.

"I've told Leo and Tristan where to wait for us," he said. "They should be on their way."

Outside, the mist had grown so dense that the cross at the top of the chapel had all but vanished. The windows were opaque with condensation. In the distance, a dog howled.

There were a handful of people outside, though it was even colder now than it had been earlier. A boy sat on a bench with the hood of his jacket pulled up. Two women stood in between a pair of columns in the cloistered walkway that ran the length of the quad—one older, a faculty member, and the other a student. Nelle stopped short, her hand still holding the chapel door open. As they hesitated, the boy stood, and the women began to walk in their direction.

"We've been seen," she told Dion.

"Change of plans," he said. "Go back inside. First, try the door to the right of the chapel's entrance, past the cabinets. If it's locked, take the stairs down again. Two flights below, there's an exit to a rear courtyard. From there, I can meet you at a faculty parking lot."

But the courtyard had been overtaken by the same unnatural fog; they couldn't see more than an arm's length in front of them in any direction. That dog howled again, closer—it was a howl like a claxon, high and shrieking. Through the cold, clinging haze, the dark silhouettes of strangers came toward them. She and Nelle retreated into the stairwell and let the door slam.

"We're surrounded," Nelle said, leaning close to Aziza to speak into the phone.

"Not yet," Dion said.

He directed them upstairs once again, one level up, to the bustling hallway with the entrance to the Divinity Library. They passed the circulation desk manned by a pair of students, went down another hall and then into the rotunda, a circular space that contained a double set of curving staircases to an open second level. She couldn't hear the howling anymore, but there were footsteps behind them, moving just quickly enough to keep pace.

"Find the Trowbridge room," Dion said. Aziza chanced a look backward and made eye contact with the old woman she was sure she'd seen outside. She had a wrinkled, hawkish face, with a small chin and a large nose, and wore a smart navy blazer and a pair of spectacles. She did not deign to chase them, only made her leisurely way up the stairs as if she had all the time in the world. She must have known where they were going. Even Aziza didn't know where they were going.

The Trowbridge Reference Room was full of students working at the study tables; she and Nelle earned a few irritated glances when they burst inside.

"Nelle, use your glasses and look for another way out," Dion said. "It'll be in the back."

White bookcases lined the walls. On one end of the room, a portrait of a pair of children hung over an unlit fireplace and a set of armchairs; on the other end, there was a small corridor with an elevator.

"You said the jackdaw collection wasn't here anymore," Aziza whispered into the phone, following Nelle that way.

Yale's jackdaw collection had migrated several times over the years. The Divinity Library had been its original host, but it had later been moved to the more centrally located Sterling Memorial Library. As the university had grown in size and prestige, and New Haven had flourished around it, traffic in the library had increased—so the jackdaw collection had been moved once again to the lesser-used classics library, to make it easier for witches to come and go unnoticed.

Unlike the abandoned library at Martin College, which was still connected to the Flight Paths, the Divinity Library's link to the network had been severed once another location on campus was chosen to host the jackdaw collection.

"It's not on the Flight Paths anymore," Dion said, "but if I'm right, Castor and Professor Serapion would have repurposed the old passage to—"

"*If* you're right?" Aziza said.

"It's a figure of speech. Obviously I'm right."

"Here!" Nelle said. She was jabbing the elevator button.

"How did you know . . . ?" Aziza asked.

"That exit at the end of the hall you're in is the same locked door you found next to the chapel," Dion said. "It's part of why I was sure Castor would have hidden the lantern there—because of the chapel's proximity to a former jackdaw collection. But I can't control what happens after this. Please be careful."

"What now?" Nelle prompted. The woman who had been following them was crossing the study room as they shuffled into the elevator.

"Press the button for the lowest level and hold it down," he said.

The elevator descended for what felt like an agonizingly long time before it rumbled to a stop. The door rippled, liquid-like, and split open to let them through to a dark passage. There was no library here, not even one with empty shelves; no torches, either, or any other light source. Just rough-hewn stone walls and stagnant, damp air.

Flashlights in hand, they raced through a long, curving tunnel. She heard the rattle of the elevator behind them as it was called back.

"Where does this let out?" Nelle asked.

"I don't know," Dion said. "It won't be far. Castor would have used this passage to enter and exit the Divinity School without being seen. Wherever it leads, it has to be someplace he can easily get to. I'm picking up Leo and Tristan. As soon as you reach the end of the tunnel, tell me where you are, and we'll come get you. All you have to do is not get caught before then."

"Oh, that's all?" Nelle said. "Castor will have people waiting for us at the end."

"I know. Be careful."

Aziza didn't waste her breath on conversation. She had a handful of charms in the pocket of her coat; in her mind, she was sorting through them, weighing her options. She had defended herself from the fae before; she'd never had to fight another witch. Which spell would serve her here?

The rising and falling tones of that high-pitched howl came again, echoing up and down the passage now. There were footsteps, too, but it was impossible to tell how many or how close they were. It was several minutes of hard running before she felt the touch of cool, fresh air on her flushed face. Her lungs burned, and there was a cramp in her side that felt like another arrow between her ribs. She clutched the strap of her backpack in hopes of holding it still so the lantern wouldn't bounce around inside; she kept picturing the latch popping open by accident and blowing the passage apart.

But then they were flying up a set of stairs and pushing open a trapdoor, dirt raining down on them. They climbed out in the shadow of a large stone cross. A weathered, one-handed stone angel leaned against it, head sorrowfully bowed. The name *Trowbridge* was carved into its base. The fog from the Divinity School had followed them here. Through a complete whiteout, they glimpsed the shape of a few trees and a row of upright slabs that Aziza belatedly recognized as gravestones.

"We're in the cemetery," Nelle said into the phone.

"Right. We're on the way," Dion said. "There's only one entrance—it's on the southwest side. Meet us there."

Something in his voice caught Aziza's attention. That was the way he sounded when he was avoiding her eyes. When he had been asked a question he didn't want to answer. She was unpleasantly reminded of his sudden calculated apathy on the battlefield during the autumn equinox.

"What's wrong?" Aziza demanded.

A pause. "I'll tell you when we see you."

"Put Leo and Tristan on."

A longer pause, and some rustling as the phone changed hands.

"Zee, something happened, but we're okay." That was Leo, and he didn't sound the least bit okay. More like shaken and barely holding it together. "Or . . . I mean . . . we're alive and we're not hurt. It's hard to explain. Just focus on getting out of there."

Tristan was conspicuously silent. She should have known something was wrong when Lucky hadn't immediately materialized beside her at the first sign of danger.

"Southwest," Nelle muttered. "Where the fuck is southwest?"

They picked a direction at random and took off running, sticking to the path. It was that or trip over the gravestones and sculptures, which surrounded them on all sides like a sea of silent spectators—towering obelisks, tablets with weathered lettering beside bare flower beds, mourning figures with hands clasped in prayer. They surfaced from the fog, looming, and then disappeared.

Their enemies came up on them like the fog had, gradually at first. They were only faceless shadows and that eerie howl that had dogged them all the way from the chapel. And then Aziza and Nelle were skidding over a layer of ice that had formed on the ground, grabbing hold of each other to keep their balance. From the fog, demonic figures with impossibly long limbs and sharp claws lurched toward them, circling, surrounding them. They were constructs made of mist—whoever was responsible for them must have also cast the spell to summon the fog that hung over the campus. It would stop any outsiders from seeing what was about to happen.

"Nelle Osorio?" a girl said, coming into view between two of the mist constructs. "Tell me that's not you."

Aziza recognized her, with her long black hair and wide cheekbones, as one of the duelists she'd watched at her first Half Moon Market, though she wasn't wearing her jackdaw pin now. She held something in her hands—an oddly shaped whistle.

"Didn't you hear?" another voice said—a boy this time, not one she remembered, though he held a knife like they used in the duels, engraved with sigils that marked it as an enchanted weapon. "Nelle is a traitor to her family line. Her and Dion Legrand. They've been compromising our secrecy with public acts of witchcraft, and now they've stolen a priceless magical artifact from Castor."

"That doesn't look like Dion Legrand to me," said another girl, a redhead who flipped her own enchanted knife end over end through the air.

Aziza had a hand in her pocket. Next to her phone—the call with Dion was still connected, though he and Leo were silent on the other end—she found one of her charm vials.

"No, that's Anne Sterling's apprentice," the boy drawled. Two more of the constructs loomed over his shoulder, staring down at Aziza and Nelle through the shifting, shadowy holes they had for eyes. "Some small-town hedgewitch. Anne mentioned she was missing, when she came here the other week snooping around. Seems like half the Clattering can't keep track of their students."

"Ready?" Nelle said under her breath. Aziza gave an incremental nod. Nelle had her revolver; she could take care of the constructs. That would leave the witches to Aziza.

Aziza and her one spell. She doubted she'd have time to cast another. But a good witch shouldn't need more than one.

Right, Castor? she thought.

"Enough chatter," a final voice said, and was instantly obeyed. This was the witch Aziza had seen in the library—the old woman—and where she had looked so forgettable there, now she had drawn her power around her like a shawl. The mist tangled with the ends of her long, graying dark hair. She carried no weapon. Her gnarled hands rested at her sides. "Miss Osorio, your aunt is my lifelong friend, so I will give you the opportunity to return what you've stolen before we take it back by force. Will you cooperate?"

Nelle's answer was to draw her revolver. She fired at one of the mist constructs, and it dissipated with a little puff of air, like a cough.

And then everything descended into chaos. From one direction, lightning crackled off the blade of a knife, throwing razor-sharp shadows. From another, that unnerving howl again filled the air as the first witch raised the whistle to her lips. It was like a small, crescent-shaped flute, her fingers moving across the tone holes in its surface as she whistled a different sequence of long and short notes. The ice under their feet thickened and began to creep over their shoes as if to freeze them to the ground.

Nelle swung her revolver around and fired at the girl—only over her head—but it was close enough that she squeaked in terror, flinching hard, which interrupted the spell. Nelle shot down another one of the mist demons, and she and Aziza both took off running in the opening she'd made, splitting off in different directions.

"Kill the other one if you have to—but don't hurt Miss Osorio!" the old woman cried behind them.

As Aziza ran, she drew out the charm she'd chosen. She could tell them apart by their weight; this one was the heaviest. Ducking behind an obelisk, she worked the cap open. Her magic poured into the charm, prepared with a spell for gargoyle mimicry—the spell which would bring stone to life.

Gunshots rang out as Nelle fired at the mist constructs. There was a *crack* as a bolt of lightning hit the obelisk inches from Aziza's face, leaving behind a fissure in its surface, black at the edges. She darted away, listening to the footsteps behind her—wondering if her spell had even worked—and then another sound reached her through the mayhem. Slow, impossibly heavy wingbeats.

Her heart leapt. It *had* worked.

Layers of fog burst apart as two of the constructs came up on either side of her. They were hard to see, their misty outlines blending into their surroundings, but their eyes and mouths were dark gashes in a sea of white. When one grasped at her arm, it didn't feel like anything—it wasn't solid—but it made her jerk to a stop. She flipped open her pocketknife and slashed at it; the silver blade went straight through its ghostly limb, breaking its grip. Aziza tried to flee, but the other mist demon snatched at her backpack; when she twisted to avoid it, her heel caught on a flat grave marker. She stumbled and took the fall on her shoulder, terror shooting through her as she felt her backpack collide with the ground—but there was no blast of unleashed energy. The lantern was intact. She scrambled to her knees, the mist demons towering over her.

But those wingbeats were close. With the *whoosh* of something very large hurtling through the air, two stone sphinxes crashed through the mist constructs and landed in front of her. The statues were identical winged lions with the heads of human women. They'd stood sentinel over the graves until Aziza's spell had woken them. As Aziza approached the nearest one, it turned its face as if to look at her with her blank stone eyes. It was all white marble, smooth and weather-streaked. Under its headdress, its hair had been carved in painstaking detail, strand by strand. Its lips and cheeks had a deceptive, lifelike softness, and its huge paws flexed, each one tipped with a long marble claw.

"Thank you," Aziza said. She had seen these sculptures earlier and had visualized them when she'd cast, hoping at least one of them would react to her spell; this was a better result than she could have anticipated. Despite everything, she grinned. She'd even used some of Lucky's fur in the charm. She couldn't wait to tell Dion that.

As lightning flashed in her peripheral vision, she climbed onto the sphinx's back.

"Stay on the ground," she said. "I need to find Nelle."

It was less comfortable than being carried by a blækhound, but only just. The other sphinx followed them from the air, circling Aziza. It blocked another bolt of lightning and shielded her from a burst of flame that burned away the fog, briefly allowing her a glimpse of their surroundings—the clouded sky, the dead trees, and the gate—*there,* the red gate that marked the entrance where Dion was waiting for them with the car.

The fog washed over the world again, but Aziza knew where she was going now. If she could just find Nelle.

The sphinx leapt over tablet headstones and swerved around the statues and obelisks. When the next flash of lightning came, Aziza said, "Go that way!" and the sphinx turned swiftly, its enormous strides carrying her toward the source of the lightning—the red-haired apprentice witch, close enough now to be visible through the mist, going wide-eyed with terror as the stone sphinx barreled toward her.

She fired off another whip of lightning and missed; then she gave in to the urge to flee. But there was no outrunning Aziza now. The second sphinx alighted in her path; the girl stopped too late. The sphinx knocked her legs out from under her with a swipe of its paw and then pinned her with its claws resting at the base of her neck, an implicit threat. As she slashed at the sphinx, little shocks of lightning sparked up wherever her blade touched it.

"Give me the knife," Aziza said.

The weather witch glared up at her in silent defiance.

"Or," Aziza said, "I can break your arm and take it myself."

The knife was discarded. Aziza picked it up and returned to her sphinx. They dodged and outran the mist constructs, following the sound of gunshots.

"Nelle!" Aziza shouted.

"Over here!" Nelle's voice called back.

Aziza sent the other sphinx ahead of her. "The statue is mine, don't shoot."

"What sta—Oh my god."

"Get on!" Aziza told her.

Nelle looked as if she really did not want to do that. But she did it anyway, and Aziza led them toward the gate. Once they saw its silhouette through the fog, they dismounted. They didn't know how far the mist reached and couldn't let the living statues be seen out there. The lantern in her bag jostled against her back as they continued on foot.

Her next step hit something smooth and slippery, and Aziza skidded, barely keeping her balance—and narrowly avoiding a collision with the spear of solid ice pointed at her chest. It was pale blue, mottled with frost, and sharpened to a glinting edge. The girl who'd played the crescent flute was holding it; her eyes were uncertain, but her hands were steady.

Nelle aimed her revolver squarely at the girl's head.

"You wouldn't," the apprentice said.

"Try me," Nelle said. Even Aziza couldn't tell if she was bluffing.

Aziza felt something coming, then, without knowing what it was. Her skin crawled, goosebumps prickling up her arms and her scalp tingling. A metallic taste flooded her mouth, as if she'd bitten her tongue.

Then lightning struck. True lightning, from the heavens, far more powerful than the bolts of electricity from the apprentice witch Aziza had disarmed earlier. It wasn't close to them—she didn't think—but still it was overwhelmingly powerful. The flash was so bright it blinded her for several seconds; the accompanying clap of thunder was more like an explosion, a bomb going off over her head. The shock wave rolled over them with a pulse of heat and the stinging, metallic smell of ozone.

When her vision cleared, the master weather witch from before was standing between them and the gate. The apprentice's spear had cracked in her hands, and she'd fallen on her backside, looking stunned; Nelle was the only one who hadn't moved at all.

"Are you kidding?" Nelle said angrily.

"That strike was fifty feet away," the elder witch said. "I don't have to hit you directly. Within thirty feet, the ground current that spreads from the point of impact is enough to cause muscle paralysis, burns, cardiac arrest, and neurological damage. It could even kill you." She paused, allowing those words to sink in. "Are you going to make that necessary? I don't want to harm you, Nelle. But I'll do what I must."

"You won't," Nelle said. "You know what we have. You know it's fragile."

The apprentice witch looked between them in confusion as she got to her feet. "What do you mean?"

But the elder witch did know; Aziza could see it on her face.

Before she could respond—or even make a move—the stone sphinxes swooped down from the mist. Aziza had almost sent them back to their pedestals, but had thought better of it. One of them crashed into the elder witch, who cried out in pain. The collision had no doubt broken a couple of bones. Aziza felt that crawling feeling of building electricity again, but she and Nelle didn't wait to see what happened next; they fled. The apprentice made no move to stop them.

The gate loomed over them. The fog wasn't limited to the cemetery; it had spilled out into the surrounding streets, too, maybe even the entire campus. But the car was right there, Dion and Leo in the front. Tristan was nowhere to be seen. She and Nelle piled into the backseat, and Dion was speeding away almost before they'd gotten the door closed.

"You all right?" Leo said.

"Fine," Aziza replied. "Where's Tristan?"

"We ran into Professor Serapion. We fought him, and . . . well, Serapion is dead. I think. And Tristan left," Leo said hollowly. "He has Lucky. He's okay, unless he . . ."

It seemed he couldn't bring himself to finish. Aziza cursed herself for not demanding answers from Tristan when she'd suspected something was wrong the other night.

"We'll find him later. Do you have it?" Dion asked.

She unzipped her backpack, and the lantern's light flooded the car. "Where can we get rid of this?"

"Somewhere outdoors and out of sight," Dion said. "Maybe a park, or—"

It started to rain—a torrential downpour that turned the entire world the color of steel. The rain came fast and hard, mingled with hailstones that struck the car with such force Aziza feared the windshield would actually shatter. The street was instantly flooded, reflecting their headlights like a mirror; Dion was forced to slow the car to little more than a crawl. Another weather witch tactic to delay them—and to conceal any magical activity. The buildings were a blur through the rain-streaked windows, and not a soul was left outside.

"He'll have someone guarding the Flight Paths," Dion said. "And probably every route out of the city. So if we have to take our chances with a fight, I think we should go to the jackdaw collection."

"Wait," Aziza said. "Take us to the coast instead."

As they veered toward the wharf, the rain softened—they had chosen a route the weather witches had not expected them to take. Dion sped up, and they were at the pier minutes later. They left the car on the street and walked out onto the rocky jetty next to the pier. Between the storm and the waist-high waves, they were quickly drenched.

Overhead, something bright and winged streaked through the rain. A flock of them. And then one broke off, circling above their heads. Castor's constructs had found them—and that meant Castor himself could not be far behind.

Aziza didn't let it distract her. She pricked her finger on the tip of her pocketknife and let the blood drip into the water, whispering into the rain about the time when she had been chased all the way back to the train station by an unruly pair of kelpies. Out there in the churning waves, three sets of pricked ears broke the water's surface. They were followed by three pairs of glassy eyes, three snouts, and three long manes afloat in the water. Very soon, the kelpies were climbing ashore, their backward hooves leaving reverse prints in a trail that led back to the sea. She kept whispering her story-spell as Leo passed her braided ropes of seaweed to wind around the first one's neck and between its sharp teeth as a makeshift bridle. They were docile, listening.

The spell to soothe kelpies had been one of the first she'd asked Anne to teach her. Anne had been reluctant, warning her that it was a higher-level spell that apprentices with years of training had trouble mastering. Aziza had insisted, even after the close calls she'd had practicing it under Anne's supervision. Now she was glad she had been stubborn in prioritizing this particular spell.

She had just finished the second one when Dion said, "Aziza. He's here."

"Everyone get on," she said, letting the third kelpie lick the blood off her finger to keep it still.

Looking back, she saw what Dion had—Castor Thorne, in his sealskin coat, his blond hair slick with rain. He was accompanied by three witches, running toward them from the shore.

She whispered an instruction to the final kelpie, and it cantered away to intercept their enemies, its hooves clapping against the rocks. Dion and Nelle had climbed onto the first kelpie already; Leo offered a hand to pull her up, and she swung onto the second mount behind him.

"So, how much, uh, skill is this going to take?" Leo asked, clutching the reins. "Remember when we got Fox to turn into a car because we all agreed we didn't know anything about horseback riding?"

"Zero skill," she said. A kind of thrill mounted in her chest. Secretly, she had always wanted to do this. "Just hold on."

Behind them, there were screams as the third kelpie attacked. Aziza didn't look back again. Their mounts kicked off the shore and trotted away. Leo gave a strangled yell at the shock of cold water. She felt the weightlessness when their hooves left the ground, and then they were swimming, even faster than they could have galloped. They sank in the water until only their eyes and ears were visible. Aziza was submerged to the shoulders. They rose and fell with the waves. The rain was in her eyes; she hung on to Leo as they sailed into deep, dark water.

Then a streak of light flashed next to her face. She flinched, expecting to struck by lightning—but instead, she felt a weight lift off her back, and gasped. Her hand flew up to feel at her bag, which was—torn. Empty. Twisting, she saw one of Castor's constructs. It fluttered in midair, looking back at her, the ring of the glowing lantern clutched in its beak.

The witches on the shore had slain the kelpie. Castor was visible, his distant figure shrinking fast as they swam away. Still, she could see his face. His blazing eyes met hers. Gone was the smiling, amiable gentleman she'd met at the Half Moon Market. He was *furious.*

Then the high waves blocked her view of the shore, and he was gone.

A knot of frustration tightened in her chest. They'd come *so close* only to be thwarted at the last minute. Worse, Tristan was gone—missing, apparently. Even their narrow escape held no triumph.

She'd failed—but Castor had, too. If Serapion was really dead, then he'd lost one of his best allies today. His master weather witches and their Ivy-educated apprentices couldn't lay a hand on her. She had walked right into his hands and escaped.

And she would be the winner of their next match. No matter what it took.

CHAPTER 35
TRISTAN

He had turned up on Jun's doorstep in part because he didn't know where else to go—and partly because he had needed to make sure that Jun was still himself. But then Jun was standing there looking so completely normal—Tristan must have interrupted him in the middle of making dinner, because he was in sweatpants and an apron, with a headband pinning his messy black hair out of his face—and Tristan was in his doorway with Professor Serapion's blood under his fingernails.

Tristan took a step backward. "Sorry. I—Never mind. Sorry."

"Hang on," Jun said. "Why don't you come in?"

"It's not safe," Tristan blurted. What he meant was *I'm not safe.*

He made himself explain what he'd done as best he could, stuttering and fragmented and barely coherent. Jun said, "Okay, but I really think you should come inside now."

And that was how Tristan ended up at the kitchen table across from Jun's sister, Hana, while Jun stirred a pot of curry and made his own confession. Yes, Professor Serapion had given him a book of the infernal arts and ordered Jun to attempt some of the spells, under his supervision. No, Jun had not transformed, not even partially.

"I never succeeded in casting any of the spells, that's why," Jun said. "I'm a medium. My power level is nowhere near his other apprentices. I managed with your serpent spell, but the kind of craft he wants—*wanted*—from me is something else. I've tried—"

"Stop trying," Tristan said, as Jun put a plate of curry in front of him.

"Is that asshole really dead?" Hana asked him. Jun had tried to shoo her away earlier; it hadn't worked. They were so close in age Tristan couldn't tell which of them was the elder sibling. Hana had the bossiness of a little sister and the protectiveness of an older one.

"I . . . don't know," Tristan said. "He was breathing. I think."

She scooped up a heaping spoonful of curry. "But you're sure that you—"

"Hana, enough," Jun said, taking the seat next to her. His fingers absently rotated the beads on his wrist. "I know I should have walked away. But he gave up on me pretty quick. It was only a matter of time before he would have officially dropped me as his apprentice."

Tristan's shoulders slumped with relief. "Good. That's . . . really good."

"It is," Jun said reluctantly, and then grimaced as if embarrassed by his own reluctance. "I *know* he was a monster. But getting dropped by a master would've made it really hard to ever find another apprenticeship. I feel like I blew my one shot to—to make something of myself."

Tristan forced down a bite of curry. The warmth was comforting, even if the taste had little effect on him now. "You don't want to be what he would have made you."

"He can't drop you anymore," Hana said. "Problem solved."

Jun sighed. "There have always been rumors about him mistreating his apprentices, but I didn't know exactly what I was signing up for."

"He found ways to abuse both his living *and* dead apprentices,"

Tristan said, thinking of the molars he'd saved from the bone wolves, still stashed in his backpack. "Why did he do it?"

"You'd be surprised by how many necromancers are afraid to die," Jun said. "And believe that being necromancers should make them exempt. He wanted power and immortality without the drawbacks. So he made his apprentices work through corruptive spells, and when some of them began to change, he experimented with methods to reverse the process. He never succeeded, as far as I know."

"The girl in his office wanted us to kill her," Tristan said. "And I would have done it if we hadn't been interrupted. Was that . . . ? Should I have . . . ?"

"It's the only thing you could have done for her," Jun said. "It's what will happen when the Clattering finds her. I'm sorry to say it, but she's beyond help."

"I see," Tristan said. It was the confirmation he had both hoped for and dreaded. Though he had believed the girl when she'd said there was no saving her, he hadn't known for certain until now. His decision to grant her request had been impulsive. He had insisted on it, almost let Leo do it for him—and what if there actually had been another way? But he'd let his fear take over—his fear of the hag.

No, that wasn't quite true. He was past the fear. It was the shame he had never managed to shake. Maybe he shouldn't. Didn't he deserve to feel like this?

"You said that the professor attempted a ghostly possession on you," Jun said. "That's what triggered your new . . . instincts. If he'd known about your condition, he'd never have done that."

"My condition," Tristan repeated. It was such an astoundingly mundane way of putting it—as if he had the flu, or perhaps a bad case of the vapors. "Which is what? Am I a hag?"

"No," Jun said, and it was like Tristan was finally allowed to breathe after a long time underwater. "The resurrection was powerfully corruptive magic, and it's changed you. But soul-siphoning is a lich quality. A hag will sap their victim's life force and kill them in the process, but doesn't consume their soul. A lich devours the soul, leaving the body alive but essentially brain-dead. They feed on anima, too, so they can eat ghosts. The professor is still breathing, but he's not a person anymore. Just an empty shell."

"Poetic justice," Hana said, dabbing a bit of curry sauce off the corner of her mouth.

"So I'm a . . . lich," Tristan said. It sounded like the difference between being a lich and being a hag was negligible, practically semantic, but still—it *felt* better to him. He remembered the way the hag had trapped spirits in the web of magic that spanned her territory, hoarding them; she hadn't consumed them, and maybe that was why. Only liches did that.

Either way, it wouldn't matter for very much longer. He gathered his courage to ask Jun for one last favor.

"Not a true lich," Jun said, before he could steel his nerves. "But it wouldn't take much more to turn you. You'll be fighting this for the rest of your life, so you're going to have to take precautions."

Tristan had to rewind those words in his head several times before he understood them.

"You think . . . there's a way for me to resist this?"

"Isn't that why you came here?" Hana asked. Her eyebrows crept up at Tristan's blank look.

"I wasn't his apprentice for very long," Jun said, "but the professor did teach me a thing or two."

TRISTAN SLEPT IN a public park. It was almost nostalgic. Jun and Hana had started working on something that would help him manage the "symptoms" of his new "condition," but it would take them a few days at least. In the meantime, Tristan wouldn't risk being around other people, especially Jun's family.

And he couldn't face Leo or the others. Not yet. They would have questions he couldn't answer, things he didn't even know himself. Would he get worse? How much worse? Could Jun really help him? Or would his best friends one day have to be his executioners? He felt a pang each time he recalled Leo offering to kill the half hag so that Tristan wouldn't have to. Maybe the best thing Tristan could do, the most loving thing he could do, would be to remove himself from Leo's life before he ruined him.

He spent most of his time studying *The Book of Fenrisúlfr*, practicing the spell to make new blækhounds. If New Haven had taught him anything, it was that one hound was not enough. He shaped his new hounds carefully, but even when he managed to give them the correct overall form with the right number of limbs in the right places, they still weren't up to his standards. Sometimes they were monstrous, with hulking, muscled shoulders and too much rage; or they were skeletal, with too many teeth and a high-pitched growl like metal grinding on metal, lashing out at him in fear. He hated to make them just to take them apart, but he kept trying. Lucky needed its pack, and so did Tristan.

To cast that spell even once should have left him completely drained. But his foray into soul-siphoning had given him a surge of power. Tristan had needed an outlet for that energy; he didn't want to hang on to it. And where before he'd found the hound creation spell terribly difficult—to focus his mind and his magic, and to summon the strength of will it required—now it felt downright easy. Jun wasn't surprised; he said that corruptive magic always made you feel more powerful at first. That was part of what made it so dangerous—it was easy to become addicted.

He sent Lucky to watch over the others periodically, in secret and never for very long. He couldn't work on the creation spell without Lucky around to protect him from his failed attempts.

But one night, when Lucky was checking in on Hazel, it tugged at Tristan's attention. He followed the pull into its mind.

He expected to see the Winter Court. But Lucky was outside; it was running next to two riders on a shared mount, each in a cloak with their hoods up. The snow was deep underfoot, muffling the sound of galloping hooves. Lucky's paws sank into it, and a dense forest of fir trees filled its nose with their crisp, piney scent. A starry sky could be glimpsed overhead, through their needles.

"Lucky!" Hazel said, fluttering down to eye level. Where the other two figures rode on horseback, Hazel flew; but she wore a matching cloak, plain and rough-hewn, nothing like the fine garments she had been given in the Winter Court. The hood fell to her shoulders, revealing her pointed green ears and silvery eyes. Her dark hair was unbound from its usual intricate plait.

The riders on horseback pulled up to a halt. Lucky stopped, too. Hazel alighted on the ground and flung her arms around its neck.

"Excellent timing," one of the riders said, lowering his hood. It was Prince Senna. And the smaller figure in front of him, slumped against his chest, was Vetiver.

"Tris, are you listening?" Hazel said. "We have a lot to tell you."

Prince Senna took a rolled-up piece of parchment from his saddlebag. "This will explain everything. Give it to Leo, please. I can't send a sandman until he goes to sleep, and I'd rather not wait even that long."

Lucky grabbed it carefully with its teeth, allowed Hazel to pat it between its ears, and left.

CHAPTER 36

LEO

AFTER NEW HAVEN, they regrouped in an empty jackdaw collection. They'd gotten food and dry clothing, pushed the tables aside and spread a couple of stolen motel blankets between the bookcases, and traded stories, piecing together everything they'd learned that day. The apprentices had known they'd taken something important, but only the master had known what it was—how much had Castor told them? How many of them were in on his plans?

As for the terrible secret they'd uncovered in Professor Serapion's office, they had managed to identify the student from a picture in the news, which bore a faint but close-enough resemblance to the half hag. Or whatever she was. She had gone missing a month ago.

These revelations answered some of Dion's questions about the professor's partnership with Castor. With his resources and authority as a fellow member of the Clattering, Castor could vouch for Serapion and shield him from scrutiny when the occasional apprentice died or went missing; in turn, Serapion supplied the occasional monster to guard the lantern at the Half Moon Market. It may have even been Serapion who had told Castor about Blackthorn's hag.

Dion had also been able to explain what Tristan had done.

Leo would have given anything to be by Tristan's side right now. But maybe he'd lost that right when he had stood there and said nothing after Tristan had told him he loved him. If he had answered differently, would Tristan still have run away? Leo had sensed then that he'd done the wrong thing; now the vague feeling he'd fucked up was more an inescapable certainty. Tristan wasn't here, not because Leo couldn't bring himself to admit how he really felt—but because, in withholding that truth from him, he had essentially said there were things that mattered more to him than the way he and Tristan felt about each other. That it didn't make any difference.

And now he was . . . where?

Leo remembered the chained girl saying, *Kill me while I'm still myself*, and had to fight a dizzying wave of panic.

"He'll come back on his own when he's ready," Aziza said firmly.

"Uh-huh," Leo said, sending Tristan another half dozen forlorn texts. Then he realized he had Tristan's phone charger, tossed in his backpack as they'd haphazardly moved out of that last motel. He still had the silver knife that Tristan never went anywhere without, too. In the days that followed, he kept it close at hand and found himself touching the hilt now and then without thinking about it, as if to reassure himself it was still there.

Dion believed the third lantern was in Sanctum, West Virginia—which technically no longer existed. It was a tiny coal-mining town and Castor's birthplace. The mine had come first; later, a fringe of residences and farms had formed around it like a patina on the edges of a penny. There were a few ramshackle wooden houses, a chapel, and a population in the low hundreds, which was vastly outnumbered by goats, cattle, and chickens.

Castor had been a teenager when a flash flood had washed Sanctum away. Buildings were flattened; parts of the mine had collapsed; people died, including Castor's parents. The survivors tried to rebuild, but it never quite took, and Sanctum was abandoned. Dion didn't even know how much of it was still standing.

They pored over maps and local newspaper archives from nearby counties, trying to determine precisely where Sanctum had been located. If they couldn't, their only option would be to get as close as they could and search on foot.

The Half Moon Market fell in the middle of that week; Nelle went alone—against everyone's protests—and returned unscathed, with charm components to replenish Aziza's stock and a fresh supply of silver bullets. She heard that Serapion's body had been found by one of his apprentices, along with the half hag. Serapion was being placed in hospice care. Lacking a soul, his body would eventually fail. And the girl had been euthanized on the spot. Anne had seized the contents of his library and was leading the investigation into what he'd done to her and his other apprentices; she must have been very close by to have beaten Castor there.

They never spent two consecutive days in the same place. They slept in the car, in motel rooms, and in abandoned or little-used jackdaw collections that Dion knew of, like the one at Martin College. Aziza and Dion worked on lessons in spell theory in the evenings, Dion helping her compose arrays and experiment with advanced spells that she and Anne hadn't yet gotten around to trying.

"Spells where you borrow, reflect, or mimic power typically require symmetrical guiding lines and doubles of every component," Dion explained, as she sketched a practice array under his supervision. "Eventually, you'll have a lexicon of your own sigils that can represent words or concepts, and you'll incorporate those into your arrays. For now, speaking the story-spell aloud will suffice."

"Do you use story-spells?" she asked.

"No. Some hearth witches do, but I've never been able to make them work for me."

"Then why do you know so much about them?"

"*Ipsa scientia potestas est*," he intoned.

"Really?" she grumbled. "You're so pretentious."

Aziza had defended her continued use of blækhound fur to fill out her charms, citing her successful casting of the gargoyle spell in New Haven. Dion had said, "Of course it worked that time."

He stopped as if he was going to leave it at that.

"It worked because . . ." she prompted.

"I shouldn't lecture you," he said, smirking. "I wouldn't want to sound pretentious."

"Don't let me rob you of the things that make you happy."

"Well, since I have your permission," he drawled. "The problem isn't that you use blækhound fur—it's when you use it in your charms carelessly, with no real thought to the function it serves. Lucky's fur worked as a charm component *this time* firstly because it was a gargoyle spell, which requires a telluric offering, and secondly . . ."

A rustling sound distracted Leo from the rest of this exchange. He didn't know how he heard it. It was as quiet as a breath. Either way, *something* made him turn around. A rolled-up note sat on the edge of the table Aziza and Dion weren't using, as if it had been there all along, waiting for him to notice.

He picked it up, but he was looking into the shadows outside the lamplight and between the bookcases, searching for a ripple of dark fur or the flick of a tail. His heart stung with a searing electricity, like when you moved a limb that had fallen asleep.

He scanned the note. It was from Prince Senna.

"Guys?" he said. "Can I call a team meeting?"

"What's wrong? Is it Hazel?" Aziza asked. Wordlessly, he passed the note to her.

Prince Senna had kidnapped Vetiver and fled the Winter Court, taking Hazel with him. They were joining forces with Princess Kova and several of the low courts to make Vetiver the new Summer King. By dawn, or even sooner than that, Queen Ceresia would know of their betrayal.

I have the elixir of renewal already. I was the one she sent on the Wild Hunt to retrieve it, Prince Senna had written. *But Ceresia and her army will beat us to the summertide lord's domain. They'll bring Princess Narra with them. To complete the solstice ceremony, we'll have to battle through her forces or find a way to sneak Vetiver past them. And they will fight to take the elixir from us.*

In the meantime, she will dispatch a small troop to infiltrate the Summer Court's castle. That is the real reason I am writing to you now.

Prince Senna believed that Ceresia would have a back-up plan in the event that Autumn and Spring's rebel alliance managed to put Vetiver on the throne. Once the ceremony was complete and the jade rot cleansed from the castle, the safe room would be exposed. The surviving members of the Summer Court would be healed, but weakened, and unable to defend themselves. Ceresia's knights would slaughter the Summer Gallowglass and take hostages: Vetiver's family, the enchantresses that would have rebuilt the castle illusions, the lords and ladies that would have become Vetiver's retinue and guided him as he learned to rule. That way, even if Vetiver became the Summer King, he would still be at her mercy.

Unless someone stopped her. Prince Senna wanted Leo to evacuate the Summer Court from the castle the moment they woke up. To ensure he beat the Winter Gallowglass to the safe room, he'd have to be inside and ready to take action *before* the ceremony was complete—which could only happen between midnight and sunrise on the solstice.

"That's in two days," Dion said. Somehow Leo had already

known that, even though he'd long since stopped keeping track of the date.

"I know we were supposed to go to West Virginia," Leo said. "But I think we're going to have to make a detour first."

THOUGH IT WAS late December, the fields around the castle were in full bloom. Wildflowers had sprung forth all over and sweet-scented breezes twined through the grass, sometimes whispering stolen secrets in the voices of strangers.

On the human side of the boundary, there wasn't a field anymore. The one-time battleground had washed away into Elphame, and the surrounding land had sewn itself shut over its absence. The neighboring farmlands were borderland places now, where—if they'd checked the news—they would've seen reports of bizarre weather, eerie lights and voices in the night, bouts of pestilence, and mysterious disappearances. At the witching hour, when the veil was thin, the people who resided in the scattered farms or towns nearby might look up at just the right time and glimpse a strange shape in the clouds, something like silhouetted towers, there for a few heartbeats and then gone. But the castle didn't reveal itself in full until they had crossed Elphame's boundary.

It was an hour before midnight. They'd spent yesterday preparing. Right now, a battle was beginning in that place Senna had described, the trees all ablaze like giant matchsticks. By midnight, either Vetiver would be dragged unconscious through the solstice ceremony or a collared and shackled Princess Narra would.

Everything had happened so fast since they had gotten Prince Senna's note. The last two days were a blur of planning and preparing and worrying and wondering where Tristan was right now—expecting Tristan to appear around every corner—and his memory of that time had been distilled into a few vivid, sharp snapshots.

Even now, he felt like he was watching himself from outside his body. He and Aziza were crossing the field, her arm hooked around his so that the shade mimicry spell concealed them both. It was like looking through a sheer black curtain. The Summer Court's Gallowglass no longer patrolled the way they had at the equinox. Some had fallen during that battle, and young birch trees marked their resting places. The others had been killed by Ceresia's assassins.

A few of the Winter Gallowglass lingered outside the castle to keep watch. Leo saw them through their illusions and look-away charms, the fanged mandibles of their helmets and the sleek beetle-like carapaces of their chest plates; the one crouching in the long grass with a halberd across his thighs, another with a shield covered in bright yellow needle-thin barbs, still more in the air with bows and full quivers of arrows.

Then he was prying open the door to the side entrance. They traversed the castle swiftly and were crossing the entrance hall when something moved above them in the blackness of the ceiling.

He flipped the hilt of his sword up and unsheathed its icy blade from the air. "Zee," he murmured, which was all the warning he had time to give. A *whoosh* of motion, a flicker overhead as translucent wings caught the barely-there ambient light, and then four Gallowglass were diving at them, their own weapons drawn. They moved so fast he could barely see them—they were only a blur of color, the dull sheen of their armor, the flash of their blades and eyes.

Leo met the first one with his sword up, their blades ringing on collision, bracing himself as the fairy bore down on him. Aziza darted away in another direction, disappearing behind a pillar and her shade mimicry spell. Two of the fairies followed her—the shade spell didn't make her invisible, just a little harder to see in the dark—but she had Tristan's knife and a few other charms ready to go.

He lost track of her almost instantly; this fight required all his concentration. Unlike his dueling partners, these fairies put all their strength into every blow, and even with the amber eye, no human was a match for the Fair Folk when it came to raw power. He resorted to petty tricks—moves he would have been embarrassed to use against a Salt-Scale fairy. He knocked away his opponent's rapier, hooked his foot behind his ankle, and sent him crashing to the ground. Then he brought his foot down on the fairy's wrist and—when he hissed and dropped his weapon—kicked the rapier away. The whistle of a blade cutting through air was his only warning before the other fairy almost lopped his head off. He threw himself forward to avoid the blow, tripped *over* his first opponent—if the Salt-Scale fairies heard about this he would never live it down, actually—and landed on his hands and knees, barely avoiding a face-first collision with his own blade.

The second fairy had come up from behind. She had a double set of wings—a transparent, membranous inner pair beneath thick, opaque elytra. Fishlike scales covered her neck. Her hair was so light it was almost translucent, like strands of glass. She flew circles above and around Leo, stabbing at him with a glaive. Its blade was almost as long as Leo's sword, and its six-foot shaft kept him at a distance. All Leo could do was dodge and parry, unable to get close enough to land a blow.

From elsewhere, he heard the thud of an armored body falling to the ground. Aziza must have gotten one of the fairies with a sleeping charm. But then she gave a strangled cry and it distracted him for a fraction of a second. Enough to slow him down. His heart missed a beat as the glaive flashed toward his face. He leapt back, narrowly dodging—but pain exploded across his left shoulder. It was the first fairy, the one with the rapier; he'd recovered and snuck up from behind while the winged one had distracted him. Leo had practically fallen onto his blade. He twisted away, his shoulder throbbing, heat seeping down the back of his shirt—blood, potentially a lot of it, but he could still move his arm at least. He raised his sword, shifting into a defensive stance, as both Gallowglass bore down on him.

They moved in unison. He braced himself.

But something halted the glaive in midair—an enormous gloved hand closed on the top of the shaft, catching it in the arc of its slash. Leo reacted before he understood what was happening, parrying as the rapier swung at his skull. Beside him, the glaive was being yanked from the fish-scale fairy's hand—and Beor the Huntsman was tossing it aside. He caught the fairy's wrist in his iron grip and snapped it. The fairy gave a hoarse scream and dropped to the ground on her knees.

Leo's opponent attacked him with single-minded focus. His next blow came at full strength, and it was all Leo could do to defend, to dodge, to anticipate the next swing and get the hell out of the way, while Beor decapitated the other fairy with his silver sword. Leo's stomach turned over as her skull rolled across the floor, trailing blood. Distracted, again, his own blade dipped an inch or so just as the one with the rapier gave a wordless cry of rage and moved into a thrust that would have pierced Leo through the stomach. Leo could see his face underneath the helmet, twisted in a snarl. He backed up, evading, but too slowly—and then Beor was in front of him, deflecting the blow Leo couldn't have dodged, his huge frame like a wall between him and the Gallowglass. He didn't see what happened next, but he heard a snap, a clatter as the rapier fell against the tiles, and then the thud of a body following.

Beor turned to him, wiping his sword clean on the hem of his cloak.

"I see someone's finally taught you how to hold a sword," he said with a raspy laugh. "But it will be of no benefit if you refuse to use it properly."

"Not my best performance, that's for sure. I—" He broke off, remembering suddenly that he had lost track of Aziza. He spun in the direction she'd gone. "Zee? Where are you?"

"Here," she said, jogging toward them, unharmed except for a couple of new bruises and scrapes. "You're bleeding—let me see."

"I don't think it's deep," Leo said, as she pulled down the neck of his shirt and examined the gash that ran from above his collarbone to the back of his shoulder, almost deep enough to have nicked his collarbone. It was hurting more and more by the second.

"It is necessary to be capable of taking blows as well as dealing them," Beor said approvingly. Aziza took out the first aid kit and quickly cleaned the wound, patching it up with some gauze and tape.

"Thanks for the save," Leo said. "I never thought I'd be saying this, but I'm really relieved to see you."

Beor was haggard, much thinner than when they'd seen him last, and the jade rot had left a smattering of pitted pockmarks over his gaunt cheeks, pale in the center and blackish at the edges. His veins were a webbing of livid green, as stark as a tattoo, over patches of discoloration like yellow-brown bruises. But unlike the other Summer fairies, he was clear-headed and calm, studying them critically with his sharp fire-fleck eyes. Prince Senna had helped him escape from the Winter Court's infirmary on the night he'd spirited Vetiver away, and had sent him here to the castle to assist Leo.

"Where is the summoner whelp?" Beor asked, his eyes dragging over the two of them. "Not hiding in the shadows with his hounds, surely?"

Leo had been trying not to think about Tristan. That ambush just now—there had been so many close calls. And maybe he hadn't fought quite as hard as he should have because deep down he was sure that if he was *really* in trouble, Lucky would be there to save him. But Leo had looked at every dark corner, had glanced obsessively down at his own shadow with almost every step he'd taken in the castle, and had seen nothing to suggest that Lucky was with them. Now he knew for sure the hound wasn't there, and it felt like the moment Tristan had vanished all over again.

"We'll explain later," Aziza said, when it became clear that Leo wasn't going to answer. "Come on. We're running out of time."

From the entrance hall, it was easy to locate the safe room. Easy for Leo, anyway; not for the Winter Gallowglass haunting the castle's shattered halls. Beor took in a sharp, dismayed breath as they pulled the doors open and he saw what had become of the Summer Court. He lagged behind them as Leo and Aziza made their way to the back of the chamber. Leo didn't look back, leaving him to his private grief.

In better times, the safe room was probably a banquet hall, from the looks of its high ceiling, the empty stretches of wall where Leo had a feeling there used to be windows, and the wide spaces in between the pillars where long tables could have stood. The distance to the other end of the room felt interminable, and the fact that dead fairies sprouted into birch trees didn't make him feel any better about the sheer number of bodies they passed. Those who were still alive had curled up unconscious beneath the saplings, their breathing shallow and wet, their deformed antlers and bruised hands knocking against the slender trunks. But he and Aziza had a job to focus on, and that made things easier. Dion had written the array they needed into a notebook. Aziza found a spot in a back corner that was suitable for it, and Leo held the page open for her while she copied the guiding lines onto the floor, extending up the wall like chalk vines.

It was a collaborative spell with elements of both hearthcraft and hedgecraft. They'd worked on it all of yesterday and into this morning, up until the last minute; their whole plan hinged on it. The sigils were from Dion's personal lexicon, which she had studied for this purpose; it was extensive enough that she could assemble a rough story-spell from the symbols. Etching them into the array meant neither she nor Dion would need to cast the story-spell aloud. At a jackdaw collection in Maine, she and Dion had consulted a few journals written by a hedgewitch a century ago, in which she had recorded several of her arrays and even the stories she had used with them. That had helped, but it couldn't give them all the answers. They were trying to do something that had never been done before.

The finished array was a series of interlocking crescents, arranged in a spiral that widened gradually until it was at least ten feet across. Standing at the edge of the chalk boundaries and looking down, it was almost like an optical illusion—he could have sworn that the spiral drilled down into the earth, and if he tipped forward, he would fall. But when he blinked, it was just chalk again.

They arranged the candles and set down the small clay bowl, into which Aziza gave her blood offering. She stood over the array and examined it critically, one last time.

"It looks right to me," Leo said, comparing the chalk array to the one in the notebook.

"I know. But what if . . ." She trailed off. "Never mind."

She struck a match and tossed it into the offering bowl. The flame met the small pool of blood and didn't go out. It floated there, burning.

The Summer Court couldn't fight off Queen Ceresia's assassins. Their own Gallowglass were dead; the intruders were in the castle and waiting for them out in the fields. So they had to escape the castle *without* going outside. This was how. The spell was supposed to connect the castle to the Flight Paths. It was based on the same spell that was used to link new jackdaw collections to the network—but it had to be altered so that it could cross Elphame's boundary. That was where her hedgecraft came in.

The match burned steadily. They both held their breath.

Then the flame spread, engulfing the clay bowl and spilling over the rim to run down the chalk lines in streams of molten light. Leo turned his face away, squinting at the conflagration through the corner of his natural eye, his hand raised defensively against the heat.

It burned for several long seconds. When the fire died out, the chalk markings vanished with it, and the candles that had been brand-new were burned down to stubs. And part of the wall was gone, too. There was a ragged opening now—and through the opening, in a dark concrete corridor that didn't belong to the castle at all, there was a second offering bowl and a second cluster of used-up candles. Dion knelt there in the Flight Paths, across from Aziza over the remnants of their twin arrays.

"Good work," he said, with a wry smile.

"Were you starting to worry?" she asked.

"Not in the slightest."

"Are you sure you don't want me to come with you?" Nelle said, cautiously approaching from down the hall, where she had watched Dion cast from a safe distance.

"We need you here," Dion said. "The next part shouldn't take long."

They'd successfully created their escape route, but they couldn't evacuate the Summer Court until they woke up. According to Senna, that *should* happen as soon as the ceremony was complete. At the same time, the castle's illusions would begin to repair themselves—which meant that the Winter Gallowglass would easily find the safe room. If all went according to plan, they'd just send the Summer Court into the Flight Paths and then seal the opening Aziza and

Dion had created, making it impossible for the Gallowglass to follow them.

But Leo had one more thing he needed to do first. With Aziza and Dion's help. If the fairies woke before they returned, it would be Nelle's job to lead the Summer Court to safety. Dion had shown her a winding route to take through the Flight Paths—had even spelled it so that it wouldn't move like the rest of the tunnels did. She'd have her silver bullets and Beor to help defend them.

Beor didn't approve of this part of the plan. He didn't try to stop them, but he did catch Leo's arm before they left the safe room, saying, "Wait."

Leo looked up at him expectantly. He was impatient to get moving. To not pause long enough to think about who wasn't there with them, and how Prince Senna's battle was going, and the seven years of warfare that would follow if the ceremony failed and no monarch was chosen at all—or if the wrong one was.

"You met the Winter Gallowglass in battle once today, and your hesitation nearly cost you your life. I won't be there to save you," Beor said gruffly. "If you hesitate again, someone else may have to bear the cost. Remember that."

THE STAFF DORMITORY was down in the basement level, where spreading root systems crept over the walls, opening deep cracks in the stone. Like the fairies in the safe room, their human servants were as he'd seen them last, though they hadn't lost consciousness as an effect of the rot—they'd been placed in a magical stasis. The sound of soft breathing filled the room. The solstice ceremony wouldn't wake them, Prince Senna had said; only a member of the Summer Court's royal family could do that.

Since Leo couldn't evacuate them, he was going to hide them instead. Dion would layer his strongest protective spells onto the entrance of the dormitory. One spell would vanish the door if anyone approached it with malicious intent. Another was a spell of minor obfuscation, so that anyone who came within range would suddenly forget what they'd come downstairs for, or perhaps become distracted by other thoughts. And there were a couple of others Leo couldn't remember, but it had all sounded good to him. Leo didn't trust the Winter Gallowglass to leave a group of vulnerable humans unharmed if they happened across them, but no one would be actively looking for the servants. As long as they just . . . stayed out of sight, they would be fine.

While Leo tried not to think about the last time he'd been here—the desperation he'd felt, and how Tristan had to forcibly pull him out of it—Aziza watched Dion draw his arrays with rapt attention.

"I was thinking about something Anne told me," she was saying. "That the purpose of a coven is to pursue magical goals together. It was after Castor showed me the energy capture spell that he and Leila came up with, the one on his cuff links. It makes me wonder what else he's still using their spells for. My parents' and Emil's, I mean."

"I've been thinking it over, too," Dion said, looking up from his array. "I searched Emil's office for notes, but he didn't keep anything from that time in his life. But some of the things Castor says make me think—"

Leo didn't hear the rest. Something was happening in the castle. No changes yet were visible—Aziza and Dion hadn't noticed it—but he somehow knew a change was present, in the same way his internal clock could tell him that night was coming, whether or not he could see the fading of light from the sky.

"Zee?" he said. They both stopped talking. He put a hand to his chest, which ached. It wasn't exactly pain. "I feel . . . weird."

Aziza said something to him, but he wasn't listening. It was hard to focus. The change he'd felt in the castle was inside *him* now. It radiated through him in slow-growing tendrils; it was less like power and more a kind of longing, a warm and wistful pull toward something his instincts told him he lacked.

"Leo!" Aziza said. It sounded like she had been trying to get his attention for some time.

"What?" Leo said, tilting toward her. Her hand was on his arm, as if she thought he might fall.

"Tell me what's wrong."

"Nothing," he said, and it was the truth. "It's Hazel. She changed her mind."

"What?" she said, not understanding. He couldn't find the words to explain. There was too much in his head right now; the castle enchantments, which before he could only observe with the limited comprehension of an outsider, were like a part of him now—part of him but also not, like the breath he exhaled.

So this was the difference between pretending to be a Prince of Summer based on a technicality, and actually being one. The status and authority he had theoretically wielded, and that the fairies of the low courts had entertained to a degree, were now written into the magical laws of Elphame.

He moved to the door, ignoring Dion's indignant protests as he walked over his unfinished array. Entering, he found the servants' quarters had expanded. There were more doors, and a couple of smaller passages that branched off from the main one. He went inside the first chamber. Most of the servants had huddled there to hide together. Too many people on not enough cots.

Leo hesitated at the threshold. Was he wrong? What if he couldn't do anything for them, even now?

Focusing with his amber eye, he traced the shining threads of enchantment with his truesight, which felt sharper and more perceptive now than it had ever been before. As he ventured farther into the room, a shiver ran through the magic—it recognized him. It responded to his presence, skittering back from his footsteps like metal flakes repelled by a magnetic force.

He found the cot where Evan slept, slumped over on someone's shoulder. His slow, steady breathing hitched as he began to wake.

"Evan?" Leo said. He put a hand on his shoulder. "Evan, wake up."

His eyes opened, squinting as if the low light hurt.

"Leo?" he mumbled. "What happened? Is it over?"

He thought it was still midsummer.

"Not exactly," Leo said.

CHAPTER 37

AZIZA

THE DISSOLUTION OF the sleeping enchantment forced a change in their plans. They couldn't leave all these people behind now that they were awake. So they went upstairs together, Leo leading the way and the servants following him.

Around them, the castle started to bloom like the wildflowers outside, in spite of the long winter, as gleaming and vibrant as if it had never known ruin. The hovering, enchanted lights winked back into existence. The staircase with the carved wooden rail gleamed enticingly when she looked toward it, and doors nudged themselves open as they passed, hanging ajar. Even the shadows seemed somehow less sinister. But as the enchantments rebuilt themselves, the castle grew larger on the inside, so that there always seemed to be just one more corridor between them and the safe room.

It would be impossible to avoid detection in such a large and conspicuous group, and they'd move more slowly. So while Leo shepherded the servants to the former safe room, Aziza and Dion broke off in another direction.

The Winter Gallowglass would find them soon. They might get to the safe room before Leo did. She and Dion would do what they could to stop them. They'd cause a diversion, lead the Gallowglass away, and hopefully buy Leo time to get everyone into the Flight Paths.

It was Leo's least favorite kind of plan.

"Something always goes wrong when we split up!" he had complained when they'd discussed it earlier, while Evan rallied the drowsy staff and hustled them out into the hall.

"Something always goes wrong when we don't, too," she said, rather than point out that they were already split up, technically. Since Tristan wasn't there. Leo didn't need reminding; she'd never seen him look so miserable as he had the last few days.

"I'm not leaving here without you," Leo told her, sounding almost angry, as if he'd heard what she hadn't said.

"You won't have to. We'll make it back in time," she said. "Right, Dion?"

"Oh, are we in a hurry? You'd never know it from the way we're dawdling here," he said, brushing the chalk dust off his hands from the arrays he'd just wiped away, uncast. "I'm a witch, not a miracle worker. The sooner we get moving, the better off we'll be."

Asshole, she thought, but even in her head it sounded fond.

THEY HEARD THE Gallowglass prowling through the halls, searching for the Summer Court. She and Dion stalked them, laying trap spells and luring the Gallowglass toward them. Dion had spells to muddle people's minds, make them walk in circles or think they'd hit a dead end when they hadn't; together, they knotted the castle into a labyrinth again. Had the situation been less urgent, it would have almost been fun, puzzling out ways to make Dion's hearth witch tricks lead his victims into Aziza's traps.

"They just keep coming," Dion said. "We have to go back. By now most of the Summer Court should have escaped."

They retraced their steps, and this time they didn't stop when they heard the Gallowglass close by; they only hid behind locked doors that yielded to Dion's touch, or waited around corners for the threat to pass. She was sure they had gotten themselves hopelessly lost when at last they found a hallway she recognized—one that led to the entrance hall.

It was full of sunlight.

Or something like it. It couldn't be coming from outside, where it was nighttime.

"That looks like . . ." Dion trailed off. "Aziza, wait!"

Silently, furiously, she followed the light into the entrance hall, which had been restored almost to its former glory. The sweeping staircase had folded open until it was thrice the width it had been earlier, the running deer carved into the balustrade kicking their hooves. A splash of gold in the corner of her eye was the dust sloughing off the frame of a landscape painting that had popped out where before there had only been a blank wall. The great double doors at the castle's main entrance hung open, so that the night crouched at the threshold like a dog asking to be let in.

The source of the sunlight was a lantern. A hooded figure was seated on the floor beside it, looking intently down, as if scrying in its shadows for visions of the future. The light inside pulsed like a throat, swallowing the energy of the castle as it came back to life. She looked at Dion and saw in his face that he was thinking the same thing she was—that they should have expected this.

They had thought Castor would focus on strengthening his defenses around the third lantern, knowing that they were coming for it. But the surge of power the Summer Court would experience as it was restored presented an opportunity he had been unable to resist. He had stolen into Elphame one last time to siphon off a little more magic.

"What now?" Castor said, sounding bored. "I told you I'd stay out of your way. Don't you have better things to—"

He broke off mid-sentence as he looked up and saw who was there. He'd thought he was speaking to the Winter Gallowglass. The troops outside had flooded in already to ambush the Summer Court's survivors the moment their haven was revealed.

At the sight of Aziza and Dion, he laughed. It wasn't the measured, genteel laugh of his stage persona; it wasn't even a villain's cackle, sharp or cruel or mocking. It was self-deprecating, a kind of genuine, surprised mirth at his own expense.

"Forgive me," he said, rising to his feet. "I wasn't expecting company. I thought you'd be in Sanctum by now. Or stumbling around in the woods where Sanctum used to be, I suppose."

Aziza was silent. Dion, too.

"And let me guess," Castor went on, smiling. "You thought I'd be in Sanctum, too."

"Why aren't you?" Aziza asked.

"Because then I'd have needed to send someone else here, and there was no one I felt equal to the task. Did you think I had an endless supply of fae princesses and their faithful knights prepared to do my bidding? If only." Castor gave a careless shrug, the velvety shoulders of the coat aglow with the light of the lantern. "Viren is dead, and Princess Narra got herself captured by the Winter Court. Some things, I'm afraid, you simply have to do yourself. But you know all about that. What a task you've undertaken, Aziza. Such initiative you've shown. And you, too, Dion. You've inconvenienced me, but as your mentor, I must say I'm proud."

They didn't move, though she heard Dion make a sound, a retort he'd bitten back. Castor's smile widened, a flash of white teeth and a narrowing of his brilliant blue eyes.

"This is the one you destroyed at the Half Moon Market," he said, tapping the lantern with the side of his foot. "The replacement for it, that is. And you won't leave without it, will you? So then, let's talk. Before it comes to a fight."

"What could we possibly have to talk about?" Dion asked.

Aziza was taking a mental inventory of the spells they each had at their disposal. Neither she nor Dion had the kind of witchcraft that was suitable for combat. Hedgecraft could do damage, but not the spells she had prioritized learning this year. A sleeping charm would have helped them get away, but she'd used her last one against the Gallowglass earlier. Dion didn't even use charms; he worked from memory or composed his arrays on the spot, which took time. Even a few seconds or minutes would be too much.

Aziza did have one spell that might work, but she'd prefer not to have to use it. Not in front of Dion.

"I'd like to tell you a story," Castor said. "Story is the language of hedgecraft, and so it's the best way I can think of to make you understand, Aziza. It's the story of what happened to Sanctum. Do you know it?"

Dion answered for her, giving her time to think. "It was destroyed during a storm, and much of the population was wiped out," he said, as if reciting facts out of a history book, academic and impersonal. "Your parents, Ruth and Stephen Thorne, were among the victims."

"You only have half the story. Less than that," Castor said. His stance had shifted subtly; he had drawn himself up in some indefinable way, as if he were speaking to them from onstage at the Half Moon Market. He even projected his voice, slipping naturally into the showmanship that suited him so well. "Sanctum was the kind of place where any whiff of the occult was dreaded, magnified, and seen as proof of wrongdoing—worthy of social exile, if not outright violence. It was the kind of place where the Satanic Panic never ended. My parents were two immensely talented weather witches who had to hide their craft from their neighbors just to coexist peacefully." His smile didn't waver; it was warm and inviting, and his voice had a captivating quality that would have made it hard to stop listening to him. "But they took pride in their hometown. It was conservative and superstitious, but it was also a beautiful place with people they believed to be inherently good. I think many witches have stories just like theirs."

Elsewhere in the castle, there was a rising clamor. Banging, as if on a distant door. Voices shouting over each other. It was the Winter Gallowglass—they had found the safe room.

"My parents knew about the storm that would destroy Sanctum," Castor went on. "Do you know what they did? They compromised their own secrecy and tried to warn the others of what was to come—tried to couch it in terms that wouldn't frighten them—and still they were answered with suspicion and hostility. From people they had known for most of their lives."

They didn't have to hear him out. She didn't care what he had to say; she wanted to go back to where Leo was, and to go right this second. But the lantern was right there—and the coat. Her fist clenched with the urge to walk over there, grab on to the collar, and refuse to let go until Castor relinquished it, no matter what he did to her.

"Still, they refused to leave," Castor said. "They stayed and tried to protect Sanctum from the storm, single-handedly. And . . . well, Dion already told you how that ended. What do you think, Aziza? Does any of this sound familiar?"

It did; it sounded so familiar she had to wonder how much of it was true. It felt like the start of a myth he had constructed around himself. It felt *targeted*. Of course Aziza knew what it was like to refuse to leave your hometown even in the face of near-certain doom. She knew what it was like to be made an outcast because her peers could sense there was something different about her, even if they didn't know what. She'd never had a human friend before Leo. Had he made Meryl tell him those things about her?

But it didn't matter. Even if every word of it was true.

"What's your point? That your parents were better people than you are?" Aziza said.

"My point is that each generation they find new ways to reinvent the witch trials," Castor said. "Through it all, we survive and do more than that—we try to protect the very people who fear and despise us from disasters of their own making. Why is that?"

"I think I see where this is going," Dion said. "Aziza, you haven't heard any of these tiresome arguments before, so I'll summarize. For as long as the Crow Mandate has existed, there have been witches who wanted to abolish it and stage some sort of magical uprising. But I never thought you'd be susceptible to such juvenile, short-sighted ideology, Castor."

"I would never endorse the removal of the Crow Mandate. Not with the way things stand now. Our secrecy is the only thing that protects us. But we *shouldn't* have to hide away in the shadows, living and dying at the mercy of our inferiors." Dion's expression of unmitigated disgust at the word *inferiors* would have been comical at any other moment. But Castor was still going. "And soon, we won't have to. We'll have a place that's just ours—somewhere that belongs to witches the way Elphame belongs to the Fair Folk. A rookery, of sorts. Consider this my formal invitation," he said, sweeping his arms out wide in a grand gesture of welcome. "You can refuse, if you wish, but all I ask is that you don't take the choice away from the others."

A place that belongs to witches the way Elphame belongs to the Fair Folk. Aziza couldn't begin to imagine what that meant. Her gaze went to the lantern again. She couldn't make a move toward it. Castor hadn't picked it up yet. He was prolonging this conversation, she knew, to give the lantern time to fill up with magical energy. But knowing that didn't help her stop it from happening.

"Another place?" Dion said. "Like what? A walled city?"

"Something like that," Castor said, amicable in the face of Dion's overt scorn.

"It sounds like a glorified prison. And you can't just—conjure places out of thin air. Even you. You'd have to take it from somewhere else," Dion said.

"That's true," Castor said. "I won't be conjuring; I'll be repurposing. Redeveloping. That's my area of expertise."

She was missing something. Something probably obvious.

"You can't stop me," Castor said. "Like Emil, you'll simply stand aside when the time comes."

"Don't talk about Emil!" Dion snapped. "You're the one who killed him. You—you lured him to the hag, and—"

He had told Aziza before that he couldn't be sure of the circumstances around Emil's death; but this, she knew, was what he believed deep down to be true.

"You're wrong," Castor said, growing solemn as suddenly as Dion's temper had surged. "I asked Professor Serapion to wake the hag again, it's true. But I never sent Emil there. Why would I? I had too much respect for her to use her in that way; she taught me a great deal, more than some of my best mentors. And if I could have had anyone by my side at the founding of our new world, it would have been him. But he never forgave me for the mistakes I made in our youth. And he never forgave himself for staying behind when Leila and Ahmed fought the hag. He was arrogant enough to think he could handle her alone this time, and prideful enough to think it was his duty to do so. The truth is that Emil killed himself."

Dion took a jerky step forward, as if he hadn't meant to do it. His fists were clenched. Aziza's hand shot out to catch his arm and hold him back.

"I hated him for that," Castor said. "All that time—I always thought he'd come around, eventually. We had never had a fight we couldn't work through. Whether it took a year, ten years, twenty, in the end I was so sure he would—But, no, he decided to punish himself forever for doing what any rational person would have done and staying out of a fight that didn't involve him." His gaze shifted to Aziza, but she had the unsettling sense he couldn't see her at all. "Leila and Ahmed were even worse. Dying for people who wouldn't even mourn them. I loved your parents. You know what it's like—the bond between a coven. How intense it can be. I would have given them the world, and they thanked me with betrayal. And they left *you* alone." With what must have been a conscious effort, his faltering smile returned, twice as bright. "They put their ideals above their children. It's them you should be angry with."

She feared Dion would actually lunge at him.

"Would you really believe us if we said we'd stand aside and let you do whatever you wanted?" she asked.

"I suppose not. It's more that I believe you might change your mind once all is said and done. After all, it's not really that you want to stop me. It's that you want this." He smoothed a hand down the lapel of the coat. "Without this, would you even consider me an enemy? Or might we have been friends? What if I offer to give it back to you right now—would you accept it as an apology?"

She hated that she hesitated before she said, "No. I don't want an apology."

"Then how about a duel?" he said, with an indulgent laugh. "There's no shame in winning it back from me, is there? If you can make me concede, I'll hand it right over. It's a promise."

"Not the lantern?" she tried.

"No, I won't patronize you. You and I both know I wouldn't give up the lantern," he said. "The coat, though, has served its purpose, and I think I can bear to part with it. Well?"

The impulse to say yes, to throw every spell she had at him, was almost irresistible. But her hatred of him was just one more thing Castor could use to his advantage. Any spell she cast would only enhance the lantern's power.

"I don't want to duel you," she said.

"Are you sure?" Castor said, his smile as fixed as a mask. He opened his hands, bringing them together palm up as if in offering. "Think fast, Aziza."

All the light in the room dwindled and died—and it was as if Castor had pulled it to him, gathering it up like a flood of tiny gold coins, until everything was pitch-black except for the lantern and Castor himself. There was something between his open hands. The stolen light was gathering there, so bright she couldn't look at it directly. Oppressive waves of heat rolled over the room. Her skin stung and reddened, as if sunburned.

"We have to go before he finishes," Dion said, with a sudden urgent fear, grabbing her hand and trying to pull her back the way they'd come.

"What's he doing?" she asked Dion, shielding her eyes.

"Keep your eyes shut!" Dion said. "That spell can blind you—it'll burn a person's eyes out—"

It was so dark they could barely see where they were walking, let alone the exit. If the range of Castor's spell extended as far as the light he'd stolen, they would never get away in time. And Dion had told her to shut her eyes while presumably keeping his own open as he pulled her with him across the entrance hall.

"Now would be a good time to counter my attack, Aziza!" Castor called helpfully. "It'll be too late in three . . . two . . ."

Maybe he was lying. But she couldn't risk it.

Out of options, she took her hand back from Dion and shoved it into the collar of her shirt, where a charm hung on a cord around her neck. She had kept it separate from the others, not wanting to risk using it by mistake.

She pushed her magic into the charm, casting the spell. It was made with an everlasting spark from a fire sprite, a matchstick Dion had used to cast one of his spells, and a sliver of a black serpent scale she had taken from the Legrand house. She had imbued it with the story of a fire that ate everything in its path, and a long, restless sleep.

It was a summoning charm.

Outside, the sky blazed with a sudden light—harsher than the sun, all scorching crimson and brimstone yellow, as if the castle had fallen into the earth's core. The salamander crashed through the doors with a wave of blistering heat and a shower of flame. It had been pulled here from the ruins of the Legrand house by the force of Aziza's spell.

What Aziza had seen of it before was a fraction of its true form; back then, it had been half-asleep, much of its body still embedded in the serpentine trails of ash on the walls. When it had attacked them, it had barely done more than lift its head.

Here, in its full glory, it was massive—so wide it could barely fit through the castle's magnificent double doors. It wound its way through the entrance hall, dragging its endless curves and coils over the floor, rearing up so high its great horned head nearly brushed the ceiling. Everywhere it touched, little flames sprang up—even on things that weren't flammable, like stone—and soon the inferno climbed the walls, where it devoured the tapestries and paintings and lapped up the shadows of the distant ceiling.

The salamander's fanged mouth dropped open, and it roared at them, smoke and flames pouring from its jaws.

The light dissolved from Castor's hands as his concentration broke, his spell failing. The salamander's vast body slithered between them, separating him from Aziza and Dion. The smoke was so thick she could barely see, barely breathe.

"We have to get out of here!" Dion coughed, hooking a hand around her elbow. Her stunned grip on the charm vial was so tight the glass could have shattered in her palm. Dazedly, she followed him. As the roar of the fire drowned out the sounds of the battle unfolding elsewhere in the castle, the flames crept toward the threshold of the hallway that would take them back to the safe room, threatening to block their only escape route.

Castor was laughing again. "I concede, Aziza," he said, raising his voice to be heard. "You win."

Through the chaos, looking back, she glimpsed him. He had picked up his lantern; it was pulling in the fire, feeding on it. His eyes gleamed with triumph as he gave her a jaunty wave and turned toward the castle doors.

And then the most mundane thing happened. The most trivial little accident. Because not even Castor Thorne was immune to accidents.

His sleeve caught fire.

"Wait," Aziza said. She dug in her heels, stopping Dion with her.

"What?" Dion said, muffled through the collar of his shirt, which he'd pulled up as a makeshift mask.

The salamander thrashed with fury, slithering around the pillars, which crumbled under its strength. At this rate, the ceiling would collapse soon. But all she could see was the flame eating away at the end of Castor's sleeve. He whipped off the coat and dropped it on the ground. As if it were nothing but a rag. Aziza let go of Dion and ran toward it—even as the flames spread—even as the fire engulfed it—

Before she could get more than a few feet away, Dion caught her around the middle and hauled her backward.

"NO!" she screamed. "Let go! *Let me go!*"

She knew she wasn't making sense. There was a growing wall of fire between her and what was left of that coat. She couldn't get to it. She couldn't leave it. How could she leave it? How could she have let that happen? How could it be burning to cinders before her eyes while she stood on the other side of the room—

"Not even you can walk through fire," Dion snapped, pulling her into the corridor, taking her by the shoulders and forcing her around to face him. "We can't stay here! Aziza, *look at me*!"

She stopped trying to twist away. His face was pink from the heat, his hair sticking to his brow with sweat. His gray eyes reflected the flames, like an arctic lake set ablaze.

This was the same fire that had killed his whole family, and she was trying to throw herself into it. And he wasn't going to leave if she didn't.

It was too late, anyway. She knew that.

She had failed to do the one thing Meryl needed from her, and failed in the most catastrophic way possible. No matter what happened now, Meryl could never go back to the sea. Aziza had taken that from her. Forever.

"Okay," she said. Still, he held her hand in a vise grip, as if worried she might try to escape again. They fled, and the inferno chased them.

CHAPTER 38
TRISTAN

THERE HAD BEEN another Wild Hunt in late autumn; it had been no competition, but a secret mission Queen Ceresia had entrusted to her best ally. She had been so sure of Prince Senna's loyalty that when he returned, victorious, she had not bothered to test the contents of the silver flask he presented to her.

So Prince Senna was in possession of the elixir of renewal, and Queen Ceresia had a flask of plain water and an army hell-bent on switching the two. The Winter Court was in possession of the summertide lord's domain by virtue of being the first to reach it, erecting fortifications to stave off Prince Senna and Princess Kova's incursion into the valley.

Prince Senna needed to get Vetiver and the elixir of renewal past all of them, and he needed to do it before sunrise to complete the solstice ceremony.

Tristan just didn't understand why he had *brought Hazel with him.*

Why hadn't Senna sequestered her someplace else for her safety? When he had broken away from the battle to carry Vetiver through a secret route across the valley's lower slopes, why had Hazel come out of hiding to flit along beside the two of them?

Senna had placed Vetiver on Lucky's back so that he could draw his sword. The ash mixed into the soil made it so dry and loose underfoot it was like walking on a sand dune. Below them, in the burned valley, the battle raged. Tristan couldn't tell the knights of Autumn and Spring apart from the Winter Gallowglass, but he recognized the ice-white figure in the midst of the fighting as the Winter Queen. Somewhere, Princess Narra was in chains, waiting to be crowned.

He watched it all unfold from behind Lucky's eyes. They found the cave in the cliff littered with cast-off scales. Hazel alighted inside its shelter as Prince Senna lowered Vetiver to the ground, propping him up against the wall beside her. The boy was fast asleep and breathing shallowly.

Prince Senna straightened and retreated to the cave's entrance, watching as the fringes of the battle inched higher and higher up the slopes. The figures of the clashing warriors were distorted by a curtain of heat haze. Hazel was the one who took out the silver flask, holding it wrapped in a cloth. She uncapped it.

"Make sure he finishes it," he told her. "Don't leave a single drop."

She clutched the flask tightly, her fingers digging into the soft covering. "I can't," she said. "I know what we agreed, but I can't."

"Then there is only one other choice."

He didn't sound surprised. In fact, Tristan had a feeling Prince Senna was getting exactly what he'd wanted all along.

This time, Hazel didn't hesitate. She brought the flask to her lips and drank. Head tipped all the way back, wings fanning slowly, the firelight from the valley falling across her with a diffuse reddish glow like golden hour. When she lowered the flask, she had a faint mark on her lips—a burn where the rim of the silver container had touched them.

"I'm sorry I couldn't warn Leo first," she told Lucky. "I wasn't sure I was going to go through with it." She set down the flask and came over to hide her face against Lucky's neck. "I couldn't force Vetiver to do it. That's what Princess Narra was trying to do to me, and what Queen Ceresia wanted to do to her. I don't want to be like them. So I guess . . . I can't go home now, no matter how many costume illusions I learn."

Vetiver was mumbling in pain, his eyelashes flickering as he stirred. Prince Senna knelt to rest a hand on his shoulder.

"But I'll visit," Hazel said. "Really soon. Will you tell him that?"

By THE TIME he found Leo, all hell had broken loose. The surviving Summer fairies fled on shaky legs, or flew unsteadily, or leaned against each other as they staggered through the ragged opening into the Flight Paths. There were humans with them, too—the servants of the Summer Court.

"Up!" Beor roared at the stragglers. Compared to how he'd looked when Tristan had last seen him, he was transformed. In the short time since Hazel had completed the solstice ceremony, his complexion had regained the flush of health and vitality, and the lesions of the rot had started to vanish. His booming voice cut over the chatter of building panic. "Get up, all of you! That way, now! You leave your dead or you join them!"

If Beor could have picked up the few who sat weeping beside the bodies of loved ones and thrown them into the Flight Paths himself, Tristan was sure he would have. But he and Leo had their hands full. The doors to the safe room had cracked open, and the two of them were barely managing to hold them against the Winter Gallowglass attempting to force their way in. Through the narrow gap, barely a body's width, their enemies were visible, teeth bared behind their helms, reaching inside to claw at them.

Beor braced his shoulder against the door, flipped his silver sword around, and skewered one of the Gallowglass knights with a merciless backward thrust. The dead knight collapsed into his companions behind him. Beor and Leo slammed the doors—but not before six winged Gallowglass managed to squeeze in from above, shooting inside one after the other to descend on the Summer Court. Beor gave chase; gunshots rang out as Nelle fired at them from the Flight Paths entrance. The Gallowglass were fast, but she got one through the wing and sent her tumbling out of the air. Meanwhile, Leo's hand made a twisting motion against the closed doors, and there was a sound like a heavy bolt grinding into place as the magical lock connected. The Gallowglass on the other side rammed against them, intent on knocking them down, the doors shuddering with the force of the onslaught.

All this had happened in seconds. No one had seen Tristan yet. He stayed in the shadowed corner from which he had appeared and sent Lucky out into the hall. Screams could be heard from the other side of the door as Lucky laid waste to the intruders. This, too, went unnoticed; Leo had already dashed away to help Beor.

Tristan opened the grimoire he had brought: *Liber Os*, the book of intermediate bone magic. With Serapion dead—or as good as—he'd deemed it safe to return to the Wulfsige house and collect it. Now he crept up to the body of one of the fairies that had succumbed to the rot. As he opened the grimoire and began to read aloud, the cool metal of his mask brushed against his lips.

He kept an eye on the others while he cast. Leo had stationed himself next to Nelle at the entrance to the Flight Paths; the Gallowglass would have to land if they wanted to go through. When Nelle ducked inside to reload her gun, one fairy took the opportunity to rush at Leo. Leo parried their strike, but another foe hovered near the high ceiling, firing arrows at him. A wind stirred through the chamber, knocking the arrows off course. The source of the magic was one of the Summer fairies, among a cluster of survivors that had yet to make it through the exit—an enchantress with her hand outstretched and visibly shaking as she used what must have been all the strength in her depleted body to protect him. The other four Gallowglass were doing their best to restrain Beor, who laughed as he fended them off.

"This is nothing!" Beor roared. "I could best three times as many of you!"

Where were Aziza and Dion? Why hadn't they sealed the Flight Paths? Outside, Lucky had been killed for the third time and tossed aside. The Gallowglass were using the reprieve to continue their assault on the safe room doors.

Tristan's spell slowly took effect as he progressed through the incantation. The cold flesh of the cadaver's thigh separated layer by layer, cleanly, as if he had taken a scalpel to it. He pressed his fingers inside. It didn't feel like touching a body; it felt more like wax than flesh. The dark, tacky remnants of congealed blood and the grayish-purple muscle parted until his fingers brushed against the femur. It was already changing shape, detaching from the skeleton, until the hilt of a bone knife was sliding up into his palm, as if the body offered it to him willingly. He had left his silver knife with Leo, back in Serapion's office. This would have to do.

He crossed the chamber, staying low behind the saplings growing from the bodies, keeping to the shadows. The violence on the threshold of the Flight Paths had escalated. The archer dove at the enchantress with a roar of anger; Leo left his post at the tunnel opening to intervene; and the other Gallowglass—all five, including the ones that had been fighting Beor—abandoned everything else and charged at the Flight Paths entrance. Nelle, left to guard it alone, fired at them until she ran out of bullets; she hit one right in the face, killing him, but only clipped a second in the arm, and the others she missed.

"Run!" Beor shouted at her, as he wrenched one of the Gallowglass back by the neck before he could escape. One turned back to help her fellow knight; the other two shot into the Flight Paths after Nelle.

One of Beor's attackers leapt on his back and clawed at his eyes. Then Tristan was there; he plunged his knife into the side of the fairy's throat, felt the blade catch on the top of his spine, and used it like a hook to drag him off Beor. Beor made quick work of his remaining enemy. Tristan watched over their heads as Leo pinned his opponent to the ground with a knee on their stomach and plunged his sword through their chest plate.

He didn't know if he should be glad that he was no longer the only person Leo would kill for.

Leo's curls were damp with sweat, and his shoulders heaved as he caught his breath. His eyes were very wide. *"Tris,"* he said, so quietly Tristan couldn't hear it from where he stood, only read it on his lips.

Then Beor grabbed Tristan by the collar and lifted him clear off his feet.

"What did you do?" he growled.

"Helped, I thought," Tristan said flatly. "You're welcome."

Beor's eyes bored into him. The medicinal scent of the Winter Court's infirmary clung to him, but his grip was unbreakable, as if he'd never been sick a day in his life. When he and Beor had first met, Beor had said that untrained summoners were too dangerous to live. He'd almost killed Tristan on the spot. Later, he had given Tristan his first real lesson in necromancy—but even so, as soon as Tristan stood in the way of what Beor viewed as his duty, Beor had once again become his enemy.

What would Beor do now?

The bone knife in his hand hung at his side. He couldn't summon the will to lift it, to even pretend to defend himself.

"Hey!" Leo said, staggering to his feet. When he let go of the frost sword—which was still embedded in the dead Gallowglass—the blade vanished, and the hilt clattered to the floor. "What are you doing? Put him down!"

"It's okay," Tristan said without looking away from Beor.

"Is it?" Beor snarled. "Do you think that—contraption is enough?"

He meant the mask covering the lower half of Tristan's face, that Jun and Hana had made for him. It was a lattice of delicate, interlocking silver bars, almost as fine as mesh, held in place by leather straps embroidered on the inside with Jun's sigils.

"I don't know," Tristan said honestly.

"How bad is it?" Beor demanded. "Tell me."

"I cast a forbidden spell," Tristan admitted, hating to say it out loud in front of Leo, even though by now Leo had to know everything. "And ever since then, I've felt . . . really, really—"

"Hungry," Beor finished. "Starving. And have you sated that hunger?"

"Once," Tristan said. "My friend made this." His free hand fluttered up toward the mask but didn't make contact. He let it fall back to his side. "He said that . . . if I lose control again, and try to . . . feed . . . it will stop me."

He was supposed to wear it around the dead or dying, and especially when he practiced necromancy. Souls couldn't pass through it even if he tried to consume them. Jun said the fact that he could wear it without descending into a feral rage and ripping it off was proof his transformation hadn't progressed to the point of no return—the point where he was no longer human. A true lich couldn't abide direct contact with silver and wouldn't have consented to wear such a thing. The half hag in Serapion's office would never have borne it.

"It will stop you *if* you don't take it off," Beor hissed. "Do you trust yourself not to slip?"

"Not really," Tristan said.

"Beor, *let him go*!" Leo said, right next to them. He had retrieved his sword, and it was clutched in his hand, the blade drawn but not yet raised.

"Don't think you can command *me*, Your Highness," Beor sneered without breaking eye contact with Tristan. Finally, after a long moment, he dropped him. Tristan landed on his feet, swaying slightly. "If you had answered yes, I would have killed you. To fight this, you must never trust yourself again."

Tristan would have laughed—what other response was there, but to laugh?

Only, then, there was a terrible sound—wood splintering. They all looked up as one. Tristan watched through Lucky's eyes as the Winter Gallowglass flooded into the corridor outside. Their numbers had increased, as if all the knights in the castle and outside had converged on this place. Maybe they had.

There was no time to react. The doors burst open, or maybe they blew apart. And the Winter Gallowglass streamed inside.

The ensuing moments—minutes—were a blur. Tristan didn't know how many there were, only a lot, too many for the three of them and one hound to contend with. Leo fought back his opponents with his sword and Tristan circled him, sliding with his hound in and out of their shadows, cutting throats. Beor was an army all by himself. Literally. Soon the spirits of the dead—of both Winter and Summer—were rising. And the spirits of the hunting party that had followed Beor during the Wild Hunt, ghostly riders on translucent steeds. They filled the air with a haze, like a cold mist; and though there were no windows in the safe room, he felt the night fall on the castle like an axe.

It was chaos. He didn't know how many of the Gallowglass made it into the Flight Paths; probably at least a few did, and Tristan could only hope that Nelle had gotten far enough away to lose them. In the presence of the spirits, Tristan's hunger was very nearly debilitating.

But it was still only hunger, insignificant compared to the all-consuming need to stay close to Leo, to watch his back, to wield his bone knife against anyone who dared lift a hand against him.

And then—as abruptly as they had come—the Gallowglass retreated. One of them called an order to the others, but Tristan's ears were ringing—he couldn't understand the message being passed frantically through their ranks, only that all at once the safe room was emptying out.

Had they really won? Just like that? Even Beor looked puzzled as his opponents abandoned him, until only the three of them and the ghosts remained.

In the subsequent silence, Tristan heard it. A roar, in the near distance, somewhere in the castle. The smell of smoke. Something was burning. The spirits of Beor's hunting party dissipated.

"What is that?" Beor growled.

Then someone else was racing through the broken doors—Aziza and Dion. They were flushed—sunburned?—and Aziza had to cough into her elbow before she said, hoarsely, "We need to go. This whole place is going to burn to the ground."

Dion knelt with a stick of chalk to disconnect the Flight Paths—not to keep out the Gallowglass, but the fire. They all waited inside the corridor behind him.

Light blazed down the end of the hallway beyond the safe room doors—the inferno had reached them already. It traveled quickly into the safe room, devouring the dead. But Dion worked even faster. In minutes, he had drawn a new array from memory. Aziza had spare candles in her backpack, and Dion pricked his finger on the tip of her pocketknife to provide the blood offering.

By then, the flames were like a cresting wave. Tristan's scalp prickled with sweat as the stifling heat enveloped them. Then Dion ignited the array, and the fire of his witchcraft sprang up like a veil between them and the castle. When it subsided, there was nothing but a solid stone wall in front of them. They were in a dead-end Flight Path, alone in a stifling silence.

CHAPTER 39

LEO

They caught up with Nelle and the refugees at the jackdaw collection they had chosen as their meeting place, where they'd planned to reconvene if they were separated. She had barricaded the door, and there was no sign of the Gallowglass who'd pursued them. They had probably gotten lost in the Flight Paths, which was a problem in itself—to have fairies wandering around in there—but they couldn't do anything about it for now.

No one had yet commented on Tristan's absence or sudden return. There hadn't been time to talk. Leo had the sense that Tristan preferred it that way. He hadn't met Leo's eyes once since that moment he'd first appeared in the safe room.

As they trekked through the tunnels to their next destination, Evan jogged ahead of the other servants so he could walk next to Leo.

"I can't find Sophia," he said. Sophia was one of the higher-ranking staff members, answering directly to Princess Narra. "I don't think she was with us in the dorm. Do you know where . . . ?"

He trailed off when he noticed the look on Leo's face.

"She tried to escape with Princess Narra and Viren," Leo said. "But there was . . . an accident. I'm sorry."

"What kind of . . . ? Never mind," Evan said, to Leo's relief. He really didn't want to explain what Sophia's final moments had been like.

"I can break your contract with the Summer Court," Leo said. With his truesight, he could see the servants' bonds like loops of shining, braided twine at their wrists and around their necks. "I'll release the magic that ties you to them. I'm sort of the, uh . . ."

It still felt mortifying to call himself a prince of anything. He was really going to have to get over that.

"Not a chance," Evan said. "If I leave them, I don't know if I'll ever find them again. It was only luck the first time. And who knows if they'd make the same deal with me."

"Figured you'd say that," Leo said, shaking his head. Evan had made it clear before that he served the Fair Folk willingly. But Leo had to admire it. Evan knew exactly what he wanted, and he didn't care if it was right or wrong, or what anyone else thought.

"Ask the others," Evan said. "I know May will want to leave. But won't the Folk be angry with you? Letting us all go without consulting anyone."

"They have bigger things to worry about," Leo said, glancing up at the head of the procession, which was being led by Beor. The fairies stuck close to him. They had given him a hero's welcome; some of the children were clinging to him, including Hazel's friend Ephira, who was hanging off his massive shoulders and chatting his ear off as she demanded news of Hazel and Vetiver. Beor was flustered by the attention—to Leo's amusement—and was handling it with his usual ill humor, but his admirers were undeterred.

Leo spoke to each of the servants in turn, making the same offer he'd given to Evan. A lot of them took him up on it—but not as many as he'd expected.

If his true love was here among the servants—as Leo had suspected—none of them gave him any sign. They probably didn't remember him, either. Evan had told him that their memories became clouded the longer they spent in Elphame. But their memories would return over time if they went back to the human realm. Once this was all over, and Castor was dealt with, he'd renew his efforts to break the curse. He'd find his true love and start undoing the damage his curse had inflicted on their life. They could talk; he would beg forgiveness. He'd make sure they were going to be okay. That was all he really wanted.

So then why was it that he could barely make eye contact with any of these people? Why did he let their faces blur together when he could have searched them carefully, attentively, the way he used to search every time he passed a stranger on the street, alert for any flicker of recognition within his own heart?

When he was feeling really paranoid, mistrustful of himself, he'd think that this was just another twisted facet of the curse—that the closer he came to breaking it, the less he seemed to care if he did. One final test of his faith.

He practically ran away from the last group of servants and came face-to-face with Tristan, whose efforts to skulk on the edges of the party all by himself had been thwarted by Aziza. She hadn't left his side since he'd returned. Leo felt a rush of gratitude for her. That was what he should have done, too. He shouldn't have avoided this conversation. Falling into step with them, he cast around for something to say.

What came out of his mouth was "So, like, is that a muzzle?"

Why. Why, *why* was that the first thing he said to him?

Tristan looked about as mortified as Leo felt. "It's a *mask*. It's why I took so long to come back," he added, his voice strangled and a little defensive. "Jun made it for me. I was afraid to come back without it—I didn't want to put any of you in danger."

That was *such* bullshit. A reasonable explanation but also a convenient excuse. Leo would have called him out on that if they were alone, but he wasn't going to argue with Tristan in front of the entire Summer Court, a gaggle of bleary-eyed and frightened servants, and all their closest friends.

Actually, no, he wouldn't have said anything if they were alone, either. He probably would have done something he shouldn't, like looped a finger through one of the leather straps on the side of Tristan's mask and kissed him through it, cool metal against his lips, his teeth glancing off it in his desperation. He'd have torn off the mask, fisted a hand in his hair, and silenced all the justifications and half lies he had planned on telling. Did Leo feel this wound up because it had been months—*months*—since he had kissed Tristan? Or—

Oh. He was mad, he realized dimly. He was happy to see Tristan again, and so relieved it was like he hadn't been able to breathe properly until just this moment—but he was angry, too, a kind of simmering, under-the-skin, frustrated anger where he knew there would be no resolution for it, nothing he could do about it, not for a while. Up until Tristan was standing in front of him, he had only missed him, and now that Tristan was here he was *mad*. That Tristan had up and left. Shut him out. *Ghosted him.* Ha-ha. It wasn't funny at all. He could have called them on Jun's phone. On a payphone. He could have gone to the library and sent an email—Dion still checked his email, something Nelle had mocked him for relentlessly. Hell, he could have attached a sticky note to the letter Lucky had dropped off from Prince Senna. Even if they weren't together, even if they were just friends—after everything they'd been through, was Leo not entitled to a few words from him, just to let him know that he hadn't *killed himself*?

He didn't know what to say, how to feel—how to broach this subject without making it about himself when Tristan was the one who had been through something so . . . something that had changed him forever. And done it for them. And no sooner had the thought finished forming than the anger was gone, the sparks smothered before they could catch. Now he just felt drained.

How was he supposed to get through to him? How could he explain to this self-destructive, self-loathing, flighty, traumatized, stubborn boy he devoutly adored that there was nothing in the world he wouldn't forgive him for? Nothing he could do that would make Leo not want him around. He had to choose his words carefully this time. Anything that made Tristan walk away from him again was the wrong thing to say.

(And he had gone with *Is that a muzzle?* Christ.)

"You could have let us know you were okay," Aziza said. A solid opening gambit. Leo decided to pretend that was how the conversation had started.

"Sorry," Tristan said quietly, a few long strands of his white-blond hair falling into his eyes. "I know. I should have."

Even when Leo had been mad just now, he hadn't actually wanted an apology. He didn't want Tristan to feel sorry, ever.

"What did Jun say?" she asked.

Dion had explained it to them, but they both wanted to hear it from Tristan.

It was hard to read his expression under the mask, so Leo focused on his voice, close and quiet.

"Using corruptive magic triggered . . . a transformation. Or the start of one," he explained haltingly. "Continuing to cast corruptive spells would eventually turn me into a full lich. And so would . . . feeding. On souls. Which is . . . what I did to Professor Serapion." He had to stop, cringing, and actually turn his face away from them before he continued. "Certain things will make the . . . hunger feel worse, like practicing necromancy at all. The mask won't help me resist it. It's only there as a fail-safe in case I'm not strong enough."

"But it *can* be resisted?" Leo said. "You won't end up like that girl we found?"

"She was much further along in the transformation than I am. The urge to follow that path will always be part of me now, and I have to fight it. But I'm used to evil things whispering in my ear." His eyes were fixed on a spot off to the side of the path, his frost-blond eyelashes fanned down. "I know it was wrong of me to stay away for so long and make you worry. I didn't know how to explain myself, or if I was still . . . human. You must be so . . ."

He trailed off. Leo couldn't imagine how that sentence would have ended.

"We were worried about you," Leo said. "You scared us when you ran away without saying anything."

Us, he kept saying. *Us,* when he really meant *me*. Leo was the one who couldn't bear it when Tristan was out of arm's reach.

"If Jun said there was no way to resist it, what were you going to do?" Aziza asked, getting straight to the point. "Were you going to ask him to kill you? Or maybe you'd have asked Beor."

"If I had really become a lich . . . if I still do, someday . . . I wouldn't be myself anymore," Tristan said. "I'd be no different from the hag. I don't want that. I'm relieved to say that I would rather die." For a moment his voice had gained a steel undercurrent of true conviction, but it wavered again as he said, "But I wouldn't want you to have to be the ones to . . . stop me. I'm sorry."

Aziza stopped walking, so Leo and Tristan did, too, letting the distance between them and the rest of the party grow.

"What exactly are you sorry for?" Aziza said. "Something that happened to you because of what you did to save us?"

"To *save* you? Right. I ripped you from the peace of death and into a world that only wants to hurt you. I didn't do it for you," he said, with that borderline masochistic honesty he had lately adopted. "I did it for me, because I wanted you back. It was selfish. And I don't regret it. Even now, knowing what it's done to me. What it might still do to me."

Leo watched his chest rise and fall as he breathed. His voice was so calm. He had been thinking these terrible thoughts for weeks, letting them poison him.

"You're not going to turn," Aziza said, without a modicum of doubt.

"Tris, death wasn't peaceful. It was just . . . nothing," Leo said. "I don't know, maybe there was a better place that I don't remember. Does it matter?"

"The things you don't remember matter a lot to you," Tristan reminded him, a little wary.

"That's different," Leo said, rather than confess that none of the things he didn't remember mattered to him as much as Tristan did. "Even if there *was* something better, do you think I'd be happy leaving my parents and Hazel behind? Do you think Aziza would have rested easy knowing that Khaled was alone and Meryl was still a prisoner?"

"Do you think we want Castor to *win*?" Aziza said.

"No," Tristan said. "You're right. I know. But . . ."

"But what?" Aziza said. "Go on."

Tristan glanced pleadingly at Leo as if for help, which, at any other point in time, would have gotten him whatever he wanted. Now Leo said, "Don't give me that look. All of this could've been avoided with a text."

Under the mask, his lips twitched with the beginnings of a smile.

"Okay," he conceded. "You're not upset about being resurrected without your consent, and you're willing to overlook the magical corruption. But you must be a little grossed out, at least."

"Because you ate a human soul," Aziza said.

"Yes. Because I did that."

"I guess it was kind of gross," Leo admitted, "but mostly because the soul in question was, like, way past its sell-by date. Probably tasted awful."

"Like spoiled milk," Aziza said. "I bet it put you off souls for life."

Tristan ducked his head to hide a grin.

Being in the Flight Paths had this way of making you lose all sense of time. When they emerged at Bishop Library, it was almost midnight. Outside, the wind howled, and thunder rumbled.

"You can get to the woods from here, but you'll have to go through Blackthorn. Do you think you'll all be able to use look-away charms?" Leo asked Beor.

"With our power restored, even in this pathetic condition, we can do that much," Beor said. "We won't be seen."

Out in the parking lot, with the trees on the side of the road whipping violently in the storm, the Summer Court's enchanters wove the rain into an illusion of winged horses, their fur a dull gleam like the surface of a puddle, their eyes an overcast gray. Very soon, the fairies and their handful of remaining servants took flight and vanished into the clouds, which had broken open and unleashed curtains of icy rain and thunder down on Blackthorn.

"We have to pick up where we left off," Dion was saying when Leo came back in. "Go to Sanctum, get the third lantern, and figure out where he moved the other two. We can't afford to slow down now."

"At the castle, after I summoned the salamander," Aziza said quietly, "he looked at me like I'd done him a favor. My spell—it gave that lantern the boost he needed. I don't think we have very long now. And I think—before we go to Sanctum—we're going to need some help."

About ten minutes later, they were knocking on Khaled's door.

CHAPTER 40

AZIZA

IT WAS STRANGE to be home. When she'd left, she had been so certain she was doing the right thing, and was expecting to be back in a day or so. And now almost two months had passed and she wasn't certain about anything at all.

There were a few empty take-out containers on the kitchen counter, yet to be discarded, and mugs in the sink, stained inside with the dried residue of days-old tea and coffee. Her grandfather's work laptop was on the table with stacks of papers beside it. The couch had been made up with pillows and a blanket, which he gathered up and stuffed away before she could make a move to help. He must have been sleeping downstairs, doubtless so that he'd hear the door open if she tried to sneak back in. A wave of guilt crashed over her.

If he was angry—and he had to be angry—he must have decided it could wait. He had not said much of anything yet—had seen her standing there on the front step and only pulled her into a tight, wordless embrace, with a grip that felt like it belonged to someone twenty years younger. His familiar scent of tea leaves and aftershave had made her eyes prickle with tears, which didn't fall. It was too soon to feel relieved. Nothing was over yet.

He rounded on Leo first.

"Call your parents," he said gruffly. "Or I will."

"I was totally going to do that," Leo said, sounding very much like someone who had planned on doing no such thing. I just . . . uh . . . Maybe it would be better if I . . ."

Before he could stumble his way to the end of that sentence, Jiddo was already taking out his phone and dialing. He pushed it into Leo's hands as the ringback tone sounded from the speaker. It rang once before it clicked and Greg's voice came over the line.

Leo raised the phone to his ear and shuffled into the hallway to take the call. "Hi, Dad. It's me."

"Sit down," Jiddo told the rest of them. "And for god's sake put that gun away."

"Sorry," Nelle said, ejecting the cartridges and dropping them and the weapon back into her bag.

"It's a pleasure to meet you, sir," Dion said, with a glittering smile. Like the rest of them, he was sopping wet from the walk over, but he had managed to surreptitiously smooth back his damp hair and straighten his collar. "I apologize for all of us dropping in unannounced. You have a lovely home."

Dion was the most exasperatingly brilliant witch she had ever met, but when he found himself in an unfamiliar social situation, he turned into a human pull-string toy programmed with a vocabulary made exclusively of insincere pleasantries. She was aghast at the discovery that she had started to find it endearing.

She nudged him toward the couch, where Nelle immediately threw her legs over his lap. Tristan hovered at Aziza's shoulder, avoiding eye contact with her grandfather.

"Your hound tripped my wards," Jiddo said, thankfully deciding not to comment on the mask. "I know you've been checking in on me. I appreciate it, but there was no need. Castor couldn't have forced his way in here if he tried."

Tristan only blinked at him over the mask like a dog waiting to be kicked. Her grandfather gave him an awkward pat on the shoulder.

"I know you have questions," Aziza said, as Tristan slinked past her to join the others. "But I have to talk to Anne first."

"She's already on her way," he said, and not half an hour later a knock came at the door. Apparently Jiddo had sent her a message the moment they'd crossed the boundary of his wards. By now, she would have gotten wind of some of what had happened in Elphame—the outcome of the solstice ceremony, at least, and perhaps the Summer Court's escape from Queen Ceresia's assassins.

Anne looked exhausted. It wasn't obvious; it never was, with her. Her eyes traveled swiftly over all of them, as if taking a head count, before settling on Aziza. Everyone had fallen silent, waiting for Anne to speak, but for once Aziza couldn't keep quiet.

"I'm sorry," she said. Unconsciously, she sat straight up when Anne walked in, her posture as rigid as Dion's. Her left hand was clenched in her lap. "Everything that happened—the three of us disappearing—I can't explain it, but it was all my fault."

"I'm sorry, too," Anne said, holding up a hand to stop her. "To be honest, I didn't think I was going to see any of you again. I thought I had failed you completely."

Failed them? Aziza didn't understand that at all.

"We didn't tell you where we were going," she said. "There was nothing you could've done to stop us. Especially me. And if I had just listened to you from the start—"

She broke off. She didn't even know where to begin listing all of the things that had gone wrong, that she could have done better.

"You felt you couldn't trust me," Anne said. "There was a time I wouldn't have been able to ignore the suffering of an imprisoned selkie, either. Or put it on a shelf until I could address it later, when it was convenient for me. You couldn't do that, and I shouldn't have expected you to."

Aziza looked away. "Maybe it would have been better if I had."

With help from the rest of them, she told her grandfather and Anne what had happened. Most of it. They neatly avoided the topic of deaths and resurrections, being vague about the timeline to cover up the weeks they couldn't account for. But they confessed to tracking Meryl to the Legrand house, hiding from Castor at Emil Wulfsige's place, being chased out and embarking on their hunt for the lanterns, and finally, the confrontation at the Summer Court's castle. They'd left the human refugees at Bishop Library in the librarian's quarters upstairs. Hopefully, by morning, they'd remember enough of their former lives to make their way home. If not, Anne would connect them with AJA resources for victims of fae mischief and help them find their feet.

No one breathed a word about their role in Professor Serapion's demise, and when Anne asked what the mask was for, Tristan said, "It's a spellcasting aid. I'm testing it for a friend."

"Right," Anne said, poker-faced.

"What about Meryl?" Aziza asked. "Can Castor still control her? Or is she free?"

"She can't shift out of her human form anymore, but his hold on her is broken now that her sealskin is no longer in his possession," Anne said. "He wouldn't have bothered locking her up. With the sealskin, there would have been no need. I'm hopeful she'll be able to escape on her own, but he hid her very well—I was never able to track her down."

"You didn't?" Aziza said. "But—I sent Fox with her. It was supposed to come back to you after it followed her to wherever Castor was keeping her."

"I haven't seen Fox since before you three disappeared. I assumed it was with you."

Aziza's heart plummeted. Maybe Fox hadn't understood what she was asking for—or maybe it had reached the stage of maturity where it had finally decided to cast off on its own, and none of them would ever see it again. She really had failed Meryl in every conceivable way. If Meryl didn't find a way to escape, what would Castor do to her? Though he'd taunted Aziza with the possibility that he'd give up the sealskin coat, he surely wouldn't let her go—not knowing everything she knew about him after serving him for nearly twenty years.

When Aziza and Dion repeated the things Castor had told them—it was everyone else's first time hearing it, too—Anne wasn't surprised.

"You've been busy for the past couple of months," she said. "But so have I. Your misadventure at Yale was an unexpected stroke of luck for me. A couple of the apprentice weather witches you encountered there sought me out afterward. They were having doubts about the orders they'd received from Castor. They regretted having engaged you in combat."

"Of course they regretted it," Aziza muttered. "They lost."

Anne pressed her lips together to suppress a smile. "They claimed to have gone easy on you when they realized you weren't even out of high school." Before Aziza could object to this—patently ridiculous—assertion, Anne added, "And they weren't comfortable with being asked to hunt down an Osorio witch as if she were a common criminal. They wanted to pass on their deepest apologies to your aunt."

Nelle groaned in disbelief. "Great."

"In any case, they were able to supply some information I was lacking about Castor's plans," Anne said. "And Professor Serapion's office was thoroughly searched after his body was discovered. He kept extensive notes on his meetings and correspondence with Castor over the years. With what you've told me today, I have everything I need to call on the Clattering to apprehend him, have his magic bound, and put him on trial for his crimes."

"How many of them will support you?" Dion asked, leaning forward.

"Enough," Anne said. "This is the first time in a few generations that such a serious rift has formed within the Clattering. Some of my colleagues aren't convinced by the evidence I've gathered against Castor, and have opted to maintain their neutrality for now. Including Penelope Osorio, which likely means—"

"She can't get a clear grasp on the future," Nelle finished. "She doesn't know what the winning side is yet."

"Yes. But I have enough support to move forward. I don't have a choice," Anne said. "Castor has already set his plan in motion."

"What do you mean?" Aziza asked.

Anne's response was to turn on the TV.

There was a middle-of-the-night breaking news report on every channel. A chain of mega-storms had formed over the East Coast with no warning. There was flooding, landslides, hurricane-force winds, ten-and twenty-foot ocean waves. Every station had a different parade of experts commenting on the situation—meteorologists, climate scientists, government officials doing a commendable job of pretending they hadn't just rolled out of bed—but no one could explain it.

"Castor's doing this?" Leo asked.

"His followers are," Anne said. "This is his way of covering up the effects of the spell he's casting—until it's all over and it's too late to stop him."

"You've figured out what his end goal is, then," Dion said eagerly. "All I could do was speculate. When he talked about his . . . *rookery* . . . I honestly still have no idea what he was getting at."

"He also talked like he had been . . . studying the hag," Aziza said. "We thought the hag was only a source of power for his lantern. But he learned something from her, too. And I think I know what. The hag was so old and so powerful, and had consumed so much magical energy, that her territory was like its own little world. It wasn't part of Elphame or the human realm—it was something else, and its existence was wearing down Elphame's boundary."

"You think he's creating a pocket realm, modeled after the hag's," Dion said, following her train of thought.

"No, I think he can do better than that," Aziza said. "He's aiming higher."

"You two were so close to cracking it," Anne said, with a weary smile. "Given more time, you would have had him. But we don't have time, so let me speed things up a little bit. He plans to stitch together his Rookery using Elphame's borderlands."

"But . . ." Aziza said, trailing off as she tried to wrap her mind around that. The magnitude of the destruction it would cause. Elphame's boundary wasn't a wall. It wasn't fixed. It was a force of nature—porous, adaptable, constantly shifting. The boundary was the entry point between the two realms, but the borderlands—where they overlapped—were what allowed them to coexist. Without the borderlands, the boundary would fall apart. It would just be gone, beyond mending, and the two realms would merge.

It would be complete disaster. She thought of wights and doppelgangers and worse roaming freely through the human realm; and she thought of bombs and missiles being deployed against Gallowglass knights. A nymph, Eirlys, had once told her that it wasn't only her job to protect humans from the fae—she had to protect the fae from humans, too. With no boundary, that would be impossible.

"Once this third realm—this Rookery—is complete, I imagine it will be closed off from both the human realm and fairyland. He'll have entry points for witches, but they will be tightly guarded. For now, though, while the boundary still exists, we can still use it to cross into the borderlands and reach the Rookery. So that's what I intend to do." Anne was checking her phone and getting to her feet. "Parts of the country are already disappearing. Entire forests and fields, miles of coastline. Those of my colleagues who had trouble believing me are beginning to see reason. I've contacted every hedgewitch I can reach, and my allies in the Clattering are assembling their own people. We're going to stop him. Nelle, can I ask you to join us?"

"Wouldn't miss it," Nelle said. "Sorry, guys. Looks like you're down a party member."

"I'm coming with you, too," Aziza said, standing, but Anne shook her head.

"My stance on bringing teenagers to battlefields hasn't changed," Anne said. "You're staying put."

"You have got to be kidding," Aziza snapped.

"Try and argue with me about it," Anne said.

Jiddo stood beside her. "I believe I can be of service."

"Your assistance would make things go a little more smoothly, I'm sure," Anne agreed.

"What? Jiddo, no!" Aziza said, swinging around to look at him in horror. "You can't—"

"Castor Thorne is the reason my daughter is dead," Jiddo said. "I want to be there to see justice delivered."

She was gearing up to argue when Dion said, smoothly, "They're right. Surely you see the sense in letting experienced witches like themselves handle this."

She knew that tone of voice. It meant he was going to smile politely, say whatever would make everyone happy and comfortable, wait until they weren't looking, and then do exactly what he wanted and damn the consequences. With his eyes, he was silently advising her to do the same.

Aziza shut her mouth, teeth grinding with the urge to argue anyway.

"I know you're going to try to follow us," Anne said. "You won't be able to. Castor's Rookery will be small and partially formed, but it's still quite the distance to traverse on foot to the place where I believe he's hiding."

Stepping closer, Anne placed her hands on Aziza's shoulders. "This isn't your job, or your responsibility. There are so many people who should have stopped Castor before he went this far. It never should have fallen on you." She looked over at Dion. "For Emil's sake, if nothing else, please let me do this."

"For Leila and Ahmed," Jiddo added. "Let *me* do this, Aziza."

Promising to be careful and to come back soon, they departed, leaving behind a silence that no one seemed to want to break. With a sudden dread, she realized Leo and Tristan were waiting for her to make the next call. Or perhaps they assumed she already had. That she would pursue Castor as relentlessly as before. And she wanted to do it. Despite mounting evidence that she was no match for him, that her entire coven combined was no match for him, she still wasn't ready to admit defeat. She didn't know what to call that emotion. Stubbornness didn't feel strong enough. Determination felt too noble. It didn't feel noble. It was a feeling that had teeth.

She looked at Leo's injured shoulder, the bandages peeking above his collar, and at Tristan's eyes over the mask, unreadable even to her.

"Dion," she said, stalling. "You know how to follow them, right? If we want to."

"I do," he said. "But this isn't a decision we have to make as a team. I want anyone who's coming to do it for purely selfish reasons. Because that's why I'm going."

Despite everything, she smiled. "What's your selfish reason, then?"

"I'm going on the off chance I have the opportunity to kill Castor Thorne myself," Dion said pleasantly. "I have a dozen different fantasies about how I'd do it and none of them involve magic. I don't want him apprehended and put on trial. I want him dead. So I am going to make sure that nobody makes the mistake of trying to show him mercy."

His certainty made her own mind feel clearer; that nebulous desire for vengeance solidified into something lucid and purposeful. It was a relief; she *needed* to have a purpose, could not function without one. She'd felt lost the moment she saw Meryl's sealskin burn, and coming home hadn't been enough to center her. But she remembered herself now; Dion had reminded her. It wasn't just that she wanted Castor beaten. Aziza wanted to be the one to beat him. The same way she hadn't just wanted Meryl to be saved; she wanted to be the one to save her. Wasn't she Blackthorn's hedgewitch? Wasn't that library hers, this city hers, those borderlands in the forest and the sea hers? Not hers to own, the way Castor Thorne owned places, but hers to defend and preserve. And if she couldn't do that much, then what was the point?

Anne was wrong—this was her responsibility. And her choice.

"He's right," she said, turning back to Leo and Tristan. "Before, he had us cornered and there was nothing we could do but fight back. Things are different now."

She already knew what they would say. Dion was right; they *were* always making decisions as a team. As a coven. But that was when they were at their best.

"I'm not finished with Castor yet," Tristan said, teeth gritted behind the mask.

"I didn't go to all that trouble to save the Summer Court from a fairy war just for him to start one," Leo said. "And I sort of forgot to mention this to Anne, but I have a favor I can call in."

IT CAME DOWN to a guess, or perhaps a strong hypothesis based on the information Castor had freely given them. They knew he meant to bring other witches to the Rookery—it was supposed to be a home for all of them. And the easiest way for a jackdaw to travel a long distance was through the Flight Paths.

When Tristan sent Lucky to scout ahead, he reported that weather witches had been posted outside the front and back entrances to Bishop Library. Did Castor know that they had returned to Blackthorn, or had he simply guessed? Where else did he have people searching for them—guarding against them? It was almost flattering that he viewed them as being worth the effort. It also indicated that Castor had a reason to keep them out of the Flight Paths at this crucial time. Which meant their hypothesis was probably correct.

But Aziza and Leo had another way into the library, one that even Castor didn't know about.

The storm had turned the street into a river. The water was ankle-deep in some places, and the wind blew so hard it was a struggle to walk against it. There weren't any cars on the road, but the trains were still running to the beach, where the ocean waves were so large they engulfed the narrow coastline and poured seafoam into the street. (And soon, she knew, this coast, those cliffs, would be part of Castor's Rookery—what would Blackthorn even look like after that?) The kelpies were hunting closer to the shore than they had dared in months; they came quickly when Aziza summoned them, unbothered by the turbulence of the currents. Three of them again, one each for her, Leo, and Dion. She kept an eye on the others as they cantered into the icy sea. Leo had his eyes screwed shut and probably a death grip on the reins. Dion's eyes were very much open, watching the water whip by.

The kelpies swam toward the rocky outcropping where the selkie pod used to rest. Here, the water was rougher, the current trying to drag her off the kelpie's back. They skated over the base of the cliffs; occasionally, through the thunder, she heard the crack of their hooves striking the rocks as they pushed off with renewed speed.

Soon the mouth of the cave was visible—a dark smudge, half-submerged, with a slight overhang so that it couldn't be seen from above. The water lapped inside, so that it was as if the cliffs were drinking the sea. The kelpies swam into the opening. Soon, their hooves found solid ground, and they walked up the tunnel's gradual slope, the water receding until the three of them could dismount. Once, there had been a saltwater river here, carved by the local selkie pod so that they could sing to their captive daughter. Since the selkies had left Blackthorn, the tunnel had dried up. Someone turned on a flashlight while she unwound the seaweed from the kelpies' necks. They nickered softly in farewell as they withdrew, trotting back into the sea.

Tristan had shadow-traveled there and was waiting a little way ahead with a change of clothing for all of them. It took about half an hour to hike up the rest of the tunnel. The sound of the waves and thunder echoed after them. Blue-green patches of algae still mottled the earthen walls, which had been scoured smooth by the river. Soon, they reached the place where the tunnel branched off and led them back to the library. They climbed up a ladder tucked into the corner and emerged in the storage space that used to be Meryl's office. Outside, the storm was only getting worse. They descended into the jackdaw collection, where it was muffled, but still audible.

They were sure the Rookery would be connected to the Flight Paths, but where was the entry point? This was where the real guesswork came into play. But Dion was fairly confident the doorway was in Sanctum.

"After Sanctum was destroyed, what was left of it could have become part of Elphame's borderlands, the way abandoned places tend to do," Dion said. "I thought Sanctum was only a hiding place for one of his lanterns, but the way he talked about it when we met him in the castle made me realize I'd underestimated how important that place still is to him."

Aziza was inclined to agree. All of this was Castor's way of righting a wrong, and Sanctum represented everything he thought was wrong with the world.

The Flight Path enchantments could not cross Elphame's boundary—not without a collaborative spell, like the one Aziza and Dion had created to evacuate the Summer Court. But if Anne was right, and Castor's spell would weaken and ultimately destroy the boundary over the course of this night—then the Flight Path to Sanctum that Castor would have prepared in advance, if it existed, would be open now.

At the threshold of the other Bishop Library, Dion paused, his expression inscrutable.

"Dion," she said, before he could speak. She didn't want to hear any last-minute doubts.

"What?" he asked.

"If you really want to kill Castor Thorne, you'd better be fast. Or I'll beat you to it."

His answering smile was on the edge of vicious. "We'll see about that."

CHAPTER 41

LEO

THE FLIGHT PATHS exit was technically outside Sanctum—about a mile away, in the old coal mine. There wasn't actually a door, just a gradual shift from a hallway to a tunnel, the air growing stale and acrid with coal dust. Their flashlights cast deep, pitted shadows on the rock walls and wooden shoring.

Outside, it was snowing lightly. They squeezed around a mine cart left abandoned just inside the entrance and followed the tracks past an empty loading dock, a toolshed, and a chain-link fence. The tracks would lead them to Sanctum, but they climbed part of the way up the slope of the mountainside to get their bearings first. To see what they were walking into.

From their vantage point, what they saw was the mine rail disappearing into the woods and the woods tumbling into a solid wall of gunmetal storm clouds, which piled overhead higher than the surrounding mountain peaks. The snowfall over the mine was only the wispy excess of that tempest in the near distance. It was Castor's weather witches, protecting Sanctum.

In the other direction, the Rookery was visibly half-finished. An alien landscape unfurled beyond the hills. Forests grew in patches like fur, and then receded into the murky distance as the land stretched. Roads trailed away into empty grasslands. The stars came on in waves. There wasn't a moon yet, only a void where it should have hung. A nearby river churned and flooded its banks, as if being fed with rainfall from another realm. Which it was. Beyond that, just—blackness.

He had understood that the Rookery was small and partially formed, that it would expand as more of the borderlands merged into it. But it was one thing to hear about Castor's spell and another to stand there and watch a world be shaped as if by a divine hand.

Even Lucky couldn't penetrate the storm ring.

"It's warded," Tristan said. "The storm wraps around Sanctum completely. I don't see anyone, either. They're hidden, probably inside the storm, because Lucky can't even pick up their scents."

And the woods were full of Castor's winged constructs, entire flocks of them perched in the trees, keeping watch.

It came as no surprise that Castor's defenses were airtight. But Anne was on her way, hopefully with an army of her own. And Leo had scrawled a letter to Prince Senna before they'd left, which Lucky had delivered. *If ever you should find yourself in need of aid, send for me,* Prince Senna had said; Leo was asking him to make good on that promise now. Chances were slim that Prince Senna could spare more than a few knights, after the hit his forces had taken in their battle against the Winter Court, but even that would be better than nothing.

As for the four of them, they would wait for an opening and make their move.

He felt sick with anticipation. And a little superfluous, maybe. He wasn't a witch. He was the only one who wouldn't be able to help with the most important part of the plan—finding Castor's array and reversing what he'd done. Leo had already done the most important thing he could, which was write to Prince Senna. Other than that, all he had was the frost sword and the nauseating prospect of having to use it against a misguided apprentice witch.

The crystal hilt was tucked in his pocket, cold enough for him to feel it through the cloth. The convenient thing about an enchanted blade that disappeared when you weren't using it was that, no matter how bloody it had been when you put it away, it was always clean when it materialized again. He wasn't sure if that was a good thing. Maybe he'd feel less numb to everything that had happened today if he'd had to wipe off his blood-spattered sword afterward.

His gaze settled on Tristan. To say he felt numb to "everything" wasn't true at all.

They put some distance between themselves and the mine as fast as they could, in case Castor was watching it, taking shelter in a shallow cave that reminded him of hiding out during the Wild Hunt. The woods were silent except for the intermittent growl of thunder. Tristan stood at the entrance, looking out in the direction Lucky had gone, through the tall hemlocks shivering in their coats of needles. Dion was paging through a set of notes he'd been keeping on the lanterns, searching for one more clue, for anything he'd missed, for some small but vital detail that could be the key to Castor's undoing. And Aziza was next to Leo. She had stayed close to him as they'd walked through the Flight Paths; belatedly he recognized it as the gesture of silent support that it was, the same way she had planted herself beside Tristan as they fled from the castle. She knew there was something on his mind.

He took her hand to get her attention. All he had to do was look at Tristan, and then at her, imploringly, for her to understand. She squeezed his hand and stood. "I'm going to look around nearby," she said to the others. "Send Lucky if you need me back."

"Look around for what?" Dion said, predictably rising to his feet when she did.

"We're in the borderlands. If any of the fae got caught up in this, they might be willing to help us."

"I'll come with you. None of us should wander off alone right now."

"Stray cats wander off. Hedgewitches in Elphame's borderlands don't *wander* anywhere. I'm not going far, anyway," she said, putting up a token protest. But she waited for him to put his notebook away and follow her outside.

When they were out of earshot, Tristan looked over his shoulder at Leo, his eyes faintly amused above the mask.

"Very subtle, both of you," he said.

"Give us a gold star for trying," Leo replied, grinning, and walked over to him. "I was so pissed off at you earlier." He finally lifted his hands to the back of the mask as he'd been wanting to do from the second he'd seen Tristan again, undoing the buckle he found there, buried in his hair. Tristan's eyes widened, but he didn't move. Leo kept talking as he pulled the mask free and let it drop. "And it was only partly because you disappeared on us. Though I hated that, too."

Tristan's face seemed more open than Leo had ever seen it, as if, in the short time he had been wearing the mask, he had gotten accustomed to not having to hide his expression. Leo's hand settled on the back of his neck, his hair brushing against his fingers. This close, he could tell that Tristan's breathing had grown shallow.

"Then why?" Tristan asked.

"It was when you said that, if you turned, you wouldn't ask us to stop you," Leo said. "I couldn't believe that you'd leave me without even saying goodbye and spend your last moments with someone else."

"You're angry," Tristan said, "that I didn't want to ask you to kill me?"

"Yeah."

"Would you do it?" Tristan asked. "If it became necessary."

"No. If it came right down to it, I'd let you take my soul," Leo said. "I'd hand myself over to you and make sure I was your last one."

Tristan's hand flew up to clutch at his wrist, fingers digging into his flesh.

"My last what?" Tristan said, in a sudden bitter fury that sharpened his voice to a frigid point. "Victim? *Meal?* You're failing to convince me I did the wrong thing when I left. Maybe I'll leave as soon as this is all over, and you'll never see me again."

His anger confirmed Leo's worst suspicions.

"You're doing it again," Leo observed. "Like you did when you were looking for that book of the infernal arts without telling us. You're thinking that if we're cornered, you'll rip the mask off and do whatever you have to do, to beat Castor and make sure we survive." He pulled Tristan close, knocked their foreheads lightly together. Tristan was shaking under his hands; his whole body was taut, as if he might spring away, but he didn't. Leo said, "I just want you to know that I'll be right next to you, and if you lose yourself, I'm not going to stop you, and I'm not going to run away. I'm staying with you. Even if it means we *both* lose ourselves, together."

"Fuck you," Tristan said, and kissed him hard. It was such a relief to be close to him again without holding anything back that Leo could only laugh deliriously into it at first. But Tristan deepened the kiss and shoved him against the wall, and Leo clutched at him, and then he wasn't laughing anymore.

He separated from Tristan briefly to say, "After this—"

He spoke against Tristan's lips and felt his shuddering exhalation in response. Tristan had gone still, and Leo wondered if he felt the same superstitious anxiety that Leo did, at daring to give voice to the hope of an "after." But he had to say it. This wasn't the right time, but it could be the only time.

"What is it?" Tristan said. His weight in Leo's arms was grounding, even more than the wall against Leo's back. He was pinned, immobilized as if by a pleasurable fear, and if he could've stayed right there and never moved again, he would have been content.

"After this, can we . . . try again?" Leo asked. "For real this time."

"For . . . real?" Tristan echoed, as if he didn't understand the meaning of the words. He put another inch of space between them. That transparent expression was back, his wide eyes and parted lips, and the signs of Leo's affection were visible all over him, his mussed hair and open collar and flushed skin. He looked vulnerable, taken aback, a little hopeful. Cautiously so.

"Because it was serious for me, too," Leo said. "I do love you, Tris. I don't know why I thought denying it would change that. I don't even want to change it. I shouldn't have wasted so much time pretending you weren't everything to me."

"Even now?" Tristan asked. "Now that I'm . . . like this?"

"Now more than ever. Any way I can have you."

"What about your true love?" he asked, without bitterness.

And Leo hadn't given up on his true love—but what it meant to not give up had changed, somewhere along the line. If his true love wasn't among the servants he'd freed from the Summer Court, he would keep looking. He wanted to rescue them from whatever suffering his curse had caused them. His love for the person in his missing memories was real. But what he felt for Tristan was real, too. Why should it matter less? Because some long-dead enchantress said so? Did he need the curse to legitimize his feelings? What could magic tell him that his own heart couldn't?

He had allowed the curse to rule his life for years. It had been a factor in almost every decision he made. And he had always found something comforting in the idea of true love. If it was fated, then there was no question it would all work out—that the curse was meant to be broken, and inevitably would be. But lately it had felt more like a shackle he had put on himself. He had limited his own choices, or perhaps not even realized he had a choice. But he did, and he'd pick uncertainty with Tristan over a destiny with anyone else. Even if it meant he never got his memories back.

Tristan was waiting for his answer.

"*This* is true," Leo said. "It's true enough for me."

It wasn't the right time, and it definitely wasn't the right place, and those weren't the right words. But he knew what the right thing was to do, at least, and it was to press in for another kiss, which Tristan accepted unhesitatingly. If Leo never had another chance, he needed to have kissed him just once and meant it the way he should have meant it all along.

It was only a brush of their lips together, almost a peck, like a hello or goodbye—casual, absent-minded, familiar. It reminded him of kissing Tristan for the very first time, innocent and painfully sincere; Leo had acted on a wild impulse and caught him off guard, lost his nerve halfway through and scrambled away almost before Tristan could react. Later, Tristan had admitted he hadn't dared let himself hope that Leo felt the same way he did—

And as that impossible thought crossed Leo's mind, it ran up against a resistance inside him—not like a wall, but like a door that had gotten stuck. It didn't need to be broken down, only given a decisive push. The thought—the memory—was followed by a cascade of them. And it was all Tristan. A scrawny eleven-year-old Tristan with his head down, talking to no one, glimpsed in passing and from a distance. A twelve-year-old Tristan looking up at him with those arresting green eyes, the tip of a pencil scratching absently at the corner of his sketchbook as he quietly replied to Leo's persistent attempts to draw him into conversation. Tristan at age thirteen, practicing sign language with Leo's mom over dinner.

Tristan at fourteen, clumsily kissing him back. Tristan, who the curse had erased from his mind. Tristan, whose absence had haunted him. Tristan, who had come back to him and—even when Leo had pushed him away—had never given up on him.

"What's wrong?" Tristan said. His thumb swiped at Leo's cheek, wiping away the tears Leo hadn't noticed falling.

"Sorry," he croaked, rubbing his sleeve across his right eye. The amber one couldn't weep.

"We're going to get out of this," Tristan said. "And I won't . . . turn. I'll keep the mask on. I promise."

Tristan thought that Leo was afraid of the fight they were about to walk into. He didn't realize what had just happened. That Leo's curse was broken. That true love's kiss had broken the curse.

Was it destiny after all? Or was it that Tristan had only become Leo's true love when Leo had decided that he was?

"I know," Leo said. He couldn't find the words to tell him the rest yet. He was overwhelmed, sorting through memories from before the curse—almost reliving them, his heart twisting with fondness as he held them up against present-day Tristan—and from after, moments that had gained new meaning in light of this revelation.

He would keep it to himself for now, until he could speak without tearing up again. It just wasn't . . . important. Not important enough to waste what could be their last few minutes alone talking about it. Leo had done enough talking and had better things he could be doing with his mouth.

Besides—Tristan had promised they would get out, and that meant they'd have time later. He had to trust that. Because as far as he could remember, Tristan always kept his promises.

WITH NO SIGN of Anne or the Autumn knights, the four of them were conducting a quiet debate about how much longer they could afford to wait. Maybe Anne hadn't managed to get the support she'd counted on from the Clattering after all. Maybe no one else was coming.

And then the darkness at the mouth of the cave lifted away. Leo looked up. One of the little jackdaw constructs, like feathered sunshine, had landed on a lower branch of a nearby tree. It shuffled its feet, talons digging in, and cocked its head in their direction.

Two more fluttered down next to it, the swoosh of their wings audible in the sudden thick silence.

They'd been found.

Probably the wisest course of action would've been to return to the Flight Paths, but they didn't do that and they didn't even need to talk about it. They ran toward the storm.

The understory was a snarl of dead thickets and shriveled yellow ferns, and perilous slicks of ice that dwindled as the light snowfall gave way to a cold, hard rain. The constructs soared after them, calling to each other; they had a sharp, chattering call that sounded like laughter, bouncing back and forth over their heads.

Lucky scaled a tree and bounded through the forest canopy; it jumped, caught one of the constructs between its jaws, and clamped down, snuffing out the light. As it plummeted through the rain, it twisted and vanished into the shadows again. It materialized above and to Leo's other side, and leapt once more—but then Leo realized this one wasn't Lucky. From below, he could see that the hound—which was snatching another construct from the air and swallowing it like a bite-sized sun—didn't have Lucky's distinctive scars. But Tristan was grinning under the mask.

"Got them," he said, breathing hard as they ran. One by one, the laughing calls broke off until there was only one voice, crying out *jack-jack-jack* to no reply; and then that was gone, too, a last light vanishing like a birthday candle being blown out, and it was just them and the pelting rain and the woods. They huddled together in a relatively dry spot beneath a tree, silent, waiting, unwilling to risk turning on a flashlight. Minutes passed, but no other constructs appeared. The two hounds had returned and sat in front of them like sentinel statues. The rumbling thunder was so close it felt like it came right in his ear, a growl against the back of his neck.

"Did we lose them?" Dion asked, breaking first.

Then they heard a bang, echoing. Another. It was gunfire.

"Wait here," Leo said, and put a hand on Lucky's flank, a silent request for it to follow him. They crept out of hiding, Leo scanning the gaps between the dark, sodden silhouettes of the trees. The sky flashed with lightning, on and off and on and off, and there was no way of telling now which of those blasts were gunshots and which were thunder. There were voices shouting to each other, sounding at this distance not unlike the back-and-forth cackle of the constructs. And where his natural eye could see nothing through the rain, with his truesight he could discern the spectacular explosion of spellwork beginning to rend the storm apart.

The Clattering was finally here.

THE PLAN HAD been to sneak around the worst of the fighting, to let Anne's assault on Castor's defenses distract him while they slipped under his guard. But when Leo had described the scene, or what he could make out of it, Aziza said, "I don't want to wait anymore. We have to help them."

Her riotous curls were flattened to her shoulders by the rain. She was leaning into the other hound, Laelaps, which dwarfed her; the fingers of her good hand were woven into its fur. He was reminded of his first impression of her, this slight and frizzy-haired witch who had stood between him and a snarling bloodthirsty creature he didn't yet know the name of, and then had regarded him with a look of focused intensity he'd never seen on anyone else, let alone anyone their age. He had thought then it was magic that made him feel drawn to her, an intuition that, with her help, he could solve all his life's mysteries. Now he knew it wasn't magic at all; it was just her, how formidable she became when she bent the full, relentless force of her attention and tenacity to a specific target. She directed that look at Dion now, perhaps because he was the only one she could not be absolutely certain would follow her lead. It rendered him speechless for just long enough to be noticeable to everyone except Aziza.

"All right," Dion said, averting his eyes. "We help as much as we can until we see our opening. And then we take it, without hesitation."

Leo and the two hounds were their eyes and ears on the battle. He didn't know how many people there were, and who was on Anne's side and who was on Castor's; he only got glimpses of the fighting as they stayed on the outskirts, circling the heart of the storm where the rainfall fell thick as a veil, shrouding the forest in its folds. He saw lightning strikes skewering the woods only to bounce off a luminous barrier of wards, visible only to him. He saw constructs of every kind locked in battle, tall and humanoid and clawed like the ones Aziza had described at the cemetery in New Haven. Some of them were weather witch creations—mist, ice, rain—but others were shadow made tangible or wooden puppets with gauntlets of carved sigils that seared themselves into Leo's mind.

Castor's winged constructs zipped through the air and were dispelled with silver bullets. That was where the gunfire was directed, at the constructs. The weather witches were visible only in glimpses, surfacing from the cover of fog and rain to fire off bolts of electricity and blue flame before retreating. He spared a thought for Nelle, hoping she was okay, but trusting Anne would keep her close. Anne's people were moving in clusters, each with a ward-keeper to shield them from the lightning, but the smell of ozone permeated the air, even the rain failing to wash it away.

Laelaps stayed with them. It was Tristan's first successful attempt to create his own blækhound, a feat he'd accomplished mere hours before he had returned to them during the battle at the Summer Court's castle. He said he couldn't trust his new hound to obey him completely just yet; their bond was too young. So he kept it close while Lucky dove into the fray, hunting down those weather witches who weren't deep enough into the storm to be behind the layer of wards that kept out blækhounds.

"I won't kill them," Tristan said, his gaze distant as he followed Lucky's progress. "But I'll take their charms, their spell books, their enchanted weapons. Their hands, if I have to."

And Aziza had found some of the borderland fae after all, and soon the mesmerizing glow of the wills-o'-the-wisp flickered on in the woods. Tristan reported that Lucky had seen some poor apprentice weather witch stumble out of hiding, following the trail into enemy hands. And the trees came alive, roots snaking out of the mud and winding around ankles, branches catching hold of wrists, binding them in place. And hungry shades oozed through rivulets of black-brown water, into the worst of the storm, and from somewhere beyond the howl of the wind they could all hear the screaming.

And then—the opening they needed.

He didn't know what was happening at first. Overhead, the clouds were whipping to a point, a plume, reaching toward the earth as if to touch down and twist into a tornado. But as he followed it with his eyes, tracing the line of its narrowing funnel, he saw it led like a rope directly into the cupped brown hands of a slim, straight-backed figure standing alone—no other witch, no ward-keeper to protect her. Anne Sterling.

The length of it undulated, snakelike; its celestial coils filled the sky, flashing here and there with little shocks of violet lightning. The wind picked up, spinning about its funnel, as if to sculpt it. But Anne stood firm, hands outstretched, so that it looked as if she held a tether to the heavens.

"It's a sylph," Aziza said, barely audible through the gale, eyes huge with awe. An ancient air elemental, like the undine from which the elixir of renewal was drawn, or the salamander. The sylph roared with a hurricane's voice, a howl and a boom and the shattering of a dozen lightning strikes at once, making the sky quake.

Anne's lips were moving as she spoke to the sylph. And then she blew gently into her cupped palms, where the flute of the storm met her skin. The cyclone swayed, oscillating, though its connection to Anne never broke.

The sylph began to eat the weather witches' storm.

As the storm dwindled, lifting, and as they made their way closer to Sanctum's borders, he caught glimpses of it through the wall of rain and fog—abandoned houses, the fragments of old fencing, plots of empty land, a couple of rusted cars smothered by blankets of kudzu, though this time of year it looked like nothing but tangles of brown yarn. And something else. Sunlight. Not from a construct. These were sunbeams that thrust through the thinning clouds and sent golden light streaming into the woods. It wasn't coming from the sky; it was coming from somewhere within Sanctum.

And then the world darkened again, the rain doubling down, a gust of wind blowing so hard it almost knocked him off his feet. The storm clouds prowled over them. The weather witches were fighting the sylph back. He turned to the others, to say something like, *now what?*

A bolt of lightning flashed past his shoulder and struck a nearby tree, setting it on fire for an instant before the rain extinguished it. The fog that rolled in was as thick as the clouds above, and though they couldn't have been more than a few steps apart, he lost sight of the others. The ground slid away underneath him. It was ice; he skidded over it, barely keeping his balance. It caught at his heels and built up in clinging layers until he was frozen to the ankle. It wasn't that strong—he pulled himself free, stomping out of the ice trap, but then light flashed in his eyes and he cringed away from it, throwing an arm up to shield himself. It was lightning, but not like before—it was a whip of pale blue that wrapped around the blade of his sword. It crawled up the blade to the hilt and stung his hand, which seized up as the shock ran through it, the sword slipping from his grasp. Cursing, he shook his hand, which tingled—but there didn't seem to be lasting damage. He dove to scoop up the hilt of the sword before it could roll away from him.

"Lucky!" he shouted, though he had no idea if the hound was close enough to hear. They had been separated so suddenly, and there were voices around him, through the wind—

"Stand down!" someone said. "Drop your weapon, and nobody will harm you!"

He took off running, trying his best to make a racket—either Lucky would find him or he'd draw their attackers away from the others. The rain wasn't falling anymore; it was spiraling, faster and faster in circles around him as the wind picked up. The bottlebrush branches of the trees rasped together and shed streams of needles. He held on to the sword with all his might as the cyclone trapped him. He couldn't take another step; it was a solid barrier of wind.

Something slammed into him, knocking him off his feet.

All at once the voices were gone—the wind was gone—and when he looked up, a beautiful, golden-haired fairy woman was above him, pinning him down with a knee to his chest, the blade of her sword against his neck. She wielded it one-handed; he'd cut the other hand off the last time they met, and she held the stump protectively to her side. She smiled down at him; and her smile still had that pure sincerity that would have fooled him completely, truesight or no, if he hadn't known better.

"Princess Narra," he wheezed, catching his breath. "How did you escape from the Winter Court?"

"Should I call you by your title, too? Your Highness?" She laughed mockingly.

"Aren't you happy?" he asked. "You got what you wanted. Hazel is the Summer Queen, and you're free."

"Yes. Hazel is the Summer Queen. And everything I endured because of you was for nothing," she said through her teeth. "I spent the past half year ravaged by the jade rot, fleeing from the Winter Court, losing Viren—only for that child to change her mind on a whim and take the crown I would have surrendered to her from the start." She leaned in, his own reflection in her glassy dark brown eyes. "And now you would destroy this realm. Where would I go then? What would I do?"

"Let me guess," Leo said, squirming slightly to test the strength of her hold, rainwater streaming around him. The flowing skirts of her gown pooled on either side. "Castor made you all kinds of promises he couldn't keep, and now you're realizing you gave up Elphame for a patchwork realm that won't even exist anymore come sunrise. Did he even try to save you from the Winter Queen? Or did he leave you for dead?"

She pressed the edge of the sword against his neck, and he felt a sting as it nicked him. "Castor will make sure I get what he owes me. But you, too, owe me a debt. Hold out your hand."

The weather witches had left him to her, so she held at least some sway with Castor and his followers. That Lucky and Laelaps hadn't come to his rescue meant his friends were otherwise occupied. He didn't have time for this.

And yet—his eyes dropped to the burn mark around her neck in the shape of a collar. Her own family had done that to her. She'd crossed paths with Castor somehow and he had sensed her vulnerability, her weakness, and exploited it. How many times had Leo seen how easy it was for someone to be taken in by a magical entity, to be tricked or persuaded, to be ensnared? And when someone was backed into a corner and felt like they were out of options—that was when they were at their worst. He couldn't forgive her for anything she'd done, but he could give her a choice. A way out. Maybe that was all she needed.

"You asked where you'd go," Leo said. "The Summer Court would take you back."

"I won't let anyone collar me again," she hissed, putting more pressure on the sword, so that he actually feared she might behead him by accident.

"They won't," Leo said. "I'm not saying you'd be welcomed back with open arms, but my sister would never collar you. You don't have to keep doing this. You can just go home."

Her face was blank for an instant, slack and emotionless. For a heartbeat, he thought he might have gotten through to her. But then rage flashed across her features, and he knew what her answer would be. His hands flew up to her sword arm, clamping down on it, and turned her wrist so the flat of the blade pressed to his throat rather than the edge. Then he twisted, rolling them over. She made a sound of wordless anger, almost a screech, as they grappled for the sword—he had dropped his own when she'd knocked him over and didn't know where it was now.

He pried the sword from her hand, but she heaved him off her and tackled him to the ground—any fairy had an edge on any human when it came to sheer physical strength—and then he'd lost the weapon almost as soon as he'd gotten it. He was on his back again, pinned, and this time she wasn't interested in just taking off his hand. She drew the blade up high, pointing straight down, poised to plunge through his throat.

And then something roared. The trees shook with it. It was so loud that even Narra flinched, looking up. Another roar, deafening, his chest vibrating with it, and it was suddenly unbearably hot in the woods, despite the rain. Narra saw whatever it was before he did. Her eyes widened with shock, anger, and no small amount of fear.

He pushed her off him, wrenching the blade from her slack fingers and shooting to his feet. There was a fire somewhere, strong enough that the rain couldn't put it out, its flickering light washing over them. Knights on winged horses—frost illusions—soared down through the storm clouds. One of them wore golden armor.

Leo laughed in sheer relief, barely able to believe it. He knew exactly who that was.

Another roar, and the clouds dropped lower in the sky—only they weren't clouds. The massive, shifting bulk over his head was the salamander's coiling, ash-colored body. Despite its size, its flight was more of a float—like smoke, billowing and portentous.

Something very small and very green was perched on top of its horned crown. That something was waving excitedly and calling, "Leo! Leo, over here!"

He hadn't fully registered what he was looking at before Hazel jumped off the salamander, her wings working so fast they blurred to invisibility, and shot toward him at full speed. She crashed into his chest and they both went down, his arms coming up around her automatically as she practically shouted into his ear, "I've been looking for you everywhere!"

"You have?" he said, dazed. He was terrified to see her here—and also, so happy to see her at all he could hardly stand it. He climbed to his feet and picked her up with him while she rambled without pausing for breath. A circlet of woven gold inlaid with topaz and ruby sat in her dark hair.

"We met up with the Summer Court and then Prince Senna noticed something weird happening to the borderlands—they weren't where they used to be or something? I don't really get it, but then we found out the summertide lord was in our castle—that's him, by the way, he's friends with the Summer Court—" She meant the salamander; it was having a grand time snaking through the forest canopy, which burst into flame wherever its scales touched. Somewhere on the ground, people were screaming in terror. "And then we got your letter, so Prince Senna said—Are you tearing up?"

"No!" he snapped. And then: "Hang on—" And he pulled Hazel behind him as Princess Narra rose to her feet and advanced on them. But in a flash of gold, Prince Senna was leaping off his winged steed, coming to his and Hazel's aid. In moments, he and three of his knights had surrounded Narra.

Senna glanced at him over his shoulder. "I'm glad you held on until we could reach you."

"You were right in the nick of time," he said. "Thank you."

"I assure you it is my greatest pleasure," Prince Senna said. "Catch me up, please."

Leo explained, very quickly, about Castor Thorne and his third realm made of stolen borderlands. "We're trying to stop him, but I need to get through the storm so my friends can break the spell."

"Understood. We'll help Anne Sterling round up your traitor witches," Prince Senna said. "As for breaking through the storm, your sister can handle that."

"She can?" He had found the hilt of the frost sword lodged against a tree root nearby and was wiping the mud off it, replacing it safely in his pocket. Lucky appeared then, lunging through the ranks of the Autumn knights—"It's okay!" Leo said before they could attack. Hazel gasped with delight and flung her arms around the hound's neck.

"He's right! I can get all of you through the storm!" she chirped, half-buried in Lucky's fur. "And then I have so much to tell you after this!"

"After this," he agreed. "Thanks for coming. You totally saved me."

"I did?"

"Definitely."

"I'll follow you once I'm finished here," Senna said. He gave a cold glance in Narra's direction. Someone had bound her arms together with rope, and she was glaring hatefully up at her captors. "And once I've dealt with her."

"Wait," Leo said. "Can I ask you not to collar her? Please. I sort of promised."

If Prince Senna was exasperated by this request, he was too poised to show it. But it hadn't escaped Leo's notice that while he had been so concerned about Queen Ceresia maneuvering Hazel onto the throne, it was Prince Senna who had essentially done just that. While it had been Hazel's choice in the end, and Leo wouldn't take that from her, certainly the Autumn Prince had crafted the circumstances that had made such a choice possible. And he'd done it in such a way that both Hazel and Leo still trusted and relied on him. He was just as formidable as the Winter Queen when he wanted something.

But right now, it looked like what he wanted was still to ingratiate himself with Hazel. He turned to her, smiling, and gave a short bow. "Princess Narra is your subject," he said. "Her punishment will be yours to decide."

Lucky led him and Hazel back to the others, who had managed to escape the weather witches and had been searching for him. At a glance, they didn't look hurt—maybe a little scratched up from their dash through the woods, but they were all in one piece. Aziza had a small swarm of pixies at her feet and was doling out little shining tokens into their spindly mantis hands, whispering, "Thank you. Now go and hide until all of this is over."

Hazel was so excited to see them she hopped up into the air and flew the rest of the way. She threw herself at Tristan and then Aziza in turn. The moment she'd released him, Tristan dragged Leo into his arms.

"I thought you were going to stay next to me," Tristan said accusingly, the cold silver lattice of his mask pressing into Leo's neck. Leo laughed tiredly, leaning his weight against him.

The storm came alive again with wind and lightning, and that was how he knew Prince Senna's knights had found the weather witches. The salamander's roar echoed over the trees.

"Hazel says she has a way through the storm," Leo said.

Hazel beamed. She pointed up at the salamander. "It's easy. He can just carry us."

CHAPTER 42
TRISTAN

THEY FLEW UP into the storm clouds—so high the air grew thin. The sounds of the ongoing battle were swallowed by the rain. The loudest thing in the world was the thunder, and the sonorous rumble of the salamander's body. He didn't know if that sound was its breathing, a growl, or a purr of some sort; absurdly, he was reminded of Fox.

The salamander's claws brushed the tops of the trees, which surfaced from the woolen clouds as if from the ocean, their passage leaving a rippling wake in the canopy. Little fires sprang up here and there, but didn't spread. Its scales were hot—not hot like the hounds, where you felt the sting immediately, but a sort of slow-building heat you wouldn't notice until it had been hurting for a while, like a sunburn, settling into your skin and compounding with time. They'd pulled their sleeves down over their hands so that their bare skin wouldn't touch its scales, other than Hazel, who sat criss-cross between its horns and sometimes leaned down to peer into one of its large eyes and speak to it. If it was responding to her, none of them could hear it.

Beside him, Leo shone with relief and pride, despite his bruised and battered state, as he watched Hazel. Aziza wore a look of concentration that probably meant she was probing at the salamander's magic with her own. Dion appeared to be doing a breathing exercise and was carefully not looking down.

And Tristan was thinking about contingency plans. What was off the table, and what wasn't. He hadn't actively planned on taking off the mask and solving the problem of Castor Thorne in the single most decisive way he could think of . . . but it had crossed his mind that the option was there. That it would always be there. Unlike others who had walked the path of corruptive magic before him, he wasn't tempted by the power that soul-siphoning could give him. But temptation had never been his greatest weakness; it was desperation and need. Those were the things that had always driven him to do the worst things he'd done.

But now that Leo—his *boyfriend*, and he really hoped he would live long enough to get used to that—had thrown him a curveball with a profession of utmost devotion that somehow managed to be a threat, an ultimatum, and a suicide pact all in one . . . taking off the mask was no longer on the table.

Castor Thorne had already killed them once. Tristan wasn't going to let it happen again. What could he do? Which spells could he confidently pull off? What would he have the time to cast?

They burst through the final ring of storm clouds and into a gilded impersonation of daylight. Sanctum was a sprawl below them—far, far below them. Tin roofs and empty porches, a dirt road that twisted between the scattered homes. And a chapel with an ivy-wrapped steeple and wooden cross, and sunlight spilling from its broken windows. Whatever was in there burned brightly enough to fill all of Sanctum with its light; maybe to fill all of the Rookery, once the storms were dispelled.

"Drop us there!" Aziza called to Hazel over the wind. Hazel urged the salamander to descend, and they plummeted—the four of them clutching each other while Hazel laughed giddily and leaned forward, arms and wings open. By some miracle, none of them flew off. The salamander spiraled down and landed, more gently than something of its size should have been able, before the chapel's front steps.

It was like being in the eye of a hurricane. The wall of storms encircled Sanctum completely, obscuring the mountains. The creek behind the chapel had flooded its banks, the water frothing over the rocky stretches of its channel.

They slid carefully off the salamander's head. Hazel patted the ridge under its good eye, which regarded her with recognition and an ancient wisdom. The other eye, the one Leo had stabbed, was scarred over. As its gaze roved slowly over them, Tristan had to wonder if it remembered them. It studied Aziza fixedly for some moments, Aziza looking back with the closest thing to reverence he had ever seen on her face.

"Should we burn it down?" Hazel asked, looking up at the chapel. If there had been guards here, they had gone to the storm ring to defend Sanctum's borders. Anne, the Clattering, and the Autumn knights must have been keeping them busy, because there wasn't a soul left to stop them from going inside.

"We can't," Dion said. "I don't know what will happen to the borderlands if we just destroy the spell while it's in the middle of creating this realm. We have to take it apart piece by piece."

"How do we do that?" Aziza asked.

"The lanterns will be in there, feeding the enchantment," he said. "If we can remove them from the chapel—separate them from the array somehow—we can starve the enchantment, and the magic it's already gathered will dissipate."

"Is it really possible to separate the lanterns without destroying the rest of the spell? None of us is a weather witch," Aziza said.

"This isn't weather magic. No witch could perform an enchantment of this magnitude on their own. It's a collaborative spell," Dion said. "I'm sure he composed the array—his signature is certainly all over it." He directed his gaze up at the sunlight streaming from the windows. "But we'll find elements of other crafts in it, too. The protective enchantments of a ward-keeper, the shadow magic of necromancy to balance out his light-based spells. Things our parents probably taught him. And hedgecraft, of course." He turned his back on the chapel and looked at all of them. "No matter what else happens in there, finding the lanterns is still our priority."

"I have something that might help," Aziza said. She opened her backpack and showed them what was inside. It turned out Tristan wasn't the only one who had been thinking of contingency plans.

"Are you sure you want to do that?" Leo said after she had explained, as if she ever changed her mind about anything.

"No asking me if I'm sure," Aziza said. "I'm adding that to the Coven Blackthorn code of conduct."

"Amendments are provisional until the board approves," Tristan said.

"You need to stop hanging out with Dion."

"What about me?" Hazel said, bouncing on the balls of her feet. Leo reached over to straighten her circlet, which was askew after their flight. "Can I help?"

FROM THE OUTSIDE, the chapel was a kind of giant lantern, pouring its light into the Rookery. Inside, it was a cathedral. Mirrors lined the walls, multiplying each other in an endless spiral of reflections and making the nave appear three or more times its size. There were no pews. Most of the interior had been taken over by the tree that grew straight up from the middle of the room. Its roots crushed what had once been wooden floorboards and its branches stretched up to the ceiling, around the false sun, which was so bright it hurt. He held back a shudder. It struck him as eerily similar to the gateway tree—the real one, the monstrosity that sprawled underneath the hag's clearing, cradling her poisoned heart. This was like the light that had cast that terrible shadow. Surrounded by infinite echoes of itself, it was the center of its own recursive forest.

"Leo, since the lanterns are actively feeding the array, there should be a bond between *that*"—Dion glanced up at the sun—"and the lanterns. They're here, somewhere. Can you follow the connection?"

Leo scanned the mirrors, turning slowly to take them all in. "I see the link, but it's reflected in the mirrors like everything else. It's hard to make out where it leads. And I can barely see it at all when it's this bright in here. Hang on—maybe if I get closer."

They spoke in an urgent hush. Leo picked his way over the upraised roots of the tree, his eyes following an invisible trail. Aziza lagged behind the rest of them, silent, though she stared at the tree with rapt interest. Unlike the hag's gateway tree, which had been only a grotesque imitation of life, this one was—real. An aged oak with a healthy, knotted trunk and sturdy branches, and a blanket of fallen leaves beneath it. He could have found dozens like it outside.

"Found it," Leo said. "One of them, anyway."

He had moved to the side of the room, to the mirrored wall. The lantern was there, inside the mirror, resting upon one of the fractal reflections of the oak tree's roots. It didn't exist in the real world, only in the reflection. Tentatively, Leo touched the mirror's surface—and his hand passed through it, the same way it did when he touched the enchanted wall that led to Bishop Library's jackdaw collection.

They walked through the mirror and into—the chapel, again. But the lantern wasn't here, either; it was in another mirror, its light almost impossible to see amid the brilliance of the false sun. They soon glimpsed the other two lanterns through the mirror portals, too—the second dangling from one of the tree branches, the third tucked into a hollow in the trunk. They passed through the mirrors like open doorways, through tunneling reflection loops and back into the shadow of the old oak, or some version of it, their own doubles pacing alongside them. It made him dizzy to look too long into the mirrors, so he tried not to.

"It's like the castle illusions on the Summer Court," Leo said. "The reflection world coexists with the real world without taking up extra space."

Tristan kept an eye on Aziza, who didn't speak. His hounds padded behind them all, and he paid more attention to their senses than his own, listening with their sharper ears.

Then the lantern was there—not in a mirror, but right in front of them.

Outside the windows, the blistering red-black scales of the salamander slithered past. It had wrapped itself around the chapel and was so large it could rest its head on the slanted roof. Hazel was in charge of persuading it to eat Castor if he appeared. But they had also been prepared for the likely scenario that Castor was already inside. Almost the moment they laid eyes on the lantern, his voice cut through the silence.

"Really, now? I was expecting Anne," he said, stepping out from one of the mirrors. In a pristine dark blue suit with glinting gold cuff links, his smile as radiant and intent as a fallen star, he looked like a benevolent god come to bless them.

"You're outnumbered," Dion said, "your followers are overwhelmed, and the rest of the Clattering will get through the storm and be here soon. You can't keep this up. It's over."

Tristan rested a hand on Lucky's side.

"Outnumbered," Castor said, amused. "Is that what you think? I suppose we'll see."

The four of them and Castor were on opposite ends of the chamber, almost equidistant from the lantern. As he started toward it, Aziza moved, too, walking forward as if to beat him to it. Castor grinned.

"Don't tell me you want a rematch already," he said. But Aziza didn't reply. She only kept walking, even as Castor faltered, steps from the lantern. He was frowning curiously at her. And it appeared, as she walked, that she grew . . . taller.

Castor stopped in his tracks.

The many mirrors reflected her from every angle. She *was* taller now. Her hair was receding into her skull, becoming shorter and blond. Countless sets of dark eyes flashed a striking two-toned blue. The thing that had looked like Aziza no longer looked anything like her at all. And it wasn't going for the lantern. It was going for Castor.

The doppelganger lunged at him, wearing a perfect facsimile of his own smile. And the rest of them leapt into action. Leo and Dion fled into the mirror maze, in pursuit of the other two lanterns. The doppelganger knocked Castor to the ground, its hands on his neck, its jaws dropping open—far wider than humanly possible—to rip his throat out. But Castor opened his hands, and his flock of jackdaw constructs shot from his cuff links. They drove their beaks at the doppelganger's eyes and raked their talons at its skin, and it hissed, crawling away on its hands and knees. The constructs followed it, and it shrank, shivering away Castor's features, returning to the formless, slippery, shadowy thing that it was underneath its mimicry. It squirmed beneath the tree roots, disappearing from view.

Castor got to his feet, looking truly furious for the first time.

"Where is Aziza?" he snapped.

Tristan had already shadow-traveled to the lantern, had picked it up and was backing away, Lucky at his side. He was supposed to take it straight to Dion.

But he had remembered something. Not a spell that he could do—a spell he *couldn't* do.

As Castor rounded on him, and his constructs swarmed, Tristan darted forward to meet him. Castor had a fraction of a second to react—to look stunned—as Tristan grasped his collar and pushed him into the shadow plane.

He didn't shadow-travel with passengers. He had never managed to bring anything larger than a mouse through it unscathed.

But when he reappeared beside Leo and Dion, he wasn't holding Castor Thorne's deformed corpse. His hand was empty. And Castor was—everywhere. A dozen or more reflections, stepping out of the mirrors. A reflection was what Tristan had destroyed just now, that was all. It was like the spell they'd once seen him do at the Half Moon Market, but far more elaborate. Castor was his own army.

"Tristan," Dion said. He was looking down at the lantern in Tristan's hand. Shadow travel had had an effect on it, too, one that none of them had anticipated. The light inside of it, that had been feeding Castor's array, had been snuffed out. The shadow magic of necromancy had canceled out the sunshine of Castor's weather-craft, weakening the spell without shattering it. Tristan looked up at Dion, stunned. Even as Castor's reflections surrounded them, Dion started to smile. "Do you think you can do that again?"

CHAPTER 43

AZIZA

Upon their arrival in the Rookery, as they had waited for the Clattering to bring reinforcements, she had ventured out of their hiding place in search of the borderland fae. She had mostly just wanted to give Leo and Tristan a moment alone, but the Rookery really *was* teeming with frightened, angry fae eager to make their complaints known to the local gatewalker. That was Aziza, by virtue of being the Rookery's *only* gatewalker.

She had found a nest of pixies and bribed them for their help. She'd whispered to the wills-o'-the-wisp of a catastrophic storm and all the lost souls desperately in need of guidance within it. She'd fed her blood to a doppelganger and urged it into her backpack, promising to show it a face she would happily allow it to steal. And at the edge of a spring that ran into a nearby creek, she met a group of confused nixies who agreed to trade their intimate knowledge of the Rookery's waterways for news from on land. They had not failed to notice that their spring was no longer in the same place it had been a few hours ago. It was extremely rude, they said, to move a nixie's spring without asking.

They had a lot to say, these nixies.

In the creek over there, next to a haunted little town sunken long ago from the human realm into the borderlands, sometimes they received visits from a fish that wasn't a fish.

"That is, sometimes it's a fish, and sometimes it's a toad," the nixie said, arms folded on the edge of the spring. "But usually it likes to be a fox."

"It's a pooka," Aziza said, her heartbeat quickening. She glanced over her shoulder at Dion, who was watching this exchange with wary curiosity. He didn't understand why these nixies had yet to turn into murderous reptilian beasts and seemed to feel it could happen at any moment. They also kept eyeing him hungrily, but they wanted information from Aziza more than they wanted to drown and eat him, which in Aziza's opinion made them all good friends.

"Those don't swim," the nixie said. "They like to fly."

"This one is special," Aziza explained. "Has it told you anything interesting?"

BECAUSE OF THE NIXIES, she knew a little of what was waiting for them in the chapel. She knew there was a labyrinth of some kind, a confusing place where Fox got lost every time it left and returned. Fox spent its days going back and forth from the creek—where it played with its new friends—to the chapel, which was occupied by an old nymph who didn't surface from her host tree anymore, and a woman who smelled like the ocean and spent most of her days curled up under the nymph's branches, asleep.

According to the nixies, a gatewalker had asked Fox to watch over the woman. Fox was supposed to do something else, too. But it had forgotten what.

Meryl had always been one of Castor's lantern guardians; he had removed her from Blackthorn, but her responsibilities remained the same. So he had sent her to Sanctum with the lantern she had taken from Bishop Library, and ordered her to watch over the array that would create the Rookery. The question was, what had happened to her after her sealskin had burned? Castor had probably come straight here with his newly completed third lantern. He had almost immediately started casting his final spell.

Had Meryl managed to escape before he got to the chapel? Before he found and disposed of her, now that she would no longer obey him? But then, she couldn't have left—she wouldn't have made it through the storms.

Unable to escape, she would have hidden.

Aziza sent the doppelganger into the chapel with the others. Then she slipped inside after them, under the concealment of a shade spell, to search for Meryl. If there was even the slightest chance that she had managed to evade Castor, Aziza had to go to her. She made her own way through the mirror maze. Through layers of reflections, she caught glimpses of the ensuing fight. She saw the doppelganger attack Castor; she saw Tristan steal the first lantern; she saw Castor's reflections give chase. The hounds tore into them. Leo cut through them with the frost sword, and Tristan with his silver knife.

Two lanterns left. Castor knew this place; he had made it. While they were occupied fighting a mirage, he could go and secure the other lanterns. Aziza should be there, helping the others, but—

But she had a promise to keep.

She crept through the labyrinth, quietly calling out Meryl's name. Then—finally—something moved in the shadows. A small, twitchy something that froze at first, and then, with a *pop* like an engine backfiring, leapt joyfully at her. It was Fox.

She scooped it up into her arms, and it rumbled contentedly.

"Where is she?" Aziza whispered into its pricked ear.

A few minutes and countless reflections later, she was walking around the side of the oak nymph's trunk and peering up into the crook of its branches. She held her breath.

The wood creaked above her as something moved. And then a pair of dark blue eyes looked back down at her.

WHEN MERYL WANTED to see into the sleeping nymph's dreams and memories, she held her cupped her hands underneath her canopy and drank from the rain that fell inside through the holes in the chapel's roof, dripping off her branches. She saw Castor as a boy Aziza's age, stumbling into the borderlands when the storm that could not be withstood came down on Sanctum. He had sheltered in the nymph's arms. She was the reason he had survived. Already an old crone back then, the nymph had felt sympathy for the boy, the way he shivered as the rain pummeled the earth, his meager spells for warmth barely enough to sustain him through the night. She pitied the way he wept and raged. She had revealed herself, speaking to him, and told him stories of Elphame so that he would know there was more to the world than the cold, cruel place that took everything from him.

Sometimes he still visited her, even after she had entered her silent years. He had a princess of the Summer Court coax her into wakefulness one last time, convinced her to uproot herself and come here, to the chapel, where she could be a part of his world forever.

Meryl thought the nymph was the one thing he still loved.

And as Meryl told Aziza the story, Aziza repeated it back to the nymph. The real nymph, not the one in the reflections. She cut her hand on her pocketknife and pressed a few drops of blood into her bark.

"There you are," Castor said. Next to her, Meryl flinched at the sound of his voice.

Aziza turned without removing her hand from the nymph's trunk. "Don't worry," she said. "I'm not going to hurt her."

His eyes narrowed. He opened his hand so that a few of his constructs came fluttering down into his palm. They merged, changing shape, and became a long, deadly blade—shorter than Leo's sword, but shining as brilliantly as the false sun overhead.

More brilliantly, even. Because ever since Tristan had snuffed out that first lantern, it had started to dim. Just a little bit at a time.

"Move away from there," Castor said.

She dropped her hand and stepped forward, losing contact with the nymph. But it didn't matter; her story-spell was begun, her blood offering given, and her magic working under the guidance of her focused intentions. She just had to finish it.

"I heard a rumor, Castor," she said. "I was hoping you could tell me if it was true. It's about how you survived the storm that washed Sanctum away."

He made no move to lift the sword. But his reflections in the mirrors now held conjured swords of their own. They waited for Leo and the others around every corner, as they worked their way through the mirror maze, heading for the lantern that hung from one of the nymph's branches. Aziza tried not to let their fight distract her. Leo and Tristan could fight, and Dion was smart enough to stay close to the hounds for protection. It was Dion leading them now that Leo and Tristan were occupied, scrawling a navigation spell directly onto the surface of a mirror with a stick of chalk and burning it away—manipulating the mirror maze as he did the Flight Paths.

They would be fine, and those Castor Thornes were only fakes. The real one was right in front of her, and this conversation required her full attention. Castor tilted his head, no longer smiling, but not quite looking upset, either. Not as upset as she felt he should be.

"Do you think distracting me will save your friends?" he asked. "They're trapped. Lost. It's only a matter of time before they tire and I catch up with them."

He thought she was the diversion. That was funny.

"I heard that when your parents gave their lives trying to protect Sanctum, you were too afraid to stay and help them," she said. "You ran away and hid until it was all over."

"I did precisely that," he said, unabashed. "If I'd stayed, I would have died, too. I suppose you think I'm a coward."

"No," she said. "That's not the part I wanted to know about. It was afterward, when people tried to rebuild, and you sabotaged them. You brought down floods, landslides, and twisters. You made sure Sanctum stayed dead. Was it to punish those people? The ones who didn't listen when your parents tried to warn them?"

As she repeated Castor's story to him—or a version of it—the nymph's branches creaked, as if straining against a wind no one else could feel.

Castor's eyes flicked up in response to the sound, and then down, at Aziza's hand slowly dripping blood.

"Or was it that you were already thinking about the Rookery back then? Did you decide to start preparing Sanctum for the day you could set that plan in motion? I don't think that's it, though," she continued. "I doubt you were thinking that clearly. You were just lashing out in pain at the easiest target."

The nymph's branches creaked again, stretching subtly.

It was an improvised spell, cobbled together and full of blanks she filled with speculation. But story spells were designed to be made up on the spot, and to be changed with every repetition, and they didn't even have to be true. Retellings made a tale stronger, and gave the spell a firmer foundation; spontaneous editing, based on whim and intuition, could produce new results, and the same story might work for many different spells based on the details she added or altered.

Normally, a story about death would have served her best in a sleeping spell, the kind she favored almost as much as her trap circles. This one would do the reverse. It was a spell for waking up.

"Stop talking," Castor snarled, coming toward her, that gleaming blade held stiffly at his side. She pressed her back against the trunk, which almost thrummed. As the nymph stirred, Aziza saw in one of the mirrors over Castor's shoulder as the hanging lantern slipped from its branch—a reflection of the real thing—and fell. Tristan caught it before it could shatter. He shadow-traveled a few feet away, and the lantern in his hands was dark when he reappeared.

Above, the sun dimmed still further; it was even more noticeable now. The shadows grew deeper, especially between the roots, which were filled with shallow pools of stagnant water.

Castor stalked toward her, and she backed away without taking her eyes off him. Her boots splashed into the dark puddles and scraped over the roots of the tree, which shifted, flexing. Meryl had vanished; Aziza didn't see where she'd gone, but she trusted that Fox was still watching over her.

"Nothing you do to me will save the Rookery," she told Castor. "It's over."

The nymph shifted again, an old woman turning over in her sleep, her roots sliding. Aziza staggered as she lost her footing, catching herself before she fell. The foundations of the chapel shuddered. Cracks ran up the walls, and mirrors crashed to the ground, shards flying everywhere.

Dion had told her once that the first thing you did when composing a spell array was define its boundaries. She had seen herself how easy it was to break her trap spells just by scuffing the edge of the circle. The chapel walls formed the boundaries of this array; the paths of the mirror maze were its guiding lines. Now, as her coven sapped the energy that powered the spell, weakening it until it could be safely tampered with, she had broken its boundaries.

"Maybe that's true. But I can at least save myself some trouble next time," Castor said calmly, and brought the sword down at her neck. She dove out of the way, but he caught her wrist in a bruising grip and reeled her back in.

"Next time?" she repeated, looking up into his face, composed even now, as he held the blade up to her throat.

"I'm not done," he said. "Far from it. I won't need years of trial and error to figure out the spell again. I'll have more support—more witches who will have seen how very close we were to remaking the world, and will do what must be done to make that vision a reality. But there is something I've learned from this first, failed attempt. A mistake I won't repeat."

More of the mirrors were breaking—maybe all of them—filling the air with a rainlike sound of shattering. Where were the others? Had they found the last lantern? If the mirror maze fell apart while they were still inside the reflections, would they be trapped? But she couldn't look for them, couldn't look away from Castor's face illuminated by the golden blade, which was now the brightest thing in the room.

"I know now that you are a problem I have to solve myself," he said.

Outside, the salamander rumbled and unwound itself from the chapel, which was no longer the stable perch it had been moments ago. Pieces of the roof caved in as it moved. The debris caught in the nymph's branches. The false sun dimmed until it was hardly brighter than a candle.

The sword flashed, and she screwed her eyes shut, bracing for the pain. But it never came.

Castor was torn from her, but his grip on her wrist dragged her down with him. The toe of her boot caught on a jutting root, and she fell on her knees into—several inches of cold water. The hollows between the tree roots were filling up with it, as if it were raining. It wasn't, but still, the water rose, soon submerging the roots completely. And Castor was—gone. If not for the ring of bruises encircling her wrist, she would have thought he had been merely another reflection.

Something splashed in the water a few feet away from her, struggling.

And there he was. Castor was in the water, being pulled under the surface by the front of his jacket. He thrashed, lifting his face for a few gasps of breath before he was dragged down again. And down, and down, even though the water wasn't—couldn't be—that deep, until not even a single blond hair was visible.

Bubbles rose to the surface, and a few dark curls of blood.

Aziza watched, waiting for Castor to reappear. When he didn't, she inched closer, looking into the inexplicably deep pool. Something was swimming up as if from a long way down. It grew in size as it got closer; and then a pale face broke the surface, with sleek, dark hair floating in a halo around it, and deep-sea blue eyes that were, at present, a little too large. She smiled, revealing sharp canine teeth that fit oddly in her mouth; she was only capable of a partial transformation now. But it had been enough.

By the time Meryl climbed out, her face was back to normal. She unfolded her water-streaked glasses from the pocket of her cardigan, pushed them up her nose, and wrung out her hair.

Then she held out her arms to Aziza.

Aziza fell into them gladly and clung to her.

CHAPTER 44
LEO

As the pieces of Castor's third realm had broken apart and gone back to where they belonged, Sanctum had returned to the borderlands between Elphame and West Virginia. That meant they had something like a thirteen-hour drive home. It ended up taking longer than that, since a lot of roads were damaged or blocked by fallen trees.

Prince Senna was taking Narra to the Spring Court, where she would be imprisoned for her role in the theft of the borderlands, until she could be relinquished to the Summer fairies. Then he would attempt to make what amends he could with the Winter Court.

"You're going to talk to Queen Ceresia?" Leo asked, taken aback. "Are you sure that's a good idea?"

"But I'm so good at talking," Prince Senna said. At Leo's skeptical look, he laughed. "I did plan to refrain from entering the palace. Ceresia will forgive me . . . one day, I'm sure . . . and in the meantime, it will be best if I keep my distance, lest she make a decision she and I will both regret."

The Summer Court would spend the coming months rebuilding their castle, replenishing the ranks of their Gallowglass, and reforging their friendships with the low courts. Leo had helped a little with that part, and Princess Kova and Prince Senna's support would do the rest. Still, Hazel had become queen at all of fourteen years old to a people who barely knew her. She had a long road ahead of her.

The same could be said of AJA and the Clattering. Castor's weather witches had scattered. Anne and her allies had swiftly taken control of the Clattering, choosing provisional replacements for those of their colleagues who had thrown in their lot with him. If Castor and Serapion weren't both dead, there would have been a power struggle for control over AJA. As it was, Anne reluctantly filled the void Castor had left, shepherding the others through the beginning of what would hopefully be a fresh start for them all.

As for Coven Blackthorn, they had agreed to worry about all of that later. Right now, he was parking their latest rental car in his parents' driveway. The others were climbing out—Nelle, carrying a gallon-sized soda cup and a half-eaten bag of fries; Dion, who somehow managed to look alert and refreshed even though he hadn't slept at all on the drive back; Aziza, who had spent most of the ride napping on Tristan's shoulder and was still only half-conscious; and Tristan, who met Leo's eyes over the roof of the car in a shared look of relief. They were both glad to be home.

Winter had settled over Blackthorn. They left footprints in a tissue-thin layer of snow.

"Go inside. I'll be there in a sec," Leo said. He had never let Tristan return his key to the Merritt house. So they went to the front door while Leo continued around to the back. There was a little forested preserve behind the house, a pond where the amphibians Mom spoke into the world could safely escape, and the neighbors on either side were just far enough away to make it unlikely they'd overhear Spot's middle-of-the-night antics.

He didn't see anyone outside, but she'd told him she would beat him here. She didn't like being trapped in a car when she could fly; she'd promised she'd find her own way back.

"You better not chicken out," he said now.

"I'm not," Hazel grumbled from somewhere overhead. She was sitting on the roof, her legs dangling over the edge, wearing a pair of jeans and a tank top she must have found time to steal from her old bedroom. She seemed not to notice the cold. She swung her legs idly and then tipped forward off the roof, her wings catching her in the air, allowing her to drift slowly downward.

Standing, she was less poised. She shoved her hands in her pockets and kicked lightly at the ground. "Are you sure about this?" she asked.

"Trust me," he said.

She trailed along after him as he returned to the driveway. His friends were inside already. But the front door flew open again before he could get there. Light spilled out of the house. His dad was in the threshold, looking frantically around.

"Leo! Thank God," he said, his voice breaking with relief. Before he could take another step, Mom's face appeared at his shoulder. Then she was running outside barefoot and flinging her arms around Leo, who had to bend to embrace her as she wept.

For a second, he was worried they hadn't recognized Hazel. Then he realized she wasn't next to him anymore, though the tip of a pointy green ear was visible behind the hood of the car.

"Come on," he said. "It's okay."

Mom pulled away to give him a questioning look, wiping at her eyes. Dad had started to follow her, leaving the door open behind him, when he stopped short.

Hazel had crept into view, tugging self-consciously at the hem of her shirt. She was so nervous she had started, probably by accident, to hover about a foot off the ground.

It wasn't that Leo was *worried* about how his parents would react to seeing her without the glamour. He had faith in them. But there was always that tiny little one percent of doubt—which was put to rest forever as Mom clapped a hand over her mouth to muffle a cry of happiness and threw herself at Hazel, gathering her up in a hug so tight it was a miracle if Hazel could breathe.

Over Mom's shoulder, Leo gave Hazel a look that he hoped she would interpret as: *Told you so.* Sniffling, she tucked her face against Mom's neck and hung off her like a little girl.

A hand landed on Leo's shoulder.

"I should have believed you when you said you'd bring her back home," Dad said.

"It's not forever," Leo said cautiously. "She can't stay. She can just visit for a few days now and then."

"Maybe *we* can visit her," Dad suggested.

Leo opened his mouth and then closed it. "Uh. Well. Maybe."

His friends stayed over that night. He insisted. Dion was still exhausted from rearranging Castor's mirror maze enchantment, and couldn't have managed even something as simple as the door spell that would take him home—and anyway, Leo preferred not to send Dion back to the empty Wulfsige house alone after the day they'd all had. Ditto for Nelle, who had been staying in a tiny apartment near Bishop Library while she'd filled in for Tristan as librarian. As for Aziza, Khaled wasn't home; Anne had convinced him to fill in as the Clattering's rook, which he had agreed to on the condition that it was temporary. So Dion slept on the couch in the living room; Aziza and Nelle took the guest room; and Tristan needed no invitation before following Leo into his room and claiming his rightful place in Leo's bed.

"I don't think I can keep my eyes open for another second," Tristan said, muffled against the pillow. When Leo didn't reply, he sat up. "What are you waiting for? Get over here."

Too tired to keep his eyes open, but not too tired to order Leo around with the confidence of someone who knew there was no possibility that he would be denied. Tristan looked increasingly puzzled in the face of what was probably the world's most pathetically besotted stare, but Leo couldn't help it.

"Hey, Tris?" he said, a grin starting to pull at the corners of his mouth, and he couldn't help that either. "I have to tell you something."

CHAPTER 45
TRISTAN

When he woke up the next morning, he felt unusually well rested. He was sore—he had accumulated a number of bruises during last night's misadventure in the Rookery. But their days—weeks—of being on the run were over. They were home—and *he* was home, in all the ways that mattered most. His mind was peacefully, blessedly quiet.

Leo was next to him, close enough to share the same pillow. Tristan breathed in time with him, waiting with detached curiosity to see whether he might trick his body into falling back asleep.

It was early. But if he lingered too much longer, he knew he'd give in to the urge to wake Leo up. *Good morning*, he'd say. *Do you still remember me? What about now? Tell me again how we met. Tell me again how long you've loved me for.*

He pressed a kiss to the back of Leo's wrist and slid out of bed. It was the first time in months he hadn't woken up to gray skies. Through the window, he could see the pink of an uninhibited dawn.

Downstairs, the couch had two occupants instead of the one he'd expected. Dion had fallen asleep half-sitting up with Leo's school laptop balanced precariously on his knees, the screen black. Aziza was slumped against his shoulder, the blanket spread across both their laps. He was sure they hadn't meant to fall asleep like that. Probably they had passed out mid-argument. He moved the laptop to the table and, because he was a good friend, woke Aziza up before anyone else could find them.

"I thought you were sharing the guest room with Nelle," Tristan said, once they had gone outside with mugs of instant coffee.

"I knew Dion would stay up and work if no one kept an eye on him," Aziza grumbled. "It's his default reaction to stress. Why did Leo let him borrow his laptop? Who is he emailing, anyway? What's so urgent it can't wait a day?"

In other words, she had gone downstairs to keep him company because she didn't want him to be alone.

Tristan stifled a laugh and let it go. They drank their coffee in silence for a little bit. After a while, he felt Aziza's eyes on him.

"What's wrong?" she asked as he met her gaze. When he only tilted his head in confusion—his mind was still pleasantly empty—she clarified, "I thought you'd be happier."

She knew what had happened, then. That the curse was broken.

"Don't tell me Leo told you before he told me," Tristan said, still a little disgruntled about how long Leo had waited to inform him.

"Not on purpose. I guessed," she said unrepentantly. "He just confirmed it."

"I am happy," Tristan said. "But I'm also a little . . . afraid?"

He hadn't known that was the word he was going to use until it was already out of his mouth. Aziza was silent, waiting for him to continue.

"What if this is too good to be true? What if he liked having a—a quest, and the reality of just being together will be . . . boring in comparison?" Tristan said, which was a little to the left of what he really meant.

"You don't actually believe that," Aziza said flatly, not fooled for a second.

He almost objected on principle. But he was too tired to fend off the instinct to spill his guts at her feet. If they'd still been bonded, his emotions could have materialized in her head before he'd properly felt them himself. Part of him still believed that was true, like nothing he could say would surprise her, and that much was probably accurate.

"Maybe not," he admitted. "Not really. I just can't stop thinking of everything that could go wrong. I think . . . I know I don't deserve this."

"Not your call to make."

She wasn't wrong. People got things they didn't deserve all the time. Why not him, too? Why did he have to question it? Why couldn't he just be grateful that things had worked out in his favor for once? His hand rose unconsciously to cover his mouth, the way the mask would have, before he forced himself to let it fall. He still felt that low-level hunger that might never leave him again; he also felt a little sick.

"I got exactly what I wanted and I still haven't atoned for everything I did wrong," he said, a confession he could make only to her.

"What would atonement look like to you?" she asked.

"I don't know yet."

He thought about those college applications he had filled out mainly to appease Leo and his parents. He had felt his time would be better spent working rather than going to college. Maybe he was starting to reconsider that. He didn't want to just survive, worrying about nothing but himself and the people closest to him. He wanted—*needed*—to justify his continued existence by using it to make the world better than it was now.

The question was how.

"I can think of something, at least for today," Aziza said. "It's not much, but it'll be a good start."

IT WAS THE second year in a row that disaster had interrupted the holiday fair at St. Sithney's Park. Of all the tragedies Castor and his weather witches had caused with last night's storms, here were some of the smallest ones: torn string lights, a three-story Christmas tree toppled on its side, the colorful debris of muddied tinsel and shattered candy canes. The volunteers cleaning it up were in good spirits; they all agreed that this was better than the thing with the wolves that had happened last year. If they were quick about it, the fair would be back up and running by tomorrow.

The three of them signed up for a volunteer shift in the evening. Aziza had spent the better part of the afternoon beginning her work on mending the boundary with Elphame. All over the country, other hedgewitches would be doing the same thing. She wanted to be close by at sunset. Inevitably, the borderland fae would slip through the torn boundary: the flocks of lesser fairies, the burrowing imps and their wreaths of pestilence, the creeping shades. She would send them home—and Tristan and Leo would help, or at least they'd distract the other volunteers while Aziza worked.

Dion showed up in the middle of their shift.

"What are you doing here?" Tristan asked, pausing on his way to throw out a bag of recycling.

"Looking for the three of you," Dion said.

"Aziza is in the woods. Leo is over there, on painting duty." Tristan studied him curiously. "I didn't think we'd see you for a while."

"Yes, well. I'm here with a formal invitation to join AJA," Dion said. He opened his hand and showed Tristan one of the golden jackdaw pins they'd once seen on the duelists at the Half Moon Market. Tristan must have made a face, because Dion gave a wry smile. "I told the others that no one would want these anymore, but they didn't listen."

As the Clattering's hearth witch had turned out to be one of Castor's followers, she had been ousted from the coven; Nelle said they were talking about bringing Dion onboard as her replacement, a temporary post that would likely become permanent. It was unheard of, to join the Clattering that young, but it sounded like they were desperate. Desperate enough to put the consequences of a problem they'd helped create on the shoulders of a person who'd already lost more than almost anyone else because of it.

But Anne would be looking out for him. And if anyone was equal to the challenge of reforming the Clattering, it was Dion.

Still, Tristan didn't need to think very hard about his answer.

"Thanks for the invitation. I decline," Tristan said. "No offense."

Dion was unsurprised. He pocketed the pin. "I know it's flawed. AJA, and the Clattering. But I think we can fix it. I hope you'll help me. All of you."

Tristan still felt that he could not have denied Dion anything he asked.

"We will," he said. "If it can be fixed. But maybe we don't have to. I think we could start over and build something better."

He even believed it. That they really could.

CHAPTER 46

AZIZA

THE WHARFS HADN'T completely survived the storm. Some of the docks had broken off and been swept out to sea, setting many of the vessels adrift. But a few of them had held. Aziza stood on one of them now as it rocked gently under her feet. It was late, but the sky was clear and the moon shined down on Blackthorn's coast for the first time in months.

It was as good a time as any for seafaring. With a view of the stars, there could be no risk of getting lost. Plenty of other risks out there, though, for a lone sailor with a whole ocean to cross.

"Are you sure this is safe?" Aziza couldn't help but ask. It was freezing cold, even bundled up in her warmest jacket.

"Positive," Meryl said. She was getting her father's skiff ready for the voyage. He'd left it behind when the pod had moved on. Now Meryl would take it and follow their trail. She had donned his yellow rain slicker and a wide-brimmed hat. Her glasses were already speckled with droplets of sea spray. When she straightened and turned back to Aziza, she was beaming. Aziza had never seen her so happy—it was the kind of happiness that had no limits, no borders, no end in sight.

"It's going to be a long trip," Aziza said, though Meryl's joy was infectious, and she couldn't suppress a smile of her own.

"Yes," Meryl said. "But when I come back to visit, I'll bring everyone."

Aziza had tried to apologize a dozen times for what had happened to her sealskin. Meryl wouldn't hear it. The sealskin had burned while it was in Castor's possession, so it was Castor's fault, she said, no matter the cause of the fire. She said it was because of Aziza that she was free. She would find her father and the rest of their pod. She would return to the sea—not the way she would have done if she'd had her sealskin, but a homecoming was still a homecoming.

Aziza wanted to ask *when* she'd come back. But even that would feel too much like tying her down.

"Safe travels," she said instead. "Tell Marinus I said hello."

Meryl leaned out of the skiff to wrap her arms around Aziza in a final embrace. A few minutes later, the motor was rumbling, and Meryl was at the console guiding the vessel out into deep waters. Aziza watched until it had disappeared into the horizon, and there was nothing to see but the waves. Then she turned back to the lights of Blackthorn and started for home.

ACKNOWLEDGMENTS

COUNTING THE TIME before the first book's publication, I've been working on the *Buried and the Bound* trilogy on and off for about ten years. It's been a constant fixture in my life, always in the back of my mind even as I took breaks and branched out into other projects. I'll forever be thankful I had the chance to share it with readers—and that I got to work with so many incredible and talented people in the process.

Firstly, thank you to my agent, Erica Bauman, for being there every step of the way, and my editor, Mekisha Telfer, for her insightful feedback throughout the trilogy but especially on this final installment, which was the most challenging project I've ever taken on. Her input on *Unraveling* helped me transform those messy early drafts into a book I'm proud of.

Thank you to my friend Chelsea Abdullah for the feedback and the brainstorming sessions, and especially for talking some sense into me when I needed it, which was often. Without her, this book *probably* still would have gotten done, but it would have taken at least twice as long. For the chapters set at Yale, I owe a million thanks to Jude Morrissey, librarian at the Divinity School, who was kind enough to show me around and answer dozens of questions.

Thank you to the team at Roaring Brook Press/Macmillan: Kathy Wielgosz, Sara Elroubi, Carlee Maurier, Gaby Salpeter, Jennifer Healey, Elizabeth Peskin, Raymond Ernesto Colón, Molly Ellis, Gretchen Fredericksen, Taylor Armstrong, Shawn Foster, Beth Clark, Mallory Grigg, Jordan Winch, Kristin Dulaney—and everyone else who played any part in getting this book out into the world, no matter how small. As always, particular thanks to designer Samira Iravani and illustrator Helen Mask for the beautiful cover art.

Thank you to my family and friends for their unwavering support. In addition, a huge thank-you to the booksellers, librarians, and educators who work so hard to put books into readers' hands, especially now, at a time of prevalent book bans and censorship attempts.

Finally, thank you to my readers. Everyone who reached out with kind messages; who posted reviews, memes, graphics, and fanwork; who talked about these books to their friends; and who gave any of their time to this series. Watching people connect with this story and find something meaningful in it has been one of the most rewarding things about this journey. I'll always be grateful our paths crossed.